Embodiment

AJ EASTERLING

Fulton Books, Inc.
Meadville, PA

Published by Fulton Books 2021

ISBN 978-1-63710-617-4 (paperback)
ISBN 978-1-63710-619-8 (hardcover)
ISBN 978-1-63710-618-1 (digital)

Printed in the United States of America

To my loving and supportive husband, Mark.
Thank you for believing in me.
To our children, Bryant Scot, Alexandra (Lexy), Starla and Shelby.
Thank you for always being supportive and
a constant source of inspiration.
I love you all very much!

Acknowledgements

I would like to take this opportunity to thank the following people for your assistance, support, encouragement, and inspiration in writing and getting this book published. Ms. Linda McKibben Whitt for your years of patience and encouragement with a class full of unruly pre-teens and your years of dedication as a teacher. Even today, years later (I won't mention how many years!) you still find the time and kindness to encourage me from afar. Dr. Robert S. Friedman for your support, encouragement, and inspiration. I sincerely value all of our conversations! Dr. Ann Hanlon for your support, encouragement, and reassurance. Thank you for always taking the time to listen! Mike Maloles, Emily J. Rogers-Flaker, and Lyndon Jones for taking the time to read my rough drafts and being brave enough to offer criticism and suggestions! I would not have gotten to this point without all of you! Thank you so much!

Chapter 1

The envelope was simply addressed to Dr. Myra Christie. It had been placed in the center of her desk. No return address, nothing to indicate who it was from. Just a simple white business style envelope addressed in handwritten block style letters. There was no postmark in the upper right corner and no postage paid, indicating the envelope must have been hand delivered at some point.

Dr. Christie deposited her briefcase on the floor beside her desk, sat her mocha latte on the coaster on her credenza, flipped her computer on, and sat down in her office chair. She automatically reached out with her left hand, lifting the receiver of her office telephone. Tapping in her four-digit code for personal messages, she grabbed a legal pad and pen from her middle desk drawer. Quickly, she played through the messages and dotted notes on the pad.

It was going to be great day, she thought. There were only three messages. One was from her mother trying to find her the night before. The second message was from a colleague requesting assistance on a case. The third message was from a patient. The patient suffered from extreme anxiety and posttraumatic stress disorder (PTSD) as a result of being taken hostage in a bank robbery two years ago. The patient also had her cell phone number because she had been in crisis mode and Myra had talked with her in length the night before. Notes from the call and a comprehensive and detailed report was saved on the USB drive in her briefcase. She jotted herself a reminder to post them to the client's chart. Replacing the receiver back in the cradle of the telephone, she scribbled a few more reminders for the day then set the notepad to the side.

"Doughnuts in the break room," a male voice rang out in the hallway. She ignored the voice and sliced into the envelope with the carved turtle ebony letter opener she had received as a gift from her mother when she graduated from college. It had once belonged to her father, and she cherished it greatly.

The handwritten letter inside the envelope was good quality heavy linen paper. She didn't recognize the handwriting, and it wasn't signed with a name. She took a sip of her mocha latte as she began to read:

My Dearest Myra,

Let me tell you a story. It was so very long ago, but sometimes it seems like only yesterday. I have been waiting patiently for this day to arrive. Okay, so maybe not totally patiently. I have done my best with the time allotted. I have honored my father's wishes to the very best of my abilities during that time whilst I waited. Waited for you, you see. Ah, but I get ahead of myself. Where to start? I suppose I should start where first our paths entwined.

It was a hot summer day in Virginia Beach, Virginia. I was enjoying the beach on that particular day. The ocean breeze tasted salty, and white fluffy clouds were sparse in the sky. Scantily clad people modeling the latest in swimwear dotted the beach around me. A redhead was doing her best to gain my attention, but I was riveted by the young girl with long blond hair drawn back in a ponytail. She was building a castle in the sand, completely oblivious to everything and everyone around her.

Ah, she was the most beautiful thing I had ever seen, and I knew immediately she was going to be mine. You see, in another life, my father had promised her to me. I had been waiting many long years for her to arrive. At last, here was my very own angel. I was nearly giddy with excitement. My bride sat just a few feet before me.

I watched her until midafternoon. I so wanted to approach, to talk and get to know her. Her mother lounged nearby, reading a book. As far as I could tell, it was just the two of them in attendance. She was as beautiful as the day, and I simply sat and watched her. When her mother began packing up their belongings, I offered to help her carry them to her car. You can imagine my surprise when the little girl slipped her hand into mine as we made our way to the parking lot. I could feel the heat of her passion melt into my own. Like a bolt of lightning, it raced up my arm and exploded in my chest as fireworks. I gave her hand a little tug to take her to my chariot, but her little hand slipped from mine, and she was settled in her car before I realized it.

I would have reached for her in that moment, tore the seat belt from her small trim waist. However, her mother chose that exact moment to shut the door and wish me well before settling in the car and driving away. I nearly wept right there in the parking lot over my loss. But then I heard my father's whisper on the wind that it was not yet time for me to reap my reward. He insisted that I should wait. I had much to do before I could claim her.

And so, I focused on my father's work while watching my love from afar. I have celebrated every milestone in your life with you...every birthday...every accomplishment... I have been there. You were so radiant and proud the day you graduated with your doctorate. Oh, how I longed for you that day. I so wanted to take you that very day…but still my father insisted I wait.

My time has finally arrived, my darling. I'm coming for you soon!

With all my love

Myra stared at the letter in shock. She felt the color drain from her face. For several minutes, she could do nothing but simply stare at the letter. She couldn't breathe, and the room began to spin in a kaleidoscope of color. A migraine sprang up behind her eyes. Her stomach lurched, and she felt sick. She jumped up and ran down the hall to the staff bathroom. So much for the bran muffin and mocha latte she had for breakfast, she thought as she flushed her sickness down the toilet. She was shaking so hard she could barely stand.

The mirror above the sink where she rinsed the vomit from her mouth and washed her face with cold water featured an extremely pale woman in her late twenties with long blond hair fashioned into a bun. Her brilliant green eyes were wide with shock, swimming with unshed tears. With shaking hands, she turned off the water tap, patted her face dry, then ran them over her hair and down her sides before clasping them in front her.

Chapter 2

"Your testimony for the prosecution, Ms. Christie, was a little vague in areas to me…and I'm sure the jury may feel the same way. You did not specifically state that my client, the defendant, Owen Johnson, was guilty of the crimes he has been charged with, specifically the murders of three women and female teenager. Is it your testimony that my client is innocent?"

"My title is Dr. Myra Christie. As stated in my prior testimony this morning, I am a forensic psychologist. It is not my job to determine the innocence or guilt of any client. That is the responsibility of the jury and the court. My job is specifically to determine if the accused is fit for trial and to make sentence recommendations in the event the accused is deemed guilty by the jury and the court."

"Do you think he is guilty of these crimes? You have spent a number of hours with him during your consultation, much more than any member of the jury."

"Again, it is not my position to make such determinations. I only perform such tests and interviews as needed to determine his mental status for the purpose of determining if he is able to follow the court process, understand what he has been accused of, and is able to assist in his own defense." She avoided looking at the defense attorney questioning her to address the jury firsthand. She wanted to make sure the jury understood her position. The defense attorney, Greg Huntington Bordeaux, was one of the best defense attorneys in the area, and he was purposely trying to trip her up and make the jury question her testimony. Any doubt on the part of the jury could mean that his client could receive a not guilty sentence.

"Ms. Christie, as a part of your evaluation process, can you give this court and the jury a guarantee that the defendant, Owen Johnson, is not dangerous or that he will not be dangerous in the future?"

"No, I can't, and my title is Dr. Christie," Myra reminded the defense attorney for the fourth time. Sometimes she really hated being an expert witness, and this was one of those moments.

"In fact," he went on, ignoring her correction of her title, "you can't really predict his behavior at all, can you?"

"Behavior is response of environmental circumstances. No one can predict how someone is going to respond under an unknown variety of conditions. Stressors, however, do seem to bring out the worst in some people."

"So you are saying that it was some sort of stressor in the environment that led to Mr. Johnson allegedly brutally and methodically killing three women and a teenager all on separate occasions? Tell me, Ms. Christie, what type of stressor would it take to incite a person to act in such a manner?" His deep baritone seemed to vibrate throughout the room. The volley of his questions and her responses had the jury members following along as though they were watching a tennis match.

"My title is Dr. Christie," she reiterated more firmly. She knew it was a tactic to discredit her testimony with the jury.

"My apologies, *Doctor*," he emphasized for effect. "Could you please respond to my question?"

"I did not say a specific stressor incited Mr. Johnson to perform those murders. I only said that no one could definitively predict how another person would respond to a variety of unknown stressors and other unknown environmental circumstances." She really hated this type of questioning. In fact, she did not like being an expert witness at all, but the court had appointed her to do an evaluation on the defendant, and testifying in court came with the territory.

"Okay, I'm confused." He smirked. "Are you telling the court that stressors caused him to allegedly murder four innocent females or that it was something in the environment?" the defense attorney persisted his line of questioning.

"I can't answer that question at all. You asked me if I could predict his behavior. I am responding to that question with the reply that behavior is a response to our environment."

"You can only talk about your personal guess as to his future behavior, your guess as to what kind of person he is and what he supposedly did to these women. Isn't that correct?"

"No. My diagnosis and report is based upon the battery of psychometric tests, evaluation of the client, reviewing of crime scene information, police reports, client history, witness reports, educational records, and medical records," she replied. She was already exhausted. After an unsettling dream last night and going on the third hour of testimony, she was frustrated and fighting to keep her emotions blank, her responses matter-of-fact and professional.

The immaculately dressed defense attorney, in his black suit and his signature power red tie, walked back to his table and reviewed some of his notes for a moment before facing the jury and asking yet another question. "Would you say that the defendant acted in accordance with his personality?"

"Yes."

"He knew exactly what he was doing and that it was wrong. Is that correct?"

"Yes."

"Has the defendant shown any type of remorse for what he did to those women?" he asked.

"I did not witness him exhibiting any remorse during my evaluation."

"Do you think he is remorseful?"

"I cannot answer that question."

"Why not, Dr. Christie?"

"That question is suggestive of a personal opinion," she replied. She longed to rub her aching temple but kept her hands in her lap as a measure of control and relaxation. Any type of emotion on her part could unduly bias the jury.

He lifted one brow in a quizzical manner. "Isn't all of your testimony just your personal opinion?" His back was to the jury, and they could not see the slight smirk on his face. The man was so smug!

"No. It is based on empirical science, background, experience, the psychometric testing we discussed earlier, and my personal evaluation of the defendant."

"I see," he mused as he rubbed the beginning of his five-o'clock shadow on his chin apparently absently with his thumb and forefinger. Myra knew differently, however. It was one of his signature moves in court and a delay tactic. He was a great defense attorney. One of the best in the area, actually, but he was extremely narcissistic as well. "Psychology is an exact science, then," he stated matter-of-factly.

"To an extent, psychology is a science, but it is mostly objective," she rejoined.

"So when you say that the defendant did not exhibit any remorse in your presence, is that an opinion or an objective statement on your part?"

"It is my statement that I personally did not witness the defendant exhibiting any remorse during my evaluation," she replied, trying hard not to grit her teeth.

"So because you did not witness any remorse during your evaluation, you are assuming that the defendant is not remorseful?"

"I do not understand your question," she replied, trying to flip the tables on him without being a hostile witness.

"Dr. Christie, is it possible that the defendant is remorseful without having exhibited it in your presence?"

"The defendant has exhibited antisocial behaviors as a child and as an adult. According to his school records and prior law enforcement records, his antisocial behaviors have been rather consistent throughout most of his life. In most cases, it is extremely unlikely that a person exhibiting antisocial behaviors such as this will have emotional responses. In most cases, persons with antisocial personality disorders are manipulative, lack empathy, and have become accustomed to manipulating conversations and people to hide their own lack of emotional responses."

"You have stated that the defendant exhibits antisocial behaviors."

"Yes."

"Antisocial behavior and criminal behavior are the same?"

"No. Some criminal behavior is rooted in antisocial behavior, but not all antisocial behavior leads to criminal behaviors."

They had already been through all this when they discussed her medical report to the court earlier during this testimony.

"Dr. Christie." He paused for a moment as he rubbed his chin in thought. "Would you expect an innocent individual to exhibit remorse for a crime they did not commit? Say, a crime or crimes of murder, as in this case?"

"I would expect an individual I was evaluating that had been accused of such crimes to at least express empathy for the victims and their families," she addressed the jury instead of the defense attorney.

"Thank you, Dr. Christie. That is all I have for this witness at this time, Your Honor," he directed to the Honorable Judge Anthony Hawkins presiding over the case. "I would, however, like to reserve the right to recall this witness in the future."

"Very well. Dr. Christie, you may step down, but please remain in the courtroom. You may call your next witness, Mr. Bordeaux," the judge directed the defense.

It was nearly five o'clock in the afternoon before the court took a break for the day. Thankfully, Myra's testimony was completed, and she headed for the nearest water fountain while rummaging in her briefcase for the bottle of aspirin she kept there for just such occasions. She had just extracted two tablets from the small bottle and popped them into her mouth when she heard the prosecutor, Frazer Remington III, address her from behind.

She held up a finger before pulling her long blond hair back to get a drink from the fountain. She tipped her head back to swallow the pills and took another drink before addressing him.

"I'm sorry. What were you saying?"

"Bad headache?" he asked as she rubbed her left temple at last.

"Yes. I feel a migraine coming on, unfortunately," she replied as she watched the spectators file out of the courtroom.

"Sorry about that. Those things can be horrible. Greg was in top form today, and I'm sure that didn't help your headache any." He referred to the defense attorney, Greg Huntington Bordeaux.

"I'll agree it was grueling. I feel like I've been on the witness stand all day. Oh wait! I have!" She gave Frazer a lopsided grin.

"You did great today," he praised her. "I think that was one of the best testimonies you have ever given."

"I just did my job, although I do have to admit that a few times I wanted to strangle Greg. I know he was just doing his job, but jeez."

He laughed at her grimace. "Can I buy you dinner to make up for his bad behavior in court? Maybe having a bit of food in your stomach will help your headache."

"Thanks. I appreciate the invitation, but I really have to get going. I need to stop by my office. I'm sure I have a ton of messages and e-mails that need responses as soon as possible." She watched the defense attorney stroll from the courtroom with his briefcase. He was talking to a petite redheaded woman that, on first glance, appeared to be quite young, but closer inspection put her around forty or older. Myra surmised it must be a relative of the defendant she had not met during her evaluations.

"I hate to even look at the number of messages waiting for me." He laughed.

Myra laughed with him and was about to say something when she was startled by a tall dark-haired man strolling out of the courtroom behind Greg. He looked straight at Myra, smiled, and winked as though they knew each other and was sharing a private moment. An involuntary shiver ran up her spine, and a feeling of déjà vu spread over her. He was familiar and yet he wasn't. She had the uncanny feeling he was looking straight into her soul.

"Another time then," Frazer offered as she continued to watch the dark-haired man walk toward the exit.

Frazer was a nice guy. He was one of the most-well respected and best prosecutors Charleston, South Carolina, had ever had. In fact, he could run for just about any political office in the state and win it. The public loved him, and it didn't hurt that he was very easy on the eyes and very single. Eye candy, one of the girls in her office had called him once, and she had to agree. But he was a prosecutor, and she was frequently an expert witness as a forensic psychologist, and she just couldn't afford to get involved with him. She couldn't afford for any gossip to start flying around about them having a meal together either. And in the South, especially Charleston, it didn't take much to get tongues wagging with gossip.

"Yes. I wasn't expecting to spend all day here, and it has really thrown off my schedule." She soothed his hurt feelings. "And this headache is not helping either. I just need to catch up with things in my office and then have an early night."

"Well, just don't forget to eat something. I noticed that you didn't eat much for lunch while you were going over your notes before the defense started its cross."

"I was expecting to just have a late lunch on my way to my office. Guess I won't make that mistake again!" She sighed, realizing that the stranger was nowhere in sight. For some reason, that realization frightened her. Was he the one that had sent her that terrifying letter?

Chapter 3

Myra headed immediately for the guards running the x-ray and weapons scanners at the entrance to the building. This morning, there had been four guards on duty at the doors scanning visitors into the building, checking for weapons and explosives. Since it was past five in the afternoon, the courthouse was now closed, and only two guards were running the entrance scanners and monitoring everyone leaving the courthouse and mulling about the entrance doors on the outside of the building. The other guards were checking rooms to make sure all visitors had left the area.

"Hey, Doc! How did it go?" Officer Abercrombie asked. They had met a few years before when she first started filling the position of expert witness in cases.

"Grueling is the only thing that comes to mind at the moment," she replied. She didn't know the other officer, a vicious-looking petite African American woman. She smiled briefly at Myra in greeting before replacing it with the scowl she had previously been exhibiting. Myra had a feeling that the woman could easily take down any man that had been in the courtroom earlier. She might be small and beautiful, but Myra could sense the power in the woman, like a tiger ready to pounce.

"Here's your phone," Officer Abercrombie said as he handed her the phone. He was a very nice-looking tall light brown man of an indistinct heritage with grass green eyes. He made many hearts flutter, including her own. Because court was in session, the guards were required to collect all electronic devices for the safety of the court.

"Thank you. I hope you have a nice evening and a great weekend." She smiled. "Do you get out of here soon?"

"Our shift ends at seven." He indicated his partner as well with a nod. "Oh, and this was left for you." He reached under his desktop and pulled out an envelope that had *Dr. Myra Christie* neatly printed in block style letters.

"That's strange," she muttered. "I don't typically receive correspondence here." Their fingers collided as she retrieved the envelope from him. Long, warm, and strong fingers bumped with her cold stiff fingers, alerting her just how cold she really was. It had been chilly in the courtroom. It always seemed to be chilly in there despite the suits she wore.

"We don't get many people dropping off notes either." He was still smiling. "I hope it's not bad news."

"Any idea what time this was dropped off?" she asked as she studied the block print. It didn't look familiar to her.

"I can't be certain. It was during the returning lunch break rush. Sorry I can't be more helpful, but we had more than one courtroom going today, so it has been really busy in here."

His partner had left her post at the walk-through scanner and was approaching two gentlemen arguing near the door. With a hand on her gun, she approached cautiously but with purpose and power. "Move it along, gentlemen. It's been a long day for everyone. The courthouse is now closed, and I must ask you to quietly leave the building," Myra heard her tell the two men.

"Thanks anyway. It just surprised me that I got a letter here of all places." Myra eyed the two men as they exited the building before going in separate directions. Neither looked happy about their conversation or the interruption to leave. She had not realized their argument had caused her to tense until she felt herself relaxing at the sight of the men going their own way. "Time I got out of here too. I still have to go to my office. Have a good one!" She waved as she exited the building.

The wind was beginning to pick up, and dark clouds were rolling in from the west as she hurried down the sidewalk to the parking garage. It was late February, and soon there would be beautiful flowers all around the courthouse. She had never really noticed just how many azalea bushes surrounded the courthouse until just now;

the cool wind brushed through their bare branches like old withered beggars reaching out for help. Soon, those same bare branches would be holding up a chorus of beautiful blossoms that set Charleston apart from other cities in the spring.

Cold rain was just beginning to spatter to the ground as Myra ducked into the dark parking garage. Most of the earlier patrons had already left the premises. Just a few stragglers were now making their way to their vehicles, just as she was, the echoes of their footsteps on the concrete sounding eerie and ominous. Perhaps it was due to the letter she held in her hand with her briefcase or maybe the memory of that dark-haired guy in the courthouse who unnerved her, or perhaps it was just a combination of the darkening sky, the rain, exhaustion, hunger, and the reverberations of footsteps in the lonely parking garage. Regardless, Myra felt as though she was being watched. Without being overtly obvious, she scanned the area as she reached her Jeep. She waited till she was quite close to it before pressing the unlock button on her keychain. The hazard lights flashed, and she heard the distinct slide of the driver's side only door unlocking as she reached the Jeep.

Quickly, she flung her briefcase and purse in the passenger seat as she scanned her vehicle for unwanted occupants. She slipped inside and slammed the door shut as though the hounds of hell were on her heels. Immediately, she hit the lock on the door and started the Jeep. The soft sounds of jazz from the radio filled the interior, helping to calm her. Rarely had she ever felt so unsettled walking through a parking garage.

Slipping on her seat belt, she checked her rearview mirror and began trembling when she recognized the man from the courthouse standing behind her Jeep. Heart racing and feeling out of breath, she was terrified. Who was this man? He acted as though he knew her, but it was an instinctive vibe that had her in full panic mode. He was dangerous. She could sense it as though it were tattooed across his forehead.

She knew deep down that she needed to fear this man. She needed to escape this stranger above all else. He was not what he seemed. But then what was he representing? He had simply smiled and winked at her as he exited the courthouse. She had been fumbling in her purse for her cell phone to call the police without taking her eyes off him. But what was she going to tell the dispatch? "Yeah, uh, I just got out of court as a witness today and this good-looking dark-haired guy exited after me. He winked and smiled before leaving the building, and now he's standing behind my vehicle in the parking garage?" They would think she was nuts. Maybe she was nuts, but she had a feeling about him that she couldn't shake off, and that alarmed her to a terrifying level.

She quickly looked around to see if anyone else was nearby. She was utterly alone with this stranger, which was terrifying. However, when she glanced back in her mirror, the man was gone, frightening her even more. Frantically, she looked around but saw no one. It was as though he had simply vanished. She sat there for a moment, willing her breathing and heart rate to return to normal before easing out of her parking spot. As she made her way to the exit of the garage, a guard was making his rounds. Chastising herself for acting like an idiot, she waved at the guard and left the parking lot. *What is wrong with me?* she thought. *I'm really losing it today!*

Chapter 4

Rain was coming down in torrents, the poor windshield wipers barely able to keep up with deluge. Traffic was at a standstill on Interstate 26. The radio announcer had just read off a long list of accidents on the interstate and connecting highways, indicating that she was going nowhere for a while. "Just great," she muttered to herself as her stomach rumbled and her head throbbed. She reached for her briefcase where she frequently kept a granola bar or two in case of such situations to keep the hunger pains at bay until she was able to eat a decent meal. Myra noticed the unopened letter addressed to her.

In her erratic, at best undignified, escape to her vehicle and out of the parking garage earlier, she had completely forgotten the envelope she held in her hand with the briefcase. When she flung the briefcase into the passenger seat, somehow the letter had come to rest squarely on top of the briefcase. Casting a quick look about, as though she were about to commit a crime or something, Myra hesitantly picked up the envelope.

She took another quick look at the nonmoving traffic, then slit the envelope open with her nail. A slip of high quality plain card-stock paper fell out. It had been neatly folded into thirds, and she took her time unfolding it.

My Dearest Myra,

Seeing you in court today made my heart leap with joy. I have waited so long for you. Your hair reminds me of liquid gold and your eyes of emeralds, and I shudder. Oh, what a joy it will be to dine on your luscious pink lips.

But I am getting carried away with my longing for you. I have watched and waited. Our time is nearing. It won't be long now. You will be mine, my love! Just know that I am near to you. Soon, my love, soon!

Always yours

Her appetite was suddenly nonexistent. Her cold fingers were shaking as she read the unsigned letter. She dropped it on top of her briefcase, staring at it as though it were about to attack her. She had never received a stalking letter before. Oh, she had received her share of hate mail and fan mail from her position as a forensic psychologist, especially in the two high profile cases she had appeared as an expert witness. Two specific letters had stood out. However, Myra had not taken any of them seriously. She simply handed them over to the authorities to investigate. One had been from the wife of a defendant accused of murdering their child. He had been sentenced to life in prison. The other had been anonymous, much like this one. However, there the similarities stop. It had been a fan letter. It was a young girl wanting advice and information on her occupation, and Myra had let the authorities respond to that one as well, just in case it was a poser—a person pretending to be something or someone they are not.

This letter, however, was totally different. This was the work of a stalker, someone who knew her and was watching her. But who? She had only noticed the dark-haired guy today as he had exited the courtroom. Had he been watching her? Had that innocent smile and wink that had unnerved her been more than innocent? What if it was someone else entirely? This was a serious situation, and she wasn't sure how to handle it. Should she just ignore it as though she was supposed to have received the letter prior to her afternoon testimony to rattle her and throw her off?

As she sat in the nonmoving traffic, an unrelenting train of theories, questions, and fears ran through her head. She tried to call her office, but the storm was interrupting service. That severely limited her choices to simply sitting in the traffic and worrying. She had never felt lonelier and an unsuspecting target in her life. She nervously checked her rearview mirror and glanced out the side windows. "Get a hold of yourself!" she chastised herself. "It's not like whomever is sending these letters is standing in the rain or in the car behind you!"

After several minutes, she finally shook it off. Obviously, whoever had written the letter was not with her at the moment. She was stuck in traffic that had just slightly begun moving. Her doors were locked, and she was safe. She cranked up her radio and attempted to get lost in the strains of a Laura Marling song and the rain beating down on her Jeep.

It was late by the time the snarled-up traffic cleared and Myra finally made it to her office. Everyone had left hours ago, and she was too exhausted to play catch-up with her work. She picked up the written messages and her mail that had been left on her desk. She listened to her voice mail, making notes of the urgent messages that needed a response first thing in the morning. The rest, and there were at least twenty messages, she took notes so she could respond when she had some extra time. It was nearly thirty minutes later when she finally left for home.

The rain had finally let up to a lazy drizzle by the time she drove into her apartment complex. As usual, someone had parked in her assigned parking place. Myra was going to have to talk to the management office about it as soon as she had some spare time. She circled the parking lot before finding a place several apartments down and on the back side, which meant she had to walk across the entire parking lot in the dark and rain. She was not happy as she collected her purse and briefcase.

After a quick walk and three flights of stairs, she was unlocking her apartment, when her neighbor's door suddenly swung open, causing her to jump violently.

Selina stuck her head out. "I thought I heard you!" she exclaimed in her strong Central American accent.

"Hello, Selina. Yes, it's been a long day for me." Myra tried to end the conversation before it began. It wasn't that she didn't like Selina. She actually did, but she was beyond exhausted.

"You poor thing. You want to come eat? I made enchiladas and much left over."

"Thank you for the offer, but to be honest, I'm too tired to even eat. I think I'm just going to take a long hot shower and go straight to bed. Rain check?" Myra offered as she opened her door and turned on the lights.

"Okay. I could bring them to you while you shower. You need to eat. Not good to miss meals. I bring to you. I also have something that was delivered to you today. I'll go get it," she said as she disappeared into her apartment.

Realizing that she was not going to get away from Selina so easily, Myra slipped into her own apartment, leaving the door opened for Selina. Depositing her purse and briefcase on the sofa, she went into the kitchen to get a glass of water. Moments later, Selina came in carrying a large bouquet of the reddest roses Myra had ever seen and a plate piled high with delicious smelling enchiladas.

"Those can't be for me," she referred to the roses. "I don't know anyone that would send them for one thing, and I'm not dating anyone," she explained.

Selina laughed. "They are from your admirer. I confess, I read the note. Very mysterious. So sweet. He's a keeper, if you ask me. Romantic and mysterious always good relationships and great in bed." She laughed. "I leave you now. You eat and sleep, and I see you tomorrow." Selina turned and headed to the door.

"Thank you for being such a great friend and for the food." Myra smiled tiredly.

"You good friend too." Selina smiled just before she stepped outside, pulling the door closed behind her.

Myra crossed to the door and locked it, including the dead bolt she had added for extra security. A rumbling stomach superseded her curiosity, so she grabbed a fork from a drawer and dove into the scrumptious enchiladas. Instead of sitting at her table or the bar, she ate as she made her way down the hallway to her bathroom, flipping on lights as she went. Instead of taking a shower, she decided soaking in a hot bath might be more relaxing after the day she had experienced.

Turning on the water and adding some lavender-scented bubble bath, she began filling the tub as she continued devouring the enchiladas. Selina had been right. The food was what she needed, and she was already feeling a bit better. Selina was an incredible cook. Myra could not understand how Selina and her boyfriend didn't weigh a ton eating like this all the time. It was extraordinarily delicious!

She took the empty plate back into the kitchen, and the sight of the roses raised her curiosity. They smelled wonderful, and the blooms were majestically open, showing off their full beauty. The card was in an envelope with the name and address of the flower shop with Myra's name and address scrawled across the top. It was a local flower shop, she noted, as she pulled out the card. As she read it, her heart nearly stopped. She was shaking as the card dropped to the floor from her suddenly cold fingers. She was beginning to hyperventilate and sat down in a nearby chair, putting her head between her knees.

"For all our future memories to come! I know they are going to be grand, Myra. It is almost time, my love," the card stated and was not signed. It did not need to be signed though. She instinctively knew who the flowers were from. They were from the same person who had left the note for her in the courthouse.

She had no idea what to do. For now, she left the flowers where they were and picked up the card with shaking fingers to place it on the counter next to the roses. She had to escape the room and think. Remembering the tub was filling with water, she felt that was the best step she could take at the moment.

She downed her glass of water and refilled the glass with some fruit-flavored wine from the refrigerator and headed to the bathroom. Within minutes, she was surrounded by sweet smelling bubbles, warm relaxing water, a glass of chilled wine, and a book she had been reading. She was hoping it would take her mind off the horrible day she had undergone.

Sometime later, feeling relaxed, calm, and more than a little drowsy, Myra fell into bed, almost asleep before her head even hit the pillow. At first, her dream was about the characters in the book she had just been reading, but as some point, her dream became real. A mist fell over the darkened room, and someone was teasing her lips and eyelids with rose petals.

Drowsily, she opened her eyes. She could not see his face in the darkened room, but she felt the fire of his kisses on her neck and shoulders. His hands were roaming her body freely as if she had invited him to do so. Maybe she had and she didn't remember. They felt so good that she didn't want it to stop. He nibbled on her earlobe and whispered in her ear, "Ah, my love. I have missed you so much. Soon we will be together daily, I promise."

Something about the way he had said it had her bolting upright in bed, suddenly awake. The room was dark with streaks of light filtering through the blinds on the windows. She flipped on the bedside lamp, and no one was there. Jumping from bed, she hurried from one room to the other, checking for intruders. She double-checked the locks on the door then began checking the locks on all the windows, which was rather eccentric considering she lived on the third floor of the apartment building. Everything was locked, and no one was found. Had it really just been a dream? she thought. It felt so real. She could still feel the tingle of his hands on her body and the heat of his kisses on her shoulder and neck. It was more than unnerving. Checking the clock, she realized she had only been asleep a few hours, but she felt more than wide awake at the moment. It was going to be a long night and an even longer day tomorrow.

Chapter 5

Daybreak found Myra at the desk in her home office going over files and making notes. She had already left several messages for her office assistant and e-mailed her instructions and notes on even more things in the several hours she had been awake. She was dressed in a powder blue suit for court and drank at least five cups of coffee. She was beginning to buzz from all the caffeine, but she was going to need it in order to get through the day.

After she had awoken and ran through the apartment looking for intruders like a madwoman in the middle of the night, she had returned to her bedroom to find a lone rose lying on her pillow. It had freaked her out even more. How had it gotten there? Had she been sleepwalking, collected it from the vase on the kitchen counter, and placed it there in her sleep? She doubted it. She was not prone to sleepwalking, but she had not found anyone in the apartment. All doors and windows had been locked. She had even double-checked!

She had left her room virtually untouched and was careful about what she touched in her apartment, going so far as to keep a list. She had also taken a picture of the rose on the pillow. She was not sure what to do about it. It was more than spooky. It was downright terrifying at this point.

She wished she could call her dad right now. He had been one of the top special agents in the FBI. He had an uncanny sixth sense about things. Unfortunately, he had been killed several years ago. He would have known exactly what to do or what was going on. He would have comforted her. He had always comforted her and encouraged her when she was feeling out of sorts. Presently, however, she was beginning to feel a bit unhinged.

The dreams were not normal for her, and she was beginning to feel a bit frightened about them. The letters and then the roses on top of it had her panic and anxiety levels high. Too high, in fact, especially when she was due back in court thanks to that defense attorney. Still, the rose on her pillow was just horrifying. There had to be a reasonable explanation. She just wasn't ready to analyze it. She needed to put it all in the back of her mind for the time being. She needed to focus on the court case at hand. Then she would put a stop to the stalker or whatever he or she was. She just had to concentrate, one thing at a time.

She was armed with the resolve that she was not going to put up with such nonsense, and she was going to get help in getting to the bottom of it, possibly even pressing charges against the creep doing it so that he or she would not be able to approach some other more vulnerable woman or person. She grabbed her things and headed out of the apartment into the day with an early sky streaked with pinks and purples. It was picturesque and beautiful, and Myra decided to take it as a good omen.

She made it through the parking lot with no mishaps, and a quick inspection inside and outside of the Jeep appeared all well. It was starting off good, she thought. She just needed to stay positive and strong. She played some upbeat music from a pop station on the way to the courthouse to keep her spirits up and whatever else was going on at bay.

She left so early that she escaped most of the rush hour traffic and slipped into her normal parking spot at the courthouse nearly two and a half hours before court was even scheduled to be in session. On a hunch, she grabbed her things and headed to the main courthouse door to see if it was open yet as it was not scheduled to open for at least another thirty minutes or so.

As she expected, the door was still locked, but a familiar officer waved at her and motioned that she wait just a moment. She was having difficulty remembering his name. Officer Jones… Officer Johnson… Officer James? Once he got closer, she was able to read his name tag—Officer Johans.

"You're mighty early." He smiled at her. "I was just doing the exterior security check."

"Yeah, I couldn't sleep last night so I've been working for hours. Thought I would try to get ahead of some of that rush hour traffic in Columbia. I was lucky and hit light traffic on I-26 coming into Charleston this morning. I don't know what that was all about."

"I noticed traffic was light this morning as well. Guess that means everyone is going to be running a little late this morning, and accidents will be everywhere here shortly. People just don't get they are driving into a peninsula here, and there is only so much room for parking. It all gets bottlenecked, and then people get frustrated, start switching back and forth in the lanes, and bam! A fender bender that wrecks everyone's travel to work."

"Exactly. It's so annoying. Say, since I'm here early, how about a good coffee from the shop around the corner? My treat?" she asked.

"I would say that sounds wonderful. Sometimes the coffee here is like motor oil. You stick a spoon in it to add sugar, and the spoon stands straight up by itself!" He laughed.

Myra laughed with him. "How do you like your coffee normally?" she asked, still chuckling.

He gave her the particulars, and she headed down the sidewalk to the coffee shop. She was surprised to find even light foot traffic in the coffee shop. It wasn't even eight o'clock yet, so she had expected it to be packed. Within minutes, she had both her order and Officer Johans's in hand and was headed back to the courthouse.

He had been waiting by the door for her return and opened it especially for her before relocking it. "Strict orders that we don't open till eight o'clock," he told her, gratefully accepting the coffee. He took a sip and moaned his delight. "The best cup of coffee I've had in a while. Thank you."

"Not a problem. I don't want to cause you any problems. I can wait outside until eight," she offered, heading back to the door.

"You're no problem. I'm just waiting for the other officers to get finished with their rounds. I can go ahead and x-ray your stuff and scan you. Then you can have a seat out here with us till eight. Sorry, but I can't allow you to go anywhere else in the courthouse yet."

"Don't worry about it. I knew I was early. I was actually planning on sitting on one of the benches outside until you opened, but this works." She smiled as she placed her purse, laptop, and briefcase in the x-ray scanner. She slowly walked through the scanning machine then raised her arms perpendicular to her body so he could run the hand scanner over her. Once cleared, she accepted all her things. She went ahead and gave him her cell phone for safekeeping.

Taking a seat at a nearby guard desk, she opened her laptop and took files from her briefcase. She wasn't sure what else the defense attorney could ask her that he hadn't asked the day before, but she planned to be ready for whatever he threw at her. The other three officers trailed into the entrance area and gave her a strange look. Thankfully, Officer Johans filled them in so she would not be disturbed. There were three entrances to the courthouse, which meant that a total of twelve officers were in the building doing security checks and what have you prior to the general public entry.

At eight o'clock, one of the officers whom she did not know unlocked the door. Instantly, several people lined up at the scanners, awaiting entry. She recognized the judge, Anthony Hawkins III, as being one of the people and nodded a greeting at him. Judge Hawkins came from a long line of attorneys. His father had served in the South Carolina Senate for a number of years and even ran for governor, but he lost. He was well liked and known to be fair and objective even in the worst of cases. Myra had met him in various circles over the past few years, but this was the first case she had ever worked with him. So far, he had lived up to his reputation as far as she was concerned.

A big man, Judge Hawkins was nearly six feet eight inches but kept a trim physique for being nearly sixty years of age. His hair was mostly salt-and-pepper with a bit more salt than pepper, which suited him well. He was a nice-looking man. Myra often thought he resembled the actor Sam Elliott. She watched as he made his way through the line and was scanned like everyone else for admittance. After he had been granted entry, he made his way over to her.

"So how did you get in here so early?" he asked with a bewildered smile.

"I arrived early with good coffee." She laughed. "I've only been here a few minutes. How are you today, Your Honor?"

"Tired. Looking forward to this case being over and moving on to the next one. I have vacation coming up soon, and I'm more than looking forward to it."

"Ah, vacation. Is that where you take off work for an undetermined amount of time, go someplace exotic, and leave all your worries behind you?"

"You forgot about sinking your feet into sand and drinking margaritas all day while listening to the waves on a warm sunny beach." He laughed.

"It's been so long since I've had a vacation. I'm afraid I've forgotten all the specifics." She grinned sheepishly. "Where are you headed?"

"My wife planned a surprise vacation. Said it was someplace warm and inviting with lots of beaches. I'm guessing it's either somewhere in the Caribbean or Hawaii."

"Nice! I may tuck myself into a piece of luggage and join you!" Myra teased him.

They had a laugh as she gathered up her things. "I've got to check into my office before court. I guess I'll see you in there. You did great yesterday, by the way. Bordeaux can be quite the grandstander at times."

"I know he was just doing his job. It's just that I had a migraine beginning, and his rhetoric and questioning were beginning to wear me down. I'm feeling better today." The lie about feeling better just fell off her lips. The fact that she was running on about three hours of sleep and about a gallon of coffee was making her a bit jumpy and hyper at the moment. She feared the moment when all the caffeine wore off. She just hoped the defense attorney called her to the stand before it happened. It would be embarrassing to crash on the stand!

Chapter 6

Court recommenced at nine o'clock. Mr. Bordeaux, the defense attorney, called two other witnesses before the defense rested. She had wasted a trip down to Charleston for the case on the grounds that Mr. Bordeaux had reserved the right to call her again to the stand for more questions, only to not call her at all. She was fuming! By noon, the closing arguments had been presented from both sides, and court was in recess pending the verdict from the jury.

Myra was at the guard desk collecting her phone when Mr. Bordeaux came up behind her.

"Excuse me, Dr. Christie. May I have a word with you?" he asked to her back.

She jumped at the unexpected address before turning to look at him expectantly. "What is it?"

"In private, if you don't mind," he suggested, taking her right elbow in his hand and steering her back down the hall. They entered a small room with a table and few chairs. A television monitor was mounted to one wall, and what looked like devices for playing tapes, CDs, and other forms of media sat on a glass table under the television. Another wall had a dry-erase board that had been wiped clean.

"You must be upset that I did not recall you to the stand today," he began.

"I'm not upset that you didn't recall me. I'm upset that you reserved the right to recall me when you knew you had no intention of recalling me to begin with!" she stormed.

"Well, at first I thought perhaps something might come up, but it didn't. I did have an ulterior motive, however. I had intended to talk to you yesterday after recess, but I had an emergency come up with the case. I wanted to ask you out for dinner. Now that the case has all but ended, how about a long lunch? It might be a while before the verdict is in."

"You reserved the right to recall me in order to ask me to dinner?" she asked incredulously.

"Well, I realize now that it sounds a bit lame on my part, but yes. I thought we hit it off well yesterday. I know you were working for the prosecution, but I wanted to talk to you about perhaps working for the defense on occasion."

"Sorry, Mr. Bordeaux, but I only work cases when requested by the court. I do not do evaluations for the defense. I'm much too busy in my practice and in working at the local prison in Columbia. As for dinner, I make it a habit not to date colleagues and attorneys. I have seen too many cases where quagmires result, and the lingering mess often leads to someone's professional reputation getting injured in some way. Thank you for the invitation, but I really must get to my office. I've been away too long already." She pointedly looked at her watch.

"But what about the verdict? Surely you want to wait around and hear it?" he asked.

"The verdict is none of my concern. I was directed by the court to evaluate the client and provide a potential sentence recommendation. The verdict is the concern of you, your client, and the prosecution," she responded as she headed back to the door.

"You are not the least bit curious?" he asked in surprise.

"I'll read about in the papers if I need my curiosity quenched. Good day and good luck, Mr. Bordeaux."

With that, Myra left the room and headed straight to the exit. What was with these attorneys all of a sudden? She was no beauty queen, though she was not totally unfortunate in the looks department, she thought. She had long blond hair and green eyes which she felt were her two best assets. She had always thought her nose was too big for her face—aquiline, probably from the Native American ancestry from her father's side of the family. Her olive skin tone made it look almost as though she had a year-round tan, which gave her a more striking look than she realized. She was also tall with a nice build that did not require dieting or much exercise. She was fortunate, she supposed, but still.

She had a few boyfriends over the years, but no one seriously since she had graduated college. In fact, she rarely got asked out on dates. Of course, she worked long hours and was a bit of a hermit when she was off work, but still, what was with the last couple of days? Two attorneys had asked her out, she had received two letters from a stalker, and roses from an unknown admirer. She felt like she went to bed one night and awoke in an alternate universe the next morning. This was a bit ridiculous!

She had a ton of things to do, beginning with returning phone calls that were mounting up. She was just about to walk out the door when Officer Johans called out to her. She thought he was going to thank her for the coffee again, but instead he held up an envelope for her.

"This arrived for you just before the court recessed. I was about to hand it to you when the attorney steered you away."

"Thank you." She smiled at him. "Have a great day!"

The winds of yesterday had calmed, and it was bright and sunny. She slipped on sunglasses and raised her face to the bright sunlight for a moment, enjoying the beautiful day. It was a bit unseasonably warm for February, but she would take it. As she started toward the garage, she glanced down at the envelope. The hand-printed block style lettering brought sudden chills. She dreaded opening it.

She tried not to show any emotion at the envelope and furtively looked around as she continued to the garage. A couple was across the courtyard talking, and a young man was riding his bike down the sidewalk across from the courthouse. A couple of men were looking at a large paper they held between them—what looked like to be building plans of some sort. A few people were headed into the courthouse and looked to be couriers going to file important documents. She saw no one lurking around or looking in her direction.

Unlike the day before, she strolled to her Jeep with purpose, all the while being alert but striving to not look rattled. She unlocked it, surreptitiously checking the entire Jeep for unwanted occupants as she placed her belongings in the passenger seat and climbed in.

Immediately, she locked her doors and started the engine. People were coming and going as she slowly backed out of her parking space and continued out of the garage. "Great, just great," she muttered to herself. "Now I'm exhibiting paranoid behavior."

She refused to read the letter before she arrived back at her office. She stopped for a sandwich and drink at a popular shop on her way out of town and ate as she drove the nearly two-hour trip to her office. Traffic was light, so she put on her cruise control and glided up the interstate, periodically checking her rearview mirror to see if anyone was following her.

Her father had once showed her how to monitor traffic to see if anyone was following when she was a teenager. It had been a fun and amusing thing at the time, but he had insisted it was a good defense skill to have. She knew it was important in his occupation, but seriously, how many people followed teenagers around, she had thought at the time. She never really thought she would need that skill. Now, however, she felt much differently.

She was nearly to Columbia and still had not identified any particular vehicle following her. She continued straight to her office, parked in her assigned spot, and collected her things, including the letter. She needed some serious advice, and she hoped one of her associates was available to talk.

She had not been in her office ten minutes when Nathan, one of her business associates, popped his head into her office. "You're back! How did it go?"

"The case? It went as they usually do with the exception that the defense attorney was Bordeaux, a great attorney but with an ego the size of Canada!" She paused as she reached for the letters. Nathan was the perfect person to address her concerns. "You got a few minutes? I have something serious that I need to talk with someone about. I feel like I'm going crazy." She smoothed her updo hair style and fidgeted with anxiety.

"Sure, what's up?" he asked with concern as he plopped down in one of the wingback chairs across her desk.

So much had been going on. She had to think a moment about where to start. She decided to start at the beginning of the bizarre events—the first letter. She handed him the first two letters in the order she had received them and gave him a quick narrative of everything, including the dream. Once she started, everything came pouring out. She was nearly in tears by the time she finished.

"I know the dream is just my subconscious responding to the stress of receiving the letters, but I just can't shake it. It was like someone was really there. And the rose? How on earth did that get there?"

Nathan didn't answer her, but his expression spoke volumes. He was concerned. He frowned as he unfolded the letters. While he read the first letter, she opened the third one.

My Dearest Myra,

You looked amazing in your blue suit today. With your hair all done up in that French twist, you looked so cool and professional. As always, so totally beautiful. Soon we will not have to deal with only our late night visits. We will be together for life. You are my promised one, my dear. I will explain everything soon.

My work is nearly finished here. Then we can go anywhere and do anything you wish. I do so much enjoy our time together. By the way, did you like the roses? I thought they looked nice on the kitchen bar. Sort of brightened up the whole room, made it cheery. The one I brushed your tender skin with last night looked so good next to you. I want to make love to you on a bed of rose petals. Ah, just talking about it gets me so excited.

Soon, my love, all of your dreams will come true, and I will be there with you. Until then.

All my love

Myra was shaking with fear and apprehension by the time she finished the letter. It was like he was in her head, her apartment, her dreams…he was everywhere and nowhere. Tears fell from her bright green eyes to flow down her face. Nathan simply held his hand out for the letter. She handed it over, staring at him in shock. She had no idea what to do.

Nathan finished reading the letter and simply placed it on top of the others on the corner of her desk. "We need to call the police," he informed her.

"What are they going to be able to do? Three anonymous letters, a vase of roses, and my weird dream does not make a case. It might add up to getting me hospitalized and heavily medicated. There is no evidence pointing to a specific person or persons. There is nothing here to check. He hasn't really done anything except send letters and flowers. It's like he's reading my mind and knows what I'm dreaming. The cops can't follow any of that. Trust me, I know. My dad worked for the FBI."

"They can at least put someone on you to watch your place and follow you to make sure you stay safe," Nathan offered. "Perhaps they can get fingerprints from the letters and DNA from the envelopes. Don't give up before we have even begun to fight back!"

She could feel the hysteria bubbling up inside of her. She had only ever had one meltdown like this before, and that was the day she learned her father had died. "Trust me, Nathan, they won't do anything. This guy has made no threats against me of any kind. They will look at these and laugh and say I have an admirer. It wouldn't bother me so much if it were not for the dreams. Am I going crazy?"

Nathan got up from his chair and rounded her desk. He put his arms around her and simply held her. "No, you're not crazy. This is simply weird. Maybe the guy entered your apartment before as a maintenance person and installed cameras. That could account how he knows where the roses are. Maybe you really did sleepwalk and took one of the roses to your bedroom last night and just didn't notice it when you first woke up. A camera in your bedroom could account for that knowledge as well. And as for knowing what you are wearing today, well, he simply was in the courtroom when he wrote this letter."

"Cameras in my apartment? Are you serious? Oh God! I hadn't even considered that! How do I get my apartment checked for those?" She shivered even more as she thought of the potential consequences of cameras hidden throughout her apartment. He could be watching her change her clothes, bathe, basically all the intimate details of her life on view for him. The thought was horrifying!

"Like I said, we need to call the cops. They can check out your apartment and fingerprint these letters. Maybe he even licked the envelopes, so they can gather DNA. He sounds like a professional to me, like he has done this before. Let me at least call them," he pleaded.

She was quiet for several moments, staring at the letters, remembering the flowers, the dreams, and that guy at the courthouse. Finally, she nodded in agreement. Maybe it was time to call the cavalry. She was certain she knew what they were going to say, but maybe they could offer some guidance. She felt a little calmer as she watched Nathan's strong hand lift the handset of her phone.

Chapter 7

Several hours after Nathan called the police, they were finally leaving her apartment. They had first arrived at her office to take her statement and the letters, including the envelopes into evidence for fingerprinting. Judging by their facial expressions, they were thinking exactly what she had thought they would until they read the third letter.

At that point, they became concerned about the possibility of cameras in her apartment as well. They followed her to her home and took the note from the roses into evidence and the rose from her pillow as well. They fingerprinted nearly everything in the house and scanned every room with electronic devices, but to no avail. No cameras were found, thereby perplexing everyone even more.

They asked if she had her shades up and drapes open during the past few days. She denied it. They asked her who her recent visitors had been. She denied having any. They asked about maintenance personnel, and she denied having any issues within the apartment. They asked her so many questions and then asked them all over again.

By the time they left, she was exhausted with a horrible headache, and her apartment was a mess. Fingerprint dust was literally on every surface of the entire apartment. They tried not to destroy her things when they checked all her furniture for cameras and microphones, as well as the vents, light fixtures, and outlets, but still things were in major disarray. She had expected only one or two officers to arrive, but had that quickly turned into a few crime scene investigators as well.

There really had not been that many people in her apartment, but they had gone in and out so many times that even the floors were a mess. Someone had even tracked mud or something onto her carpets, which meant that she also needed to clean those as well. Simply looking about the apartment made her burst into tears. She was too tired to do any cleaning, especially since she had not slept the night before, and she was too tired to think. She simply took a shower and climbed into bed.

*****

The jury deliberated two full days before returning with a guilty verdict on all counts. It was all over the local network news and radio stations. Owen Johnson was now up for either multiple life sentences or the death penalty. As a part of Myra's evaluation report to the court, sentencing recommendations had been approached as with most evaluations of this type. She had recommended heavy counseling among other things if he were given life sentences.

The court would reconvene within the month so the jury could give their sentencing recommendations to the court. All in all, Myra felt that Owen would likely get life despite South Carolina still being a major capital punishment state. Most of the evidence against him had been circumstantial, which she felt helped to keep the death sentence off the table. Either way, it was totally out of her hands at this point. She had done her job and was now back in her office.

During those same two days, she had been busily scrubbing nearly every surface of her apartment in an attempt to rid it of the fingerprint dust and God only knew what else had been tracked in and deposited on her surfaces and floors. And with trying to play catch-up in the office, it had her feeling sleep-deprived. Although truth be told, much of the sleep deprivation was due to anxiety over the dreams and that last letter.

Though she had not heard or received anything since that last letter, the thought that someone might be there lurking was frightening, whether she wanted to admit it to herself or not. It was the unknowing that was the worst part. The what if. What if there really was a stalker? What if someone had been able to enter her apartment without her knowledge? What if that someone was watching her every moment of every day by an unknown method.

The what ifs were driving her crazy, and she really needed to get a grip. Fingers and toes crossed, the police were right, and it was just someone playing games with her. She had to believe the police. She could not afford to let herself think otherwise, despite herself. She also had to trust the police to be there to help if needed. To be on the safe side, they put extra patrols in her neighborhood for the time being. It wasn't much, but it was better than nothing and the most they could actually do under the current circumstances. The detective in charge of her case had called earlier that morning to notify her they didn't find any fingerprints on the letters and no DNA on the envelope. He assured her they were taking the situation seriously, but with no evidence, it was going to take a while.

She was doing her best to push those unsettling thoughts aside, and everything else was essentially falling back into a natural rhythm. Phone calls had all been caught up, paperwork was…well…paperwork, and always needed something done. But most importantly, she had just begun seeing her patients again. What should have been only one day of court and out of the office turned into almost a week of not seeing any patients. As Nathan had so eloquently pointed out, "You have to have your own head on in the correct position before you can effectively help others."

He had been correct. She knew that and would have told him the same thing had the tables been turned. Nevertheless, it had not made her feel any better. After those two days of court, those letters, dreams, and roses, she had been so jumpy she actually jumped at her own reflection in the bathroom mirror. Patients would pick up on that, maybe not noticeably, but possibly on a subconscious level, and that would not be good for them. In fact, it could potentially be downright detrimental to the patients, not to mention being unethical.

In the end, she simply decided to take it one day at a time and do her best to forget the unpleasant things. Just one step at a time, one phone call at a time, one patient at a time. It was all anyone could do.

In the meantime, the detective had suggested that she go through her files to look for anyone who might have a grudge or unhealthy obsession with her. She had looked around her office and scanned her computer for all the cases she had ever worked on. There were so many cases and patients, both past and present, she realized it would take the rest of the week scrutinizing records. She could literally feel depression and anxiety wrapping her in their dark suffocating grips.

Chapter 8

Nearly one month to the day of the verdict, court convened on the case of the *State of South Carolina v. Owen Johnson* for sentencing. It was said that Mr. Johnson nearly fainted in the courtroom when he was given the death sentence for the death of the three women and the teenaged girl. A hush of quiet shock had even fallen over the courtroom as the general consensus had been that Mr. Owen would receive four consecutive life sentences for the murders based on a purely circumstantial case at best. It had definitely been a shock for everyone and a victory for the state and the families of the victims.

Myra heard the news while eating lunch at a local hot spot with Nathan. She had mixed feelings on the controversy of capital punishment and could see the pros and cons of both arguments. Neither of which, however, made her feel any better about the sentence.

"It's not your fault, you know," Nathan reminded her. "You did your job. The jury did their job. The cops, the investigators, the judge…everyone did their jobs in this case. Anyone who commits a murder knows that there is always the possibility of getting caught and getting the death penalty."

"I realize that. It's just that…well…this was my case, and he got the death penalty. I've never had a case that actually received the death penalty before." Myra's eyes were glued to the television playing the breaking story quietly in the corner of the restaurant. A pale Owen Johnson was being led out of the courtroom in an orange jumpsuit and shackles.

"Unfortunately, it probably won't be your last either. As long as there have been men on earth, there has been deceit and murder, and it will continue until man vanishes from the earth. My grandmother used to say we are all victims of our humanity and cruelty. I didn't understand what she meant when I was a kid, but she's right. We all, no matter whether we want to admit it or not, have humanity and cruelty within us." Nathan sipped his iced mocha latte as he dispensed his grandmother's wisdom of years gone by.

"My father used to say that we are all capable of everything, but it is our choices that make all the difference on who we are as individuals. It's sad, really, that some people take the lives of others so casually and insignificantly. Life is to be treasured and cherished. I've talked to so many killers over the years, and not a single one has been able to give me a good reason for killing another human being. I just don't understand people sometimes." She stirred a sweet tea and pushed her lunch around on her plate, mostly uneaten.

"I know what you mean. Are they born psychopaths? Is it nature versus nurture? Maybe we will never truly know the correct answer. All we can do is keep doing what we are doing until a better way comes along. In the meantime, some people will get off, and others get life or the death penalty. The ones who are truly responsible are the ones who do the deed."

"True. It's just a sad state all around, and no one really wins," she said thoughtfully. "What if he's really innocent though?"

"That's what the appeal process is for. Myra, you didn't present the evidence. You are not the prosecutor. You simply did an evaluation and presented your evidence."

"I suppose," she murmured, tearing her eyes from the screen.

With that, they cleaned up their table and headed back to the office. Myra had patients at the local prison scheduled for the entire afternoon. They were more of those same people who played roulette with other people's lives, and they all lost.

*****

Nearly a month passed without any more letters or contact from Myra's unwanted stalker. She was finally beginning to relax. Perhaps it had just been some nut in the courtroom watching the trial that had decided to play head games with her. Perhaps it had been one of

Mr. Johnson's family members, thinking that it might make a difference in the case. She didn't really care so long as it had all stopped.

Rhonda, Myra's assistant and intern, finally began to break the serious shell that Myra had built around herself. She was beginning to joke and laugh again. Darrell, another therapist in the office and who Rhonda secretly thought had a crush on Myra, had even been hanging around her office more lately. He had been away from the office due to a family emergency while Myra had been in court and had missed most of the upheaval.

Upon hearing about everything, however, he began hovering. Rhonda had even taken to calling him UFO behind his back in jest. Even after a month of no harassment of any kind, he still continued to hover.

Nathan had even taken it upon himself to act as her personal protector. He took her to lunch every day, followed her to and from work, and had notified the front desk to screen the mail for envelopes and notes such as the ones Myra had previously received. He checked on her frequently throughout the day. Truth be told, she was beginning to feel suffocated by Nathan.

All in all, everything was beginning to look better. February had rolled into March, and now April was on the horizon. They all had a bit of spring fever in the office.

On the drive into the office one particular morning, Myra was feeling particularly happy for no apparent reason. She had been sleeping much better of late. The temperature had been climbing, and it felt wonderful outside. The days were getting longer, and spring flowers were beginning to bloom everywhere, she noticed.

She swept into the office with a surprise box of Krispy Kreme donuts for the office staff and a big smile on her face. "Have you noticed how beautiful it is outside these days?" she asked Rhonda. "Flowers are blooming everywhere! I don't think I've seen such an abundance of blooms this time of year before. I guess it's because it's been a little warmer so far this year than normal." Myra continued to chatter away as she selected a donut for herself before heading to her office.

"Ah, Myra," Rhonda began hesitantly.

At the tone of seriousness in Rhonda's normally cheerful voice, Myra turned and made eye contact, finally noticing that something was significantly amiss. "What's wrong?" she asked, suddenly filled with dread.

"I just received a phone call not more than five minutes before you arrived from Judge Hawkins's office. His secretary said it was urgent that you contact them as soon as you arrived. I taped the message with the phone number to your chair so you would see it in case I missed you coming in."

"Thank you, Rhonda. I'll call them right now," she said as she made her way to her office. She started dialing the number before she even sat down in her chair.

"Good morning, Judge Hawkins's office," a friendly voice said after the second ring.

"Good morning. This is Dr. Myra Christie. I was just given a message that I needed to contact your office immediately," she explained.

"One moment, please, Dr. Christie. Judge Hawkins is waiting for your call. I'll put you through to him," the voice replied.

A moment later, the deep baritone voice of Judge Hawkins was on the line. "Good morning, Dr. Christie. I hate to disturb you, but would it be possible for you to attend an emergency meeting in my office at noon today? It's concerning the Owen Johnson case."

"I have some appointments. Could you hold on a moment?" she asked.

"Certainly," he replied.

Rhonda, sensing trouble, had fetched Nathan and Darrell from the break room as soon as she had delivered the message to Myra, and they were all hovering outside Myra's office door. "What's wrong?" Rhonda asked as Myra put the judge on hold.

"I'm not sure, but I have a feeling it's definitely not good. They need me in the judge's chambers at noon in Charleston. I have the prison most of today."

"My eleven o'clock cancelled yesterday afternoon," Darrell volunteered. "I can cover for you till one o'clock."

"I know Stephanie has some free time this afternoon. I'm sure we can juggle things around," Rhonda assured her.

"If you are going to need more than just this afternoon down there, just give me a call on my cell and we will take care of things up here. I have the prison tomorrow, so I have more flexibility than the others," Nathan told her. "I can always push some of your schedule for today to tomorrow. I'm sure the prison staff will alert the inmates on the schedule today."

"Thanks, guys. I'll let you know what's going on as soon as possible." She gave them an appreciative smile as she reconnected the call with the judge. "I just talked with my staff, Your Honor. They can cover for me. I have nine and ten o'clock appointments, so I may be a few minutes late, but I'll be there as quickly as I can."

"Thank you. I really appreciate it," the judge responded.

"May I ask what the problem is?" she asked.

"He committed suicide last night in his cell. I can't discuss all the details at the moment. I'm afraid it will have to wait until you get here," he answered.

"I see. I'll be there as quickly as I can."

"Thank you, Dr. Christie. See you at twelve," he said just before the call ended.

"That didn't sound good. What's going on?" Nathan asked.

"Apparently, Mr. Owen Johnson committed suicide last night in his cell. I certainly didn't see that one coming. I didn't get any indications of suicidal tendencies during my evaluation," Myra answered, frowning.

"He may not have exhibited any. We are not psychics, Myra. We can't see the future or read minds. He received the death penalty for his crimes. For some people, it's much easier to take another life than to face their own mortality. You need to give yourself a break on this case," he told her.

"I know. But something is not right here. Why would the judge call an emergency meeting for a convicted criminal awaiting death row who just committed suicide? And why would he need me there?"

"Good question," Rhonda answered. "Guess you can let us know after your appointment with the judge."

"Amazing how a great day can go down the tubes so fast," she muttered as she turned her computer on and got ready for her first appointment of the morning.

Chapter 9

It had been a harried morning trying to get as much done before her first appointment and between appointments. She had to cut her ten o'clock appointment short and apologized profusely to her client, who was more than understanding. As soon as her ten o'clock patient left, Myra grabbed her recorder, laptop, briefcase, and all her information and files on the *State of South Carolina v. Owen Johnson* case. She pulled up her case notes for Darrell on her eleven o'clock appointment and made quick notes for Stephanie, another therapist in the office, to cover her afternoon appointments at the prison.

Before heading out of Columbia, she stopped at her apartment and packed an overnight bag just in case and was back on the interstate by eleven o'clock. It normally took almost two hours to reach Charleston from her office, but her apartment was between the two cities, which helped cut down on some time. Traffic was also in her favor. The lunch rush had just begun to pick up as she headed out of Columbia, so she missed most of that as well.

It was twelve thirty when she pulled into the parking garage at the courthouse. Juggling her briefcase, laptop, purse, and a box containing all the information she had collected on Owen Johnson, she made her way to the courthouse doors. An officer she didn't know held the door open for her, and she swept in, practically dumping everything on the conveyor for the security checks.

"Sorry about all the stuff, but I'm here for an appointment with Judge Hawkins," Myra offered, a bit out of breath.

"He told us to be 'specting ya," another guard spoke up. "I'll help ya up to his office," he stated as yet another guard did a quick scan with a wand over her body.

"Thank you. I would appreciate that since I'm not sure where his office is located." She smiled.

The officer's name turned out to be Jesse James, which brought a smile to Myra's lips at the coincidence of a federal officer having the same name as one of the most famous outlaws in American history. He grabbed the box of information while Myra collected the rest of her belongings. She followed him down the hallway to an elevator, and they got off on the second floor. After a couple of turns down hallways, Officer James opened a door that led to an office with three women typing away on computers.

The women looked up, but no one spoke to them as they walked through the office to another door. This time, Officer James knocked. Myra heard someone shout, "Come on in!" from the other side of the closed door, just before Officer James opened it.

"The doc's here, Yaw Onoah," he informed the judge and several other men in the room as he went forward and placed her box on the conference table in the judge's office.

"Ah, Dr. Christie! I'm so glad you could join us," Judge Hawkins addressed her as Officer James turned on his heel and exited the room. "Come in, come in. Won't you please have a seat? While we were waiting for you, I ordered lunch to be delivered. I got a variety of sandwiches and chips, so just grab what you want. I'm sure you didn't have time to eat on the way here considering your schedule, and I know you are not alone in that department," the judge went on. "This has taken all of us by surprise, but first, let's all get acquainted while we eat, and then we will discuss this unpleasantness.

"Dr. Christie, I believe you are already well acquainted with Mr. Johnson's attorney, Greg Bordeaux, and the prosecutor, Frazer Remington. This is Alex Rhodes, the warden at the prison where Mr. Johnson was incarcerated." He indicated an older balding gentlemen to his right who reached out to shake her hand.

"Nice to meet ya." He smiled in a distinct Southern drawl.

"Likewise." Myra smiled.

"Mayor Jeff Reece." He introduced a broody-looking man with round glasses that made his perpetual red face look even more severe. He looked like he was nearing his eighties.

"Mayor Reece," she repeated with a nod and a smile.

"And last but not least, Attorney General Warren Zeeke," he finished the introductions.

"Mr. Zeeke, sir." She shook his hand.

"It's a pleasure, Dr. Christie. I've heard great things about you." He smiled.

Judge Hawkins removed the box of information from the conference table and placed it on his already overflowing desk. Then he took his position at the head of the table like a father at the dinner table and announced that it was time to eat. The eatery that had catered the lunch had done a great job. Myra had chicken salad croissant with a side of cottage cheese and a chocolate brownie for dessert that was divine. The conversation around the table was congenial and informative for Myra, who rarely saw this side of the legal profession.

Some good-hearted jawing between the judge and the attorney general exhibited they had been longtime friends. She was surprised, however, to learn that the judge and Mayor Reece had grown up together. She would have sworn the mayor was at least twenty years Judge Hawkins's senior.

As lunch was winding down, the judge finally announced that it was time to "get down to some unpleasant business," as he put it. He buzzed one of his secretaries, who quickly cleaned away the luncheon things to make room for the real business at hand. As she left the room, the judge got right to the point.

"Dr. Christie, since the rest of us are all on a first-name basis, would you mind if we called you Myra?" he asked.

"I would be delighted." She smiled.

"Thank you, Myra. Let me catch you up on what is going on here. Everyone else in the room is more or less up-to-date, but I didn't want to discuss this on the phone this morning. As you know, Mr. Johnson was found deceased in his cell this morning by the prison guards. He had a cell to himself pending his transfer to another prison where death row inmates are housed. It appears that it was suicide. He used his sheets to hang himself from the bars of his cell. Rarely have we had inmates commit suicide in our prisons here. What is especially disturbing about this case is that you did not note any suicide concerns in your official evaluation report," the judge explained. All the men looked at her expectantly.

"I did not observe any suicidal concerns, Your Honor. I brought all my research on this case along with testing results so you could see for yourself that none of those markers were a concern at the time of evaluation." She rose to collect her box.

"That's not necessary." Judge Hawkins stalled her. "We'll take your word for it. The problem is a bit more complex than just his mere suicide. You see, he left a sealed letter addressed to you. We have not opened it as it was addressed to you, but we"—he glanced around at all the men at the table as a collective—"feel that since this case received such headlines, and considering the nature of the case, we need to see the contents of the letter as well."

"Of course! Frankly, I'm shocked that he left any correspondence, especially for me. All I did was evaluate him for the court proceedings."

The judge had risen and crossed to his desk where he retrieved a sealed envelope. He handed it to her before taking his place at the table again. Myra carefully examined her name scrawled on the envelope. Mr. Johnson had nice penmanship. Her name was listed simply as Dr. Christie. There was absolutely no resemblance to the other letters she had received in weeks past. Despite the relief that passed over her that the handwriting was not the same, trepidation passed over as she opened the letter.

Dr. Christie,

During your enterview and valation of me, I told you many times that I was innocent. Still you said I was some sort of anti-social maniak, and now everyone believes I'm the killer of those women and that poor teenage girl. I don't have many friends, but that is by my own choice. It has always been my experience that "friends" always want some thing—more time than I'm willing to give, borrow things that they don't return, and lead me down paths that I wouldn't normaly have taken. Paths that have led to trouble with the police on more than one okasun in my life. I'm not as smart as you and most people, and I followed these so-called friends because I ain't never been encluded in the group. I've been the out cast, even as a small kid. I was the out cast in my own family. From an early age, I knew my Ma and Pop didn't want me around. They told me that almost daily. I have always been the unwanted and often wished I had never been born. It's funny how things work out. And now I'm an out cast of the intire world, thanks to you. I'm not a monster, and I ain't never been a monster. I only ever wanted what others get so easy— love, under standing, frend ship, and to belong. I will never have any of those things. Now more than ever. I under stand the world ain't never wanted me in it. I don't know why. I guess some times it jut chooses kids at random and says hey, we don't want that one here. Maybe if we are mean and egnor him, he will just go away and die. I ain't never hurt nobody, but I have been hurt by many over the years. After a while, I just quit trying. What's the point? I just want to die to end my own mizery in this shit hole of life. I guess I should be thanking you for that. I am dying now, but this is not exactly how I thought I would go. I never thought I be labbeled a monster and a killer on the way out though. I think that hurts most of all out of every thing I have lived through over the years. I was too chicken to end my own life all these years, but now as a monster and killer—well, I just can't live with that, and now I have a purpus for the 1st time in my life. I akshully have the courage to die. I am still not a monster, but now I guess I'm a killer as I'll be dieing by my own hand tonight. I had hoped that you would under stand me and what I had been through, but I was wrong. No body ever understood me. Maybe if there really is an after life, I will find some peace or perhaps I'll just go to a nother kind of hell. I guess I'll find out soon. I just wanted to you know that even at this late hour of my life that I have always been innocent. I hope that in the futur, if you happen to run into a nother soul like me, that you will try to under stand him or her before you jump to your labeling that all you doctors are so fond of. A label that may seem so innocent but that kills a sole so easily.

Owen Johnson

Myra was so stunned by the contents of the letter that she merely sat and stared at it. It was not at all what she had expected, not that she had expected anything. A declaration at suicide as to his innocence was astounding and revealing. Though it had never been her place to judge Mr. Johnson, she had also felt the evidence compelling. It was heartbreaking to read his declaration at this late hour and to realize he might have been telling the truth all along.

With unshed tears in her eyes, she looked up to find six pairs of eyes looking at her expectantly. She took a sip of water to clear her throat and composed herself. Then she began reading the letter to the others at the table. When she had finished, the room was quiet for several moments as everyone contemplated the revelation. Mr. Johnson had been innocent of the killings. That meant that the real killer was still out there and might still be killing. Did Charleston have a serial killer on the loose?

Chapter 10

"Good God! What a mess!" Attorney General Warren Zeeke blurted out, startling Myra so badly that she jumped.

"It was circumstantial evidence, but it was all compelling." Frazer defended his position as the prosecutor.

"I knew he couldn't have killed those women. I worked with him for over a year waiting for the trial. He had problems like he said, but he wasn't a bad guy. Just sort of always in the wrong place at the wrong time kind of thing," Greg Bordeaux, the defense attorney, spoke up.

"So basically what I'm hearing," the mayor spoke up, "is that the residents of South Carolina just wasted millions on this case and the state had the wrong guy the whole time?"

"Really, Mayor? Dat's da first thang dat comes to yar mind? Money matters?" asked the warden incredulously in his strong Southern drawl. "What about da fact dat we still have a killer out thare on da loose? Don't ya think dat should take preceedeence o're how much a court case costs da citizens?" he barked.

Suddenly, it seemed that all the men were arguing at the same time. How could this have happened? Who was ultimately responsible? What were they going to do now? On and on the questions flew back and forth until one question stopped them all in their tracks. Who would be making the announcement to the media, and how was it going to be made?

It was just a matter of time before the media got wind of Mr. Johnson's death while in prison. If they found out he was really innocent, it was going to be a shitstorm for a lot of people. The most frightening aspect yet was the fact that the real killer was still out there and would be even more dangerous once he or she realized authorities were reopening the case.

Myra merely sat in her chair and kept her mouth shut and her thoughts to herself. Technically, none of this concerned her. She had only been designated by the court to do the evaluation of Mr. Johnson. She had done that. Evidence collection and case building were not her areas of expertise.

"Myra," Judge Hawkins addressed her in the break of arguments. "What is your take on this?"

"Well, Your Honor, a death confession of declaration of innocence is pretty compelling. I'm fully aware of the evidence in this case, and yes, it was circumstantial. Not being an attorney, I do not want to overstep any boundaries, but begging your forgiveness, you did ask my opinion. Cases have been won and lost with much less circumstantial evidence than this one had at hand. Considering Mr. Johnson's background history of being easily manipulated into questionable circumstances that often led him to trouble with the law, I'm inclined to think that perhaps Mr. Johnson knew the killer unwittingly."

"Makes sense, Your Honor," Frazer agreed with her.

"I agree. If the killer was manipulating him, it would be easy to plant circumstantial evidence that would point to him. The only problem I see is that my client was a loner. He never mentioned any friends to me during our time together," Greg spoke up.

"What if the killer was not considered a friend by Mr. Johnson? What about a family member or coworker? Being a forensic psychologist, from my point of view, the real killer would have to have known Mr. Johnson's routines, schedules, places he hung out, basically nearly every detail of his life. It would have to be someone who is carefully observant but does not call attention to himself. It could even be a neighbor or a friend of a neighbor," she mused out loud.

"Dammit! We needa get da authorities working on dis ASAP!" Alex piped up. "Did da 'riginal investagators look into dis case really good or just collect all da breadcrumbs and say, 'Hey, look what we found'?"

"What do you mean by that?" barked Frazer.

"I think what he means is how was this case investigated? We have four dead females in a relatively close proximity to each other with similar but not exact MOs. Does anyone know if they ran the MOs through CODIS?" Myra asked. CODIS, the acronym for the Combined DNA Index System run by the FBI, looked for links between violent crimes entered by other investigators.

At Myra's question, everyone glared at each other around the table, demanding an answer that none of them had readily. There was entirely too much testosterone in the room.

"Give me a minute," she said in frustration as she walked across the judge's chambers to his desk. She removed the lid from the box of documents she had brought with her to the meeting. She ruffled through a few files and other miscellaneous information for a couple of minutes before dialing a number on her cell phone, which she placed on speaker so the entire room could hear the conversation.

"Any hits in CODIS could mean the killer has a larger killing zone than previously thought or may have victims in other states. In the event similarities were connected by the computer software, the authorities would have been notified who and where similar crimes are being investigated. It is my understanding that it was not necessary in this case since we already had a suspect," Frazier replied.

Several rings were heard throughout the office before a deep male voice answered, "Officer Jett Houston."

"Officer Houston, this is Dr. Myra Christie. I'm the forensic psychologist who worked the Owen Johnson case. I have with me here several individuals including Judge Hawkins, who presided over the case, Attorney Bordeaux, the defense attorney, Attorney Remington, the prosecutor, and the attorney general, Mr. Zeeke."

"What can I do for y'all, Dr. Christie?" he asked.

"We have had some rather unpleasant developments in this case over the past twenty-four hours. As I understand it, you were the lead investigator on this case. Is that correct?" she asked.

"Yes, ma'am."

"During the investigation, I understand you interviewed neighbors and potential witnesses who came forward. There was quite a bit of evidence that led you to Mr. Johnson, as I'm sure everyone in this room would agree with me." She paused for effect as a rumbling of agreements from the others came forth. "I'm curious. As a part of the investigation, did you by chance run any of the deaths and evidence through CODIS?"

"We didn't feel we needed to. SLED [South Carolina Law Enforcement Division] was on board with us during the investigation and running the evidence for us. The more we investigated, the more it pointed directly to Johnson."

"I see. Would it be possible to run that evidence through CODIS at this point?"

"I don't see the need since Johnson was already convicted and sentenced."

"Officer Houston, this is Judge Hawkins. I would appreciate your assistance in running this evidence immediately. As Dr. Christie has stated, some...er...developments have just arisen, and we need this done ASAP!"

"I can call SLED and put in a request, sir," Officer Houston offered. "But to be perfectly honest, Your Honor, it would have more effect if you or the attorney general called SLED. They would move faster on it for you."

"Thanks. I'll do that right now," Attorney General Zeeke said.

"Thank you for your assistance," Myra said.

"Not a problem. If you need anything else, just let me know," Officer Houston responded.

"We appreciate it," she replied before hanging up the phone.

Attorney General Zeeke was already speaking to someone at the SLED office in Columbia by the time she hung up. The mayor and Judge Hawkins had their heads together in a quiet conversation. The rest of the men were watching her expectantly.

"That's all I can really think of at this point. If someone really was manipulating Mr. Johnson to hide their own crimes, it seems very organized. Like this guy has done this before," Myra offered.

Frazer had picked up a briefcase from near his chair and pulled out a legal pad and pen. "Tell me, Myra," he began as he snapped the briefcase closed and replaced it by his chair. "As a forensic psychologist, you can profile, correct?"

"I've had training, though I rarely have the opportunity to use it. Most profiling of these types of killers is done by the FBI."

"If you were doing the profiling, what would be your first impressions?" he asked, beginning to scribble something on the pad.

Myra went back to retrieve the box from the judge's desk and placed it on the conference table. She lifted the lid and began depositing the contents onto the table. After she emptied the box entirely, she shuffled through files and manila envelopes until she found one marked crime photos. She opened the clasp on the back and unceremoniously dumped the grisly crime scene photos of four dead females on the table.

Systematically, she spread them out and began studying them closely. "Allison Dunbar was the first victim," she began. "Next was Cynthia Oats, followed by our teenager, Samantha Briggs. And finally, Tenisha Jackson. The first thing I notice is that all the crime scenes are virtually clean. All the victims have been strangled, but whatever was used has been taken from the scene. Cynthia and Tenisha were both fighters as evidenced by their defensive marks on the arms and hands. Cynthia also had bruising on her face where she had been punched or hit with an object, so that tells me she fought the hardest, and he had to immobilize her by dazing her or knocking her out.

"There were no fingerprints on the bodies," she continued, "which indicates that the killer either wore gloves or cleansed the bodies before dumping them at these locations. Allison had been dumped near a wooded area and found by deer hunters. The medical examiner had stated that she had not been in full rigor yet when her body was found, which tells me that this was a body dump for him. The grassy area around the body was virtually untouched. If he had killed her there, I personally would have expected a larger area of grass to have been disturbed."

"The investigators said the same thing," Greg Bordeaux spoke up.

Myra ignored him and focused on the pictures before her, along with all the information she already knew about the case. She was mentally taking out the element that Owen Johnson was the suspect and inserting an unknown subject. "Something is really bothering me about all these killings. They are all too clean. They are too organized. This guy, in my personal opinion, may have killed before, maybe many times. Only one of the females was sexually assaulted, and that was our teenager. Why her? Why was she different? Had she appealed to him in some manner that the others had not?" She was talking to herself. She was getting into the role of a profiler. She had not done this during the evaluation process because it was not what had been asked of her.

Now that she was looking at the case from a different angle, things were not quite adding up for her. "Allison, then Cynthia, then Samantha, and finally Tenisha," she said and then repeated herself again. The third time of repeating the order of the deaths, Myra suddenly stopped midsentence. There was a pattern she had not picked up on before.

"What is it?" Frazer asked.

"Has anyone else said anything about a pattern with these women?" she asked.

Judge Hawkins and the mayor had ended their conversation at some point during Myra's studying of the pictures, and the attorney general was off the phone. She had the attention of the entire room.

"What do you mean a pattern?" Greg asked. "I don't remember anything about any patterns."

"Neither do I," Frazer spoke up.

"Allison, then Cynthia, then Samantha, and finally Tenisha." She looked up at the men as if they should be able to figure it out.

"What?" asked the judge.

"The women were killed in alphabetical order: Allison, Cynthia, Samantha, and Tenisha. Are we sure there are no other bodies in this case?" she suddenly asked.

The collective silence of the room said it all.

Chapter 11

Myra looked around the conference room at the police station. Several people were busily working and setting up computer and phone stations around the large room. Groups of men and women, some in police uniform, were standing about in quiet discussions, but the overall noise was still loud. Just after Myra had asked everyone in the judge's chambers if they had noticed that all the women were killed in alphabetical order, the judge and the attorney general had immediately gotten on their phones. Within thirty minutes, they had all gathered at the police station where a command center was quickly being set up.

A female police officer was busy tacking up the crime scene photos to a board, and her partner, Officer Jett Houston, was making notes on a white board of the case. Myra, at the request of the judge, had written out a complete profile of the killer based upon what she had reviewed in his chambers. He had cancelled the rest of his day in court and was taking an active role in the investigation for the moment.

Luckily, the media had yet to get ahold of the story of Mr. Johnson's suicide, his letter to her, or the fact that the case was being reopened. It was going to be a huge can of worms for everyone involved when it finally hit television. Despite the fact that she had only done an evaluation on Mr. Johnson, the news would put just as big a ding on her reputation as it did the rest of them involved with the case.

She grabbed her purse and stepped out into the hall, hoping it would be quieter. In fact, it was busier than the conference room. The police chief had declared that all available hands were going to be working the case nonstop for the foreseeable future. To her fairly untrained eye of the inner workings of police stations, it looked like every officer in the state was in the building.

She finally found a quiet office. She stepped inside, pulled her cell phone out of her purse, and called her office. She was surprised when Nathan answered the phone.

"Hi, Myra. It's Nathan. I saw your name pop up on the reader. What's up?"

"It's a circus here, Nathan. Owen Johnson committed suicide last night in his cell. Before he died, he wrote a letter he addressed to me stating he was innocent. Nathan." Her voice caught. "Nathan, he said I put a label of monster on him in my testimony and he couldn't take it."

"Darling, it's not your fault. You didn't give him a label. You gathered the facts, made a diagnosis, and presented them as you were supposed to do. All you did was give him a diagnosis. The media gave him the label. If anyone is responsible, it's them."

"But they weren't in the courtroom."

"Exactly! They tried him in the papers, on the radio, and on television without due process. His blood is on their hands."

"It gets worse, Nathan. Much, much worse," she whispered.

"What is it, Myra? What's wrong?" he asked with concern in his voice.

"At the meeting, they asked me to go over the crime scene photos for them. I don't really think he did it. I think we have an experienced serial killer down here. I'm pretty sure he killed them in alphabetical order. If that's the case, then there are a lot more bodies that have not been discovered yet."

She heard Nathan suck in a breath and let it out in a whistle. "Wow. I don't know what to say, Myra. Are you going to be acting as a profiler for them? Are you going to be working this case with them until the killer is found?"

"No. I've already told the judge, both attorneys, the attorney general, and the police chief that I can't do it. I don't have enough practice. They have called in the FBI, but a profiler can't get here until tomorrow. I did a rough one so they could get started. They are setting up a temporary command center here in the police station conference room for the time being. They didn't even run the case through CODIS, Nathan. Frazier and the detective who worked the case said all their evidence pointed directly to Johnson. I think someone set him up to take the fall, but they didn't expect him to die so soon."

"This is going to get really bad, isn't it?"

"It already is. They are bringing in officers from neighboring counties, SLED, FBI," she responded, peeking out into the hallway at the mass of bodies working frantically, trying to play catch up on the case.

"So when are you going to be back?" he asked.

"I'm planning on coming home tonight. I should be there tomorrow, but if something comes up, I'll let you know immediately."

"You take care of yourself and drive carefully. I'm worried about you."

"Thanks, Nathan. I really needed to hear a friendly voice. I gotta go. I have some things I need to do here before I can leave."

"Anytime. If you need me, just call."

She hung up her phone, dropped it back in her purse, and headed back to the conference room. She had just sat down with the attorney general and the police chief when someone called her name.

"Dr. Myra Christie? Is there a Dr. Christie in here?" she heard a voice yell above the droning noise of the room.

"Over here, La Rouge!" barked the police chief.

A moment later, a slightly chubby police officer in his mid-forties appeared by the chief's side. "Dr. Myra Christie?" he asked, looking at Myra.

"Yes. Can I help you?"

"This was just delivered to you by a courier." He handed her a white business-size envelope and immediately disappeared into the mass of bodies.

She flipped the envelope over and saw her name in block letters. Her breath caught in her throat, and the grip of terror squeezed her heart so tightly she couldn't catch her breath. Suddenly, the room started to spin and went dark.

The police chief, Lorenzo Decemi, had seen her startled expression when she received the envelope. As she slid unconsciously from her chair, he leaped up, rounded the table, and caught her before she hit the floor. The letter was still tightly gripped in her hand.

*****

Slowly, her eyelids began to flutter open. She looked around bewildered. "What happened? Where am I?" she asked. The chief, attorney general, and a female officer were the only other people in the room. Myra was lying on a sofa. She tried to sit up, but the female officer restrained her.

"Just lie there a moment or two longer. We don't want you passing out again."

"I passed out?" Myra asked incredulously, her face turning beet red from embarrassment.

"Are you okay?" Attorney General Zeeke asked. "You gave us a bit of a fright in there."

"I think so," she replied as she struggled into a sitting position.

"Are you sure? You took one look at this envelope La Rouge delivered to you and then literally melted from your chair. I'm just thankful you were sitting when you received it," the chief spoke, holding up the white envelope.

Myra literally felt the color drain from her face and head began to spin again. The female officer pushed her back down on the sofa.

"Obviously, you're not okay. You look like you just saw a ghost or something," the chief noted to the room.

Myra bit down on her terror and found strength from her deepest recesses. She knew who the letter was from, but still, she needed to read it. Almost like an addiction, she had to see what was written. Just when she thought the nightmare was over and her stalker had moved on, here he was again.

"May I see that letter? I'll tell you everything in just a moment. But first, I need to see what he wrote this time." She held out a shaking hand to the chief and took the letter from him. She was shaking so badly she could barely open the envelope and pull out the letter.

My Dearest Love,

And so the game is afoot, my darling. This is so exciting! I know how much you have missed me the last few weeks. I do apologize for that, but it could not be helped. Don't fret, my darling. I promise to make it up you to you.

I was working on a delicate matter for my father and could not get away to see you. My work is nearly finished, and I can't wait to tell you all about it. It's going to be big! Father planned it very well, and it's going to make us all famous. Are you excited? You will soon see it was worth a few weeks apart. I know it was difficult for the both of us, but hey, it just makes things all the more interesting, right? What is that they say about absence and making the heart grow fonder?

I was looking forward to more of our nightly rendezvous before I came for you. I have missed them sorely. I imagine you have too. Perhaps we can still get a few in for a while. What do you think? It will still be a few weeks before I can come for you. Everything must be planned exactly. For now, we will just have to make do in your dreams.

I'll do my best to be more attentive to you. Soon I shall be able to hold you tenderly in my arms for all days. I know you can't wait, but you must be patient, my darling. Soon. Very soon…

Always yours, my love

With dread, Myra dropped her hands and the letter on her stomach. For a moment, she lay there in shock and disbelief. So many emotions were running through her at once that she could not hold them, and they ran with the river of tears leaking from the corners of her eyes to fall in puddles in her luxurious hair. Finally, she took a shaking deep breath and handed the letter back to the chief.

"Please read this. I started getting these a few months ago. I've also received roses, both on my kitchen counter and on my pillow. The Richland Police Department has been notified. They did a thorough check on my apartment for cameras and signs of break-in to no avail. To date, they have yet been able to find fingerprints or DNA evidence. My staff and I have been through all my patient files, both in office and the prison files. I have no idea who this person is. I've even had dreams that I cannot explain and which he seems to know about."

The chief held the letter gingerly while he and the attorney general both read the letter. "Have they all been like this? Like a perverted love letter?" asked Attorney General Zeeke.

"Every one of them. I received the first one at my office. No one remembers it being delivered or placing it on my desk. I arrived at work one morning, and it was simply laying in the middle of my desk. The next two were delivered to the Charleston Courthouse, actually, while the Owen case was in progress."

"Have you noticed anyone following you?" the chief asked.

"No. I've been watching very carefully. My father was an FBI agent. He taught me how to notice if someone was following me and how to lose them. Trust me! I've been looking over my shoulder for months. Since I haven't heard from him since February, I thought perhaps he had moved on. Apparently, I was wrong," she explained drily as she wiped the tears from her face and sat up. "I'm sorry I fainted. I haven't done that before. I guess the letter just caught me unaware."

"You have nothing to apologize for. I'm sure any of us in this room would have done the same thing in your shoes. I can't imagine what it's like having a stalker." The female officer patted Myra's hand.

"I hope you never have to find out," Myra replied. "I can't even explain how I feel right now."

"You said you received two of the letters at the courthouse? Was that during the trial?" the chief asked.

"Yes. Why?" She looked up at the chief.

"Has it occurred to you that it could have something to do with the Owen Johnson case?"

"It did at first. I thought maybe someone was trying to freak me out to affect the case. The problem I have with that is that I received the first letter at my office. Then I received the roses at my apartment. Also, I just did a competency evaluation for the judge and sentencing suggestions as requested. Technically, I didn't have much to do with the case, so we dismissed that idea early on."

"I think you may need to reconsider. It concerns me that you received this letter here at my station. We have to ask why he would have a letter couriered to you here of all places. Whoever he is, he is definitely following you. And I would reconsider the possibility of it having something to do with all this. I think you might need some protection."

"So do I. I'll arrange for it immediately." Attorney General Zeeke pulled out his cell phone and dialed a number.

"Were you planning on heading back to Columbia this evening?" the chief asked.

"Yes. I have clients to see tomorrow. I really have nothing to do with this case. The judge and the prosecutor asked for a profile to get the ball rolling, but the FBI will be here tomorrow. They specialize in that. Once you catch the guy, you'll have to go through the Department of Mental Health in Columbia to get a psychologist or psychiatrist assigned for evaluation. It will be considered a different case. Besides, I would have a conflict of interest being that I evaluated Mr. Johnson."

"It sounds to me as if you are involved in this case up to your eyeballs, sweetie," the female officer said. "If these letters are being written by someone involved in this case, it makes you a potential target."

"Exactly!" Attorney General Zeeke spoke up as he hung up the phone. "Hell, it could be the killer playing games with you. I've assigned a unit to your apartment and your office. Another unit will be trailing you at all times. I need to head back tonight as well. I will be following you until you get home tonight."

"Do you really think that necessary?" Myra could feel the alarm and panic settling into her chest. "I've interviewed several murderers and psychopaths over the years. These letters don't sound like something any of them would write."

"Are you sure? I don't think you are looking at this clearly." The chief perched on the edge of his desk. "You are too close to this emotionally at this point to see what I see in this letter. This subject sounds extremely narcissistic to me. He writes his letters as though you are...well, lovers."

Myra was quiet for a few moments as she considered it. He was right. The letters did sound narcissistic. When she looked at them objectively, she realized they were all about what he wanted and expected. He was telling her how she was feeling—that she missed him, that she was anxious. He had put her in a role where she felt she had no choice but to react. Just thinking about that put red spots of anger in her cheeks.

"Thank you, Chief. That was very...enlightening. I've been so busy reacting that I forgot to act. I'm ready to head home when you're ready, sir." She met Attorney General Zeeke's eyes. "But I'm not going to stop living because of this guy. If any of you need me for anything, you know how to reach me."

The chief hiked one eyebrow but didn't say anything. He exchanged a quick look with the attorney general. "I'll be ready in about thirty minutes." Attorney General Zeeke checked his watch. "Will that work for you? I need to talk to a few people real quick before we go."

"Sounds good to me. I'll just gather my things and meet you out front."

"Mind if I keep this letter? I would like to run it for prints."

"Sure, Chief. I sure don't want anything to do with it."

Chapter 12

Forty-five minutes later, Myra was finally driving out of the parking lot of the police station, closely followed by the attorney general. She had hoped to beat the rush hour traffic of I-26, but instead found they were stuck in the middle of it. She flipped on the radio and tuned it to a local station to listen for traffic reports.

Traffic was moving slowly, so she pulled out her cell phone and connected to her Bluetooth earpiece. She hit Nathan's cell number and listened to the ringing on the other end.

"Hey, Myra. Everything okay?"

"Yes. I'm on my way home. Nathan, I got another letter today. It was delivered to the police station by a courier."

"What? What did it say? Did you turn it over to the police? Are they investigating it?"

"Yes. Actually, I'm so embarrassed. I fainted when an officer handed it to me. The room was full of people, and I fainted. How pathetic am I?"

"It was a normal response to a shock like that, Myra. It's not like it's the first one you have received."

"This one was a little different. He talked about a game being afoot. He said there was something big that was about to happen. The police chief thinks its all tied to the Owen Johnson case and this one because I received two letters at the courthouse and today's letter was couriered to the police station. He said he had been working for his father and that's why I hadn't heard from him in a while. That I'd be hearing from him more frequently and that he was coming for me."

"Good God! We need to put you in protective custody, Myra!"

"The attorney general already called it in. He has someone posted at my apartment and the office, and I'll be followed everywhere I go. It's like I'm being stalked by him and the police now, Nathan."

"I can't imagine what you are feeling. Do you want me to come over tonight? We can discuss it more in-depth?"

"No. It's all right. I'm fine now. It was a shock at first, but the chief of police said something that got me thinking. I've been reacting instead of acting. That's not who I am. I'm going to ask for a copy of all the letters from the detective up there handling this case. Will you help me profile this guy?"

"Of course, I will. Do you want to go over them tomorrow after work?"

"That would be great. Thanks. So how were things in the office today?"

"Everything was fine. No problems. Your eleven o'clock patient wound up cancelling his appointment. His mother fell and broke her hip this morning. Everything else was just fine."

"I owe all of you big time for covering for me on such short notice."

"Myra, you don't owe us anything. We all go through things sometimes, and someone covers for us. It's all right."

"You really are the best, Nathan. I'll see you in the morning."

"Drive safe."

"I will."

A few minutes later, a traffic report came on. Traffic snarls had accumulated. "The light rain showers we had earlier, folks, have caused a few problems on your commute home. Three car accident at Interstate 26, Exit 215 and Dorchester Road is almost clear now. Police and emergency vehicles are on the scene of I-26, Exit 211 at Aviation Road in North Charleston. Reports of multiple cars and several injuries. Bees Ferry Road and Glenn McConnell Parkway has a two-car accident with injuries. An earlier accident at Highway 61 and Cooke Crossroads has been cleared, but traffic is still slow in that area. Also, there is a report of an accident at Clements Ferry Road and Interstate 526. That has traffic backed up on Interstate 526 exiting onto Clements Ferry Road. This traffic report has been brought to you by—" Myra turned the radio off.

"So much for getting though Charleston in a timely manner tonight!" she mused. She hated rush hour traffic everywhere, but Charleston bugged her the most. In most places, if accidents occurred, there was at least a way to reroute around the accident to get where you were going in a timely manner. In Charleston, one accident could somehow morph into a dozen accidents within minutes. Plus, with Charleston being a peninsula, there were only so many direct routes getting in and out of Charleston. The Holy City was so beautiful and quaint to have such horrible infrastructure.

She reached in the console compartment and pulled out a CD of *The Beach Boys Greatest Hits*. She might be overly stressed out and a bit of a basket case over those stupid letters. The death letter from Mr. Johnson had hit her where it hurt. She took pride in her work and genuinely wanted to help people. Nathan had been right…it was the media who applied the label of monster to him, but she had put medical labels on him which could be just as damaging. Throw in the traffic calamities and she was close to her breaking point for the day. She needed something cheerful and fun. What better way to get a dose of both than the Beach Boys?

She was nearing the Aviation accident at Exit 212, and traffic was at a standstill. She took the CD out of its case, slid it into the radio/CD player, and cranked up the volume as the first strains of "Surfin' Safari" flowed over her. She leaned her head on the headrest and took calming and relaxing breaths, then she belted out the words in unison with the Beach Boys.

It was dark by the time Myra drove into her apartment complex. She didn't see the protective detail, but she assumed they were there in an unmarked vehicle. She parked her Jeep in her assigned parking spot, grabbed her purse and briefcase as she climbed out, and locked up the vehicle as she waved the attorney general off. The music had done her good on the way home, but now that she was in the dark parking lot, she couldn't stop herself from looking over her shoulders every couple of seconds. She scanned the parking lot and the stairs of her apartment building. A couple of tenants she had run into on occasion were walking across the parking lot in the opposite direction, and she heard some kids playing nearby. No creepy looking people anywhere in sight.

She quickly climbed the stairs and let herself in her apartment. As soon as she slipped in the door, she put the chain and dead bolt on before dropping her purse and briefcase on the sofa. She had gotten into the habit of leaving a living room lamp on so she wouldn't have to come home to a dark and uninviting apartment over the last couple of months, and she was really happy she had it on tonight. The overcast sky had brought darkness early this evening, and it blotted out the moon and stars, making it darker than usual.

She kicked off her shoes and made her way to the kitchen, where she put on a kettle of water for some hot tea. She was feeling relaxed tonight, the first night in a long time. She picked up the remote to her stereo and tuned to an oldies station before making her way to the bedroom.

A few minutes later, she emerged freshly showered wearing a pair of silk pajamas and carrying a crime novel by her favorite author. She fixed her cup of tea and settled in her favorite seat—an overstuffed, oversized armchair big enough for two people. She changed the radio station to an easy listening station and turned down the volume. She took a sip of chamomile tea and set about engrossing herself in some enjoyment reading.

Chapter 13

Myra was immersed in her book. She was working on her second cup of tea and beginning to feel drowsy despite the excitement of the novel she was reading. *Just one more chapter*, she thought as she flipped the page. *Then I'll go to bed.* The FBI agent in her book was closing in on his suspect. The suspect was an international jewel thief who had committed yet another burglary in the FBI agent's home turf. She had no doubt the thief was going to be taken down.

The sudden ringing of Myra's home telephone nearly caused her to jump out of the chair. Thankfully, she didn't have her teacup in her hand or she would have needed another shower. She grabbed the cordless handset off its charger. The identification screen showed all stars and no numbers. She noted that it sometimes did that when her mother called.

"Hello?" she asked, fully expecting to hear the bubbling of her mother's voice on the other end.

"Did you enjoy my letter today, love?" a rich and deep voice vibrated into her ear.

Sudden panic hit so hard she couldn't catch her breath. Her heart was pounding, and her chest hurt. "Who is this?" she finally whispered.

"Aww, darling, you cut me to the bone." He laughed. "I know it's been a few weeks, but you can't have forgotten all about me yet, have you?"

"What do you want?" She tried not to croak or show fear in her voice.

"Why, I want you, of course! Did I not tell you that in my letter? My work for Father is nearly finished. Once I have completed it,

Father says I can claim you. Won't that be a treat for both of us!" She could hear his smile through the phone, and it made her skin crawl.

I've got to keep him on the phone, she thought. "So how much longer is it going to take?" She tried to sound brave and interested. Anything to keep him talking. She hurried to her purse and grabbed her cell phone. She dialed the detective's number who was handling her case.

"Just a couple of weeks, I should think. What's the matter, darling? Getting impatient?" he asked.

"Just curious. So what type of work are you doing for him?" she asked. She hit mute so he wouldn't hear her talking to the detective who had just answered her call on the cell phone.

"Detective Parks, it's Dr. Myra Christie. I have him on the phone. Hold on."

"Why won't your father let you tell me what type of work you're doing for him?" She tried for sounding like she was pouting, and he laughed. She hit mute again.

"Sorry, Detective. My stalker! He called my home phone. He's on it now. There wasn't a number showing. Can you trace the call?" she asked as she quickly rattled off her home phone number.

She took the home phone off mute and tried to hold the cell phone far enough away that should the detective talk, her stalker would not hear him. "I just don't understand why he cares if you tell me. Does he also object to you telling me your name?" she demanded. "After all, if we are promised to each other, don't you think we should at least know each other's names?" She hit mute again and brought both phones to her ears. "Detective?"

"I'm here, Dr. Christie. We're trying to get a trace, but these things typically need to be set up in advance. It's not an instant thing like in the movies and on TV."

"I understand. Hold on."

"Sounds like your father is a bit of a control freak, if you ask me."

"Careful, love. Don't insult my father. It wouldn't be good for you," he warned. "I realize you are frustrated and impatient, darling. There is no reason to insult my father. He has done everything for us.

Perhaps you need some time to think about and remember that. And it's late. I didn't realize just how late it was. I'm sure you are exhausted after driving to and from Charleston today. Not to mention dealing with all that unpleasantness concerning Mr. Johnson. You poor thing. I think you need to put your book down and go to sleep now. You need your rest. You have a full schedule tomorrow. You'll want to be your best for your patients."

"How do you know about Mr. Johnson? It hasn't been in the news yet. Also, how do you know what my schedule looks like for tomorrow?" she demanded.

He laughed. "Ah, my darling, my love. I know everything about you. Now go get some sleep. You look tired. I'll talk to you later. Good night, love."

"Wait!" she cried into the phone, but he had already hung up. "He's hung up," she spoke defeatedly into the cell phone.

"I'm sorry, Dr. Christie. We couldn't get a trace that quick. With your permission, however, we can have a trace put on your phone in the event he calls again."

"Please do. I don't know how this guy knows so much about me. He even knew about a case I was working on today that hasn't even been in the news yet. I'm sure you've heard through the grapevine by now that he sent me another letter today," she said.

"Yes, my chief mentioned that the attorney general had requested a protective detail for you himself. Have you had any other contact with him since those letters a couple of months ago?"

"Nothing until today. First the letter delivered by courier to the police station in Charleston today, and now this phone call. Oh my god!" Myra suddenly exclaimed.

"What's wrong? Talk to me." Detective Parks started barking orders to someone in the background.

"I'm sorry," Myra apologized, her voice quivering. "Something he said just dawned on me."

"What was that?"

"He was talking about how tired I must be after a case I was working on in Charleston today. The suspect killed himself in prison last night, but they managed to keep it from the media so far. So how did he know that? He also knows I have a full schedule tomorrow at work. Detective Parks, before he called, I was sitting in my living room reading a book. He specifically told me to put my book down and go to bed because I look tired! My blinds are drawn! How could he know that?"

An abrupt banging on her door caused Myra to scream.

"Open up! Police!" came a muffled call through the door.

"What's wrong, Dr. Christie? Answer me! Are you okay?" Detective Parks barked into the phone.

"Someone is at my door," she whispered. She was shaking so badly she could barely hold the phone.

"Sorry about that. Those are my guys. They are your protective detail. You can answer the door. I sent them up to you," the detective explained.

"Are you sure? How can you be absolutely certain?"

"Hang on second, Doc." She could hear him saying something in the background to someone. "Okay, you there, Doc?"

"Yes."

"There are two officers at your door. Officer Welch and Officer Church. Go to the door and ask them the password through the door. The password is stapler."

Hesitantly, Myra crossed the living room and looked out the peephole in her door. Two officers in uniform were standing outside her door. Both were closely monitoring the surroundings. "What's the password?" she asked through the door.

The shorter of the two officers faced the door. His name tag said Officer Church. "Stapler. Detective Parks said to tell you the password is stapler, Dr. Christie. Could you please open the door?"

Myra exhaled in relief, and tears of joy sprung to her eyes. Her trembling fingers fought viciously with the locks and the chain. Finally, she had the door unlocked and flung it open. Both officers rushed into the apartment, and she slammed the door shut behind them, sliding the dead bolt again.

"It's okay now. Your officers are here."

"I'm on my way too, Dr. Christie. I'll be there in ten." He hung up abruptly.

"Are you okay, Dr. Christie? Detective Parks called us and told us to get up here immediately." Officer Church was speaking to her. Both officers had their guns drawn. Officer Church stayed near her while Officer Welch checked out the rest of the apartment.

In response, Myra collapsed onto the sofa and burst into tears. She hated feeling like this—overwhelmed, stressed, anxious, weak, defenseless, hunted…hunted! That was exactly what she felt like. She was being hunted!

Officer Welch came back into the living room and shook his head from side to side as he holstered his gun. Officer Church followed suit and holstered his gun as well. "Can you tell us what happened?" Officer Church asked, coming down on one knee in front of Myra.

Myra did her best to choke back the tears and explain what had just happened with the phone call. After she was finished, they both asked her several questions, which she also answered. They were just finishing when she heard the sound of several feet on the stair outside her apartment. A moment later, there was an insistent knock on her door.

Officer Welch opened the door to Detective Parks and three other officers. One of the officers carried a large briefcase, which he immediately opened, and took out a handheld device. He turned the device on and immediately began scanning the room, being very thorough.

Detective Parks sat down beside her on the sofa and began peppering her with more questions. After several minutes, he sat back and shook his head. "I don't know how this bastard knows so much about you!" he exclaimed.

"Me either. I feel like I'm being hunted," she complained.

"Technically, that's what a stalker does. He hunts his victim," a young female officer spoke from across the room. She received an unpleasant scowl from Detective Parks in response.

"I'm not finding any spikes from any electrical equipment. No cameras, no listening devices, nothing." The officer holding the black device was back in the living room, looking confused.

"Who did you tell about the case in Charleston today?" Detective Parks asked.

"No one except my staff. Most of them were in my office when I returned the judge's call. I had to discuss it with them so we could rearrange schedules to cover for me so I could make an emergency trip to Charleston."

"One more time…then what happened?" he asked.

"I covered my next two patients. My third one cancelled after I left. I gathered my files from the case, put them in the Jeep. Drove here to get a change of clothes just in case I had to stay there for the night. I drove straight to the parking garage of the courthouse. An officer helped me carry my things to the judge's chambers when I got there. We had our meeting.

"We realized there was a possibility a mistake had been made in the case. The attorney general had called someone at SLED about running the case through CODIS. We started getting hits immediately, so we moved the meeting to the Charleston Police Department, where they immediately started setting up a task force. In the middle of trying to get things mobilized, an officer came into the conference room of the police department and called my name. I think it was the chief who spoke up for me, and the officer delivered an envelope with my name written on it just like all the others.

"The officer said it had just been delivered to the department via a courier. The receptionist hadn't noted which courier. I'm ashamed to say I passed out from the shock. Next thing I knew, I was in the chief's office lying on his sofa." Myra wiped the tears from her face with a tissue the female officer handed her and ran her hands through her long blond hair. "I read the letter and then let the others read it. I told them about the others, about everything that had happened up here. We discussed it for a while, and then the attorney general decided I needed a protective detail.

"One of the officers down there called all the courier services, but none of them had any deliveries for their department nor had any of them recently made any deliveries. They have no idea who dropped the letter off. Anyway, then I left to come home with the attorney general following me all the way here. He watched me till I got to the stairs before he drove off."

"So no one else knew about this unplanned trip or what it was for? Did you talk to anyone on the way home about it?"

"Just my colleague, Nathan. I called him a couple of times to give him updates, and then I called him on my way home to let him know I would be back at work tomorrow."

Detective Parks gave a meaningful look to his partner who, up to this point, had been sitting quietly in Myra's favorite chair. He scribbled something down in a small notebook.

"Was he the only person you spoke with after you left your office?" Detective Parks asked.

"Yes, why?" She looked blankly at him then around the room. Everyone had the same closed look on their face. "You don't suspect Nathan, do you? You can't! I've known Nathan for years. He would never do such a thing. Besides, he was the one who urged me to call you in the beginning. He also asked you to come here the first time to look for hidden electronic equipment." She knew she was being overly defensive of Nathan, but she couldn't help it. It couldn't be Nathan. He would never do anything to hurt her or anyone else. He had always been her sounding board. They were friends. He knew everything about her, gave her counseling, and provided her support when she needed it.

Myra became very still. Nathan was her sounding board, she thought. Yes, he really did know everything about her, including how her father died. She rarely told anyone those details. But could Nathan do something like this to her? *Would* Nathan do something like this to her? He had shared just as much information about himself as she had with him.

"But the voice on the phone didn't sound like Nathan's," she said hesitantly.

The officer who had done the electronic scan spoke up. "A voice can be easily disguised with the use of equipment."

Myra frowned at him. "The writing doesn't look like his either. Nathan is left-handed and has a distinct slant to his writing."

The young female officer spoke up. "Handwriting is also easily manipulated."

Myra looked around the room. Frustration, exhaustion, and fear made her voice a bit sharper than she intended. "I'm telling you it can't be Nathan!" she declared.

"Then who do you know would be capable of this? Who knows you so well that they would know you were reading a book tonight after you got home? Who else knew you were going to Charleston? Who else knows the particulars of that case?" Detective Parks's partner fired off questions to her. She couldn't remember his name, and unlike the rest of the officers in the room, he was wearing a suit and tie like Detective Parks.

"I don't know," she whispered. "I have no idea."

Chapter 14

The next morning, Myra stared at herself in the mirror as she brushed her teeth. She didn't recognize herself. Her eyes looked dull and weary with deep dark circles that couldn't be concealed no matter how much concealer and makeup she put on. Her mouth was drawn and pinched, and she had fine lines around her eyes and mouth. A deep crease had formed practically overnight between her brows. She was ghost-white pale, which only served to make her makeup look even more like a mask.

Even her hair seemed lifeless and worn out today. After several attempts at curling it with her curling iron and several different styles, she finally gave up and just threw it up in a clip at the back of her head. For good measure, she sprayed the front with a bit of hairspray to make some semblance of an attempt at styling.

She had originally decided to wear a suit jacket with a matching skirt. But after putting runs in two new pairs of pantyhose, she let out a string of uncharacteristic curses and grabbed a pair of slacks from her closet instead. In light of the way the day was starting off, she close flat shoes with firm rubber soles. Hopefully, she wouldn't fall flat on her face with those on!

It had been the wee morning hours by the time the officers all left. The female officer was about to get off work and offered to spend the night in the apartment, but Myra assured her she would be fine. *What a crock*, she thought. *I'm not fine. Who could possibly be okay with all this?*

Myra tried going to bed, but she couldn't get over the feeling that someone could still potentially be watching her in the bedroom. Eventually, she grabbed her pillow and an extra blanket from the linen closet and camped out on the sofa. It had been a fitful sleep at best, if you could even call it sleep. She was up, showered, and had a strong cup of coffee before her alarm even went off.

As she bent to retrieve her purse and briefcase, she noticed she had aches and pains all over. She felt old and stiff and totally worn out. *Funny how stress can make one feel so awful,* she thought. She slipped out the door and locked up. Just like the night before, she was super alert on her way downstairs to her Jeep.

A few of her neighbors whom she recognized from various events the apartment complex had sponsored were either on their way to work or doing an exercise regimen. There were a couple of people she didn't recognize, but they were not paying any attention to her. As she hit the last step and made her way down the side-walk, she made eye contact with Officers Welch and Church. Officer Welch nodded a greeting, and Officer Church gave her a little salute and a smile. She gave them a small wave, climbed in her Jeep, and left for work.

Officers Welch and Church followed her all the way to work. She assumed they must have a different crew watching her house during the day since the attorney general and Detective Parks both said someone would be watching her apartment and her work at all times. As expected, she was the first to arrive at the office. Officer Welch followed her across the parking lot and into the building when she unlocked the door.

"Stay here," he ordered with no room for argument. He had his weapon pulled as he disappeared down the hallway going from room to room. Several minutes later, he returned with his weapon hol-stered. "All clear," he told her. "I checked all the offices, closets, bath-rooms, windows, and the back door. All secure. See you tonight." He nodded as he disappeared out the door.

The rest of the day passed uneventful. Thanks to Detective Parks and his partner, Myra was uncomfortable around all her coworkers, especially Nathan. She caught herself on more than one occasion of listening to everything he said with a certain amount of suspicion. Finally, she berated herself for letting her stalker and the police get to her. These were her trusted coworkers. They spent hours together most days treating those with a variety of illnesses, including emotional complaints. They had known each other for years. They were a cohesive team. They were her friends. *Or were they?* the unbidden thought sprang up in her mind.

It was a relief when her last patient of the day left the office. She had caught herself holding her entire body rigid with tension several times throughout the day. Now she ached all over. All she wanted was to leave work, get home, and soak in a hot bubble bath to release her tension and body aches.

She was in the process of logging off her computer and powering it down when Nathan poked his head in her door. "Hey, Myra, want to grab a drink at Mel's?" Mel's was a little hole-in-the-wall bar not far from the office. It was also a favorite hangout for many of the city's professional working class. Normally, she and Rhonda would accompany Nathan and a couple of other coworkers there on Friday evenings.

"I don't think so, Nathan. I haven't had a very good week. Think I'll just head home, get a glass of wine, and take a really long soak in the tub." She didn't look up at him as she stuffed a couple of files in her briefcase that she intended to review over the weekend.

"Any big plans this weekend?" he asked, walking farther into her office.

"Not really. You?" she asked.

"Are you okay, Myra? You've been a bit distant all day, and you look terrible. Did something happen last night?"

"Not really. I just haven't been sleeping well," she lied, biting her lip. She hated lying and avoiding her friends, and she had considered Nathan a very good friend for several years.

"It really bothers me that you have to go through this, Myra. I wish I could help you more."

"Don't worry, Nathan. The police are actively working the case. I'm sure they will catch him quickly." She flipped the light on her credenza off and grabbed her things. "I'm just going to head home and relax."

"Would you like some company? I'll skip Mel's, pick up some wine, and come over to your place in about an hour if you would like."

"I'm fine, Nathan. Go enjoy Mel's with Rhonda and the rest of the gang. I'm actually looking forward to a quiet evening at home. I'm probably going to fall asleep just as soon as I get out of my relaxing bath." She gave him a brief tired smile.

He followed her out of her office and out to the reception area. The days were noticeably getting longer. Daylight was still shining through the office windows. She passed by the receptionist's desk and opened the main door of the building.

"Hey, Myra!" Nathan called to her.

She paused in the open doorway to look back at him with a questioning look.

"You be careful and get some rest. If you need me, just call. I can be there quickly." Concern drew his eyes and mouth.

"Thanks, Nathan! I really appreciate it. Good night and have a great weekend."

*****

"How did I get in this mess?" Myra asked aloud. She had stopped by a favorite shop on the way home and purchased the most expensive bath milk she ever dared. Dumping a liberal amount in the tub filled with the hottest water she could stand, she stripped off her clothes and climbed in. She had not eaten since the piece of toast with coffee early that morning, and the thought of food now made her nauseous. She leaned her head back, letting her hair fall about her shoulders into the water and let the tears wreak havoc on her face. Within moments, her entire body was racked with sobs.

She always prided herself on her strong nature. She was not a weepy damsel in distress type in the slightest. In fact, she often wondered how women could allow themselves to fall apart so easily. Being that she felt herself on the far extreme of that spectrum, on occasion it had crossed her mind if perhaps there was something wrong with her. Growing up with mostly male cousins and male neighbors, she learned to toughen up if she wanted to hang out with the cool guys. In turn, she inadvertently associated emotional displays with weakness.

Of course, her outlook on that concept had changed as she had aged, and at times she found herself envying other females. Some, she had discovered, were very adept at using their emotional displays as manipulation tools. By the time she had discovered that in college, it was too late for her. She had held her emotions in check for so long, it was difficult to express them at all. Until the past couple of months, of course. Now it seemed that she was always crying, fainting, and playing the role of damsel in distress. And she was beginning to despise it.

What had happened to her? Why did it seem impossible to hold her emotions in check? She couldn't concentrate on anything. She even found her mind wandering off earlier in the day while working with a patient. With great effort, she had reigned herself in.

She was having difficulty sleeping, difficulty staying awake, and difficulty eating. A constant headache had become her unwanted companion. She was so jumpy that anything could set her off. She had been at the copier that morning when Rhonda came up behind her and stapled some papers together. Myra had jumped and let out a squeal, barely suppressing a scream of fright.

She knew most of it had to do with stress and anxiety. If she didn't get a handle on it soon, she was libel to have a heart attack or stroke. But how to stop it? That was the billion-dollar question. There was no end in sight to her dilemma. The police department was checking out all her coworkers, her patients, and other potential suspects at the prison and who knew who else. So far, they had nothing. Just a bunch of creepy letters, a weird dream, flowers, and a phone call.

To most people, love letters, flowers, and phone calls were a sign of an active and healthy love life. Of course, it would turn out to represent a deluded and crazed stalker in her case. She had attempted to get information out of him during the phone call, but he had been too smart. He had not divulged a single significant clue.

Her stomach growled, and the water had turned tepid. She contemplated adding more hot water to the bathwater, then opened the drain and climbed out. Her paranoia of being watched resulted in trying to put on a robe while still wrapped in a towel and later trying to put on pajamas while wearing the robe. One obviously couldn't be too careful in her apartment.

She padded into the kitchen. She hadn't been grocery shopping in a while, and most of the cabinets and the refrigerator were bare. After a thorough search, she found some stale crackers and a can of soup in the pantry. She put the soup on, made some iced tea to cool in the refrigerator for the weekend, and made some hot tea to go with the soup.

She tried flipping through television stations while eating but couldn't concentrate on any of the programs. She had lost total interest in the book she had been reading the night before. Just thinking about touching the book brought flashbacks of the phone call. She fidgeted around the apartment for another fifteen minutes before giving up and crawling in bed. She was asleep within seconds.

The next morning dawned with an unusual and heavy fog bank in the area. She could barely see the parking lot from her apartment windows. She was still nervous and having paranoid thoughts, so she opted to put her shopping off until the fog disappeared. Instead, she sat at her bar, nibbling on toast, sipping on coffee, and thinking. She was staring at the heating and air vents in her ceiling.

Without hesitation, she pulled the stepladder from her spare bedroom closet and set it up under the vent in the kitchen. Grabbing a couple of screwdrivers, she swiftly climbed the ladder and removed the screws holding the register in place over the vent. She checked out the vent before replacing the register, a frown on her face. Noting the position of the next vent, she moved the ladder and went through the motions again.

An hour later, she was again sitting at the bar. Frustration and disappointment creased her brow. She had checked all the vents for possible cameras, including all the pictures on the walls, all the little collectibles and such things in her apartment. She had initiated virus and malware scans on her computer, cell phone, and laptop. So far, nothing had been found. She had been hoping that the police had missed something. So where did that leave her now? *In exactly the same spot I was before*, she mused.

Possibilities began running through her head. It was a hopeless situation, and she felt helpless to stop it. What if that creep decided to take the action he kept threatening? What if he did come for her? Would she be able to stop him? Would the police notice before it was too late? What did this guy really want from her? Was it simply to control and manipulate the fear factor until his fun ran out, or was it more serious?

It was obvious that the guy was, at a minimum, delusional. But what if there were other factors she had not dared consider? What if he really was dangerous? What if he was a serial killer who liked to play with and torment his victims? She had never heard of one going to this extreme, but anything was possible, wasn't it?

"Stop it!" she yelled at herself. "This isn't helping one bit! Then again, talking to myself isn't helping either!" She growled in frustration, grabbed her purse and keys, and left the apartment. She could at least get rid of some of the nervous energy by doing her much-needed grocery shopping!

Chapter 15

Father Zachariah was great with kids. He was badly burned in a fire that took the lives of his parents, sister, and twin brother when he was ten years old. He liked working with children more than adults. They didn't stare, and they rarely judged. More often than not, they were curious about his scars. It had taken him years to come to terms with the way he looked now. His lips had been skin grafted from skin taken from his inner thighs. He had lost a thumb and pinky finger on his left hand. Plastic surgeons had restructured a new nose for him just a few years ago. Prior to that, he had had a prosthetic nose, and not the best looking one either. One of his ears had been scarred badly, and he was missing his earlobe, but the other ear had miraculously been saved. Some of his hair had returned, but he kept it cut short so it wasn't noticeable how much was actually missing. As a teenager, he had learned that over 70 percent of his body had been burned and he was a walking miracle. He should not have survived.

He always thought it strange that the doctors called him a survivor. He didn't feel like a survivor. For years after the fire, every day had been filled with horrendous pain and agony. When the physical pain had finally lessened, the emotional pain escalated. For so long, he had been kept from the public eye due to recovery and so many surgeries he had long ago lost count.

When he was declared as good as he was going to get, his aunt and uncle had enrolled in him public school. It was the biggest mistake they could have made on his behalf. They had reasoned that it would be good for him to socialize and make new friends. Instead, he had been called the class freak, and everyone had ostracized him.

They made fun of him, bullied him, and played cruel pranks whenever possible.

He begged his aunt and uncle to move him to a different school, but they refused. And so he had to endure. He hid wherever possible until one particular day, while a sophomore in high school, he had been pursued by an especially cruel group of boys that made it their mission to make his life even more miserable than it already was. The janitor was in the bathroom, so he couldn't hide in there as usual. The classroom door next to the bathroom was open, so he ducked in there.

Mr. Fralix had been sitting at his desk working when an unknown teenager slipped into his classroom prior to school starting. He ran to the back of the classroom and ducked down behind a desk in an effort to hide. Moments later, Mr. Fralix watched the other boys walk down the hall, high-fiving each other and laughing. "It's okay. They're gone," he notified Zachariah. "Want to tell me what's going on?" His eyebrows rose as the tall, gangly, and severely scarred boy stood in the back of the classroom.

"No, sir. I'm sorry if I disturbed you. I didn't notice you there," the boy said, just above a whisper.

"Do they bother you a lot? It's okay. I won't tell anybody if you don't want me to. I'm Mr. Fralix, and I teach biology and chemistry. I don't think I've seen you before. You're not in in any of my classes."

"No, sir. I'm a sophomore. I've missed a lot of school, so I'm behind everyone else. They have me in special classes," he explained as he walked up to a picture on the wall of a cell being viewed through a microscope. "Wow, this is cool! What is this?"

"It's a microscopic view of a virus cell. Do you like science?" Mr. Fralix asked, walking up to Zachariah.

"Yes, sir. When I was finally able to hold something in my hands"—he held up his scarred hands for inspection—"I asked my aunt for book about science. It was always my favorite subject."

Mr. Fralix smiled as an idea struck him. "How would you like to learn more about science? I'm usually here really early every morning. If you like, you can hang out in here and you can study science before school starts."

"You mean it?" Zachariah's eyes lit up.

"Sure. How about we start first thing tomorrow morning? We'll go over some stuff to see where you are academically in science and go from there."

The next morning, Zachariah arrived just as the school was opening. Sure enough, Mr. Fralix arrived just minutes later. Mr. Fralix had been impressed by how much Zachariah had known about science. In fact, he was confused and concerned on why the school had placed him in remedial classes when in fact, it was obvious Zachariah was an advanced student. And so began a long teacher-student friendship. By the next school year, Zachariah was moved up to the advanced classes. He was top of his class and excelled in nearly every area of science.

Every morning prior to his graduation from high school, he and Mr. Fralix worked together. He liked using the microscopes and doing experiments. He helped Mr. Fralix grade papers and develop tests for his classmates. It was almost a dream come true for him. At Mr. Fralix's encouragement, he applied for several scholarships and won a fully paid scholarship in a religious-based college. That was where he had found God. Before long, his hunger for the Word of God rivaled that of his hunger for science. After grad school, he took the oath and became an ordained priest.

Just last year, he had been transferred to Christ Our King Stella Maris Catholic Church and school in Mount Pleasant, South Carolina, a small town just across the Cooper River from Charleston. In his spare time, he enjoyed volunteering with the children and started a science club. After school and on Saturdays, he and the kids would work on experiments, take nature walks to gather materials to study, and work on various projects.

On Saturday morning, Father Zachariah was bent over a ditch with Xavier Willis and Yon Lang, studying tadpoles and collecting some in jars for classroom study. Other students were collecting specimens of various things from a list they had prepared in school earlier in the week.

"Hey, Father Zach! What kind of caterpillar is this? Would it be a good one for our classroom?" Trevor Reynolds called out, studying the worm in his hands. He looked at where Father Zachariah and his friends Xavier and Yon had just been gathering tadpoles. The collection jars had been knocked over, and their nets were scattered on the ground. "Father Zach?" he called, but there was no answer.

Chapter 16

Myra was tired. She purposely stayed away from the apartment all day. She had shopping and errands that needed to be taken care of, but mostly it was because she was afraid. Afraid that another letter might arrive for her. Afraid she might receive another phone call. Afraid she might receive more unwanted flowers or fall asleep and have another creepy dream.

The poor protection detail had followed her all over town. She knew they had to be just as exhausted as she was. It took several trips, even with them helping her, to get everything into her apartment. Feeling guilty, she had insisted on fixing them sandwiches, which they took back to their vehicle to eat. She finished putting away the groceries and the clothing from the dry cleaners, made herself a sandwich, and sat down to relax for a few minutes in front of the television.

Every local station and a few national stations were covering the news of a missing priest and two missing boys from the Charleston area. She settled in to listen to the report with concern and half interest when something caught her attention. She focused more intently on the news report. A view of the ditch where the three had been collecting tadpoles for a science project was shown to the viewers. The reporter was laying out the events of the day. There it was again! She grabbed the notepad and pen she usually kept on the bar and listened carefully for the names again. A moment later, the news anchor was rattling off the names of the missing and a phone number to contact with any information.

"Oh my god!" Myra moaned to the room. It just couldn't be a coincidence, could it? Her gut was reacting to the news in a way that said it was no coincidence. Could it be that the possible serial killer in Charleston was going after a list in alphabetical order and it didn't matter the age or sex of the victim? It was unusual but not unheard of. While most serial killers have a specific type of individual they target, others act on different details to meet their needs.

Acting on her gut, Myra immediately dialed the task force number she had helped initiate the day before. An officer she didn't know answered after the second ring. She identified herself and asked for the chief of police. He put her on hold to track down the chief, and she flipped to another station to watch their report of the same story.

"Chief Decemi here. How can I help you?"

"Chief, it's Dr. Myra Christie. I know you are overwhelmed with that investigation, but I have some information that I think you are going to want to consider. It could lead to a capture earlier rather than later."

"I'll take anything at this point. What do you have?" he asked.

"Have you heard about the disappearance of the priest and the two kids in Mount Pleasant today?"

"Yeah, but what does that have to do with this investigation?"

"Okay, yesterday, we noticed that the women we had discovered had all been killed according to the first letter of their name and in that order."

"Yes, you and the attorney general discussed that with me. We are currently looking at all missing person reports and bodies of women that have been discovered over the past ten years based upon that idea," he supplied, still obviously confused as to why she was calling.

"Exactly! But what if his victims were not only women? What if the gender of the victim didn't matter to him so much as their first name? The three individuals who were reported missing today are Xavier Willis, Yon Lang, and Father Zachariah—X, Y, and Z," she exclaimed.

"Holy cow! We've only been searching for missing women. Hang on a second!" he demanded before putting her back on hold. A minute later, he was back on the line. "Great work, Dr. Christie! I remembered seeing a report a few days ago, and I just looked it up.

Victor Shades went missing two weeks ago. His body was found in an empty lot in West Ashley on Wednesday. I'm going to have to call the ME to get the cause of death, but it's looking like that one could be connected as well. Damn! This case is getting out of hand, and it's bigger than we thought," he complained.

"That's exactly what I thought yesterday when I noticed the way the names ran in order with their deaths. I just turned on the TV and saw the news about the priest and those two boys, and I thought, what if. I wish I could help you more. I pray you find the three of them alive!" she said, her eyes glued to the pictures of the two boys and the priest being shown on the news.

"You've done a lot! You gave us a starting point and made some startling connections. I'm going to run this by the FBI agents here and get their take on it."

"Good luck, Chief!" She hung up and said a prayer that the priest and the two boys would be found alive and safe.

Chapter 17

By Monday morning, everyone was talking about the disappearance of Father Zachariah and the two boys. Myra had stopped by her favorite coffee shop on the way into the office for specialty coffees and danishes for the entire office. While waiting in line, she heard three different conversations on the subject, and when she put in her order, the employee at the register asked if she had heard about it. Like every television and radio station she had listened to since Saturday afternoon, it seemed as though everyone had an opinion on what had happened, and it didn't bode well for the priest.

Back in her car on the last leg of her trip to the office, Myra caught the tail end of a caller voicing his opinion to the radio disc jockey, who was having an informal debate on the missing trio. "If you ask me, the pervert priest kidnapped those poor boys! You know how those priests are! When I was an altar boy—"

"And I think it's time for a commercial break, folks." The disc jockey cut in on the caller and immediately sent the show to a string of commercials.

"That poor priest!" Myra muttered to herself. "If they do find them all alive, the priest will never be able to survive the public opinion of the events." She pulled into her parking space, bowed her head, and said a quick prayer for the missing priest and the boys. She carried her purchases into the building and met Rhonda at the front desk, who relieved her of some of the items and followed her to the break room.

"Did you hear what happened over the weekend?" Rhonda asked.

"If you mean the missing priest and the two boys, then yes." Myra set down the danishes, selected her coffee from the drink carrier, and headed to her office, followed by Rhonda.

"Isn't it awful? I heard they were organizing search parties all over the area. Do you think that's possible?"

"I'm sure they started those yesterday around the church and surrounding properties. They will most likely search the marshes and swamps around Charleston and Mount Pleasant before moving on to Francis Marion National Forest."

"Do you think the priest took those two boys? I was watching a reporter interview some guys he went to high school with way back when. They said he was a loner. A real odd egg."

Myra sighed. Sometimes she really hated the media. "News reporters can find anyone to say what they want them to say to drive up ratings, Rhonda. No, I don't think the priest took those boys. I think all three of them are victims of the same perpetrator. In fact, I'm almost certain of it." She dropped her purse and briefcase on her credenza and plopped down in her chair.

"Really? Why? Do you know something? Does it have anything to do with why the judge called you down there the other day?"

"Perhaps. I'm not sure yet. Since Mr. Johnson is dead, I'm no longer on the case," Myra informed Rhonda as Darrell popped his head in her office.

"Good morning, ladies. I trust you both had wonderful weekends?" Darrell was smiling as he stepped farther into the office.

"Mine was absolutely fantastic! My boyfriend took me on a surprise mini camping trip on Friday evening. We didn't get back until late last night. How about you, Darrell? Did you do anything interesting?" Rhonda filled them both in on her weekend escapades.

Darrell sat down across from Myra, stretched his legs out in front of him, and gave Myra a dazzling smile. "Nothing as interesting as your impromptu camping trip. I just took a day trip to Charleston on Saturday. I needed a change of scenery. Know what I mean, Myra?"

"Not really. I had such a busy week last week. I enjoyed spending the weekend close to home. Lots of peace and quiet for me, I'm afraid." She turned on her computer and tried to look busy. Darrell had a way of looking at her at times that made her feel distinctly uncomfortable.

"Aw, you poor baby. No excitement at all this past weekend? You need a man in your life to remedy that," Darrell suggested.

"My life is pretty full the way it is," Myra said in a clipped tone, a little sharper than she intended.

"Hey! What's going on in here? Someone having a party and I didn't get invited?" Nathan walked in carrying a coffee in one hand and a danish in the other.

"Something like that." Darrell frowned at the intrusion.

Nathan sat in the chair next to Darrell and sipped his coffee. "Not sure who brought in the life support this morning, but thanks! I really needed the caffeine this morning."

"Myra brought them in. How are the danishes? I opted for my coffee first." Rhonda was perched slightly behind and to the left of Myra, sitting on the credenza.

"They are delicious, as always. I need to buy some stock in that company."

"You can't," Myra gave the disappointing news. "They are privately owned. I already checked to see if they needed investors." She was skimming through her e-mails and jotting down notes on her legal pad.

"Did you hear about that poor priest and those two boys who have gone missing down in Charleston on Saturday?" Rhonda asked the men.

"Yeah, it's all over the news. I think it's kinda strange that a priest would abduct two boys in his care when there were at least three other adults and several other kids on the premises. What were they doing anyway?"

"He runs a science club," Rhonda supplied. "And Myra doesn't think the priest did it. She thinks someone else got all of them."

Nathan shot a surprised look at Myra. "You know something?" he asked.

Myra shook her head from side to side.

"I wouldn't put it past our darling Myra to figure it out before the police do. She is so clever." Darrell had raised a questioning eyebrow in response to Rhonda's comment before chiming in.

Myra froze. There was something about the way Darrell had said it. He had put too much emphasis on *darling*. Flashbacks of the letters fluttered through Myra's mind. She saw the word *darling* kept popping up as a common theme in the letters. Hadn't the caller also called her darling? The voice was completely different, but didn't the tech guy say it was easy to distort a voice?

No. Absolutely not! Myra couldn't believe she was actually considering the possibility that Darrell could be the stalker and the caller. He wouldn't. He hadn't worked there as long as the rest of the staff. He had only been there for about a year. Rhonda knew him much better than Myra.

"Probably because her father was an FBI Agent. She's probably been trying to solve crime since she was a baby, right, Myra?" Ronda giggled as she teased Myra.

"I think the both of you give me too much credit," she replied drily. "If I have any insight into the criminal mind, it comes from all that work I do in the prison each week. Speaking of which, I really need to go over some things before my first patient gets here."

"Fine. I can take a hint," Rhonda grumbled as she slid off the credenza. "Time to snag one of those danishes before the rest of the staff nab them all up."

"Maybe we can do lunch today, love?" Darrell suggested.

Myra's head snapped up to look at Darrell. "Sorry, buddy. I have first dibs on lunch with Myra today. We made them yesterday, right, Myra?" Nathan stood and stepped behind Darrell as soon as he saw the look she gave Darrell.

"Are you two dating or something? I thought there was an office rule about dating coworkers."

Before Myra could comment, Nathan had thrown his arm around Darrell's shoulder and began ushering him out of her office. "Not that it's any of your business, buddy, but we happen to be very close friends. What do you say we get to work now and leave Myra alone before she forcibly throws all of us out of her office?"

Darrell said something to Nathan as they went down the hall, but Myra couldn't understand what he had said. She was still reeling over the fact that in the course of a small conversation, he had called her both darling and love. Both were common enough endearments, but it just so happened that her stalker had used both many times.

She noticed her hands were visibly shaking. Dropping her pen, she slid her chair back, crossed to her door, and shut it firmly. She made a fist and relaxed her hands a couple of times while she paced her office.

Should she call Detective Parks and tell him about Darrell? Was Darrell capable of something like this? What did she really know about Darrell? Did any of them really know him? She had been a party to his hiring. As part owner in the practice, she was given a copy of every resumé and application the practice received. She was also present at each interview.

Thinking about it now, she realized she had never really spent much one-on-one time with Darrell. She didn't know anything except what was on his resumé. *People sometimes lie on their resumés*, a tiny voice spoke up in her head. Had Stephanie completely vetted his resume? She hurried to her computer to check the office calendar.

"Dang it!" she snarled in frustration. She had forgotten Stephanie had taken the day off for personal business. It was not enough to warrant disturbing Stephanie on her day off. It could wait. Maybe if she had enough time between patients, she could look through the employee files in Stephanie's office later in the day.

The intercom on her phone buzzed, making her jump. She picked up the receiver before it could buzz loudly again. "You okay? I saw the way you looked at Darrell earlier. Is anything wrong?" Nathan asked over the line.

"I'm fine. We can discuss it at lunch today. I'm trying to get ready for a new referral that is due in a few minutes." She put him off.

"Okay. I get the hint." She let the receiver fall back on the phone while she considered everything running through her head. It was going to be another long day, and she could already feel the headache beginning.

Chapter 18

As luck would have it, Myra's ten o'clock patient was running late, and her eleven o'clock patient had a total meltdown and anxiety attack in her office, which caused the appointment to run through most of her lunchtime. Thankfully, most of the staff kept a variety of frozen meals in the freezer for such an occasion. No one really cared who took what, as long as it was replaced from time to time.

With only fifteen minutes till her next appointment, she selected one at random and threw it in the microwave for the appropriate time frame. She was relaxing in the break room. waiting for the magic of technology to finish cooking her meal, when Darrell walked in.

"Hello, love," he greeted her while placing his leftover lunch in the refrigerator. "I thought you had a lunch date with Nathan."

"We had plans, yes, but my last patient went into an anxiety attack toward the end of the appointment, and it took most of my lunchtime to help her get through it."

"Poor darling. I'm sure Nathan will be demanding a reschedule. Perhaps I should make my move and demand a lunch date with you for tomorrow." He sneered.

"It was actually my request to have lunch with Nathan. I need to discuss something with him. I'm sorry, but I've already rescheduled for tomorrow with him," she explained, feeling a bit irritated at his sneer.

"Why not just discuss it with him tonight after work?" he asked, leaning against the counter.

"Believe it or not, I rarely see any of our coworkers outside of the office. I believe you have been invited to our outings together. We have an open invitation when we all go out on Friday night for dinner and/or drinks. Unfortunately, it's typically only Nathan, Rhonda, and myself who attend regularly. Occasionally, Stephanie is in attendance, but not often." Myra's hackles were raised. How dare he insinuate she and Nathan were in an illicit affair!

"The problem with those outings is that Rhonda is always in attendance. I would prefer an outing that does not include her," he stated.

"Nor include Nathan or Stephanie. Is that correct?"

"Well, well, well, Dr. Christie. Are you asking me out on a date? In that case, I accept." He smiled slyly, pushed away from the counter, and strolled out of the break room before she had an opportunity to respond.

Myra sat staring after him, her jaw hanging in disbelief at his smugness. *Bing!* The microwave announced the cook time was over. She slammed her hands down on the table in frustration as she rose. "I really don't need this right now," she muttered.

*****

Myra was in the process of shutting down her computer and collecting her things to go home at the end of the workday when Nathan walked into the office. "I missed you at lunch today. I gathered you had something you needed to discuss. Want to talk about it now?" he asked, sitting down in one of the chairs across from her.

She snarled at him before sitting back down behind her desk. "Thanks to you, I now have a lunch *date* with Darrell tomorrow." She emphasized the word *date* with air quotes. Nathan hooted with laughter. "It's not funny!" she said crossly.

"Oh, yes, it is!" He continued to laugh. "How on earth did you manage that one, and why is it my fault?"

"Your little comment about us having a lunch date today. He took that as an invitation."

"Not my fault." He shook his head with a huge smile on his face.

"It is your fault," she insisted.

"Did you accept?"

"I didn't get a chance to decline," she grumbled.

Nathan hooted with laughter again. "I wish I had been there for that one. I could have taken notes!"

"Will you stop it? This is serious!"

"It's just lunch, Myra. Maybe he needs to talk to you about something," he replied.

"I don't think so. He's been acting different all day. He's normally on the shy side and rarely talks to me. Today he's been using inappropriate endearments toward me. Then he more or less tells me I'm having lunch with him."

Nathan sobered when he saw she was really concerned. "What do you mean by endearments?"

"It's one of the things I had hoped to discuss with you at lunch. Do you remember this morning when everyone was in here? In the course of the conversation, he used both darling and love when referring to me."

"I didn't pay attention to that, but so what? I've thrown around darling and love somewhat carelessly over the years. Every time I go to a restaurant, I call the waitress darling if I can't remember her name."

"It's not the same, Nathan." She sighed. "Rhonda has told me she thinks he has…um…affections…toward me."

"I see. So you are basing this on what Rhonda says?"

"Not really. Well, perhaps a little. What really bothers me is those letters and the phone call. The stalker always calls me darling and love," she explained.

Nathan sat ramrod straight in his chair. "What phone call?" he demanded.

"That was another thing I wanted to discuss with you. I received a phone call on Thursday night on my home phone. I was relaxing and reading a book at the time, and he knew I was reading a book. My blinds were closed at the time, and it was late."

"Did you call the police?" He was very concerned. She could see that in his expression.

"Yes. I called Detective Parks while I had him on the phone. They could not trace the call quickly enough, but they have put a device on my phone in case I get another call like that one. They also swept for cameras and bugs again. They didn't find anything. How does he know what I'm doing, Nathan?"

"I don't know, but we have to get you out of that apartment!"

"I can't just move, Nathan. I signed a lease."

"You can stay with me for a while. I have an extra guest room."

"I'm not staying with you. I appreciate your concern, but I'm not leaving my apartment."

"It could be one of your neighbors. Maybe they have one of those telescopic lenses on a camera or something."

"The police have questioned most of the residents at my complex. Nothing suspicious has come up yet."

"They talked to me on Saturday too," he supplied.

"The police talked to you? What about?" she asked.

"I think any male you know is a possible suspect at this point. They were just asking me how well I knew you. Had we ever dated or slept together. Did I have any romantic notions toward you? Mostly that kind of stuff. I told them I had a girlfriend, and then Darlene came home from the hospital right after that. They asked her if we had been together the night before, and she told them we had been at that new action movie that just came out. I had told them the same thing earlier. I didn't know exactly what was going on, but you didn't call, and they said you were okay, so I didn't worry."

"They asked me if I thought you would do something like that. I told them no. I had no idea they would question you like that. I'm so sorry." She rubbed her temples. It seemed as though she constantly had a headache these days.

"Don't worry about it. I'm glad they questioned me. It shows me they are taking this threat seriously. They also took a sample of my handwriting with both hands. I'm sorry to say that my right-handed writing is not even legible. A toddler could do better." He grinned.

"Do you know if Darrell is right or left-handed?"

"I haven't noticed, but odds are that he's right-handed. We've had a beer or two over the past year. I don't know him that well. I guess just about as well as I know the rest of the staff. I can't imagine anyone in our office doing something like this."

"I can't imagine it being anyone I know. Then again, I can't imagine anyone doing it. I know it happens, but why me? I'm a nobody. I'm not a celebrity. I just live an ordinary life." She had picked up the pen on her desk and was doodling as she talked.

"I'm sorry you are going through this. I wish I knew who it was. Don't worry, Myra. I'm sure the police are closing in on him."

"Thanks, Nathan. You're a really good therapist and friend. You always make me feel a little calmer and better."

"You're very kind, Myra. I value our friendship. I just wish I could do more for you. So what are you going to do about Darrell?" he asked.

Myra thought about it for a moment before answering. "I'm going to have lunch with him. I'll keep it very professional, but I'll get to know him a little better. Maybe I'll be able to determine if he's the culprit."

"I don't like you playing detective, Myra. You need to leave that to the police. It's their job."

"I'm just going to feel him out. I can't sit back and do nothing, Nathan. It's driving me crazy."

"I know. Just please be very careful. Promise me you'll be careful," Nathan pleaded.

"I'm not going to purposely put myself in danger, Nathan." She smiled across the table at him. "And nothing is going to happen to me in a crowded restaurant at lunchtime."

Chapter 19

Darrell and Myra were sitting in a crowded restaurant. It was popular with the lunch crowd for their exceptionally fast service. Myra insisted on driving, and he let her choose where they ate. She was not as nervous as she had been the day before and earlier that morning. Having partial control by doing the driving and choosing the restaurant helped.

"Nice place," Darrell commented, taking in his surroundings.

"Yes, and the food is delicious. Care to tell me why you insisted on this?" she probed.

His gaze landed on her. "I just wanted to get to know you better, love. I've lived here a little over a year, and I still don't know that many people. I thought I should at least get to know my coworkers. You're the only one who has resisted an outing together."

"An outing?"

"Yeah. You know, one of those things where people get together somewhere...out." He used his hands to encompass their surroundings and more.

She raised a questioning eyebrow. "And you have been...out... with everyone in the office except for me?"

"Precisely." He would have elaborated, but a waitress arrived at that moment for their orders. They promptly gave them to her, and she rushed off to the kitchen. "Now where were we?"

"You were telling me that you've been out with everyone in the office."

"Ah, yes. Nathan and I had a beer or two together on a couple of occasions. Stephanie and I had dinner with her family. Dora, Marta,

Bill, and I all had drinks and then a dinner together. And now I'm having lunch with you," he explained.

"What about Rhonda? You didn't mention her," she pressed.

"Didn't I? I'm sorry. Well, Rhonda and I have been out several times. She insisted on making me feel at home here as soon as she realized I had just moved to the area. We've been to a few singles bars, a few restaurants, a couple of movies, and I've been to her boyfriend's apartment. Sometimes he comes with us when he's not working. Sometimes it's just the two of us."

"I didn't realize you and Rhonda had gotten so close."

"She was essentially my first friend here. I've made a couple in my apartment complex and one or two here and there. It's been more difficult than I expected."

"Why is that?" she asked, genuinely interested.

"I grew up just outside Seattle in a small town. Everyone knew everyone. I even lived at home with my parents while I commuted to college every day. After graduate school, as you know, I landed my first job at the practice of one of my professors. He offered me an internship in graduate school and asked that I stay on for a while."

"So what happened? Why did you leave there if you had a job?"

"Is this another job interview? It kind of feels like one." He smiled across the table at her.

The waitress arrived with their food and placed it in front of them, then she dashed off to another table.

"Whoa! That was fast!"

"Yes, it's their signature. It's why this place is always packed. And no, it's not an interview. I'm just curious." She dug into the freshly made fries on her plate and the owner's own ketchup recipe. He claimed he made it all himself and had won several awards. A few years ago, he and his restaurant had even been featured on a culinary television program.

"Well, love, I simply decided I wanted to see something of the world instead of my hometown and Seattle."

"Out of all the places in the world to go, you chose Columbia, South Carolina? That's rather odd." She was focused on trying to pick up her Veggi More Club. It was a turkey and bacon club that was four layers high with shredded lettuce, tomato, shredded carrots, pickled beets, bread-and-butter pickles, sautéed zucchini, hummus, bean sprouts, and avocado. It was her absolute favorite sandwich.

"Why is that odd?"

"You could have literally gone anywhere else, and you came here. You obviously didn't know anyone here. So why come here?"

Dubiously, he watched her lift the large sandwich and take a bite. "I wanted to see what the South was like. I've read so many books. I'm a bit of a history buff. I thought being in Columbia would afford me a fairly central area from which to travel to the other states. I spent a week in Gatlinburg, Tennessee, last year, and I've taken quick weekend trips and holiday trips to several historical areas in North and South Carolina and Georgia. I plan on spending a week in Charleston this fall, though I may go down this weekend for the Flower Town Festival. I hear it's something I need to check out. If I had known about the Ravenel Bridge Run, I would have registered for that as well."

"Flower Town is nice. They also have several things going on downtown Charleston at the same time. You should check it all out. I ran in Bridge Run once."

"Really? How was it?"

"I ran over the old Cooper River Bridges. It was exhilarating and terrifying."

"Why? Did something happen?" he asked.

"Apparently, you haven't seen any pictures of the old rickety metal bridges that used to be there until about ten years or so ago. They were so old, and they looked as though they were about to collapse at any moment," she explained.

"So then why did you attend the Bridge Run?"

"My father wanted us to run it together. He participated in the occasional marathon when his work permitted. Sometimes I ran the smaller ones with him. We had a lot of fun training for it and then running it. After the run, we tried to get as many activities in that weekend as we could. We were so exhausted afterward." She laughed at the memory. "For two weeks, we played couch potatoes after work and school."

"Hmmm…maybe I can talk you into training with me for next year's Bridge Run." He gave her an inquiring look.

"Don't count on it. I rarely run these days."

"Then perhaps I can talk you into attending Flower Town with me? You obviously are familiar with the area and I am not." She could hear the hopefulness in his voice.

"I'm sorry. I've got too many things going on at the moment."

"Things with Nathan?" he asked rather sullenly.

"I don't think that's any of your business!" she replied rather sharply.

"You're right. I'm sorry. I just think you deserve better than him." He pushed a homemade chip around his plate.

"You know we have a rule in our office procedures handbook that states coworkers are not allowed to date, right? The purpose of that is to keep relationship dramas out of the office. We are there to provide stable psychological help to our patients, not bring our drama and unrestful undertones to the office to make our patients more depressed and anxious."

"I thought perhaps you had made an exception."

"There are no exceptions. Sometimes, as psychologists and staff, we offer advice and therapy to each other to help keep all of us in relaxed and professional form. If we are not physically and psychologically healthy, our patients will pick up on it and suffer accordingly."

"I see. It just seems like you two spend an awful lot of time together."

"We have known each other for years. We are good friends, and he's also helping me deal with a rather unpleasant case I have going outside of the office."

"I'm sorry. I didn't mean to pry. Perhaps we should change the subject," he suggested.

Myra glanced at her watch and waved down the waitress. "Actually, I need to get back to the office. I have some things I need to get completed before my one o'clock patient gets there."

"You're angry with me," he stated as he pulled out his wallet.

"Not at all. I really do need to get back to the office."

"Then could we do this again sometime? I really enjoyed talking with you, even if it did seem we were talking mostly about me."

"Perhaps," she answered vaguely. He did not press her any further as he followed her out of the restaurant and to her Jeep.

Chapter 20

"So how was the lunch date?" Nathan asked Myra that day after work.

"It was…enlightening," she commented a little absently as she finished updating a patient's record.

"Enlightening? What exactly does…enlightening…mean?" he asked.

"You know…informative, educational, helpful, illuminating. Need I go on?"

"Ha…ha…very funny! Care to elaborate?" He leaned casually against the doorframe, crossing his arms across his chest.

"I learned a lot about Darrell. Where he came from and why he wound up here in Columbia."

"I could have told you all that. I've known that since a week after he started working here," Nathan replied drily.

"Well, you didn't tell me, and now I know, too, because we got to know each other a bit better today."

"But did you get any answers regarding the letters and phone calls?" he persisted.

"One phone call, Nathan. And no. I don't have any more answers than I had this morning." She looked up at Nathan, exasperated. "What would you have me do? Ask him outright? So tell me, Darrell, are you the creepy bastard sending me anonymous letters, flowers, and calling me? I'm sure that would go over tremendously well."

"Fine," he replied as he crossed the room and sat in his usual seat. "You know very well what I meant. Do you still think it might be him?"

"Honestly." She shook her head, running her fingers wearily though her hair. "I have no idea. He only used those endearments a couple of times during lunch. I don't know if it's a normal thing for him to use them, meaning does he call every woman love and darling, or do they have some sinister significance? I just don't know."

He leaned forward, interlocking his fingers between his knees. "So basically we're still at square one."

*****

The phone was ringing when she entered the apartment that afternoon. She dumped her belongings on the sofa, kicked the door shut, and grabbed the phone, a bit out of breath. "Hello?"

"Hi, sweetie! Did I catch you at a bad time?" her mother cooed into the phone.

"Hi, Mom! No, I just literally walked in the door. How was your trip?" Myra's mother and her husband, Jack Carson, had been on a two-month long trip. The first three weeks had been spent overseas, followed by nearly six weeks of traveling around Virginia.

"Long and exhausting! The first part of the trip was wonderful. Baby, we have to go to Greece together. I love it, and I know you will too. We got to see a lot of Italy and Spain. It was beautiful and great, but I personally would have preferred to spend a little more time in France. I loved the countryside over there. And the food! Please don't get me started on the food! I think I gained twenty pounds in France alone!"

Myra laughed. Her mother had a fast metabolism like Myra and was very active. Myra doubted her mother sat still long enough for the calorie-rich foods of France to attach to her. "I'll believe it when I see it." She laughed. "So how was the trip around Virginia?"

"Even longer. I learned a lot about its history and saw some beautiful places, but I also saw many desolate places. I didn't realize there were so many under privileged families in America, much less Virginia. They are scattered throughout Virginia, but I was shocked at how bad the economy was in rural areas and in the Blue Ridge Mountains. The closer we got to West Virginia, the worse the conditions were. Honey, some of those poor people live in homes not much better than a dilapidated shack!" Her mother, Camellia, was emotional.

"I know, Mom. I've seen some of them. I wish the media would report from those regions sometimes. They love to do human interest stories on the inner cities and minorities, but they forget about the struggling farmers, miners, and such in the hills and mountains of this country."

"Well, you'll be happy to know that Jack and I have discussed this thoroughly, and he's decided to really tackle this issue in his senate run. We talked to so many people in those areas and took so many notes. Jack called one of his buddies who works at the USDA and a few others. We've been working out strategies for potential cash crops and how to bring businesses into those areas to help build them up."

"That's wonderful, Mom! I take it that it's definitely happening then? Jack really is going to run for office?" she asked.

"Of course! He's more motivated now than he was before. He's already scheduled for a couple of debates coming up soon. I'll get the dates and times for you so you can watch them on our website."

"Wow! I can't believe this is happening. Jack will be a great senator. He cares so much about people and the law. He really needs to be a part of the lawmaking process," Myra said.

"Funny, your cousin Lydia said almost the same thing." Camellia laughed.

"You talked with Lydia? When? How is she? I haven't heard from her in ages." Myra kicked her shoes off and poured herself a glass of wine.

"She called me two days ago. You're not going to believe it. She's engaged! Her boyfriend, I don't believe you've met him. They met at a conference or something last year. He's gor...geous!" Her mother singsonged. "Anyway, Cecilia said it was hot and heavy right from the start. They can't look at each other without stars in their eyes. Cecilia and Richard are so impressed by him. He even went to Richard and asked for permission to marry Lydia!" Cecilia was Camellia's sister. They were only fourteen months apart and looked nearly identically; many people often thought they were twins.

"Really? I didn't know guys still did that."

"Right? Cecilia says he's very family oriented. He comes from a big Italian family up north someplace. New York, I think. Cecilia said she cried when he asked Lydia. He had asked her parents to double date with them one night. They went to a fancy restaurant then suggested a walk in a nearby park. He had arranged for white Christmas lights to be hung everywhere in this one section that had a gazebo. He had a trail of rose petals leading to the gazebo with a bouquet of roses, wineglasses, wine, and his family waiting there with some musicians. He got down on one knee and everything!"

Myra could hear her mother getting all teary-eyed just talking about it. "Wow! It definitely sounds…romantic." Myra laughed. It was a bit much, in her personal opinion. If, and when, she ever got engaged, Myra hoped the prospective groom-to-be would be a little more down-to-earth and ask her a little more privately. "Nothing like putting the prospective bride on the spot."

"Are you kidding? You know Lydia. I'm sure she was on cloud nine with all the attention."

"Yes, she probably was," Myra mused.

"Speaking of which, anyone catch your attention since I've been gone?" It was her mother's sly way of finding out if Myra was dating anyone or not.

"Nope. Not yet."

"Sweetie, you know I want only the best for you. But, darling, you have to put yourself out there on the dating scene at some point."

Myra cringed. The moment she heard that Lydia was engaged, she had been waiting for her mother to bring up her so-called aversion to dating, as her mother put it. "I know, Mom. I'm just really busy with work. I just finished that big case, you know."

"That was just as we were leaving on our trip, Myra. That was two months ago," she replied sardonically.

"Well, yes, but something big has since come up about that case, and I was called back in to help out on it. I think I'm finally out of the loop now." She didn't want to tell her mother the details of the case. She knew her mother, and her mother would worry needlessly when she needed to be focused on her husband's campaign. Myra also purposely omitted informing her mother about the letters and such. No sense in worrying her.

"Did it concern your evaluation? Everything okay?"

"Not exactly. It's a big mess, and I really don't think I should be discussing it at this point. While I was in Charleston this last time, though, I was asked to do a profile of a suspect. They were waiting for an FBI profiler to get there, but they needed to get started immediately. I gave them a temporary one to get them started, but the FBI profiler was able to get more detailed for them."

"Did they catch the suspect?"

"I really don't know. I'm out of the loop now."

They talked a while about Jack's campaign and in general. They just caught up on family news and general conversation before hanging up.

After getting off the phone, Myra changed into lounge clothes, padded into the kitchen, and began rummaging around for something to eat. She finally settled on bacon, eggs, toast, and cheesy grits with a side of fresh strawberries.

After eating and cleaning the kitchen, she settled down to watch a movie with another glass of wine. The phone rang, and the caller ID indicated the area code of her cousin Lydia. She couldn't remember Lydia's phone number offhand, but she did recognize the area code. She grabbed the phone.

"I just got off the phone with Mom. Congratulations! I can't believe you didn't call me immediately after it happened!" Myra reprimanded.

"Hello, darling! It's so nice to hear you excited." The male voice caught her off guard.

"Who is this?" she snarled into the phone. She could feel her chest getting tight with anxiety and panic.

"Come now, love. You know who this is. Did you enjoy your lunch today?"

Myra refused to answer. She was listening for signs in the voice that might indicate if she really knew the person calling as she rummaged in her purse for her cell phone.

"I'm not really surprised. You looked a little bored with the conversation. Perhaps you wanted to ask something else but held back?"

"What do you want?" she asked as she dialed Detective Parks's phone number.

"I just wanted to hear your lovely voice. I miss you."

"You don't even know me." She hit mute when she heard Detective Parks come on the line.

"Ah, but we both know that's not the truth, don't we? I know you better than anyone. I also know you intimately, don't I? Ah, now I understand. You miss me so much that you're playing hard to get. I do so love your little games, my dear. You want more intimacy, don't you? I knew you wouldn't be able to get enough of me."

As the caller went on with his bizarre and revolting discourse, Myra was quickly telling Detective Parks the creep was calling her again.

"You certainly think a lot of yourself, don't you?" Myra suggested to keep him talking so the trace could be run.

"Not as much as I think of you and I. We both know you think about me constantly now, don't we, Myra? You just can't stand not knowing where I am when I'm not with you."

"I don't think about you at all," she spat.

"Then why are you having Detective Parks run a trace on the phone line right now?"

Myra paled. How did he know she was having a trace run on the phone line? How did he know she had called Detective Parks?

"What makes you think that?" She stalled, suddenly nervous and terrified.

"Do you think me a fool, love? You have your cell phone in your other hand. Tell Detective Parks I said hello, will you, darling? I've to run right now. But don't worry. I'll be there very soon." The call was disconnected.

"He just hung up," Myra told Detective Parks. It was all she could do to keep from crying. "He said he would be here very soon."

"He wasn't on long enough for the trace to go through. The number he was calling from was not the number featured on the caller ID. What else did he say?" Detective Parks informed her.

"Nothing but a bunch of narcissistic garbage really, except the part about coming here soon." She shivered with a sudden chill.

"The protective detail reported that everything looks good from their location. Do you need someone to come to your apartment?"

"No, I'm fine. Frustrated, angry, terrified, but I'm fine. I just wish we knew who it was and we could catch him." She was staring at the landline phone as though it might attack her.

"Are you sure? You sound a bit shaky. I could send a social worker over to you," he offered.

"Oh, for Christ's sake. I'm a damn psychologist, Detective. I know exactly what a social worker can and can't do for me. I do it every day myself."

"Sorry about that. I just thought it might help. Maybe a different perspective might bring some things to the surface that might help with the case."

"I've been talking with a coworker in that capacity. I still have no idea who this bastard is, nor do I understand how your department can't come up with a single lead. No fingerprints, no DNA, no line taps, no anything!"

"I know you're frustrated, and I promise you, we are working hard on your case. Can you stop by the department tomorrow so we can discuss some things pertaining to your case? It's not something I like to discuss over the phone," he asked.

"Do I need to be worried between now and then?" she asked.

"No. I just don't want to discuss it over the phone. I really prefer to discuss it in person and in my office."

They discussed a mutual time, and Myra made a note of it on her calendar.

Chapter 21

It was hours before Myra calmed down enough from the phone call that she felt able to go to bed. With some trepidation, she finally went through her nightly regimen of readying for bed. She read for a time, hoping to further take her mind off the call and exhaust herself. Even then, she tossed and turned for quite a while before she fell into a deep slumber.

The nibbling on her earlobe combined with the heavy weight of the hand on her breast gently tweaking her nipple caused an involuntary moan of pleasure to escape from her partially parted lips. A soft whisper in her ear triggered an avalanche of involuntary shivers.

The heavy weight of the hand left her breast to be instantly replaced by a hot wet mouth. She felt unable to move as the hand was joined by another in caressing her body. After thoroughly exciting one nipple, the hot mouth moved on to play erotic games with the other. One hand began to knead her buttocks while the other continued to set off little circles of sensual pleasure down her sides, over her stomach, and across her back. At times, it felt like a thousand hands upon her body all at once.

One of the many hands found her most feminine and sacred place. It immediately took a carnal possession of her, stroking her erogenous area until her entire body arched up in desire. Her entire body was racked with pleasurable sensations, even the bottoms of her feet. It was like nothing she had ever experienced before.

Little by little, the hot mouth replaced where hands had once been, trailing whisper-like kisses all over her feverish body. Gradually, what had felt like one hot mouth felt like many. It was as though hundreds of mouths were following thousands of hands, kissing, licking, tasting every inch of her.

The sensations seemed to continue for hours. Her moans turned to sensually frustrated whimpers. She heard a deep laugh that enveloped her in its deep vibrating timbre. It was nearly more than she could take. She thrashed about wildly, seeking sexual satisfaction, her legs becoming entangled within the damp knotted sheets.

"Soon, my love, very soon." The deep timbre of the voice washed over her like ice cold water.

Myra abruptly sat up in shock, an unreleased scream on her lips. She had gone to bed and fallen asleep wearing a two-piece satin pajama set. Now she was nude with sheets knotted and tangled about her legs. Her body hummed with unreleased sexual tension. She flipped on the bedside lamp and found herself alone. Trembling with fear, she fought with the sheets to untangle her legs and stumbled into the bathroom.

There was no need to check the apartment for an intruder. By this point, she knew what she would find. Absolutely no one. Turning the shower on cold water, she stepped into it, letting it hit her in the top of the head and envelope her in its stinging grip. She soaped up thoroughly as unwanted memories of the prior sensations ran through her head. Sickness abruptly caught her, causing her to stumble, slip, and slide her way across the bathroom to the toilet.

The sickness continued to spill out of her until she was left with dry heaves. Weakly, she crawled back into the cold shower and sat on its floor, huddled in the icy cold spray. She had neither the energy nor the ability to shut the water off for the longest time. She simply sat there in its icy grip, shivering and crying, from either the cold or shock, she didn't really know.

Much, much later, Myra finally found the energy or the courage to turn off the shower. She cocooned herself in two large fluffy towels for a few moments before vigorously drying herself. It was just past four in the morning. She threw on her favorite pair of yoga pants and long sleeve shirt, took one look at the bed, and ran to the toilet where she was sick once more.

Bleary-eyed from exhaustion, she went to the kitchen where she made herself a cup of the strongest coffee she could stand. It was too quiet in the apartment, she realized. It was making her even more jumpy. She flipped on a twenty-four-hour news broadcast, wrapped herself thoroughly in an afghan from the couch, and curled up in her favorite chair.

At some point, Myra dozed off on the couch. She jerked awake, disoriented due to being in the living room. The news anchor was shifting the focus of the program to the weatherman for a weather update of the country. Myra sat there watching in a sleepy daze until the previous night's event washed over her like a freezing cold shower. The icy fingers of memory gripped her so hard, it briefly took her breath away.

The weatherman giving his report faded away as one by one, the recollections washed over her. She trembled uncontrollably with the intensity of the memories. How could she have such extreme negative reactions from just a dream? *But was it just a dream?* she asked herself. Just as quickly, she thrust the thought aside. Of course, it was just a dream! Well, maybe not exactly a dream—more like a nightmare. What should have been a wonderful and fulfilling sexual dream felt more like an invasion of privacy—a rape.

She never had those type of dreams, at least not since she was a teenager with raging hormones. So why was she suddenly having them now? It was the second one in the last couple of months. She had responded violently to both dreams afterward. Why? What was it about those dreams that felt more like rape? Like she had been drugged so she had no control over her mind or her body? The more she thought about it, the angrier she felt.

She was so preoccupied with her thoughts she didn't realize she was late for work until her cell phone rang and she saw her office number was calling. "Crap!" She snapped up the phone and answered by the third ring. "Hello?"

"Myra? This is Stephanie. Rhonda said you hadn't arrived yet this morning, and your nine o'clock patient is in the waiting room. Are you okay?"

"I'm so sorry, Stephanie. I had a terrible night and didn't fall asleep until the late this morning. I'm afraid I overslept. I'll be there within thirty minutes," she said. "Just tell Mrs. Delaney I'm running a bit late."

"Will do. Sorry for disturbing you while you're trying to get ready and get here. I was just concerned that we hadn't heard from you."

Myra smiled into the phone. She loved her job, and she worked with a great group of people. "I'm glad you called. It was just the motivation I needed to get my butt into superspeed!" She laughed.

Stephanie laughed with her. "Okay then, I guess we'll see you shortly. I'll pass your message along to Rhonda."

As she hung up the phone, she rolled her eyes at her own error for not noticing how late it was and ran for the bedroom. Twenty-eight minutes later, she was rushing in the back door of her office building and slipping into her office. She dumped her purse and briefcase under her desk, shuffled through her file cabinet for Mrs. Delaney's file, quickly reviewed the notes from their last session, then went to greet her patient.

Chapter 22

On Thursday morning, Myra flipped on the morning news while she made herself breakfast and a cup of tea. A breaking news report was being broadcasted. She wasn't really paying attention to the program until she heard a reporter saying something about a priest. She grabbed her bowl of oatmeal and her cup of tea and perched in her armchair, watching more avidly.

"Police are not reporting on the identities of the three individuals found at Charles Towne Landing early this morning. Park Manager Thomas Grooms said off camera that the site was horrifying. Grooms is a twenty-three-year park ranger who has served as the park manager for Charles Towne Landing for two years. He said he had never seen anything so horrific in his entire service as a park ranger.

"Charles Towne Landing is the first European settlement in South Carolina and was founded in 1670. A replica of one of the original cargo ships is moored at Charles Towne Landing. It is said that the bodies of the three individuals were found in the clearing near that vessel. This is Rebecca Johns reporting."

"Rebecca?" asked the anchorwoman in the studio. "Is there any connection with the three individuals found this morning and the missing priest and two young boys that went missing over the weekend from Mount Pleasant?"

"Ginger, police are not commenting at this time, but there are rumors that they are the same individuals."

"Do we know how they died?" the anchorwoman, Ginger, asked.

"Not at this time. Park Manager Grooms said he would defer to the police in this matter. One source who prefers to remain anonymous suggested all three bodies were found nude and in chilling positions. It is unclear if Father Zachariah killed the two boys and then himself or if all three were murdered by an unknown assailant," reporter Rebecca said into the camera.

"Thank you, Rebecca, for that report." Anchorwoman Ginger moved on to the next item of news on her reader. "Mount Pleasant's Mayor Tradd was asked this morning how news of these deaths would affect tourism here in the Charleston area. He said he would be meeting with his cabinet later this morning to discuss the particulars of the case and how the news would affect our area. He expressed his condolences to the families. Now time for the weather with Roger Spays."

"How horrible!" Myra muttered to the empty room. She had hoped that the priest and the two boys would have been found alive. It was evident, now, that something sinister had happened. She flipped off the television, finished her bowl of oatmeal and cup of tea, placed the dishes in the dishwasher, and proceeded to finish her morning routine.

Later at the office, the entire staff was discussing the morning news report on Father Zachariah and the two boys. The deaths at Charles Towne Landing report had been picked up by the National News syndicate. This was the type of story that reporters lived for and television loved to announce. Myra felt sorry for the families of all involved and the police working the case. There would be no happy endings, just lots of grief and an invasion of reporters comparable to the locust plagues.

Furthermore, news reports such as this often triggered depression and anxiety in patients who had tragically lost family members due to murder. Myra had at least three patients in her files that had lost loved ones tragically; one had lost a son to murder. She left a note on Rhonda's desk, asking her to call and check on the patients before calling her nine o'clock patient into her office.

Just as Myra had predicted, reporters swarmed on Charleston for the story of Father Zacharia. Friday morning, news stations were reporting that indeed, the victims were the missing trio. A park ranger doing his morning rounds had found the trio. The boys were both nude, feet bound before them, hands bound behind their backs. They had both been brutally sexually assaulted and strangled afterward. Their bodies were propped up, eyes taped open as an audience to Father Zachariah's brutal death.

It was unclear if they had died before or after Father Zachariah. What was clear, and a shock to the community, was how Father Zachariah had died. A wooden cross made of four-by-fours had been constructed upside down in the clearing to the right of the replica cargo ship in Charles Towne Landing. Father Zachariah had been found nude, also brutally sexually assaulted, and affixed to the cross upside down. He also had a stab wound on the left side of his abdomen. It was clear to the Christian members of the Charleston community that Father Zachariah's death was a statement to their religion. His death was a mockery of Christ's death. It was exactly the opposite of the crucifixion.

Charleston, nicknamed the Holy City, was in an uproar. They were demanding whatever it took to catch the murderer. What had originally been a local news article about two missing boys and a missing priest was now a worldwide news story. The Pope even made a statement about the deaths and had a prayer session in Saint Peter's Square. Bells tolled all over the world. Workplaces and schools were being closed the following week for group prayers and masses and the funerals for the trio.

Rumors were rampant that the Pope and other dignitaries from the US government and foreign governments were traveling to Charleston for the funerals. The office phones for Myra's office were ringing off the hook. People wanted appointments to help deal with the grief they were experiencing. Myra heard that many therapist offices were experiencing the same thing. Television stations had turned to twenty-four-hour news reporting and featured talking heads that included religious leaders from all over the world. Billboards were changing from advertisements to condolences and memorials to Father Zachariah and the two boys.

Myra marveled at how just days before, people had jumped to the conclusion that Father Zachariah had been behind the disappearance of the young Xavier Willis and Yon Lang. Now those same people were praising the young Father and grieving his death. They were placing flowers and other objects at the scene of their deaths and at religious houses all over.

Crime rates dropped all over the world. Fighting and bickering between families, neighbors, and enemies stopped. Cease-fire agreements had been signed between several countries where war had ravaged for years. Myra marveled at how quickly things could change. People, who before had barely recognized other people on the planet, were now being friendly and offering aid to those less fortunate. Neighbors were helping neighbors.

It was like every religious holiday in the world combined into one and on steroids. Even the prison patients Myra had were on their best behavior. Though she was surprised and a little pleased that the world seemed to be coming together, deep down she knew it would not last.

Chapter 23

A few days after the funeral of Father Zachariah, Myra walked into her office to find Darrell leaning against her closed door. "Were you waiting for me?" she asked as she unlocked her door and stepped inside.

"As a matter of fact, I was, darling." He had a crafty smile as he followed her into her office.

Myra gritted her teeth at the endearment. "What can I help you with?"

"Lunch. I did all the talking last time. I think it's only fair we have another lunch date so I can learn about you."

She flipped on her computer and tried to look as busy as possible getting ready for the day. "I'm not sure how my schedule looks today. I also have the prison this afternoon."

"I already checked with Rhonda. Your last appointment is at eleven o'clock, and you don't have to be at the prison until one o'clock. That gives us at least an hour lunch," he informed her.

His smug attitude really got under her skin. "That's just what she has on the office calendar. I've got to check my personal calendar as well. Also, it takes me a while to write up my appointments. I'm very particular about that. *And*"—she emphasized for his sake—"I prefer to get to the prison early and talk with the guards, the medics on duty, and the warden concerning my patients that I'll be seeing that day, as well as read their prison records to see what they have been up to since our last session."

"Come now, love, you don't really need to do all that for those lowlifes." He sat down in the chair Nathan usually used. He leaned back as though getting comfortable and set one ankle over the other knee.

"I don't know how you ready for your patients, Darrell, but I prefer to be thorough. And just for the record…none of the patients treated by me or anyone else in this office are lowlifes, as you call them." She used air quotes to emphasize his use of the words *lowlifes*.

"I'm sorry, love. I didn't mean any offense. I just meant that if we were a little late getting back from lunch, it wouldn't really matter since you are going to the prison today. My one o'clock patient cancelled yesterday."

"I think you have gotten the wrong idea. First of all, please stop calling me love and darling. It's inappropriate in the workplace. Secondly, I believe it always matters if I'm late to an appointment no matter where I am. Third, I'm not having lunch with you today. I'm busy. Fourth, my nine o'clock appointment is here, and I'm ready to see him. So if you don't mind, I would appreciate it if you returned to your office."

Just as she finished telling Darrell to get out of her office, Nathan stuck his head in her office. "Hey, Myra, you got a second?"

She sighed in frustration. "Actually, no, I don't. My appointment is here, and he's on a tight schedule today. You'll have to check if Stephanie is available." She crossed her office, brushed past Nathan, and headed for the waiting room, leaving Darrell and Nathan staring after her.

At noon, Myra was in the break room reading through the medical file of a newly referred patient while eating a salad. She was engrossed in the file and making notes when Darrell walked into the break room with a Styrofoam container from a nearby restaurant. He sat down across from her. "Looks like we get to have lunch together after all." He smiled across the table at her.

Myra ignored him.

"Horrible thing about those two kids dying with that priest, huh?"

Myra made a noncommittal sound and continued reading and making notes.

"It must have been terrifying for them watching that priest die like that, knowing they were going to be sexually assaulted and murdered next, don't you think?"

Her head whipped up, and she stared at Darrell in shock. "What makes you say that?" she asked with suspicion.

"Oh, you know, the way they were found and all," he replied, opening his lunch container.

"They were found dead. What makes you think they were alive when the priest died?" she questioned him.

"They were bound so they couldn't get away, eyelids taped to keep their eyes open…just things like that." He shrugged. "Not to mention the fact that they were tied to that palmetto tree."

"Don't you think they could have been posed like that after death to give the appearance of an audience for Father Zachariah's death?"

"I suppose so," he agreed without enthusiasm. "Would you like to have dinner tonight?"

Myra planted her forehead in the palm of her hand and shook her head in exasperation. She decided not to answer him. She cleaned up her lunch items, gathered the record and her notes, and left Darrell in her wake.

*****

The weekend was welcomed wholeheartedly by Myra. She was tired of trying to avoid Darrell in the office. Having that one lunch with him had obviously been a mistake. All week he had been popping up when she least expected it. He was waiting at her office door, showing up in the break room, arriving at work at precisely the same time to walk in with her, appearing in line behind her at the grocery store, and appearing at her dry cleaners just as she was paying for her items and leaving.

The coincidences were just too much, and she had begun thinking they had all been planned in advance by him. Maybe she had been right in her first instincts when he was calling her those endearments. Thankfully, that had finally stopped. She could not even use the work restroom now without finding him waiting outside the door to follow her back to her office.

Nathan had begun arriving in her office more than usual too. She had asked Nathan his opinion, and he felt she was just being paranoid. Darrell just had a simple little crush on her, per Rhonda's belief, but Myra could not shake the feeling that he might be her stalker. She had not had any strange happenings, phone calls, or letters in over a week, for which she was thankful, but that did not mean the stalker was not still there hovering in the shadows…maybe just down the office hallway.

By Friday afternoon, she had endured Darrell as much as she could handle. Having a break between her last two patients of the day, Myra had leaned back in her chair, propped her feet on her desk, and tried to relax, thinking about her last patient and the battery of psychological tests she was going to order for her.

Her last patient, Ms. Chaucer, was a new patient with a host of problems. After an extreme physical assault by her ex-boyfriend that had landed her in the hospital for a number of weeks, she had developed posttraumatic stress disorder on top of being bipolar. She had been referred by her medical doctor to Myra for treatment and review for possible dissociative identity disorder. Family members of Ms. Chaucer had noticed unusual changes and contacted her doctor about them. Despite having had only one appointment with her, Myra noticed some alarming inconsistencies in her intake analysis, warranting further testing.

Hearing voices in the hallway just outside her closed door, Myra sat forward and listened more carefully. She was concerned one of her staff was having difficulties with a patient. If so, she would need to intervene—a common enough situation with a few of the people with violent tendencies. Focusing on the voices, however, she realized it was Rhonda and Darrell having a conversation. She crossed the room, intending to tell them to take their conversation to the break room so they wouldn't disturb Stephanie and her three o'clock patient. With her hand on the doorknob about to open the door, she heard more of their conversation that caused her to pause.

"Yeah, those poor boys were tied to that palmetto tree. You know they were terrified, knowing what was going to happen to them," Darrell stated.

"I just can't imagine what they must have gone through," Rhonda said. "Do you suppose they witnessed the sexual assault as well?"

"I'm certain they did. All three of them had body fluids from the attacker on them. It's a shame the oldest boy died last. Watching the priest and his younger friend get tortured before they died. You know he knew what was coming for him."

"You mean…oh my god! They were actually tortured and killed right there in that spot where they were found?" Rhonda was impressionable, and Myra knew this type of talk about the crime in Charleston would really upset her.

"Of course! Torches had even been lit to brighten the area that night so they could see better. The killer even smoked cigarettes between each one of them. He put the finished butts in a little pile between the boys."

"Oh God! That is so horrendous! Appalling that he smoked cigarettes after each one like he enjoyed it. Unbearably disgusting and chilling! Those poor babies. They were so young and innocent."

Myra could hear tears in Rhonda's emotionally thick voice. She had heard enough of the vile details of the death of those boys and the priest from Darrell. She flung the door open, startling Rhonda. "Could you two please come in here for a moment?" She stepped back, holding the door as Darrell followed Rhonda into Myra's office. "Have a seat, please," she stated as she followed them across the room. Myra rounded her desk and took her own seat, her lips drawing a line with her anger.

Rhonda slipped a couple of tissues from the box on Myra's desk and dabbed at her eyes swimming with tears. Darrell sat beside her, looking innocent, which irritated Myra even more. "What do you think you are doing having a conversation like that in the hallway during working hours?" she demanded. "We have patients here who already have a wide range of problems. They come to us for help in resolving their problems. Instead, while they are here attempting to get help, they hear the two of you having a conversation about two innocent boys and a priest being sexually assaulted and murdered in front of each other! How do you think that makes them feel?"

"We were just—" Darrell began.

"I know exactly what you were doing!" Myra interrupted. She was having a really difficult time controlling her anger and keeping her voice down. She wanted to scream and rant at them for their repulsive behavior in the hallway. "You saw your conversation was upsetting Rhonda, yet you continued with your lewd details of a crime scene! Do you enjoy upsetting people? I'm beginning to wonder about your treatment of patients after what I just heard take place in the hallway."

Darrell's face distorted with his own anger. "How dare you eavesdrop on our conversation and then lecture me on ethics! You question my ability to treat patients when you're the one that looks like you need to be hospitalized. Your paranoia seeps out of you like a toxic waste!"

"My paranoia? Excuse me? I'm one of the owners of this establishment! It's my job as one of your bosses to make sure you fall within the ethical guidelines as set forth for our profession by the American Psychological Association! Furthermore, I was not eavesdropping. If you didn't want your conversation overheard, perhaps you shouldn't have been talking so loudly in the hallway just outside my office! We have three other psychologists treating patients in this hallway, and I'll wager all of them could hear your conversation."

"I'm sorry," Rhonda apologized tearfully. "I didn't realize we were talking so loudly. I don't even know how we got onto that subject."

Myra was in a stare down with a defiant Darrell. "I am pretty sure I know exactly how you got onto that subject," Myra growled, her deep green eyes flashing with her fury. How dare he call her paranoid!

"Are we only allowed to discuss sanctioned topics of conversation in this office?" Darrell sneered. "I must have missed that in your office operational manual."

"Watch it, Darrell! You are on very thin ice right now," Myra warned him in biting tones. "Now get back to work. I'm sure we both have patients waiting."

Red-faced with suppressed anger, and possibly a little humiliation thrown in, Darrell stormed out of her office. Rhonda, on the other hand, had to express a few more tearful apologies before Myra was able to get her out of the office and back to work. When they were both gone, she shut her door and leaned against it a moment. She took deep breaths and attempted to calm herself and clear her mind.

Paranoid? Was she really letting those letters and phone calls get to her so badly that others noticed? And what exactly did he mean by her needing to be hospitalized? She knew she had lost some weight because her clothes were getting way too loose, and she didn't know why. It wasn't like she was dieting. And she all but stopped her exercise routine. The police had recommended she completely change her personal schedule so she didn't appear so predictable. She growled in disgust. She had let Darrell get under her skin.

Thankfully, it was nearing the end of the day, and she only had the one patient left. She hated confrontations, and she especially hated having to reprimand a coworker. Days like this she wished it were her day to work the prison. At least in the prison, you knew exactly the type of person you were counseling—killers, abusers, thieves, arsonist, rapists.

A few of them were psychopaths. Some were acting out the anger and frustration of what had been done to them as children. Others were trying to make a living. A handful were addicts attempting to support their addictions. Some were aggressive, while others were charming. In the end, they were all not to be trusted, especially while incarcerated.

Outside of prison was much scarier. You never really knew who could have sinister feelings toward you. Some could smile to your face, be husbands...wives...coworkers...friends...and easily stab you in the back or slit your throat. Darrell made her uneasy on the best of the days. Now that he was truly angry with her, what could he be capable of?

Those letters had all spoken of love but smacked of ownership and control. The dreams felt of love and tenderness but were rape and domination. Even if the dreams did stem from the unconscious realms of her brain, the act of domination and control had come from the reading of the letters.

Darrell had just shown he was capable of domination and control in his conversation with Rhonda. He had known how it was affecting her, yet he went on and on. He had known there was a good possibility that patients could overhear their discussion, yet he didn't care. Beyond that, in her office, he had demonstrated a blatant insubordination and anger that he could barely control. What else was he capable of?

*****

On the way home from work, she had spontaneously decided she needed a huge break, even if it was only for the weekend. She packed a weekend bag and headed out to Charleston. She planned on finding a hotel for the weekend and spending the entire time relaxing on the beach. It had been years since she had a weekend at the beach, and she needed to get away from the office and her coworkers for a while. More importantly, it was doubtful her stalker would find her there.

By nine thirty that night, she was entering the hotel where she had been fortunate enough to find a weekend reservation. She checked in and lucked out even further. She had scored a room facing the beach. Quickly depositing her bag and purse in the room, Myra slipped off her shoes and darted outside.

She inhaled deeply, tasting the salty ocean air as she walked to the ocean's edge. Waves crashed one after another on the sand at her feet. She stood perfectly absorbed as moonbeams danced on the water like diamonds and the brisk refreshing breeze swept over her. Myra looked up and down the beach, finding she was utterly alone in the magical moonlight of the beach.

Closing her eyes, she could literally feel the weight of all the stress and worry of the past couple of months fall from her shoulders. After carrying so much around for so long, she felt weightless and free. It might not last. Actually, it wouldn't, she realized, but she would take it for as long as it lasted. She strolled along the ocean's edge, digging her toes in the damp sand, allowing the cool fingers of ocean waves to lap and massage her bare ankles.

Myra cleared her mind and focused on the sound of the waves and the smell of the air. It had been years since she had walked along a beach in the moonlight. The last time had been with Luke, her last serious boyfriend. They had literally bumped into each other coming out of class in college. Things had gotten hot and heavy very quickly, and they had spent spring break together in Myrtle Beach. A week later, her father had died.

She returned to campus after the funeral and an extended grieving period to find him in the arms of her sorority sister. Hoping to find solace and comfort, she had found deceit and heartbreak instead. She spiraled from her sorrow and anguish into severe depression. She began missing classes simply because she couldn't get out of bed in the mornings. She lost so much weight that she began to look anorexic.

On one of the rare days she dragged herself from her bed and into class, a professor took note of her condition and recommended she visit a friend of hers. The friend's name was Dr. Eugene Hull, a fellow professor at the university and a psychologist. That visit had been a huge turning point in her life. He helped her with the grief of losing her father and the subsequent betrayal of Luke.

With time, she felt she had a new lease on life. She became obsessed with learning about psychology and eventually changed her degree from business management. She now reflected on how she had thrown herself into her studies and later into her work. The only vacations she had taken since that time was to travel home to visit with her mother. *What have I been missing?* she thought as she walked.

"Have I let myself become a hermit because of an asshole?" she asked herself aloud. Myra discovered that indeed she had. She had stopped enjoying life to the fullest because her father had died and she had been betrayed at the same time. And here she was again, letting someone else dictate her life. With dread, she realized she was allowing someone to terrorize her. She was essentially giving him free reign to intimidate and frighten her. She vowed to herself, in the moonlight-soaked sand and glistening water, that she would no longer give anyone ultimate control over her own life.

She had achieved so much in the past few years, but she had sacrificed almost everything. Her father would not have been happy to see her living this way. She knew her mother was not happy with Myra's life choices. Well, tomorrow was a new day, a new beginning, the day Myra would take control of her own life, her own destiny! She was going to start living and enjoying life!

Chapter 24

The next morning, Myra awoke with the cloudy mist of a dream evaporating. There was something she was supposed to remember about the dream, she thought. She felt it had something to do with Charleston, her work, or both. She tried meditation to remember, but it didn't work. Frustrated, she took a long shower and went to the hotel lobby for the free Continental breakfast bar.

She snagged an apple danish and cup of green tea. A vacant table sat next to a window, and she commandeered it, as well as the newspaper lying folded on one of the two chairs. She scanned the headlines as she ate.

"Dear, would you mind considerably if we joined you? All the other tables are occupied, and we really don't want to go back to our room to eat." A petite gray-haired lady smiled generously with a tall big man slightly behind her.

"Of course not," Myra replied. "I'll just be on my way and let you enjoy the table and your breakfast." She folded the newspaper and rose to leave.

"Nonsense! You'll do no such thing. We can all share the table together, and frankly, my dear, if I may be so bold, you look like you could do with a few more of those danishes. Now you just sit right back down there. Leon, would you be a dear and pull up another chair?" she addressed the man with her.

Myra was momentarily speechless. "Umm…well…um…please join me," she finally stammered.

"I'm Helen, and this is my husband of forty-seven years, Leon," the woman introduced herself as she sat across from Myra.

"Myra Christie," Myra introduced herself as Leon finally found a vacant chair and joined them.

"Such a pretty name! It suits you, my dear. A pretty name for such a beautiful woman!" Helen complimented her.

"Thank you. I was named after one of my grandmothers. Are you here on vacation?" Myra asked.

"Yes. We've been here a couple of days. We are taking the cruise that leaves the Charleston Port tomorrow afternoon. Our son and his family are meeting us for an eight-day cruise. What about you? Are you here on vacation?" Helen asked.

"Just a little weekend trip to recharge," Myra explained.

"How nice! Did you bring anyone with you?"

"Helen, you're a nosy old bat!" Leon suddenly exploded, causing Myra to visibly jump.

"Now look at what you've done! You frightened the poor thing with that booming voice of yours, Leon. Are you okay, dear?" Helen cocked her head slightly to one side, looking expectantly at Myra.

"It's okay. I'm fine. Just a really bad week at work that's made me a little jumpy. I'm alone, but I intend to visit some dear friends of my family a little later today." Myra satiated Helen's curiosity.

"I'm happy to hear you're going to be visiting someone. Life is too short without making the most of time to be near those we enjoy. Isn't that right, Leon?"

"It's true," Leon's voice boomed again. It wasn't as though he were yelling but rather just had a deep strong voice. "You gotta be careful and enjoy all the little things or else life will simply pass you by, and one day you'll wake up and realize what a fool you have been. My father was like that. Always had to be working. He didn't enjoy us kids or his grandkids. Never took a vacation. Then one day...*bam*! He was in his early seventies, dying of cancer. It was too late then."

"That's awful!" Myra exclaimed.

"It truly was. On his deathbed, he broke down crying over all he had missed in life. Leon and I made a pact before we got married that no matter how rough things got, we would always be there for each other and our kids." Helen smiled at Leon, and Myra could feel the love radiating from them both. "We couldn't always afford the nice things or vacations, but we always took time to enjoy life."

"The rough times are always the best." Leon laughed. "You don't have enough money to do anything except provide the basics, so you use your imagination and creativity. Our kids are convinced the best times they had growing up was when we took them camping in the middle of nowhere and they had to forage for their own food. These cruises and expensive vacations are nice, but I really miss those camping trips the most." Leon had placed his hand over his wife's while he was reminiscing. It was so sweet. It warmed Myra's heart to see such love between two people.

Her parents had been happy, but they had their share of fights while Myra had been growing up. With her father being in the military and then later in the FBI, there had been long stretches of time without him in their lives. Times when he had been on military deployments where families could not go. Times where he was on a case, trailing criminals around the world. It had been hard on her mother at times, being the sole caretaker of Myra, the house, the financials, and everything in between.

She and her mother were both very proud of her father's work, but it was difficult and filled with personal sacrifices. He often missed holidays, birthdays, important events, Myra's volleyball games, her dance recitals, and her music recitals. After a while, she got used to his not always being there, but he always called her on those days from wherever he was. He had always taken the time to make special dates with her and her mother when he was home. He was always telling them everything would be different when he retired. He had so many plans for the three of them…and then he was gone, taken down by one of those very criminals he was trying to keep the world safe from.

Myra knew Helen and Leon were right. She had seen the very same thing from her father. Had felt the regrets of not being able to spend more time with him. You never knew what tomorrow held, and Myra knew she had to make some serious changes in her life. She had realized just how many changes she needed to make while walking on the beach in the moonlight last night. Today was the beginning of her new life. She had pledged that to herself in the mirror this morning.

"You just never know when your time is going to be up here on earth. Just like that poor priest and those two innocent little boys they found murdered here in Charleston. One day they are enjoying themselves and having fun, and then a madman comes along and cuts their lives short. It breaks my heart." Helen sniffled.

"We've been following the story from our home in Cincinnati," Leon added. "Do you know if they have caught the killer yet? We haven't watched much television in the past couple of days, so we haven't heard either way."

"Not to my knowledge."

"Those poor little boys. What an awful way to die! Tied up and abused in such a manner. I just hope they went fast and didn't have to watch that monster defile the others. It makes me so sick and angry!" Helen exclaimed in agitation. "I hope they find that bastard, lock him up, and someone in jail does the very same things to him!"

"Now, now...dear. Don't let all that sordid stuff get you all wound up again." Leon caressed Helen's hand and kissed her on the temple. "I'm sure they will catch him soon. Let's just focus on having a good time and being happy."

"I think that's great advice, Leon." Myra smiled. "You have a great cruise and safe journey. I must be off now. I have something I need to do before I visit my friends. It has been a joy talking with you this morning."

She collected her breakfast items and left the newspaper for other hotel guests. Myra had been having nagging thoughts since she had overheard Darrell's conversation with Rhonda yesterday afternoon in the office. Something about what he had said had been annoying her like a Lowcountry no-see-um.

No-see-ums were plentiful and foul little creatures with a particularly nasty little bite. They were so small they could barely be detected. One often did not notice them until they swarmed maddeningly about the head of their victim. Some people called them sand flies or sand fleas. Myra preferred to think of them as tiny flying sharks due to their painful bites. For something so tiny they could fly through the grates in screens, they could take chunks out of their victims.

Myra had even awakened thinking about Darrell and the murders this morning. Something said in the general course of Darrell and Rhonda's conversation had piqued Myra's attention. Unfortunately, she had been so angry that she did not dwell on it at the time. As a result, it had been driving her nuts trying to remember ever since. Helen's causal comments had brought it to the surface, and the more she thought about it, the more concerned she became.

Jotting down everything she could remember from their conversation on the notepad she found beside the phone in her room, she filled a couple of pages easily. The more she wrote, the more alarmed she became. Darrell had been talking about details never revealed by the police. Was he just assuming, or did he know something about these from a personal level?

She put in a call to Police Chief Decemi and left a message on his voice mail. She followed the call up with an extensive e-mail outlining the overheard conversation between Darrell and Rhonda, including everything she could remember about the details of the crime Darrell had mentioned. It could just have been conjecture and exaggeration on Darrell's behalf in trying to impress Rhonda, but given Rhonda's reaction in the conversation, Myra wasn't convinced. She also listed every detail she had found in media reports. Just as she hit send, her cell phone rang.

Dr. Eugene Hull, her old professor and friend of her father's, greeted her with genuine warmth in his voice. After a brief conversation of catching up on family news, he got right to the point. "My dear, have you been keeping up with the news?"

"I've been trying, but I'm afraid I've been swamped lately. Are you talking about the abductions and murders of the priest and the two boys in Charleston?"

"Ah, yes, that was some terrible news, but I'm afraid I have stumbled on something even worse. The day before yesterday, a man was caught speeding on a local highway in Goose Creek. It's one of the smaller townships on the edge of Charleston. When the officer pulled him over, the gentleman was acting a bit odd," he explained.

"What do you mean by odd?" she asked.

"I really don't know how to explain it. It's almost like he has no personality at all. The officer was suspicious and saw a couple of file boxes in the back seat of the vehicle and what looked like a weapon on the floorboard in the back seat. He called for backup and used probable cause to search the vehicle."

After a small pause, a puzzled Myra asked, "What did they find?" It was unlike Dr. Hull to ramble on and not get straight to the point of the matter.

"Myra, it's unlike anything any officer has ever found in a vehicle before. They found multiple weapons, but the alarming part is what was in the boxes. They were filled with files." He paused again as if it were a difficult topic for him discuss.

"Files?"

"Four boxes full of files. Files that detailed people all over the country, several here in South Carolina. Polaroid photos of the people along with details of how he had abducted and killed them. Where they were buried. What he had to done to them while they were alive. How he had desecrated their bodies. Their driver's licenses if they had one. All kinds of information. He even had clippings of their hair and other personal effects as trophies." He spilled out everything quickly.

"Oh my god! They caught the serial killer! The ABC Killer?" she exclaimed.

"The ABC Killer?" he asked, confused.

"Remember that case I had a few months ago where that guy Johnson had killed those women and that teenage girl? Well, it turns out, he may not have killed anyone. He committed suicide in jail and left a letter for me claiming his innocence. The judge called an emergency meeting where we realized, purely by accident, that the women had all been killed in alphabetical order. We were convinced there had to be more victims.

"The Charleston Police Department set up a task force and called in the FBI to assist. The priest and those two boys may have been additional victims. Their names fall into the alphabetical scheme."

"Myra, I think we are talking about two different people here. I'll double-check, but no one has mentioned anything about any of those individuals having files in these boxes. Myra, this guy has been killing for years. We're talking prolific serial killer here. There has to be at least two or three hundred files in those boxes."

"Two or three *hundred*?" she asked incredulously.

"At least. He won't speak to anyone about who he is or where he's from, or even if he has killed all those people. They had a bail hearing late Thursday, and he still wouldn't speak. He just keeps acting very strange. The judge called me after the hearing and asked if I would do an evaluation on him. I spent all day with him yesterday and I saw him early this morning. He started rambling about a bunch of nonsense that frankly creeped me out. When I pressed him about who he was and the boxes of files, he just shut down on me. He refuses to talk to anyone but you. He specifically asked to see you, Myra. He said he will only talk to you."

"Me? Why me? And how does he even know me?"

"We have no idea. I called the judge and told him what he said. We don't even know the guy's name. He didn't have any identification on him, and the vehicle turned out to be stolen."

"But the Department of Mental Health has to appoint me to the case. I can't just take on a case like this at your request, you know." She was thoroughly confused as to why Dr. Hull had contacted her when he knew the SCDMH had to do the appointment.

"The judge called the DMH this morning and explained the situation. Someone should be contacting you shortly about this from the DMH. I'm sorry this is so short notice, and on the weekend when you're trying to relax and destress from the work week, but we don't know anything about this guy, and we need help. His fingerprints are not on file. They took his blood for DNA analysis yesterday, but even with a rush, it could take weeks."

"Wow! I've heard of people not cooperating before, but this is…" She was at a loss for words.

"I know. I've never encountered anything like this before. If possible, I would like to meet with you about this before you see him.

I know it's an inconvenience for you, and I'm willing to travel to you this afternoon, if that helps."

"Actually, I'm here in Charleston. I came down to relax on Isle of Palms this weekend at one of the hotels. I can come by your house or your office today."

"You're here? Why didn't you stay with us? You know you are always welcome to stay with us, even if it's just for relaxation." Dr. Hull sounded a little offended.

"I know, but I didn't want to impose. I didn't even decide to come down here until after work yesterday. It was nearly ten by the time I got checked in last night."

"Nonsense! You are never an imposition. Just wait till I tell Clara. She is going to be miffed with you, you know."

Myra laughed. "Tell her I'll make it up to her."

"You can tell her yourself. Why don't you have lunch with us today and we can go over everything afterward? The police made a complete copy of the files for me yesterday, so I'll pass them on to you."

"What time would you like me there?"

"I've got everything here at the house. Clara is running some errands right now. How about one? Is that too late for you?"

Myra checked her watch. It was nine thirty. It would take about thirty minutes to get to Dr. Hull's house. That would give her almost three hours to bask on the beach. "I'll be coming straight from the beach. Is that okay?"

"Of course. Bring a change of clothes with you and you can shower here. You could always check out of that nasty hotel and stay with us, you know."

Myra laughed at his persistence. "It wouldn't be fair to the hotel on this visit, especially since I've already paid for the room for tonight. How about if I promise that the next time I come down, I stay with you and Clara? Would that work?"

"I'll take it under consideration and discuss it with Clara when she gets home. Just be forewarned that you're going to have to plead your case with her," he warned her with a laugh.

"Deal! I'll see you at one!" she confirmed and said goodbye.

"I just can't catch a break," she muttered to herself. She rummaged through her overnight bag and pulled out a bikini. A few minutes later, she had her hair in a messy bun, tanning lotion she had purchased at a gas station the night before, a beach towel thrown over her arm, a large insulated cup filled with ice water, a trashy romance paperback she had purchased at the same gas station, and her phone. She was trudging through the sand to find a place to relax on the beach.

Since it was a Saturday and a beautiful sunny day, it wouldn't be long before the beach would be teeming with half-naked bodies worshiping the sun god. The tide was going out, which was great because she didn't have to worry about finding high ground so she wouldn't be swamped with cold ocean water when engrossed in her book or napping. She found a place near the water's edge, spread out her towel, and plopped down. She set the alarm on her phone for 12:15, just in case she fell asleep in the warmth of the sun and settled down to reading.

Chapter 25

While Myra was soaking up the sun, she received phone calls from both the judge in the case and the SCDMH. The judge wanted to personally explain the situation, which was, more or less, precisely as Dr. Hull had described. The SCDMH called to tell her she had specifically been requested by the judge to handle the case. She had just taken on two new patients at the office and had a full load as it was. It was going to be challenging handling another case in Charleston. Her staff was going to be frustrated as well, but she decided to wait to break the news to them on Monday.

As she predicted, the sun god had lulled her into a nap with the help of the ocean god's wave rhythm. The beeping of her phone's alarm woke her. She stretched and yawned before sitting up and taking in her surroundings. The beach was packed with bodies of all sizes and shapes. She sat for a moment longer, simply enjoying all the beach had to offer—the coconut scent of tanning oils, warm sun, cool ocean breeze, crashing of the waves, squeals of children laughing, and squawking of seagulls as they dove on unsuspecting patrons, hoping for free handouts of food.

She gathered her things and headed for her hotel room. The room was downright cold after the intoxicating warmth of the beach. She threw her things in her bag, including her laptop, slipped into a pair of shorts, a tank top, and her trusty flip-flops. On her way out of the room, she caught a glimpse of herself in a mirror.

"Oh dear!" she cried. She had fallen asleep on her stomach. Her entire backside was beet red. Even her face and arms were red. With her olive skin tone, she rarely burned, but it had been years since she had been in the sun at the beach. Despite having applied her tanning lotion twice, she still turned red. At this point, all she could hope for was that it wouldn't hurt.

Forty-five minutes later, she pulled into the driveway of Dr. Eugene Hull. Traffic had been a little heavier than she had expected, but she still arrived at exactly one o'clock. She pulled her bag from the Jeep as she climbed out, and before she shut the door and locked it, Clara, Eugene's wife, was already hurrying out of the house to greet her.

"Myra! It's been ages! Why haven't you been to see us before now?" Clara enveloped her in a warm hug.

"I'm sorry, Clara. I've just been working. In fact, this is the first weekend I've taken off to just have fun in so long that I don't remember the last time."

"Eugene told me you were staying at the beach. You know you are welcome to stay with us anytime you are in Charleston."

"I know. It was a spur-of-the-moment decision last night. I've been going through some rather unpleasant stuff lately, but I'll wait to discuss all that with both of you until after lunch. It's so great to see you! I have missed you so much!" Myra wrapped her arm around Clara's shoulders in a loose hug as they walked to the house.

"There you are!" Eugene was relaxing in a leather recliner reading the newspaper when they entered the living room. "How was the beach?"

"Wonderful! Just what the doctor ordered." She grinned. "How have you been?" She leaned down and gave him a hug as he pressed a button to return the recliner to its sitting position.

"You know what they say, every day above ground is a good one, so I'm doing great. Clara has been after me to retire. I've cut back on my hours, but I just can't seem to bring myself to retire. I'm afraid I'll get lazy." He grinned mischievously.

"Too late for that," Clara playfully chided him. "You've been lazy for years."

"That's because you're too good to me and let me be lazy," he replied and blew his wife a kiss.

"Okay, no mushy stuff while I'm here!" Myra stood between them with her hands held up as though she were in a boxing ring between fighters.

"Well! I see some people don't change!" Clara huffed in a joking tone.

"All right, we will try very hard to control ourselves." Eugene looked at his wife with gooey puppy eyes.

"Some people just don't appreciate our love, sweetheart." Clara fluttered her eyelashes, returning the air kiss.

Myra rolled her eyes and pretended to be disgusted. "Think I'll take a quick shower while you two get the sappy stuff out of your systems." She laughed. "I'm claiming the guest bath!"

"You're welcome to use your usual room too," Clara called at her. "Just in case you change your mind and decide to stay the night with us."

Minutes later, Myra was seated at the breakfast table set within a bay window overlooking Clara's beautifully manicured backyard filled with flowers and greenery. Clara had fixed shrimp and grits, cornbread muffins, garden salad with pineapple-mango vinaigrette, sweet tea, and freshly sliced strawberries over old-fashioned pound cake that was still warm from the oven with a large dollop of home-made whipped cream.

"I am so miserable!" Myra complained. "That was so delicious, and I couldn't stop eating. I really don't understand how you can eat her cooking all the time and not weight six hundred pounds!" she told Eugene.

"I've learned moderation the hard way. In the first six months we were married, I gained fifty pounds. My doctor nearly had a coronary over my weight gain. I came home, told Clara, and she accused me of lying. A week later, we bumped into my doctor, and he told her himself that she needed to make sure I stayed on the diet he had put me on."

"Of course, I didn't listen to that quack. You were much too thin back then. And since I didn't want you to leave me, I made sure you were well fed!" Clara grinned across the table at Eugene.

"I'm sure I would have gained much more than fifty pounds," Myra claimed. "I have no willpower when it comes to good food. I can't believe I actually had two servings of that strawberry shortcake!"

"There's plenty more, if you want it." Clara smiled devilishly.

"Are you kidding me? Any more and I'll literally burst!"

"Then I better distract you from eating with our sordid business," Eugene stated. "Why don't we start with your news?"

"Oh, but I must help Clara clean up first. It wouldn't do to discuss something like this at the dinner table. All of it is just too much and too dark for a place as light and wonderful as this." Myra stood and began stacking dishes.

"Oh no, you won't!" Clara erupted. "Let's retire to Eugene's office to discuss your situation. While he discusses this serial killer case with you, I'll clean the kitchen by myself. You two have a lot of information to cover."

"Good idea, dear!" Eugene rose and led the way to his office. After the ladies were seated in wingback armchairs upholstered in matching charcoal paisley print fabric, Dr. Hull seated himself behind his desk in a black leather wingback office chair that swiveled. He leaned back, steepled his fingers, and looked at Myra. "Okay, so what is this situation or incident you needed to discuss?"

Myra swallowed hard. It was easier telling total strangers her predicament, she found, than it was telling friends that were more like her family. She pondered how to begin for a moment before simply blurting out, "I'm responsible for someone's death, and I have a stalker."

"What?" Clara burst out.

"A stalker? What do you mean by someone's death?" Eugene sat up and leaned over his desk.

Myra told them how everything had started. She told them about the case she had worked and Mr. Johnson's subsequent death. How the judge had called her into his chambers and showed her the suicide letter. That going over the evidence again, they realized that perhaps there was a serial killer loose in Charleston and that maybe Mr. Johnson had indeed been innocent.

Then she told them about the stalking that had started during the case. She discussed the letters before pulling copies out of her briefcase and showing them to both Eugene and Clara. She told them about the dreams, the roses, the phone calls, and what had happened at the courthouse. She even discussed her concerns about Darrell and the police's questioning about Nathan. It was some time before she finished.

"Why didn't you call me and tell me this was going on? Does your mother know about this?" Eugene looked concerned.

"No, I haven't told her. She's gearing up with Jack's senate run, and she's so busy and worried about that, I just couldn't overwhelm her with this. It's my problem, and I've been working on it. Besides, I've turned all this information over to the police, and they are actively investigating the stalker case."

"It's been well over two months, Myra. Shouldn't they have had a suspect or someone in detention on this by now?" Clara was gazing out the window, lost in thought.

"It takes time to gather enough information on stalking cases to get serious jail time from it," Eugene offered. "The letters are bad enough, but those phone calls concern me. And when you went to the courthouse and received a letter... Myra, sweetheart, this is very serious. I do hope you are taking it as such."

"I know it's serious. I find myself constantly looking over my shoulder, dreading answering the phone and collecting the mail. And then there are the dreams. What do you think about those? Am I going crazy?" she asked Eugene.

"I think the dreams are just your subconscious lashing out. It's normal for men and women to have sexually stimulating dreams, especially if they have not been sexually active in a while. Those letters are suggestive of a lover or significant other reaching out to you. My guess is that they triggered a sexual need you have been suppressing."

"That's what I was hoping. It's been a long time since I've dated anyone. Work keeps me busy, and when I get home, I just want to relax and decompress. Dating is the last thing on my mind most days."

"I understand, dear, but don't let yourself get so wrapped up in your work that you let your life get away from you. Life is for enjoying. It's much too short to spend it being only productive. Like all things, you must live in moderation." Clara patted Myra's hand with a soft look in her eyes.

Myra placed her other hand over Clara's and held it for a moment. She had known Clara and Eugene since she was a little girl. Her father and Eugene had worked together at the FBI for a while before Eugene retired and opened his own practice. Eugene was several years older than her father and was like a mentor to him. Back then, Clara had babysat Myra on occasion and given her piano lessons. Her parents frequently visited the Hulls', and the Hulls had done likewise. She had grown to think of them as her adopted grandparents.

Not having any children of their own, they had doted on Myra. Even after Eugene's retirement and their subsequent move to Charleston, Myra had visited during spring breaks and summer breaks. Often, the Hulls traveled back to Virginia to celebrate Thanksgiving and Christmas with Myra and her parents. They attended her father's funeral and grieved with Myra and her mother in the front pew of the church with them.

Dr. Hull had been there when she suffered her severe depression after her father's death. When Myra later discussed her desire to change her college major to psychology, Dr. Hull helped advise her. Both he and Clara had been there for all her college graduations. She had done her summer internships in his office, and he helped her get her license to practice on her own. He stepped up to be her stand-in father, and Clara had been a second mother. They had been there every step of the way, and now Myra felt guilty for not spending more time with them.

"Thank you so much for reminding me of that, Clara. I promise I'll make a point of paying more attention to me and my needs."

"I'll leave you two alone to discuss the case. I think I'll go piddle in my flower garden for a while. Let me know if you need anything, Eugene." Clara patted Myra on the shoulder then left the room, quietly shutting the door behind her.

Chapter 26

For the next three hours, Myra and Eugene discussed the case. They reviewed all the information the police had been able to gather on the suspect to date before moving on to the suspect's files of his victims. He had taken before and after pictures of his victims, and the photos were severely disturbing. Some victims had been posed in innocent positions, some in extremely provocative poses. Some victims simply appeared to be fully clothed and sleeping, while others were mutilated beyond belief.

After reviewing one particularly disturbing victim file, Myra ran for the bathroom and threw up. When she returned to the office, she saw Dr. Hull had the file in his hands and was extremely pale. The after picture had been particularly disturbing, but the worst part was that he had included two recipe cards with comments on the back. He had consumed some of the victim's body parts, describing in detail how he had prepared the parts and how delicious they had been. Just remembering his comments had her stomach churning again.

"Dr. Hull, I don't think I'm the right person for this case. In my professional opinion, this guy needs a psychiatric evaluation by a psychiatrist like you. A psychological evaluation is not thorough enough. This guy is so disturbed, I have no idea where to even begin."

"I actually agree with you, but he refuses to talk to anyone or submit to any evaluations until after he has discussed it with you first."

"Why me? I don't know this guy. I've never even met him, thank God for that!"

"I wish I knew. It disturbs me that he may be fixated on you. After hearing about your stalker situation, I'm inclined to think it might be this guy." Dr. Hull ran his hand through his gray hair, leaving tufts sticking up in all directions.

"That's highly unlikely. I don't know this guy. I've never met him to my knowledge." She picked up a police booking photo of the suspect. Dark hair, dark eyes, black rimmed glasses, a shaggy beard. He was actually smiling in the photo as though it was a photo shoot. "My stalker knows things about me…gained access to my apartment somehow. The police are convinced it's someone I know, perhaps someone I work with or one of my patients."

"I expect you have already gone through your patient files." He leaned back in his chair, focusing on her instead of the file in front of him.

"Yes. A couple of my staff even helped me. We also went through my records on the inmates. Frankly, I've been thinking it might be a junior psychologist in my office. He's a little off, in my opinion, and he has a bit of disregard for the office rules."

"How so?" Dr. Hull asked with interest.

"Well, he keeps calling me love and darling, just like the letters for a start. He keeps asking me on dates and has been out with several of the other staff despite our office rules stating that we refrain from it. That was my idea when we opened the office. I felt if we discouraged office romances and such, there would be less office drama."

"It's a good concept. How is it working out for you?"

"We haven't had any problems until this guy started. He's a bit too chummy with Rhonda, my assistant. Yesterday, I actually had to counsel him because he was discussing the case of the priest and the two boys in the hallway outside my office. He was loud, discussing evidence that I'm not sure how he obtained, and doing it while we had patients in several of the rooms."

"Hmmmm… I don't like that, Myra. Have you reported him to the police investigating your stalker?"

"No, but I did contact the Charleston police about the bragging he was doing about the case. He knew details that have not been published, Eugene. I'm not sure if he had something to do with it, if he's simply making up crap to impress Rhonda, or if he knows some-one working on the investigation and has gained access to pertinent information."

"I see what you mean. It could be any number of things, but I think you made the right choice in contacting the police."

"I hope so. I guess now I just have to sit back and wait for the police to look into him." Myra crossed to stand in front of the double windows overlooking the backyard where Clara was busy nipping spent blooms off her numerous flowers. "If it's not him, I'm going to feel really bad about suspecting him in the first place."

"It's better to be safe than sorry. It's a difficult decision to make."

"Extremely. I thought about it all night. It was something spe-cific that he said that initially caught my attention. After our con-frontation about it yesterday, I couldn't quite remember what he had said until this morning. He said the killer made the boys watch the degradation and killing of the priest. I looked up everything I could find on the case, and that was never released to the public. I tried calling the police chief, but he was tied up, so I sent him an e-mail about it. It might be nothing, but I have a feeling that what Darrell said is true. He might just be conjecturing, but I didn't feel I could take the chance. What if I'm wrong? What if Darrell is innocent?"

"What if you're right? What if he's your stalker? What if he's the serial killer? What ifs will drive you mad if you let it." Eugene watched her with concern.

"I was wrong about Owen Johnson. He committed suicide because I was wrong. His blood is on my hands."

"Owen Johnson committed suicide because he wasn't strong enough to fight the system. He was aware he could appeal. You were not the one who accused him. You didn't put him on trial. You did a job that you were hired to do, and you did it well. You need to stop questioning yourself. You could not have prevented his death. I'd wager that he still would have been found guilty if someone else had done his evaluation."

"Maybe, but I can't forget the part I played in his death." She returned to her seat.

"What about the detectives? If they had done a more thorough job of investigating instead of latching on to him as a suspect so quickly, perhaps Mr. Johnson would still be alive. Perhaps Mr. Johnson would have died in a car accident last week. Perhaps Mr. Johnson really was involved in the murders in some way. Hindsight, as they say, is twenty-twenty. Myra, honey, you can't beat yourself up over something that was out of your control."

"That's much easier said than done, I'm afraid. So what do you think about this guy?" Myra waved her hand over all the files they had been reviewing and successfully changing the subject.

"He's very disturbed, Myra. I don't like you going to speak with him, but the judge feels it's necessary to get him talking. Are you up for this? You've been through so much lately."

"Maybe dealing with this guy will take my mind off other things. I can't believe this guy has murdered all these people. I've reviewed at least a hundred files so far, and I don't even see a particular pattern in his crimes."

"I felt the same way when I started reading them. I think that *is* his pattern. He's extremely organized and kills for the fun of killing."

"It's like each murder victim is a new discovery of humiliation and slaughter, like he enjoys experimenting on them to see how much pain and torture they can take."

"I've read nearly all of them. I've been keeping a list putting them in order to see how he has deteriorated over time. It seems as though he started with sexual assaults and strangulations, then graduated to shootings, stabbings, before moving to total mutilations." Eugene handed her his working list on a legal pad for review.

Myra began skimming the list. "I saw you were reviewing the file I just read when I returned from the bathroom. I was violently ill after reading those index cards. He has evolved into cannibalism."

"Reminds me a horror movie I once saw. After reading most of these files, I feel we need to move him to a high-security mental health facility. I'll talk to the judge about it. In the meantime, maybe he will open up to you and we can get some much-needed information from him."

"I'll do my best. I think it was a great decision to house him in the high-security prison until trial instead of the jail. I don't think the jail could handle him." Myra made a few notes on the pad to add a couple of files she had read that were not listed.

"Yes. In light of what they found in his vehicle, they moved him there as soon as they finished booking him."

"I'm going to call Stephanie and Rhonda and let them know I'll be down here for a few days. I'll run home tomorrow afternoon and pick up some things."

"Will you be staying with us? Clara would love it."

"I think I better get a hotel since this is work related, but I promise to stop by your office at the end of each day and come over here for supper. Will that work?"

"Clara will be overjoyed. She thinks you're too thin."

"I won't be after eating here for a few days!" She laughed.

Chapter 27

"Let me tell you a story." The flat black-brown eyes watched her closely for her reaction as he paused for effect. When she refused to comment, he continued, "The kind that will make your blood run cold. The kind that will make you shiver even on the hottest of days. The kind"—he leaned forward and lowered his voice to just above a whisper—"that will haunt your dreams forever." He burst into a maniacal laugh. He was obviously enjoying the attention and was prepared to prolong it as long as possible.

He was right. His story was an evil one, and she didn't know the half of it yet. She wasn't sure she wanted to know it. If it hadn't been for his lifeless eyes and the light beige prison jumpsuit with the letters SCDC (South Carolina Department of Corrections) emblazoned in black capital block style lettering, he was the man of most women's dreams. He had thick black hair with a boyish curl that fell onto his forehead, a strong chiseled chin, dimples, and the build of a weight lifter. He was definitely an eye-catcher.

He looked much different from his booking photo. He had shaved and looked much more kempt. Myra was certain she didn't know him. While his name was definitely unfamiliar to her, she had an odd feeling that she had seen him before. She shrugged the feeling off and realized he reminded her of a movie actor. It was probably just a resemblance to the actor that was lending to the feeling. She would have remembered the dull eyes she looked into. It was like looking into a person and not seeing a soul, only an evil darkness. She shivered lightly.

She stared at him blankly. Myra was accustomed to antics and storytelling of homicidal psychopaths like him. As a forensic psychologist, she had interviewed her fair share within the confines of the prison system. From his records, police reports, and eyewitness accounts, she knew this one, however, was a little more perverse and deranged than most. He was definitely the most prolific. Possibly the most prolific the world had ever seen. From what she had seen in his files from his vehicle, he was definitely the most vicious!

The news of his capture was now the new headline "story of the moment" of every media outlet in the world, eclipsing the deaths of the priest and two boys. The exploits the newshounds had credited him with, if they could be believed, were fueling sales everywhere. She doubted it would be long before Hollywood was making a movie about it. It was the stuff of all the best and goriest of horror flicks. If the accounts were true, then God help them all.

So many families torn apart, so much grief and mourning… so many deaths! She hoped it did not give other psychopaths ideas. Stories like his held the world captive. What made him tick? What made a person like him do the horrible things he had done? Why did they not have a conscience like everyone else? While the public did not want to know people like him existed in the general public, they could not seem to get enough of the horrors. The insatiable curiosity abounded.

She knew the psychopathic brain was different. She hoped the state would let her get an fMRI (functional magnetic resonance image) of his brain at some point. She wanted to test him while images of his brain were taken. It would definitely be interesting. For now, she was here to do a simple job.

Like so many others, she had watched the news stories on every national television station since Saturday evening. When she and Dr. Hull had finished reviewing the files, they both felt too nauseated to eat the delicious supper Clara had fixed for them. Instead, they had retired to the family room to watch a bit of television before she headed back to the beach. The story was literally on every news station as a special report.

Sunday morning, she had decided to have breakfast at a local restaurant and picked up a newspaper on her way in. It was the head-line story. Normally, she would not have had reason to be sitting here before him videotaping this session as she frequently did with her interviews. This was not her case. She didn't want this case, but she had been asked to come.

Rarely did Eugene invite her to one of his cases. To her knowledge, he hadn't invited anyone to assist him since she had interned with him fresh out of college. But he had called asking for her help, and she couldn't not help him. He had done so much for her over the years since her dad had died. She owed him. If helping him on this case was what he required, then she would do it, no matter how much she hated it.

"I want you to view this case with fresh eyes, without any preconceived ideas or notions. I want to see if you get the same information I have gotten so far," Dr. Hull had explained with a worried frown.

"What do you mean?" she had asked.

"I've spent three days interviewing him. Let's just say his personal account of his life history is…interesting, at least what part of it I could get out of him. He won't talk to anyone about recent events or give us his name until he talks with you. I want to see if you get the same account," he explained.

"Why me? You know so many top psychologists and psychiatrists in the country."

"I know you're not thrilled with this case, Myra. I really don't want to pull you into this. But since he has refused to give us his information and such unless he talked with you, I felt I had no choice. I had to involve you. He is depraved, among other things, but I think you can handle it. I know you want to write a book on the criminal mind. This case may be of use to you in your research and writing," he had elucidated.

Now here she was, sitting in front of one of the worst serial killers the world had ever seen. She was only going to interview him—get his name, personal information, version of events, and life history. Dr. Hull would do the psychometric testing, and she would review the results of those tests later. After that, he would be seen by another psychiatrist his defense attorney would line up for him.

Investigators were still collecting evidence, and they needed his name and a little history to assist them in determining his background and such. The back seat of his pickup truck had detailed his crimes, and investigators were working hard to determine if the crimes were legitimate. The files had even detailed where bodies would be found.

The FBI had already been called in to assist, and a couple of files had already been matched up with John and Jane Doe cases of bodies found in various states. Presently, a task force was assisting law enforcement officials in a number of states to find missing persons. It would probably take months, if not years, to recover all the bodies if the records were accurate.

His records were immaculate with photos, newspaper clippings, and drivers' licenses being affixed next to his pictures, confirming the identities of the victims, mostly teenage girls and women, but some children, teenage boys, and men were also sprinkled throughout the volumes. It made the job a little easier for the law enforcement officers in identification, but they still had to physically follow the directions he had in his files to find the graves. So far, investigators had confirmed 176 victims from North Carolina, South Carolina, Georgia, Alabama, Mississippi, Louisiana, and Texas, but they still had several more volumes of the scrapbook files left to identify and confirm. If he had listed all his victims, by Myra's and Dr. Hull's calculations, there had to be over six hundred victims scattered throughout the United States and Mexico.

It had been a great catch, but there was a problem with that evidence. Just because he had that information in his custody when he was captured did not simply mean he was responsible for all those deaths. The fact that he did it all or that he had drivers' licenses for the majority of them was not an admission of guilt. It was circumstantial at best. Investigators had interrogated him for hours, days even, but had gotten nowhere. He simply sat in the chair and looked at them stoically. After nearly a week of frustration on the part of the investigators, he finally smiled at them and asked for his lawyer.

Authorities had no other choice but halt the interrogation. Some were working overtime in tracking down leads on the individuals in the scrapbook files. Others were working at building a profile of the suspect to explain how and why he was able to continue for so long.

Still, others were researching his background. All were major under-takings considering how much he had traveled and the sheer number of individuals in the scrapbook files. It was the biggest case of all time.

The number of individuals working the case had eclipsed a hundred; that she knew. Even the psychological profile was difficult because no one MO or modus operandi was consistent with the vic-tims. She would have to do her research in that area as well, but that would have to wait until she could determine what was going on in his head. Dr. Hull was helping her by making a list of the victims and their injuries and the dates of the crimes in order to determine how his mind had deteriorated over time.

According to Dr. Hull, the suspect had only told him that he was born and raised in Northeast Tennessee, the heart of the Smokey Mountains, near the borders of Kentucky, North Carolina, and South Carolina. He had also spent some time in his early twenties liv-ing with his elderly grandmother in West Virginia before her death. Investigators were expecting to find cases in those states as well, but first they had to know his name.

It was an investigator's nightmare. He had been captured near Charleston, South Carolina, and now sat at Lieber Correctional Institution in Ridgeville, South Carolina, a level three maximum security facility that housed death row inmates and the most danger-ous. He was assigned a solitary cell awaiting his trial.

"Why don't we start with your name?" Myra asked him.

"You might leave without me telling you my story," his deep voice resonated.

"I can't leave until we finish. You specifically asked for me. The judge decided to honor your request. Dr. Hull and I will both be interviewing you," Myra explained.

"You promise? I know you don't break your promises," he said as though he knew her.

"How do you know I don't break my promises?"

"I've read about some of the cases you have worked on."

Alarm bells began going off in Myra's head. "What do mean you've read about some of my cases? Where did you get access to that information?" she asked in a level voice, trying to keep the panic out.

"It was in the newspaper after that guy killed himself a few weeks ago. I also saw a news report about it. You promised the court to do a good job, and you did. It wasn't your fault the police didn't do their job right. You didn't convict the guy. You just interviewed him and did your evaluation. That's what you're going to do here too, right?" he asked.

Myra began to breathe a little easier. She had forgotten about the newspaper story on her after the media were notified of Mr. Johnson's death. His suicide letter had not been revealed, and the media had spared her in the story. They had not been so cordial on the investigators in the case. "Yes, that's exactly what I'm going to be doing here."

"Very well. My name is Canton Wayne Heirwick. Does it please you to know my name? Your investigators will find my birth records in Tennessee. I'm forty-four years old. My blood type is O negative. I'm a self-employed carpenter. I have no siblings and no parents. Everyone in my family is dead." His eyes never left her face.

"So why don't you tell me your story?" she invited as he continued to watch her intently.

"I'm not sure you will believe me. Not sure you are worthy." He leaned back in his metal chair, narrowing his eyes.

"You told Dr. Hull. What's the matter? Don't tell me you are afraid of the cameras," she taunted.

"Not really. Though I'm usually on the other side of the camera taking the pictures. I haven't told Dr. Hull everything. He's not worthy to know everything. He was scared of me, as he should be." He flashed a dazzling smile showing his bright white teeth; it did not quite reach his piercing eyes.

"Then what is it? You don't think I will enjoy your story? You think I will be afraid?"

He laughed again. "I know you won't enjoy it, but you won't be able to get enough of it either." He cocked his head to one side as though he were trying to figure her out. He slowly leaned forward again and, in his low deep voice, said, "Just remember, you asked for it. And yes, you will be afraid—terrified before I'm through."

Chapter 28

Canton Wayne Heirwick's life story as told to Dr. Myra L. Christie, forensic psychologist in association with Dr. Eugene Hull for the purposes of state examination for trial, Lieber Correctional Institution, Ridgeville, South Carolina. Dictation taken from audio and videotaping.

Day 1:

I am an angel of hell sent by Satan to create chaos and fear, hate and destruction in humanity. I am not delusional or insane, as some would say. I have been here for centuries, and you cannot rid yourselves of me or my brothers and sisters. You may kill this body, but I simply am reborn immediately. I am immortal…sort of. I know this because it has happened many times, and I remember everything from my previous lives. I am not the only one.

Satan, himself, sent several of us to his bidding. I have met and worked with some of my brothers and sisters over the years. Some were sent before I arrived, others much later. Never do we rest in our work. We enjoy it too much. This is the story of my reign.

My arrival was by human birth in the year 1555 in a small village called Tallow, Ireland. It was a very destitute area then. Ireland and England were at odds over English law and religion. Ah, religion—the best excuse for war and destruction by humans. Of course, frequently it is orchestrated by my siblings and me, as you will see. War was forthcoming in Ireland, but it would still take a few years before it arrived. Ah, but I'm getting ahead of myself. Let me start at the beginning.

I was a stocky child, born to fight and kill. My earthly father was weak and pathetic for a member of the Irish clans. He was no warrior, but he was patriotic to Ireland, at least. My mother was a hard worker and mother to four other children. I was a middle child. My eldest brother was much like my father, and my eldest sister was very beautiful with long blond tresses and piercing blue eyes. I'll never forget her beauty. I also had two younger brothers eventually.

We lived in squalor. Little more than indentured servants, we worked hard handling the planting, cultivation, and harvesting of crops and livestock for our master, the Earl of Desmond. Luckily, he was a fair, just man. Not all masters were so. Some were greedy, power-hungry clansmen. Others were more battle hungry. The situation with England was fueling their thirst for blood.

Queen Elizabeth I of England was trying desperately to instill her will on Ireland in a number of ways. She sent troops to police us, took the lands away from our clan leaders, and gave it to her noblemen. She also tasked a man by the name of Henry Sidney, Lord Deputy of Ireland, to protect her interests and be the enforcer. He was ruthless. Some called him little more than a well-dressed savage. Anyone who even spoke out against the queen, England, or her laws were quickly dealt with and paid a hefty price, often with their lives.

My earthly family learned this lesson the hard way. Before the English came, my family had freedoms in the clan. They grew the earl's crops and paid their taxes, but they were free. Once the English arrived, taxes increased to the point where people were starving. Freedoms were stripped. We were told what we could do and what we could not do, what we would do for England and the queen. *God rest the queen!* (Subject laughs cruelly.)

My earthly father was frustrated watching us starve. He spoke out against the English travesties. He spoke to his neighbors about rising up for the earl. I have to hand it to him, he was a slight and weak-minded man, but he hated England and stood his ground on that score. Unfortunately, Sidney heard of this and dealt a swift blow at the hands of his henchmen. They arrived at night while my family was sleeping.

I was nine years old then, lying awake and thinking. I did that often. I have never needed much sleep in any human body of which I have resided. I knew I was different. I had an awareness of my purpose and often would lie awake and think about achieving my directive. Something told me to hide that night. Perhaps it was my father in hell softly whispering. Perhaps it was just the knowledge that I was too young yet to fulfill my destiny. It has been so long. I cannot quite remember.

The henchmen suddenly broke through the door and grabbed my father as he leaped from his bed. He was forced to watch as they killed his family, our family, one by one. My mother was decapitated in her bed. Her body jerked, and blood covered everyone. My siblings were too horrified to make a sound. I watched as my siblings were slaughtered like lambs.

They killed my youngest brother first. He was just a babe. These men took pleasure in their work. They were barbaric and callous, and I watched and learned a new craft. Some of them took turns raping and sodomizing my beautiful sister before they slit her from her vagina to her chin. They all but gutted my father and brothers, but at least they cut their throats first. My sister, my lovely sister, did not get such generous treatment. It was meant to be a warning to everyone in the area.

Their intentions, however, were not so well received. A couple of other families were also butchered that night. It was a significant number for our small village at the time. Word spread like lightning. Within a couple of days, everyone in Southern Ireland knew what had happened. Their objective had been to quiet the area, to bring it into compliance with English law. Instead, it fueled a rebellion. I had heard that the Earl of Desmond was residing in nearby Cork, so I set out in search of him.

A sturdy child, I was big for my age. Tall and broad of chest and shoulder, I was ready to avenge my earthly family and do Satan's bidding. Unfortunately, my skill set in fighting was lacking. I found the earl within the week and pledged my allegiance. He attended me, and the training began. For three years, I trained diligently and daily under Master James Fitzmaurice FitzGerald, a general if you will, for the earl. Our army grew.

I was a fast learner with a sword. I quickly became most accomplished. Struck like lightning and was not afraid to die. Mind you, I did not know of my immortality at that time, but I continued to hear the whispers in the night. The soft bidding was calling to me. I knew with certainty I was on the right path.

A male's thirteenth birthday is a rite of passage in becoming a man. The voice of my father told me mine would be extra special. It was joyous and fulfilling. That day, I became more than just a mere human man. In the early morning fog, thick and cool, I began my true life. I began a journey like no other. And it started with my march to Tallow.

The day dawned with the crowing of the rooster and the trampling of feet. Our small army made our way through the town. The fog was still heavy as we made our way to the stone structure that held the still sleeping English. A sentry saw us and gave the battle cry, but we were already upon them. The Earl of Desmond and our army attacked the English garrison in Tallow with gusto.

Just over a hundred English soldiers were present, and many fled, escaping with only their lives. The rest we massacred much the way my family had died. Some had not even the time to rise from their slumber. They died where they lay. Those that did not escape or die in their beds died just the same. Their bodies were piled haphazardly so one had to step over them as they navigated the building. The floor was slick with the blood of our enemies.

I had been the first to enter, first to draw blood, and first to taste victory. I was the first to find retribution. Revenge was mine at last. My reckoning on earth, however, was just beginning. My thirteenth birthday was an awakening of sorts—for me, for Ireland, for England, for the world.

My fierceness and bravery on the battlefield earned me the nickname Swift Sword, the first of many nicknames, as you will see. But for the time being, in this initial lifetime, in this specific period, that name would strike fear into the heart and soul of all my enemies. That day, my birthday, however, I was cheered and given honor. Funny how sometimes you humans honor killers and sometimes you punish them when the end result is still the same. A person dies at the hands of another. Fate is fickle, turning at any moment, but that day I became Tallow's hero. That day I became a true son of Ireland.

That day, the earl gave me a torch to burn England out of Tallow, and I gladly accepted the assignment. My work was just beginning.

The rebellion lasted many years. My fierceness and brutality became legendary. Some equated me to godlike status. If only they had known…hahaha. My viciousness knew no bounds against my enemies. I felt empowered, alive…free. They were blood soaked, their broken bodies trampled beneath my feet. Their dying souls gave me life…gave me breath…and provided me a joy like nothing else. I gave no mercy. I accepted no surrender. I exterminated the English with unbridled passion. Like the grass beneath my feet, I crushed them. I began to thirst for it, to hunger for it.

War was my element. It fed me. It watered me. I had found my element, as it were. I now remembered my father's wishes, my mission on earth. The whispers were not just fanciful imaginings of a young child but the counselor for a man. I became a leader for skill as well as my well-thought-out plans. Luckily for me, this was a long war that eventually took over most of Ireland.

The enemy kept coming to me to be slaughtered. For many long years, I fought and won. Battle after battle, the bodies piled up. All of Ireland saw me in battle. I butchered thousands. Anyone who stood in my way was cut down. It didn't matter to me if they were English, Scottish, or Irish. I massacred entire families and earned the rejoicing of my father in hell.

Don't you find it peculiar that one minute a soldier is a hero to his nation and the next he is considered a madman? One minute he is a defender to be rejoiced, yet the next an embarrassment? Such is my tale of woe. My own people turned on me. My Irish brothers of battle declared me too bloodthirsty and insane.

Drunk on food, drink, and women, they took advantage like vultures on the dead. Like creatures of the night wind, they stole my life away. I was stabbed in the back without a weapon at my hand. They moved unseen in my drunken haze. I still remember the feel of the heavy sword's tip thrust into my being, the blade twisting against my insides and breaking my ribs, the coldness as my blood seeped from my dying body. An ungrateful thank you for bringing the hounds of hell to fight their battle for Ireland!

I was furious my life was over. I was not ready to die. And then, something amazing happened. That death brought about my first changeover, my first reincarnation. It has happened so many times since then, but still I cannot quite put it into words. One minute I am in the throes of the agony of death, and the next I am beginning a new life. So you see, they murdered that body, but they did not kill me!

Chapter 29

Perhaps a little clarification is in order at this point. Yes, I am reincarnated. I cannot truly die, nor am I truly reborn. You see, I am never carried in the womb like other infants. I die and then suddenly I am alive. I am just opening my eyes for the first time to a new life, a new start. I simply appear in another human body. I pondered this for many centuries. I suppose my father in hell takes the soul of the living child and allows me to take over.

Quite possibly, there was never living life there to begin with, merely a vessel awaiting my arrival. It is really amazing. I still have all the vivid memories of my past life, and yet I am new to the world again. I do not forget anything. I'm sure your test results will indicate that I am extremely intelligent with no memory deficiencies.

Getting back to my story…here I was opening my eyes and totally confused the first time. Ah! My rebirth! Such an exciting time! I don't just start my work, you understand. I get time to adjust to my new surroundings. Yes, if I just got right to it, things would get blurred. Humans might eventually figure it out. Even now you still doubt me.

No, my brothers and sisters and I have to wait and bide our time, learn our new life, figure out our new missions. You see, our objective doesn't really change. But the mission, ah, the mission on how we achieve our objective changes. Sometimes we are simply sent to kill, others to lead or influence, and then there are those times where we do both. Here I am getting off-track again. I do apologize. Let me see…where was I? Oh, yes.

At first, I was a bit disoriented. Here I was thinking I was still in my old life, but my surroundings were unfamiliar. It took me a few moments to realize I was in a different body, an infant body. Quite extraordinary to suddenly realize you are in a completely different body, an infant body at that, being held gently in a woman's arms. I even remember suckling every breast of every mother I have ever had. How is that for a kick! Anyway, here I was, suddenly suckling off a nice big jolly breast. The skin was creamy white, the nipple dark and rosy. My father in hell was whispering in my ear.

This mission was, I remember, an unforgettable experience. Even now your historians cannot fathom my destruction. Mystery abounds—one of the greatest mysteries of all time. The greatest secret of all time! My secret! And now it's time to share it with you. I was reborn in England on a cold, wet day in 1575. My new family was struggling, as all families seemed to do back then. I grew quickly on that breast, and soon I was a small boy caught up in the stories that abounded about the New World.

My father worked on the piers, so I was always hanging around listening to the stories of the sailors, the explorers, simply waiting for the time my earthly father would apprentice me out to a sea captain or other merchant. That's what many people did with their sons back then, you know. They couldn't always afford to feed them as they grew, so they did their best to give them a good start. I didn't have to worry about that though because I always knew my other father was always looking out for me. He would either provide or tell me how to get what I needed.

I don't remember exactly how old I was when my earthly father came home telling us about Sir Walter Raleigh seeking citizens to colonize the New World. It was the chance of a new life, of riches and wealth. This would be a difficult transition filled with promise, and we could stay together as a family, he said. Mother had some reservations at first, but the promise of opportunity soon had her head reeling as well.

We didn't have enough money for the first group that sailed, but Mother and Father soon had all of us kids working hard to scrimp and save for our journey. I remember watching the ship carrying the first group set sail for the New World. It was a big production. Women and children were waving and weeping as they watched their men folk set sail to an unknown land. Not knowing if they would ever return. Not knowing what they would encounter. Families were not allowed for the first group, you see.

They were the first on the journey. Their job was to map the area and start construction on the new colony. Several months later, the second group set sail. That group sort of set the stage for my entrance. Funny how that happened. They set out with only menfolk again, but this time was different. There were no mapmakers in this group. Several military men went along. I guess it was either to police the men while the colony grew or to protect England's claim with the new colony. Either way, it didn't work.

They returned lickety-split with horror stories about savages attacking them continuously, harsh weather, starvation, and the like. The word spread like wildfire throughout all of England despite efforts of diplomats and the royals to keep it quiet. Not long afterward, it was announced that another group would be leaving, and families were invited this time. Again, Mother had reservations, but Father soon won her over.

In no time, my two siblings and I were on a ship with our parents, sailing to the New World. We took what we could and sold the rest. The ship was small, and between our possessions, food supplies, military armament, and us, we were cramped, to say the least. So cramped, in fact, that illness was a major fear. We lost a few on the voyage to sickness and injuries. Thankfully, there were no serious illnesses that were catching. Something like that on a voyage such as ours was devastating and could kill everyone on the ship. As it was, it was a long and hard journey to the new world.

Nothing but water all around for months. Do you know what that is like? It grates on your nerves after a while. Tempers flare. The stench on the ship was sickening at times. I remember the joy and relief when we saw land for the first time. Little did the rest of them know the joy would be short-lived.

By the time we arrived, I was almost fourteen. The oldest of my siblings, I was also the largest built. I looked like a man instead of a child. We gratefully worked hard to unload our belongings and the rest of the food stores to set up our new home. Sir Walter Raleigh led us down the beach and through the jungle of sorts to a clearing he and the first explorers had called Roanoke Colony.

It was a depressing site. A few huts stood crammed within a small fort and not much else. Once again, we were packed together as we worked quickly to build lodging for families. Some started working the land for crops, and others hunted. We all had our assigned jobs. Unfortunately, it was a dry year, and the crops did poorly. Moreover, we had no idea what would grow well here and what would not. Hunting animals were scarce too. A few decided to go back to England to fetch more supplies for us when it became apparent we were going to need more help and more food in order to sustain our new colony.

They left us just as the cold weather was approaching. We had no idea what to expect, you see. We were used to the environment of England and learned to survive in those conditions. These were all new, all foreign to us. The winter was bitterly cold that year. We rationed our food, not knowing how long the winter season would last.

To top it all off, the savages, or Native Americans as you call them now, were suspicious of us. It was readily evident the last group created more problems than they solved with the inhabitants. When they saw we were struggling, they made our lives hell on earth for a while. But then the winter became even harder. Snowstorms and ice storms came one after another, and our conditions became dire.

By now, we had already lost a few men and a woman in our new surroundings. I was getting restless, and my father in hell started whispering to me again. It was so nice hearing from him. It was time I began what I had been sent here to do.

Starvation was becoming a very real possibility. Our stores were becoming increasingly low despite our efforts at rationing and fishing and hunting. Not all of us men could go hunting together as some were required to stay behind to cut firewood and protect the fort. We shared everything, including the chores, so I volunteered to go with the hunting party one day. There were supposed to be four of us, but another boy of near my age begged to go at the last minute. We set off early that morning. The other men in our group were seasoned hunters by now and had scouted the area near our colony. But since wildlife was scarce, we had to extend our hunting area much farther. It meant we had to split up.

I took the youngest in our group with me, and we set out along the designated trail pointed out by the more seasoned hunters. A plan had already been forming in my mind. We were not expected back until late that night, but they would not be seeing us that soon. We journeyed several miles from the colony before we stopped to rest. I can't recall his name, but my hunting partner was weak and whiny. He kept needing breaks to rest and complaining about being cold. Finally, thirsty and starving with only one squirrel killed between us, we decided we needed a break. We had been battling a path through dense underbrush and thicket most of the morning in the freezing temperature, so I suggested we build a small fire and rest during the noon hours.

He was so frightened of everything! I still don't know why he insisted on going in the first place, but it worked out well for me in the long run. It didn't take us long before we had a roaring fire. I skinned and cleaned our meager squirrel, and we took turns watching it while it cooked. After we ate and picked its bones thoroughly, we sat and talked for a while, listening to the crackling and popping as the flames licked at the dead wood we had found.

At some point, I made an excuse about needing to relieve myself and disappeared into the dense underbrush. I waited some time, and when I snuck back, my partner had nodded off, providing me the perfect opportunity even though I could have overtaken him any time I wanted. He was lying on his side as close to the fire as he could safely get snoozing away. Creeping slowly and quietly, I smashed the back of his head in with a rock, killing him instantly.

My belly was growling, and I was nothing but skin and bones—not a natural look for someone with my build. As poor as we were in England, we still managed to eat better than we did in Roanoke Island Colony. Miserable and starving, I promised myself this was going to end one way or another. This was the first step in keeping that promise.

I manufactured a spit out of nearby saplings and roasted me some hunting partner. Ah, he smelled so good roasting on that spit. What little fat he had sizzled as it melted and dripped into the fire. He was smaller than I and even thinner, if that was even possible, so there was not much meat on his bones. I got the most satisfaction out of eating his liver. So nutritious and flavorful! So tender! Mmmmm...he was so tasty. I gobbled him right up.

Since I had been the one in the lead on our hunt, I knew I would not get caught. I had deliberately taken us in a completely different direction in what we were instructed to follow. We were in new, undiscovered country, miles from our colony. We were so far away, no one would notice the fire. No one could smell the lusciousness of his meat sizzling over the heat.

I ate on him all day and into the night. I even used his bones to keep my fire going during the night. I had such a great time. My belly was full for the first time in months, and I slept well in my contentment. The next morning, I was lucky enough to get a few squirrels on my way back to the colony.

Of course, you can imagine the shock and worry when we had not come back the night before. Out there all alone with those savages and who knew what else! Everyone was so happy to see me. I think it was the fact that I had a few squirrels slung over my shoulder that really captured their attention. As you can guess, wimpy boy's mother was in an uproar. She insisted on knowing where her son was.

I was ready. I had already mapped out this story in my head, you see, while I was nibbling on his bones. I explained how he insisted on splitting up to increase our chances of getting something. Being as it was our first time out there, I naturally got turned around and hunkered down when it got dark. I looked and looked, called and called, and couldn't locate him. Assuming that he had made his way back to the colony on his own, I decided to do the same the next morning.

For the next week, several of us would journey out on a hunting party to look for him and to hunt for food. It was eventually decided by our leaders that he must have fallen victim to either the elements or some wild animal. We finally quit looking for him. That was fine by me.

My next big meal came about three weeks later. This one little guy, he must have been around six or seven, kept sneaking off from the fort. His papa caught him once and tanned his hide with a belt, but it didn't help. A couple of days later, he went and snuck off again. I followed him this time, telling my mum that I was going to try my hand at fishing, but in truth I wanted to see where he was going, and I was getting mighty hungry again.

Surprisingly, he had been off setting some small traps. He hadn't caught anything, of course, but he still tried. He wanted to be a big man, he confessed, when I caught him in the act. I suggested we try setting his traps farther from the camp, and he readily agreed. He was much easier to kill, but not nearly as much meat. Still I filled my stomach and gorged myself. I realized that the younger they are, the more tender they are.

I won't bore you will all the details about how I dined on most of the colony over the next two years. Or how superstition took hold and drove the pitiful few left so mad that they ran out of the fort and died in the elements. The ship never came back for us. We figured they must have gone down on the way back to England. We were on our own, and it was each man, woman, and child for itself.

Chapter 30

Myra could handle no more of his sickening rambling and beyond gross story that morning. She was in desperate need of a respite. Nauseated by his vile and twisted narrative, she suggested they take a break for a couple of hours. She called the guard, who escorted Mr. Heirwick back to his cell. She sat there at the table, and images he had conjured up were swirling in her mind. She had to remind herself it was just a story, and he was obviously setting himself up for an insanity plea. She almost wanted to tell him he already had a good case for that based on the scrapbook files found in his truck. The guy was demented!

She didn't believe him for one instant. Occasionally, she had interjected a question or comment, and he would elaborate more fully. Mr. Heirwick was, she had to admit, a great storyteller of horror. He was right up there with authors Stephen King and Edgar Allen Poe, in her opinion. Grosser than most of even the worst horror movies she had seen. Perhaps, if he had not been linked to several murders by circumstantial evidence of his own making, he might have had a great career producing horror flicks, she reflected.

She had brought a sandwich with her for lunch, but after that sickening story, she could not bring herself to eat it. Eating luncheon meat after his descriptive narrative of cannibalism was just more than she could stomach. What she really needed was some fresh air. Packing up her stuff, she made a beeline for the front door of the prison. She deposited her things in her vehicle before rubbing her eyes and inhaling deeply the sweet April air. Full of the perfumes of spring flowers, she felt immediately better. The sweet smell was a bit intoxicating.

A nice drive with windows down to blow away her thoughts was just what the doctor ordered, she suddenly decided. She needed to clear her head of his voice and sickening words. *Some of the demented things people came up with*, she thought as an involuntary shudder shook her tall thin frame, and she climbed in her vehicle and drove away from the prison. *You have to keep an open mind and be nonjudgmental*, she mentally berated herself.

Psychological ethics had been drilled into her head all during her course loads in college and even during her continuing education classes. Two sets of ethical rules, in fact—the American Psychological Association Code of Ethics and the Specialty Guidelines for Forensic Psychology. *Don't break those cardinal rules*, she reflected. He might have had a revolting sense of storytelling, but he was still a human being in need of help, and she was responsible for seeing that he received the help he needed while still protecting the rest of the population from him if need be.

Another image of his description on Roanoke Colony flashed through her mind, and she gagged despite herself. He was just trying to get under her skin, to enjoy himself and the attention he was getting, she reminded herself. It was simply a deranged and gory story designed to unsettle her, but her thoughts involuntarily flew to that file she had read with his recipes that included human body parts. She had had other criminals do the same over the years, though none had been as graphic as he was in the telling, and none had bragged about eating their victims.

A gas station ahead caught her attention and looked like a nice distraction, she thought, as she pulled up in front of the attached convenience store. Cutting off the engine, she entered and purchased a bottle of spring water and a candy bar before climbing back into her vehicle.

Chocolate candy bar melting on her tongue provided necessary soothing to her frazzled nerve endings. She could almost feel the endorphins being released in her brain as she savored the dark chocolate. It cleared her head and calmed her nerves. Finally, the lunchtime drive was becoming more settling.

Two hours later and over one hundred dollars poorer, Myra sat in her vehicle in front of the prison. She had found a small antique shop not far from the gas station and decided to browse for a while. A beautiful necklace, a gift for her mother for Mother's Day, and some art glass for herself sat in the back seat wrapped in newspaper. She had enjoyed herself. She loved treasure hunting in antique shops but didn't get to do it as much as she would have liked. It seemed she was always working.

Today, the venture had been more of a therapeutic venting for her. The long work days she had inflicted upon herself over the past few months of seeing patients, dealing with the court case, and the stalker had been taking their toll. This case, on top of all that, at long last had her admitting to herself that she needed a vacation. She jotted down some notes in her organizer before stuffing it back into her briefcase.

Running her fingers through her long blond locks, she dreaded going back into the prison. Usually, she was intrigued by the killers she interviewed and evaluated. Their methodology and abnormal minds fascinated her. Why did some people have such high morals and others had none? What had happened during the development of their brain that led to abnormal behaviors? There were so many aspects of interest. This inmate, however, was neither fascinating nor captivating. Oh, he was good-looking and had charisma, but his demented storytelling was just out there. Above all else, he was repulsive.

She shook her head and rubbed her temple just thinking about what he called himself—an angel of hell. The idea was so preposterous. What was with serial killers and the media in that they had to be labeled with such outlandish nicknames? Jack the Ripper, Son of Sam, the Zodiac Killer, the Boston Strangler, DC Sniper...there was always some outlandish title bestowed upon them. When this got out, the media was going to have a field day with it. The media had already tagged him the Butcher of the South.

She could just see the headlines. The media would be totally crazed during his hearing. She didn't even want to think about the trial. Glancing at her watch again, she determined that she could put it off no longer. The faster she finished this, the faster she could get back home. Gathering her resolve, she grabbed her things and headed back inside.

Chapter 31

Continuation of Canton Wayne Heirwick's narrative, day 1

Let's see, where were we? Ah, yes, Roanoke Colony…those were some fun days. I did well there. As I was saying earlier, during our second year, the remaining colonist had run off. Said the place was cursed. There were a couple of groups of Native Americans nearby. I guess they were a bit nomadic because we didn't see them much in the winter months. I think some of our people went to live with one of those groups. I'm not sure really. I didn't see them again.

Anyway, with the disappearance of my comrades came the great hunger pains again. Left with only a couple of knives, I could only fashion small game and fish traps. The effort was not equal to the gain, so I started hunting the Native Americans. Hunting them was not like hunting my own. They were more suspicious, more alert. Watchful! They almost got me once. I wound up with an arrow in my shoulder and was able to escape back to the fort. Since I was now lame for a while, I had to ration my kills.

Then John White and his crew came back. You can imagine my surprise when they suddenly walked into the fort. I don't know who was more shocked, to tell you the truth, me or them. They were definitely not happy. I can tell you that. My shoulder was still bum, and here I was nibbling on my last bones when they burst in on me.

They took one look around, saw only my stacks of bones I was using in my fires, and came to the conclusion that I had killed everyone. I tried to tell them that some got away, but John was totally crazed, thinking that I might have eaten his precious daughter and granddaughter. To tell you the truth, I really don't remember if I dined on them or not. I didn't get to all the children. I almost got caught when I took my little brother off for a nice meal, so I kind of shied away from the kids after that. At least for a little while. People got mighty upset when the kids disappeared, more so than any of the adults.

Nevertheless, they tied me up and burned me alive. The pain was agonizing as those flames climbed higher and higher, licking at my flesh. I could hear myself sizzle as the skin charred and the fat melted. I thought it was unusually cruel. Even I didn't burn any of my victims alive. They were all dead before I put them on a spit to cook. Most were even dead before I gutted them, or at least mostly dead.

It was a long time before I heard John's version of events, and by that time he was long dead. He and his crew had promptly gone back to England, but the story they told was much different. I didn't play the starring role. Nope! As he told it, they arrived to find the colony abandoned. Not one survivor to greet them. No corpses, no graves. Nothing!

I think it's funny that people are still trying to solve that mystery. All I can say is that maybe he and his crew never should have left us in the first place. A lame excuse he had of getting caught up in England's conflict and politics over there. He and his crew took valuable supplies for their trip back to England that we needed to survive that winter. If they had stayed, we would have been better fortified and had more men to hunt and gather food sources. Guess he didn't care *that* much about his daughter and *sweet* little granddaughter after all…little Virginia Dare.

I guess it must have been August of 1590 when I died that time. That's what the historical records state when John set foot in Roanoke Island Colony again. Records were not as accurate back then as they are today about births and deaths and such. Family Bibles kept track of most of the births and deaths, so all I really have to go on was John's ship records. Those three years John was gone were so difficult, we were more concerned with simple survival instead of paying attention to what day of the week it was or what month it was.

From what I remember, the winter spilled long into April that year. It had been warm only a couple of months when John arrived. The day I died was one of the warmest I had experienced that year, pun not intended.

I was reborn into a wealthy and noble French family that time. What a refreshing change after that brutal winter and all that poverty of the previous life. Father rewarded me with the birth into the wealthy family for doing such a great job in the previous life. This time, my family and I were *noblesse d'extraction*, which meant that we were pure-bloods. It was quite nice after the destitute and filth of my previous life.

My mother had title from her side before she married my father or noblesse uterine, but his father was also a noble. As the eldest male in the family and the only male on my mother's side, I would inherit the wealth and the extensive lands held by my parents and grandparents. Together, my family held more lands and wealth than any other except the king of France.

We were practically royalty and would have been had it not been for an ancestor that had the unfortunate business of being born the second male. As it was, my family had the distinction of holding titles of importance in France's military services as well. In fact, my father's service in the Royal Navy was what led to our fantastic fortune in the shipping and trade business. My youth was spent in luxury, and I was trained in the ways of a gentleman, but I was no gentleman. I'm afraid I was a rather bad boy every chance I had. I killed my chambermaid when I was but six. I'm rather proud of myself for that one. It's not every day a child can take out an adult, you know.

She was rather an ugly, dimwitted, and lazy bitch from a very poor family. She did her job, but barely. Thought she could tell me what I should be doing and how I should be acting when my parents and governess were not around in that vulgar language of hers. I had the last laugh, however. I pushed her down the stairs where she broke her ugly neck. Of course, no one saw me do it, so it was blamed on the stupid fool's clumsiness. She tripped and fell down the stairs! But now you really know what happened.

My mother was so embarrassed that something like me came from her womb. So much, in fact, that she left me entirely in the hands of the staff and doted on my brother and three sisters instead. She was a beautiful woman and so very kind. She simply was afraid of me from the time I was a toddler. Perhaps it was because I kicked her repeatedly in the stomach while she was carrying my brother. Who knows at this point? Maybe my real father whispered to her in the dark as well.

I was always getting into trouble, though. My parents had the doctor look at me when they found me experimenting on my sister's stupid dog. I just wanted to know what he looked like on the inside! The doctor wanted to lock me up in an institution, but my mother would not have it. She said people of nobility were not meant to be treated as animals in those places. We were too good for those horrid places. I think she started reconsidering that prospect, however, when I poisoned my aunt, my mother's older sister. She was a horrid woman and was constantly criticizing my mother and me.

She was never happy, which is probably why she never married. An old maid who thought she knew the ways of the world more so than anyone else simply because she was old. No one was ever good enough for her or her family, including my father, who was a cousin to the king! Luckily, we didn't have to see her that often. Still, when she did come to visit, she stayed for months—long tedious months of criticism, continuous complaints, nagging, and insults. The day she died, she had been particularly mean and cruel to me. I slipped some belladonna into her tea. I was around ten or eleven at the time.

Although they could never prove I was the one that had slipped her the belladonna, somehow my mother just knew. Instinct, perhaps? Maybe. At this point, I guess I'll never really know. Not that it matters. She wanted my father to lock me up in the tower of our castle, but Father refused. He said her sister was as crazy as a loon and probably slipped it in her own tea by mistake. Ultimately, Mother avoided me at all costs after that, insisting on taking her meals in her own room with the room locked. I only really saw her at family events, holidays, and when we were requested to attend royal events.

By the time I was in my late teens, my parents had had enough of me. Even my father had begun to avoid me. A couple of people disappeared, and people started to talk. I had a reputation of having quite the temper and getting even. I really only gave people a taste of their own medicine, but I was considered the bad guy. Always the bad guy.

The final straw was when rumors began about several *femme non mariée*—unmarried maidens—in the vicinity wound up pregnant. My human father rightly accused me of taking liberties with the young ladies, some without their permission. He came up with this ingenious plan to save the family name, protect the king, get rid of me, and to expand the family wealth all at the same time.

You see, I had been taught and primed to take over the family business from a rather young age. It was my birthright. Thus, my father took advantage of that training and gave me a ship. He financed a trip to the Colonies where I would be taking merchandise to market and bringing goods back to him. Really, it was seemingly the cheapest route to seeing my backside. Unfortunately, by accepting the position, I would lose my birthright at the same time. That was his condition, though I really had no choice. I believe he would have either had me killed or reported me to the king for the guillotine if I had not accepted. I didn't really mind accepting it. I was tired of France.

Now I had heard stories about piracy for years, and I knew the Caribbean was full of them. I was only too eager to go, but I did not further the family business, in case you haven't figured that out on your own yet. I docked in Saint Domingo and told my crew to go have a merry time. I sold the majority of my cargo and took on a new crew.

I chose the meanest and roughest men I could find and then set sail. It wasn't long before we attacked a Spanish ship. Unfortunately, the first ship we captured was not carrying the big payload but merely food supplies and rum, which we took anyway to sell at any number of ports in the Caribbean. Life was dangerous for captains what with the battles and then the occasional mutiny when riches were not had fast enough.

I grew wealthy and learned from the best of them. By the time I was in my mid-twenties, I was a force to be reckoned with, and my name was feared. I excelled because I had no principles and no compunction when it came to battles. I wielded a sword better than almost everyone. Of course, I had had plenty of practice, if you will remember.

I can still hear the battle sounds, smell the blood that flooded the deck, taste the salt in the air. We got lucky a time or two and captured ships headed to the Americas carrying women to their husbands. Of course, they didn't make it that far. The young ones we took to our ports and sold to the taverns after we finished having our fun with them. By then, most didn't want to see their husbands again anyway.

I joined forces for a while with an English privateer, as England liked to call their pirates. The only difference between the two was the fact that the Crown authorized her sea captains to pilfer, and as a pirate, I was an enemy of everyone on the sea. The Crown, as it turned out, felt I was too brutal and suggested the demise of our affiliation. That was fine by me. I liked being my own man and keeping my own loot.

I had a bit of democracy on my ship. It made for easier bedfellows and minimized the risk of mutiny, I found. We made our own rules and voted on what we took. We sailed when we wanted and only under our own flags of skulls and crossbones. Oh, the pirate's life was definitely for me! I had a whore in every port like the best of them—sometimes several at a time, especially when we brought in a treasure. Nowadays, people think we spent every moment we had in port, but truth be told, much of our time was at sea, hunting down those ships we heard about at port.

There is nothing like living on the sea, the boat gently rolling on the current and wind, the creaking of the wood, the slapping of the sail. I loved being on deck with the salt spray in my face. You're going to be thinking of me as some sentimental old fool. But I did love the pirate life. I can't tell you how many men I got to keelhaul. Keelhauling, in case you don't know, is where we tied ropes to both their arms and legs, threw them overboard, and dragged them from one side of the ship, under the keel, to the other. If they survived, they were good to go, but I made sure they never survived when I was the one imposing the sentence.

Sometimes I imposed it as a form of punishment to liars and thieves among the crew. Sometimes it was used on our enemies, and sometimes, well, I did it for fun after we took a ship or wanted information from someone about other ships. It was a good way to keep them from telling others what they told us. If we threatened them with it first, they often told us exactly what we wanted to know; then we did it anyway just for fun. I also often took the option of torturing, when needed, upon myself. I always took pleasure in my work, did it to the best of my ability, and I always got results. Moreover, it also put fear into my own men that they dare not cross me.

With the American colonies growing and needing labor, we also dabbled in the slave trade on occasion, but that was only when the pickings were slim. Dealing with all those chained slaves in the cargo holds, the filth, the stench…and then a good many often died, so that was always a loss of sales. Some captains preferred that trade and thought it was easy money. And it was, considering that in some areas of Africa, they caught and sold their own people to the slave markets.

For pirates working the slave markets, however, it was a big risk. Slaves had to be sold in larger markets like Plymouth and European cities. The problem was that if caught in with the wrong flag up, everyone on the ship could be hanged simply for being a pirate. Hence, we stayed mainly in the Caribbean and dealt our blows on the trade ships.

My last voyage was in the spring of 1637. We had been at sea for three weeks and just taken a nice trade ship. Her crew had put up a meager fight, so we massacred them all and threw them overboard. Unfortunately, that left me providing crews for two ships, and we were undermanned as it was. We spared what we could to the other ship and accompanied her heading toward the nearest port, but then my men spied a *flota*, what the Spanish called their treasure fleets. It was headed east toward the Windward Islands. Both crews wanted a bounty in riches, and I could tell they were considering pulling a mutiny over me. Despite being dangerously undermanned, I took all but what was needed to sail the other ship to port and set about a plan to attack the latter most Spanish ship.

The Spanish, though, had set a trap. It was counting on such an attack from pirates and fallen behind on purpose. It was setting low in the water, which usually meant great weight. My men were salivating with greed. The looking glass indicated only a sparse crew that was struggling with their sails. Unbeknownst to us, it was carrying a military crew in her belly and extra cannons they were taking to port for the port's defense.

Turning my ship, we took our chase. She was a fast girl, that ship, but with hardly any supplies save the cannons and soldiers by this point, she sailed swiftly. We pulled up and latched on to our prize and then realized our folly. Grossly outnumbered, we still fought valiantly. Reflecting, I can still feel the sword as it sliced through flesh like butter, the crunch of bones snapping with the twist of the blade. Cannonballs and limbs were flying through the air with a rain of splinters, and saltwater decorated the air. I can still hear the screams of agony and death floating on the smoke-filled air. A pirate's life is not for cowards!

Many of my men fell, mortally wounded. The rest were rounded up, and my ship confiscated. We were bound and taken below deck, where we spent the rest of the long trip to Spain. We were only given the barest of food during the trip—the majority of the food going to her crew. By the time we arrived in Spain, we were starving men.

After what barely resembled a trial, the order was given that we all be hung as pirates as a lesson to others. Like that was really going to work. Other pirates could have cared less. It just meant more money in their pockets. Just one week after our arrival in Spain, we were marched out, chained together, to the gallows. A large crowd had come to watch us die, to cheer and celebrate Spain's good fortune. I can still remember the rope tightening around my neck as I dangled. My feet kicked in the air relentlessly. My crew died quickly, one because his neck snapped when they released the door of the gallows. My death took a while. It felt like my eyeballs were going to pop out of their sockets from the pressure around my neck. The rope tightened so from my thrashing that I thought my head might just pop off my shoulders.

Chapter 32

Dr. Hull's outer office door was unlocked, and she let herself in. His receptionist was long gone as it was closing in on seven o'clock. She had not intended to stay that long at the prison, but Canton Wayne Heirwick had been in-depth with his storytelling. Still, he was not finished, according to him. She dreaded heading back there tomorrow to listen to the rest of his disgusting and horrific tale.

She lightly tapped on the inner office door before opening it. Dr. Hull was deeply engrossed in typing something on his computer, perhaps replying to e-mails or typing up notes from his patient sessions. She cleared her throat rather loudly to gain his attention.

"Good evening, Myra. I'm almost finished," he acknowledged without looking up.

Helping herself to one of his wingback chairs, she kicked off her shoes and drew her feet up beneath her. All she needed now was a long hot shower after listening to hours of Heirwick's narrative, she thought. The filth and obscenities of his words still clung to her like a grimy shroud. Shrugging out of her suit jacket, she sat back in the soft cozy armchair and closed her eyes in relaxation. Her shoulders, back, and head ached from the tension of the day.

The clicking of the computer keys was soothing and stopped all too soon. Dr. Hull removed his glasses and quietly observed her. She looked a bit pale and weary. He rubbed the bridge of his nose. "You look exhausted," he finally stated.

"I am," she opened her eyes and looked at him. He looked tired too.

"Well, what did you think?" he asked.

"He's been reading too many horror stories and is hoping for an insanity plea," she stated rather matter-of-fact.

He rubbed his neck as he looked at her. "You know," he said, readjusting in his chair to get more comfortable. "I thought the same thing at first. His story was just way too fanciful. Then on a hunch, I started doing some research. Everything he has told me is fairly accurate according to historical records."

"So he's a history buff too. So what? Don't tell me you actually believe that load of crap?"

"There is just too much...something. I can't quite put my finger on it, but I believe..." His voice trailed off. His eyes had a faraway look, as though he were trying to remember something.

"Dr. Hull," she started.

"How many times do I have to tell you to call me Eugene?" he interrupted her.

"I know...it's just that you were my professor, she stated a bit sheepishly.

"That was years ago. I would like to think us friends and colleagues. After all, I did know your father very well during my time at the FBI. I've known you since you were knee-high to a grasshopper." He smiled.

Her heart skipped a bit at the mention of her father and grasshopper. Grasshopper was her father's nickname for her. Funny how the mere mention of the word brought a stab of pain after all this time. She had lost him when she was just nineteen, her second year of college. He had been shot by a suspect during an investigation of a serial killer. It was a suspect that had been released on parole only six months before and had wasted no time getting back to his old habits. In those six months, he had killed fourteen women from Virginia to Oregon.

"I know. We're family now," she admitted. "But even as a kid, I called you Dr. Hull. It just doesn't feel natural to call you by your first name." She smiled.

He gave an exasperated sigh.

"Getting back to Mr. Heirwick," she returned. "Do you honestly believe that nonsense he was spouting?"

"Actually, I'm not sure. It is a compelling story, and I'm sure you haven't heard all of it yet," he pointed out.

"No, I obviously haven't. I have an appointment with him tomorrow for round two."

"Where did you stop him today?"

"We made it through his life as a pirate in the 1700s. Let me guess, this goes all the way to the present, doesn't it?" It was more of a statement than a question that she posed.

Dr. Hull gave her a compassionate smile. "It does, but I didn't get the whole story. I didn't believe him at first either, but the closer he got to modern day, the more similarities I was seeing in historical reports. That part about being an angel of hell... I have to admit, it gave me cold chills when I first heard it...and it still does, come to think of it."

"Seriously? How many serial killers have said 'the devil made me do it', or 'Satan was giving me orders,' or 'the Easter Bunny insisted that I had to or else'? Hell, they even gave themselves similar names. Son of Sam or Mr. Monster? Even David Berkowitz and Herbert Mullin claimed the devil was in them. He is no different than any other sadistic serial killer trying to get out of a wrap. They all think they are smarter than everyone else in the world. Why should this one be any different?" she asked.

"I hear you. Trust me, I do. It's just that...well, angel of hell. You are going to think of me as a rambling old man versus a psychiatrist. Right now, I feel like it, but I tell you, there is something about this one." He rubbed his hand over his thick silver hair.

"I know you are a devout Christian. The majority of the world practices some sort of religion or another. He knows that, and he's using it to his advantage. The odds of you believing in heaven and hell were in his favor," she explained.

"I know that too. But did you look in his eyes? Those hollow pits of nothing? They were so dark brown they looked black. No emotion whatsoever. The man has no soul, I'm telling you. I've been in this business a long time, and I've seen just about everything. This guy, though, he's different."

"Well, that's obvious just from the number of people he has slaughtered," she agreed. "I'll admit, he's a charming psychopath, and there is something off about him."

"But what if he's telling the truth?" he asked and raised his hand to silence her when she went to interrupt him. "What if he and others, for that matter, are reincarnated? I've never really thought about it before, but you have to admit some of these serial killers are really depraved, just like him. What if they do just keep coming back solely to keep killing? There are several religions that believe in reincarnation, you know."

"I think your imagination is running away from you," she responded with a soft smile to lessen her harsh comment. "It sounds too much like science fiction." She was getting concerned about Dr. Hull. He was too invested in this case already, and it was affecting him in ways she had never seen him affected before.

"The Buddhist religion preaches about reincarnation. Half the world believes in it. What if it can happen? I'm not saying it does or it doesn't, just that it could be a possibility. Where does that leave us? What happens to society when psychopaths are reincarnated? Maybe I'm just tired and need to retire."

"This guy has really gotten under your skin, hasn't he? Dr. Hull, I know South Carolina law requires evaluations by two different mental health providers for the court, but in this case, I think you should withdraw yourself from this case," she said gently.

"That's exactly why I called you. This case is becoming too much for me. Normally, I would not have requested someone to come onto a case just because the suspect demanded it. I'll tell you what," he bargained, "you listen to the rest of what he has to say, and then we will talk again."

"Dr. Hull, we are not even supposed to be discussing this case prior to submitting our opinion on the evaluation. It's unethical and illegal," she warned.

"Yes, which is exactly why Dr. Zula has also been appointed by the court to do an evaluation of him as well. Her evaluation is scheduled for next week. That's why I needed you here this week. I needed another perception to be able to put my observations and opinions into perspective. I know it's not normal and quite out of the ordinary, but under the circumstances, I do not think it unjustified. You are my personal consultant on this case. The judge actually suggested it before we both called the SCDMH. Just listen to the rest of his ramblings, and then we will talk again. In the beginning, I had your same viewpoint, but…well…let's just see if you still feel the same after he's finished. Okay?"

What could she say? He was more like an uncle to her instead of a colleague. She had known him almost her entire life. *Hey, Dr. Hull you've been drinking too much of this guy's Kool-Aid?* Instead, she gave him a dazzling smile and agreed. "Okay." She slipped her feet back into her shoes, stood up, and reached for her suit jacket.

He watched her lithe body as she stretched before she shrugged back into her jacket. She looked bone-tired, and he felt a fatherly compassion for her. He switched off his computer and gathered some files into his briefcase. He would be working from home tomorrow morning. His first appointment was not until one o'clock. "How about some dinner? My treat," he asked. "It's late, and I know you won't eat when you get back to your hotel. You're too tired. I told Clara I would be taking you to dinner tonight anyway. She had her reading group tonight with her women friends."

"Dinner sounds great."

"Good then. You are looking entirely too thin!" he admonished as he locked his outer office door.

"You sound just like Mom now!" She laughed, tucking her hand around his elbow and letting him lead her down the hallway to the elevator.

Chapter 33

Myra arrived at the prison early the next morning. She wanted to get this interview over with as soon as possible. If she were totally honest with herself and Dr. Hull, she was more than a little unnerved by the account given yesterday by Mr. Heirwick. Those flat dark eyes of his had haunted her dreams during the night.

And that laugh of his really grated on her nerves. It was cold, calculating, and emotionless. It was a hollow laugh that she couldn't quite describe. If evil had a laugh, then that would be it, she thought. Not quite sincere yet not quite insane either. Dangerous.

He played his part well, she would give him that, but she could not dispel the thought that he knew exactly what he was doing. He was not insane. He knew the difference between right and wrong. She could tell that simply by his gross and disturbing storytelling. She felt it in her bones.

Still, she had to go through the motions and do a proper evaluation. Ethically, she had to keep her personal feelings out of the process and not let Dr. Hull's opinion sway hers in any way. She could do it. She knew she could…had done it before in other cases. She would always do it.

She entered the building, slipped her shoes off, and placed them, along with her video camera bag and briefcase, in a gray bin on the conveyor belt of the x-ray machine beside the door. Her watch joined the bin before she walked through the metal detector. An alarm sounded, indicating she still had metal on her person. She was already standing facing the wall with her arms outstretched at her sides, waiting while the prison guard crossed the foyer and picked up the metal detecting wand. He waved the wand over her from head to toe. A buzzing sounded as he neared her neck and ears. It was the gold necklace and gold studs she had in her ears that had set the machine off.

Another female guard was intently viewing the x-ray machine's screen as the gray tub passed through it. "What do you have in here? I need you to open those bags," she indicated.

The other guard placed his hand on his gun as she walked to the tub and unzipped the camera bag and unlocked her briefcase. "I'm here to continue my interview with inmate Canton Wayne Heirwick," she stated. She handed the female guard her business card, indicating her name and position. "Dr. Eugene Hull arranged for me to interview him. I was here yesterday," she explained.

Both of the guards looked at each other. The male guard lifted a questioning brow.

"Is something wrong?" she asked.

"That is one wacko!" the male guard stated. "Our guards here are pretty hardened and have seen just about everything, but after returning him to his cell yesterday, one of our guards had a mental breakdown. He's in the hospital right now under observation. Are you sure you want to interview him by yourself?"

"A mental breakdown?" she repeated.

"Yep. The inmate said something to him, and he started screaming nonstop. We're not sure what was said, but something happened between those two," the female guard added.

"That's horrible. I hope he will be okay. This is a very stressful job, dealing with those men on a daily basis," Myra sympathized.

"True, but it wasn't but one man in here that did that to Joey. He was nearly catatonic when the ambulance left with him," the male guard stated as she slipped on her shoes.

"Everyone was so spooked by it that the warden said that two guards have to escort him from now on," the female guard said as she finished inspecting the video camera and zipped it back in its bag. "You're good to go if you still want to do your interview." Though her expression indicated that Myra should run as fast as she could back out the door she had just come through.

"Thank you for your concern, but I really need to finish my interview for the court." She thanked both the guards. They watched as she walked across the foyer to the cage, an area that was occupied by another guard handing out visitor passes and monitoring video screens showing all the entrances and exits to the main building.

A clipboard was hanging by a cord beside the door with a pen attached. She printed her name, address, driver's license number, and vehicle make, model, and plate number before sliding it through the four-inch-by-eighteen-inch opening in the cage door. She took her driver's license from her wallet and slid it through the opening as well.

"Who are you here to see?" the guard in the cage asked as a matter of routine.

"Canton Wayne Heirwick," she responded.

The guard's head whipped up from the clipboard where he was checking her information and adding the visitor badge number he was about to give her beside her name. "Who did you say?" he asked with a shocked look on his face.

"Canton Wayne Heirwick," she replied again. "I'm Dr. Myra Christie here to examine and interview him for the courts."

"One moment," he declared as he lifted the receiver from the phone and dialed an extension, not once taking his eyes off her. He mumbled something into the phone then hung up. He handed her the visitor's badge and placed her driver's license on a shelf behind him. "Wait here. The warden would like to speak with you. He's on his way," he explained.

She clipped the visitor's badge on the lapel on her suit jacket and readjusted her electronics bag on her shoulder before picking her briefcase off the floor where she had placed it while she completed the form on the clip board.

"Ah, Dr. Christie!" a warm deep voice welcomed her. She turned and saw her old friend, Dale Jones, entering the foyer.

"Dale! What are you doing here?" she greeted.

"I'm the warden, if you can believe that. Been here a little over a year now. I could ask you the same thing. What are you doing here?"

"Wow, Warden Jones. I can scarcely believe that! After all the trouble you used to cause everyone?" She laughed. "I would have thought you would be a resident rather than the warden." She and Dale had known each other since the third grade, when her family had moved to Fredericksburg, Virginia. Her father had just accepted a job with the Federal Bureau of Investigations and left his position in the Marine Corps. Prior to that move, they had lived just outside Camp Lejeune, North Carolina, in a growing sleepy little town called Jacksonville. After her father had died, her mother stayed in Fredericksburg until she remarried two years ago and moved to DC with her new husband, Jack Carson, currently running for the senate.

"Shhhh…they don't know about all that." He laughed. He took her elbow and gently guided her to his office. It was a large office with a huge cherry desk at the far end. The walls were covered with hunting paraphernalia and Virginia Tech memorabilia. A large bulletproof window encompassed one wall so that he could look out onto the prison yard and observe inmates and guards at any given time.

"Nice digs," she commented.

"Thanks. Most of it was already here. I just added the Virginia Tech stuff. The last warden was big into hunting. I thought it looked menacing, so I kept it as a warning to the inmates. What they don't know won't hurt them, right?" He snickered.

She laughed. "You haven't changed. I'm still blown away with the fact that you are the warden here." She laughed again.

"Yeah, well, after my stint in the Marines, I started working in the federal prison system. It was okay, but my wife worried a lot, so when this position opened here and was close to her family in Beaufort, I jumped on it. The way I hear it, the last warden retired, and his wife threatened to shoot him if he brought any of his hunting stuff in the house."

Myra laughed. "Wow, a warden, a veteran, and married. Anybody I know?" she asked.

"I doubt it. I met Sonja when I was stationed down in Beaufort a number of years ago. We've been married ten years now with two rug rats—Raymond Henry after my father, and Russell Harry after her father. They're six-year-old twins."

"Twins! Oh my! If they are anything like you, I pity your wife!" She laughed.

He blushed slightly. "Yeah, well, sometimes she really hates me." He laughed with her. "So what brings you here? Lester, the guard in the cage, said you were here to see Inmate Heirwick."

"Yes. I'm consulting with Dr. Eugene Hull on this case. We are doing a competency evaluation on the inmate for the courts. Apparently, Mr. Heirwick would only speak to me and give me his personal information, which I shared with your staff and the authorities immediately. Judge wants to make sure he's competent to stand trial and needs sentencing recommendations. Mr. Heirwick won't give me the information we need other than his name until he tells me a sordid story, which I had to listen to all day yesterday."

"Why only you? Do you know him?"

"No. Never heard of him before. He says he read about the trial I was just involved in and decided he wanted to talk to me."

"Nothing creepy about that." Dale lifted the side of his upper lip. "Where's Dr. Hull? He didn't come with you?"

"No. We wanted to do independent evaluations and interviews for comparison. I heard what happened last evening with your guard. I started the interview process with Mr. Heirwick yesterday," she explained.

"I heard about a gorgeous Dr. Christie coming in yesterday. You had all my guards drooling." He laughed. "This place has been buzzing since yesterday about you."

"Guilty." She blushed.

"Wow, it's my turn to be stunned. Last count I had you were well on your way to becoming a big shot CEO."

"Yeah, well, things change. My dad died while I was working on my business degree and it…" She paused for a moment. "It changed my perspective about a lot of things."

"Oh, Myra, I'm so sorry. I had no idea. What happened?"

"He was shot by a deranged suspect when he and his partner went to interview him about a crime spree. They thought he was a witness at the time, not the suspect."

"Gee, that's tough. I lost a couple of guys over in the Iraq War several years ago. Our guide, it turns out, was actually one of the Al-Qaeda posing as an Iraqi police officer. It sucks when you can't tell the good guys from the bad guys."

They both pondered their respective information for a moment in silence as they sat across from each other in matching leather chairs, both gazing absently out the window.

Finally, Dale broke the silence. "I'm not fond of the idea of you talking with that guy by yourself."

"I understand, but it is my job. He's not the first serial killer I have interviewed," she explained.

"There is something definitely off about that guy," he warned.

"Yes, I know. I did the Hare Psychopathy Checklist on him yesterday. He's what we would classify as a psychopath. He met all the criteria."

"I've met plenty of those over the years what with working in prisons. He's not like any other person I have ever met. I don't know exactly how to describe him, but my guards are extremely nervous around him, especially after Joey Nickerson's meltdown last night."

"I heard about that from the guards in the foyer. I understand, but it's still my job. Sometimes, I think the person's reputation follows them into these prisons and upsets the balance in the guards. I'll heed your wishes and be extra careful."

"I appreciate that, but I'm also taking my own precautions. I'm bringing him to a treatment room down from my office for you to interview. The staff psychologist is out this week for a funeral, and you can have his office. There is a restraint we can bring in there and place him in. It is the only way I'll let you interview him. Also, two guards will be placed outside the office. It has windows on two sides so the guards can see in there, but you will still have doctor-patient confidentiality."

"Very well. If those are your terms, I have no problem working within them," she agreed. Actually, it made her feel a bit more comfortable than the usual interview room for inmates and their attorneys. Although he had been in handcuffs and an officer had been in the room, she had not felt comfortable with him.

He walked her to the staff psychologist's office and helped her set her video camera up. It was painted a dull gray color with nondescript tiles on the floor. A plain gray metal desk sat to one side with an office chair behind it. A gray four-drawer filing cabinet sat on the other side of the room beside a gray folding chair. Large picture windows on either side of the door and another at the back of the office chair looked into the room. Even the door had a window in it.

She sat down at the desk. The camera would look over her right shoulder directly at a large uncomfortable metal restraint chair two guards were sitting into position. The chair had a straight back with straps that crisscrossed across the chest, straps that went over the forearms and wrists, and ankle straps. A chill shivered up her spine. She would hate to have to sit in that contraption.

All the drawers in the desk were locked, which didn't surprise her. Her office at the prison in Columbia where she worked once or twice a week looked very similar. The difference was that she didn't actually see patients in her office at the prison. She and her staff had to go to each individual's prison cell. A metal folding chair was set outside the cell for the therapist while the inmate remained firmly locked in his cell.

"Why don't you just give me a chair outside his cell? That's what I usually have in Columbia," she asked.

"He was in solitary last night. After what happened to Officer Nickerson, I didn't want to take any chances and leave him in his usual cell."

Myra made a couple of notes on her notepad. She wanted to see this Joey Nickerson and find out what had happened. She doubted it had anything to do with Mr. Heirwick. Sometimes just the stress of working in high-security facilities caused guards to snap. She needed to talk to Dale a bit more about what had happened.

A few minutes later, Inmate Heirwick was escorted in and placed in the restraint chair by three guards. He and the warden exchanged a long hostile glare before the warden turned to Myra. "If he gives you any problems, I expect you to notify the guards immediately or hit this big red button." He pointed to a big red button about four inches wide next to the door. With that, he flicked a warning glance at the inmate and left the office.

She closed the door behind him and nodded at the two guards sitting across the hall watching her through the windows. The warden was issuing orders to them, and they were nodding, their eyes never leaving the office. She turned and walked over to the camera, turned it on, then sat at the desk and turned on her separate audio recorder.

"I am Dr. Myra Christie conducting an interview with Mr. Canton Wayne Heirwick. Today is April 20. We are at Lieber Correctional Institution. Mr. Heirwick, yesterday you were telling me your personal history. We left off where you were claiming you were a pirate. Would you like to continue?"

"You still don't believe me yet, do you?" he asked with that maniacal chuckle of his. It was rather irritating and more than a little unnerving.

"Please continue, Mr. Heirwick. It is not merely a matter of whether I believe you or not. There is much more I need to consider from our…um…discussions," she responded.

He gave her a long thoughtful look before nodding his acceptance.

Chapter 34

Day 2 of the interview with Canton Wayne Heirwick

My rebirth was late in the year of 1637. It was a small fishing village on the coast of Sicily. It was a modest family and life. My youth was uneventful. The town was too small to afford my handiwork and therefore was too boring for me. I left home as soon as I was capable of providing for myself. I was in my mid-teens when I embarked upon the world in search of fun and adventure.

I traveled to Rome and left a trail of misery in my wake. It was so much fun! Being able to finally act on my mission was so fulfilling! It was like being tied up for years and then finally being set free. Anyway, rumor has it that one of my kills was someone of importance, and soon authorities were on my tail. I'm not sure how they tracked me down, but they did. It must have been that nosy old woman I caught following me. I knew I should have killed her, but truthfully, she was nothing but skin and bones, old and fragile. It really would not have been worth my time or energy.

Obviously, I had to leave Rome before I was finished in my work. I traveled north through Italy, accidentally bumping into one of my sisters in Portugal a couple of years later. Needless to say, I was overjoyed. She was the first of my brothers and sisters from Hell that I had met. She called herself La Quintrala, and she was beautiful in human form, almost as beautiful as I remembered her from home. Her hair was long and a vibrant red, reminiscent of soft rose petals. Ah, I loved her.

We became lovers. Her skin was so creamy white with those waves of red hair flowing down her shoulders and back. You should have seen her. She was such a sight to behold; so innocent looking. I think that was why we were so successful together. She loved children, and they loved her. They would follow her anywhere, especially when she baked her special treats. She would bring them home and keep them for a while, spoiling them until she tired of them. Then we would butcher them together, and she would make all kinds of delicious dishes.

I have to admit, I also had my own charms. Both the men and the women adored my good looks and charisma. I lost count of the number I brought home for my love. We would ravish them with sexual pleasures, and then they would dine on my love's wonderful cooking. The best part is when we finally got around to dining on them. As you have probably guessed, we could not stay in one place for too long. Residents always seem to protest too loudly when children go missing. It didn't even matter that a number of them were vagrants.

So together, we traveled. We went to Naples, where we stayed but a year before people took notice, and from there took a ship to England. We lived in London for a few years, but La Quintrala was unhappy with the cold wet English weather, so we went to France for a while. Viva la France! I showed La Quintrala all my old haunts. By now, my younger brother had inherited the family fortune and my title from my previous life. He was nearing his fortieth year and was married with nothing but daughters. I laughed mightily at that one, I can tell you.

I purposely bumped into him one day, but alas, he did not recognize me in my new human form. I had thought for a moment he might when he stared into my eyes, but he simply shook his head and bid me a good day. A proper gentleman he was, with his wife and daughters in tow. Our parents had been gone but just a few years, which was a pity. I would have enjoyed laying eyes on my beautiful mother once more.

La Quintrala and I enjoyed Paris. She learned new cooking techniques, which were outstanding. She also started dabbling in the art of herbs and potions. She cooked up this one potion that was so deadly that it only took a few drops to kill a man. She took to selling her wares, which were very popular, especially her deadly potion. Women were practically lining up at our door for a small bottle to give their husbands or lovers. Sometimes, if she thought it deserved and the woman could not afford it, she gave it away for free or poisoned the man herself.

My La Quintrala had some skills. She singlehandedly took out several of the nobles with her potions for one reason or another. I was so proud of her! She was so much more skilled than I. Can you believe she was only working on her second human existence at that point? What a beauty. I truly miss her. I miss our dining together, her sexual exploits. She was not shy at all, and she was so creative!

Grapevine gossip finally got back around to us that authorities were investigating the large number of deaths. They had their hands full with all the nobles demanding justice. On top of that, they had so many complaints—hundreds, I'm sure, of missing children. That doesn't even count my kills or the men and women I brought home to my love so we could kill them together. She loved bathing in their blood afterward, said it pulled the impurities out of her skin.

I don't know if that was necessarily true, but I can tell you I never found any impurities in her. She was perfect! With the rumor mill going crazy, we thought it best if we left. We spread some sort of rumor ourselves about La Quintrala's grandfather being ill and she being the only heir. We had to travel immediately to see him, but we didn't say to where we were traveling. We actually skipped around Spain for a while, settling here and there for short periods.

La Quintrala continued to pedal her wares, and I did my thing. A couple of kills in one town had townsfolk declaring that a werewolf was loose in the area. We got a laugh out of the panic that ensued. After that, I took extra care in hiding the bodies for a while. They make really good fertilizer for gardens I found. La Quintrala liked to place her herbs upon their graves sometimes.

Discovering that it was much better to nab travelers than residents, we settled down for a while on a well-traveled route. Our yard was full of corpses, so it was also full of herbs. She became well-known in the area for various potions. I guess you could say she became known as a healer of sorts. It worked out well, treating the locals and dining on the travelers. We also cut down on our sampling of the children—you know, one from here and one from there. That way, people didn't get so suspicious and call out the authorities.

We moved on to Portugal again, making sure we avoided her previous haunts. She was too afraid of bumping into someone who knew her from before, so we went back to Italy. Unfortunately, we were recognized all too quickly as we traveled through familiar towns on our way to Rome. I sent her ahead of me and created a diversion to keep her safe. Unfortunately, I was captured immediately after disemboweling a pregnant woman. I was beheaded, and I never saw my beautiful La Quintrala again, then or in any of my later lives.

I have never had a lover as good as she since. Kissing her luscious full lips was like eating strawberries ripe from the vine after a gentle rain. I so miss wrapping that luxurious full red hair around my hands and fingers. I miss her so much.

Chapter 35

One of the guards rapped on the glass of the door. Myra turned off the recorders and answered the door. "Yes?"

"It's his lunchtime, ma'am." He motioned his head toward Mr. Heirwick.

"Thank you. You can get him. I think we are in a good stopping point." She smiled as she stepped back out of his way. She tucked her notes in her briefcase and slipped out the door as they unfastened the restraints and collected the prisoner. She used the key Dale had given her to lock the office after them.

She passed by the warden's office, peeking inside to find him at his desk. She lightly tapped on his door. "I just wanted to thank you for the more private area. It is nice not having any distractions." She smiled as he raised his head from the file he was reading.

"Taking a lunch break?" he asked as he glanced at his watch.

"Yes. I'm sorry I interrupted you. I just wanted to thank you for the use of the private office." She turned to leave.

"Wait!" he called after her. She stopped, turning back to face him. "I need a break from this place too. I've been here since five this morning. I'm starving. Want to join me for lunch?"

"Sure, sounds good. Where are we going?"

"There's this little place in Summerville called Eva's Restaurant. Mostly homecooked Southern food," he replied as they left his office. "As skinny as you are, I bet it's been a while since you had any real food," he chided, as he followed her out of the front door.

Less than twenty minutes later, they were seated in a charming restaurant in the heart of downtown Summerville. An older woman about her mother's age handed them menus and took their drink orders before hurrying toward the kitchen. "The food is really good here. I especially like the fried chicken dinner, but I have never been disappointed with anything on the menu." He smiled.

"I haven't had fried chicken in forever." She laughed. "You talked me into it."

At that moment, the waitress came back with their drinks, and they gave her their orders. They spent the rest of the time catching up on old times and getting to know each other again. He told her of his time in the Marines. How he loved the camaraderie and his job, but being deployed to the Iraq War twice and the Afghanistan War three times in less than four years had taken its toll on him mentally and on his marriage.

Once, he had dreamed of retiring from the military, but that was not to be. He had gotten out after ten years. The sadness in his eyes told her more about his loss of buddies than his words. Though he denied it, she was sure it was still taking a toll on him. He skillfully evaded questions about his family as well, which she suspected meant he was still not comfortable in that regard either. He had been out five years now. In that time, he dragged his family through three different states in search of a job that he liked and made his family feel more secure.

Although they were now closer to her family and he was in a better occupational position, Myra had a hunch the marriage was still on the rocky side. War had a tendency to do that to some marriages. She was just sorry it had to happen to him.

"You were right. The chicken platter was delicious." She smiled as he drove them back to the prison.

"I told you it was good. I eat there at least once a month. My doctor would probably have nightmares if he heard me say that." He laughed.

She laughed with him. "I would have nightmares if I ate there that often! I can already hear my arteries clogging."

"Changing the subject, what do you think about Heirwick?" he asked, casting a quick glance in her direction as he drove.

"What do you mean?"

"I don't know. I guess just your overall impression."

"Well," she hedged. "I'm not really supposed to talk about a case, especially when I'm doing an evaluation for the courts." She stared out the passenger window at the endless acres of pine trees.

"I didn't mean to put you in a difficult position," he apologized. "It's just that there is something off about him. He's different than the other prisoners I have guarded or dealt with over the years."

"Yeah, I think I know what you mean. He's…definitely different," she responded.

Chapter 36

Continuation of Canton Wayne Heirwick's narrative, day 2

Let me think a moment. Earlier, we spoke of my beloved Quintrala. That means we are now on my next life. That would mean Bavaria in...hmmm...1676, I believe it was. My rebirth was in the town of Rosenheim. It had once been a bustling place on the trade routes near Prien am Chiemsee. That's a specific lake in what is now Southern Germany, close to the border of Austria.

My new father's family had been distinguished ship builders, but another bout of the plague and new trade routes had hurt the area financially for a while. Mind you, that was before I was reborn. Our family, however, had weathered the economic crisis and still held a moderate wealth.

My childhood was again rather unremarkable, save for my fighting and my secret pleasure. No, I hadn't yet started the killing, but I was wreaking havoc on the natives. I liked to experiment and hone my craft on the animals in the area. People were very superstitious, and all manner of tales were spread about the discoveries of my hobby. My teen years was when I really got active again.

By then, I was strong enough to handle most situations, so I didn't have to worry about my victims escaping before my deed was done. I remember my first victim was a rather plain-looking hefty girl. She was a little younger than I, but I did not know her. I just happened to be walking back from a fishing trip when I came upon her picking wildflowers. We talked for a while, then I gutted her like my fish. It's really quite fascinating watching intestines spill out of the body. She thought so too. She didn't even scream when I thrust my knife into her gut and jerked upward.

She just had this surprised look on her face as she watched her insides fall out in jerking loops. I slit her throat after that, just for good measure. I couldn't afford her screaming when the pain set in to alert everybody. She just sort of melted to the ground right where she stood.

That got a lot of attention, I can tell you! A manhunt was on for her killer. Rumors started up about a stranger passing through. Others said it was an animal attack because some of her innards were missing by the time they found her. I guess a dog or something got to her after I did.

I felt so alive again. I had so missed my time with Quintrala. My mother's cooking was mediocre, nothing like Quintrala's, and I knew she wouldn't cook human flesh for me, so I had to suffer for a while. I only killed on occasion and when I knew no one could suspect me of it. Sometimes I traveled several miles out of town and killed vagrants or travelers. On those occasions, I took along a kettle and stewed them myself for a little treat now and then.

My father was very angry when I told him I was leaving at the age of seventeen, especially without taking a wife he had arranged for me to marry the following week. I just grabbed a few of my belongings, my sword left to me by my grandfather, and a couple of knives, stuff like that...and I walked out. Mother was in despair as I walked down the street and headed out of town. They didn't understand my need to be on my own. Likewise, they didn't know about my mission. I stayed out of towns for the most part as I headed north toward Munich.

When I needed money, I did the odd job. If I couldn't find humans to kill, I killed animals and ate what I wanted. I had lived on my own for just less than two years when I found a pretty young woman tending to her garden. I used my charm to flatter her, which I admit worked quickly. She was a young thing and a new mother with a baby boy in a cradle.

Her body was so soft and supple. I ravaged her body, and we made love before I began to devour her. She still had milk in her breasts, from which I greedily drank as her life slowly ebbed away. Her flesh was easily torn with my knife, my hands, my teeth, as it was still soft from the child. Her blood was sweet and yet salty. I was hungry and went at her greedily, an unfortunate folly.

Her husband and a neighbor came home unexpectedly and caught me with her. You should have seen their faces—ghastly pale, horror stricken. Speechless! There I was, bent over her still hot body on all fours, blood dripping off my chin and smeared across my face, her blood up to my elbows; chewing on her flesh like the starving man I was. They called me a werewolf, among other things. Tied me up and took me into town with his wife's body.

It was a long ride to town. Several miles, I would guess. I cannot tell you the agony to which I was subjected. I was tightly bound at the hands and feet, tied to the side of the wagon so I could not reach her body. For several miles, I sat so close to her that I could smell her cooling body. I could still taste it on my tongue, my lips, but I could have no more. My stomach was tight with want, with need. And all throughout the journey, I was blasted with name-calling, scripture, and the anguished cries of the husband, the hungry cries of the babe.

Oh, the outrage over a silly woman that wasn't quite right in the head. She was a little more than a simpleton in my opinion. But she was very pretty…and tender. They were so crazed, they couldn't decide how to kill me. Some said I needed a stake through my heart, others said I had to be beheaded with a silver sword, and others said I had to be burned at the stake so my body could not roam any longer. Eventually, they settled on doing all three just to be on the safe side. I was declared the youngest werewolf any of them had ever seen. I ask you now, how many werewolves do you think they witnessed?

Chapter 37

Myra was just walking into her hotel room when her cell phone began ringing. She had cut his narrative short that afternoon. She needed a break from all the awful stuff pouring out of his mouth. She also wanted to make a list of the psychometric tests she felt Dr. Hull needed to add to his file.

She dropped her electronics bag and briefcase on the dresser before pulling her cell phone from her pocket. She did not recognize the number calling. She pondered a moment over answering it or letting it go to voice mail before hesitantly answering. "Dr. Christie."

"Myra! Are you okay?" a voice barked in her ear.

"Who is this?" she demanded.

"It's Dale."

"Dale?" she repeated blankly.

"Dammit, Myra, are you okay?" he barked again with urgency in his voice.

"Dale Jones? How did you get my number?" she asked, puzzled.

"I called one of my guards at the prison. You had to write your number down on the sign in sheet, remember? Are you okay?" he demanded, a bit frustrated.

"Yes, of course I'm okay. You sound a bit frantic. What's wrong?" she asked.

"One of the guards taking Inmate Heirwick back to his cell suddenly collapsed as they shut his cell door. They said he was struggling to breathe, and his eyes rolled back in his head. I'm on my way to the hospital now. I wanted to make sure you were okay."

"I'm fine. Which hospital?"

"Trident Medical Center. Why?" he asked.

"I'll meet you there. I'm staying at a hotel just up the interstate in Summerville. I'll meet you in the emergency area." She hung up before he had a chance to argue. Grabbing the audio recorder from her electronics bag, her purse, and her briefcase, she hurried back out the door. Within fifteen minutes, she was exiting the interstate and turning into the hospital grounds. She followed the emergency department signs and was soon parking her car and hurrying in the sliding double doors. She saw Dale talking with a nurse at the admittance desk and walked up to him.

"How is he doing?" he was asking the nurse.

"I'm not sure, sir. The doctors are with him now. If you would like, I can have one of them come speak with you," the nurse explained. "I'm not allowed to leave my post. You understand."

"Yes, of course. Please. Let the doctor know I'm the warden and Officer Garrett works for me."

"I will, sir."

"Um… I'm Dr. Myra Christie. Could you please direct me to where Officer Garrett is being treated?" she asked.

"Are you related to the patient?"

"No. I'm strictly here in a professional manner," Myra replied.

"Very well, then." The nurse checked the computer in front of her. 'Take the hallway to your right. Turn at the double doors. He is in the third room on the right," the nurse directed.

Myra took Dale's arm and led him to the waiting area. I'll check on him and come back and report to you as soon as I know what's going on."

"Thanks. I would appreciate that," he murmured as he took the closest seat.

Myra left him and disappeared down the hall. It was easy finding the room. Medical staff were coming and going frantically around the area. A nurse came out carrying what looked like blood samples and nearly ran down the hallway. Another was quickly tying a mask behind her head while trying to hold several others with her elbow next to her side. Across the hall from Garrett's room was another room that seemed to be empty at the moment.

Myra slipped inside and thoroughly washed and dried her hands before grabbing a pair of gloves to put on. She then ducked into Garrett's room, where chaos was ensuing. A pile of masks were on the counter to her left, and she grabbed one and started putting it on. The nurse she had just seen in the hall was now busy slipping masks on everyone else in the room that seemed to be too busy to do it themselves.

A middle-aged man in scrubs with a white lab jacket was issuing orders to the masses. He was applying betadine antiseptic solution to the patient's side. A battery of equipment and wires were attached to the patient, and she could tell by looking that the patient was in dire trouble. She watched as the doctor made a small incision on the man's side before placing a piece of flexible tubing into the hole. Then the doctor was again monitoring the battery of machines, and from the way his brows were drawn, she assumed he was frowning.

He barked out more orders and told someone to get a cardiologist and a pulmonologist on deck stat. He leaned over to shine a light in Garrett's eyes and rocked back on his heels. He looked up and noticed her for the first time. "And you are?" he ground out.

"Dr. Myra Christie," she offered. "I'm a forensic psychologist, and I've been doing an evaluation and interview with the inmate who Officer Garrett here was escorting when this happened. Could you tell me what exactly is going on?"

He reviewed the monitors again to make sure the patient was semi stable before nodding her to the hallway. Officer Garrett was unconscious and deathly pale, lying in the hospital bed. Fleetingly, she wondered if he had a wife and children, making a mental note to ask Dale.

She stepped into the hallway, followed by the doctor who told the head nurse to watch the patient closely. "Could you tell me exactly what happened to my patient?" he asked as he removed his bloody gloves and pulled his mask down. He walked into the vacant room to dispose of his gloves in the hazardous waste receptacle and washed his hands.

"I have no idea, I'm afraid. Warden Jones called me to tell me something had happened. He said Officer Garrett and another guard had just escorted the inmate to his cell when Officer Garrett collapsed onto the floor, struggling to breathe. Apparently, it was so sudden that everyone was stunned," she explained.

"Hmmm…well, from a medical standpoint, I've never seen anything like this. It's almost like his lungs have spontaneously collapsed then reinflated on their own, but not completely. His heart is out of rhythm, and his vitals are all over the place. He wasn't breathing when paramedics arrived on the scene, so they intubated him. Then he flatlined twice in the ambulance on the way here. Just when it appears that his vitals have stabilized, they go haywire again. He has been unconscious since the paramedics loaded him into the ambulance. This is one really sick man. I've never heard of anyone having his symptoms without a major trauma before." The doctor looked puzzled.

An elderly man with wire rimmed glasses came hurrying down the hallway toward them. "If you will excuse me," the doctor said. "The cardiologist is here, and I need to brief him."

"Of course, Doctor. If you need any more information, I'll be in the waiting room with Warden Jones," she said.

Reentering the waiting room, she saw Dale talking to a beautiful slim brunette with a very worried expression on her face. The woman clutched a tissue in her hands, twisting it to death. Myra assumed it was Officer Garrett's wife. Dale looked up to see her approaching and introduced them. "Dr. Christie, this is Eloise Garrett, Officer Garrett's wife." Both turned hopeful eyes upon her. "Well?" he asked.

"They are working on him. A cardiologist arrived, and I left so the doctors could discuss his case." She reached out and patted Mrs. Garrett's hand. "They are doing everything they can to help him. Has he ever been through anything like this before?"

"No! Never! He's always been healthy; not even so much as a broken bone as far as I know. I don't understand. They think it's his heart?" a tearful Mrs. Garrett asked.

"They are not sure yet. They are looking at every possible solution and doing lots of tests. It's going to be a long night, I'm afraid. Would you mind if I stole Warden Jones here for a moment to discuss a prison matter?"

Dale furrowed his brows but said nothing as he followed Myra to the nurse's station. "We will be just outside the emergency room doors if the doctor comes looking for me," Myra explained as she handed the nurse her business card. Then she turned and led the way outside into the cool April evening.

"What's up?" he asked.

"The doctor is very concerned. Officer Garrett is in deep trouble in there. Do you have any idea what happened?" she asked.

"I told you everything my guards told me when they called. They locked the inmate in his cell, and just as the door closed, Garrett fell to the floor."

"Well, something is not making sense! The doctor said his symptoms are consistent with a major trauma, like a car accident or something. Yet he doesn't have a scratch on him!" she exclaimed.

"I'll tell you what is not making sense! Every time one of my guards gets around Inmate Heirwick, something happens to them!" He paced on the sidewalk, running his hands through his hair in a mixture of worry and frustration.

"You can't blame someone's mental state on your inmate, and you certainly can't blame this on him." She motioned with her hands toward the hospital doors.

"You are not talking to him again. He will stay in his cell until his hearing," he declared.

"You can't do that!" she fumed. "I have a job to do, and I'm going to do it."

"I am not going to be responsible for him hurting you or anyone else!" he boomed.

"I have talked with him for two entire days, and nothing has befallen me yet. I don't know what's going on with your guards, but you cannot deny me access to him. I have a court order to evaluate and interview him!" she spat.

They stared at each other. She was right and he knew it, but he didn't have to like it. Finally, he turned toward the hospital sliding doors. "I need to get back to Mrs. Garrett, but we are going to talk about this later," he said over his shoulder.

"Well, I see some things never change!" she muttered under her breath in frustration. "Arrogant bastard!"

Chapter 38

Myra gritted her teeth in anger. Dale slipped through the automatic sliding doors and disappeared, heading toward the waiting room. She understood his frustration. He was worried about his men and the rest of the guards at the prison. He was responsible for them after all. He was not, however, responsible for her. If he tried to refuse her access, she would contact Dr. Hull and the judge. She hated to take that step, but if necessary, she would. He could not and he would not stop her from doing her job. She was through being pushed around. Between him, her stalker, Heirwick, and Darrell…well, he could just take a number and stand in line. She was going to finish that evaluation whether he liked it or not.

Taking a few calming breaths of the cool evening air, she gazed across the highway to the Charleston Southern University campus. She jumped when an ambulance siren shrilled at the intersection between the hospital and the campus. It was turning into the hospital driveway. She felt sorry for the emergency personnel. It was going to be a very busy night for them. It was going to be a long night for Mrs. Garrett and Dale as well.

Myra gathered her briefcase from her car before reentering the hospital. She nodded to Dale when she entered the waiting area and sat in a quiet corner beside an end table where she set her briefcase before opening it. She shuffled through several papers and files before she found what she was looking for.

She took the arrest report from the file and started pouring over it. A number of officers, local, county, state, and federal were involved in the investigation and subsequent arrest, but two officers specifically had been credited with the apprehension. She took her cell phone from her jacket pocket and called the police headquarters. She knew it was late, but she had some very specific questions for these two officers, and it just could not wait.

A police dispatcher answered the phone. She explained who she was before asking to speak to Detective Wilson or Detective Ameson, the two officers listed in the police report. The dispatcher put her on hold. She was on hold for so long that she began to think he had forgotten about her holding when a female answered the phone. "Captain Harover here. Is this Dr. Christie?"

"Yes, Captain. I was hoping I could acquire the numbers of Detective Wilson and Detective Ameson. I realize it is quite late, but I really need to speak with them about the Heirwick case," she explained. "It's very important."

"I'm sorry, Dr. Christie. I guess you haven't heard. Detective Ameson died right after the arrest, and Detective Wilson is in intensive care at MUSC," Captain Harover informed her.

Myra was so stunned she was speechless.

"Dr. Christie? Are you still there?" the captain asked after a long pause.

"Um, yes. I'm sorry. I don't know what to say. Could you tell me what happened?"

"Well, the doctors aren't really sure. Detective Ameson just collapsed and died just hours after the arrest, and Detective Wilson collapsed the next morning. They barely got their reports in before they collapsed."

"You said collapsed. Could you be more specific?" Myra asked as she caught Dale's attention and waved him to her.

"Not really. Detective Ameson collapsed in front of his wife, and Detective Wilson collapsed in a coffee shop. That's all I really know. Perhaps you could call the medical examiner for Detective Ameson's report. I haven't received it yet. As for Detective Wilson, you would have to contact his wife or MUSC." Myra jotted down a name and number the captain gave her as Dale sat down beside her. "May I ask why you are interested in Detective Ameson and Detective Wilson?" Chief Harover asked.

"I'm working on the evaluation of Mr. Heirwick for the court. I wanted to discuss his demeanor at arrest. Now I'm really curious. The prison where he is being housed until his hearing has had a couple of guards collapse in the past couple of days. Do you know of anyone else that has had contact with Mr. Heirwick besides Detectives Ameson and Wilson and the prison guards, Chief Harover?"

"Just the booking staff. One of them fell ill for a few days, but he seems to be fine now. I can't think of anyone else off hand."

"Could you check around your station and verify for me? It's rather important at this juncture. I'm wondering if Mr. Heirwick has come into contact with something that may be contagious."

"Sure. I'll make sure it's passed at all the shift changes and at the task force working his case. I'll call you as soon as I hear something," Chief Harover assured her.

Myra looked over at Dale. "You are not going to believe this," she said in hushed tones.

"Try me," he responded drily.

"That was the police department. The two arresting detectives in this case also collapsed. According to Captain Harover, both literally collapsed within hours of the arrest. One is dead, and the other is in intensive care at MUSC."

"I told you there was something about him. Now what?" he asked.

"I'm not sure, but I have to alert the doctors in case the inmate came into contact with something that is affecting these officers. Could you watch my briefcase?" she asked as she snapped it closed and locked it.

"Sure."

Myra hurried to Officer Garrett's room. He was in full arrest again, and there were so many people in the room working on him that she just watched from the hallway, careful to stay out of everyone's way. After about ten minutes, they finally had him stable again.

The doctor with whom she had talked earlier walked up to her. "It's not looking too good," he stated.

"I can see that. I have some information that might be beneficial. I just spoke to the police department that made the arrest of the inmate this man was in contact with in the prison. The captain I spoke to informed me that both detectives collapsed shortly after the arrest—one within hours and the other the next morning. One is still alive and is in intensive care at MUSC. His name is Detective Wilson. She didn't know the symptomology, but I was thinking that maybe the inmate came into contact with something contagious that could be causing people he comes into contact with to collapse with these symptoms."

"I wouldn't think so, considering with what we are dealing with here, but I guess at this point it couldn't hurt to call MUSC and check symptoms and treatments," he said thoughtfully. "What did you say the officer's name was again?"

"Detective Wilson. The arrest record has his name as Henry Wilson."

He poked his head back into the room and motioned to one of the other three doctors in the room that he was going to make a phone call.

*****

Several hours later, the emergency room doctor found a bleary-eyed Myra sipping some of the worst coffee of her life while jotting notes on a pad. She was using her briefcase as a makeshift tabletop on her lap. Dale was pacing the waiting room, and Mrs. Garrett finally nodded off just a few minutes before with her head propped up on her palm.

The doctor cleared his throat, and they all jumped to attention. "Are you Mrs. Garrett?" He looked at Eloise Garrett.

Eloise gave Dale and Myra a terrified look before nodding. "Yes, how is my husband?" Her husky voice was barely above a whisper. Her beautiful golden brown eyes were bloodshot with worry, and dark half-moons settled under them.

"He is finally stable. We are going to transfer him to MUSC intensive care. You were right, Dr. Christie. His symptoms are very similar to Detective Wilson's. At this point, we think isolation of the patients in the same hospital will be the best route. A chopper will be here shortly to transfer him."

"Will I be able to ride with him?" Eloise asked.

"Your husband is in very critical condition and may be contagious. I'm sorry, Mrs. Garrett, but I cannot allow you to ride with him. I wish I could tell you more, but at this time, we are just incapable of diagnosing his symptoms. MUSC has been treating a similar case, and I think they may be best able to handle your husband's care at this time. We have him stable for the moment."

"Is he going to be all right? He's going to live, right?" she choked as the tears began running like rivers down her face.

"I'm afraid it's just too early to say at this time. He's a very sick man, but we have done our best, and I know MUSC will do their very best." He took Mrs. Garrett's hand in his and held it between his palms to lessen the blow, his eyes conveying empathy.

Myra appreciated his tact and honesty. The doctors had said nothing to her or her mother for hours while they worked on her father. It was some time after he died before the attending surgeon had even come to tell them he didn't make it. It had been the worst night of her life. She knew how Mrs. Garrett was feeling. It was going to be tough for her for a while.

Mrs. Garrett dabbed at her stricken face, leaning against Dale for support. "I guess I better call our parents and his sister," she said.

"I'll drive you to MUSC and arrange to have your car brought down there sometime later today," Dale offered as he checked his watch. It was nearly four in the morning.

"I can follow you now, and you can just drop me off at my car on the way back," Myra suggested.

"Warden?"

"Yes, Doctor?"

"May I have a word in private with you and Dr. Christie?"

Dale helped to settle Mrs. Garrett in a chair lest she collapse from the strain. Myra hurriedly placed her things back in her briefcase, snapped it shut, then followed Dale and the doctor to the other side of the check-in desk.

"Warden, we think that under the circumstances, the inmate needs a thorough physical, and we would recommend he be transferred to a hospital where he can be kept in isolation until whatever is causing this can be identified."

"I don't think that is going to be possible." Dale sighed.

"Doctor, I have been in close proximity with the inmate for the past two days, and I feel fine. I realize the symptomology is pointing to a possible contagion after being in contact with the inmate, but I should have fallen ill as well, correct?"

Brows crumpled in consideration, the doctor responded, "One would think, but not necessarily. People are exposed to contagions all the time, but not everyone succumbs. How long has this inmate been in custody?"

"Almost two weeks," Dale answered. "The jail refused to hold him for hearing because of the nature of his crimes."

"The two detectives I told you about earlier collapsed within hours, not weeks," Myra added.

"Nature of his crimes?" The doctor gave Dale a puzzled look.

"The inmate is Canton Wayne Heirwick. The media has dubbed him the Butcher of the South," Myra offered.

"Good God! That's the inmate you are evaluating?" The doctor gasped. When she nodded affirmation, he continued, "I was watching the news earlier, and the reporter said that the number of homicides he was linked to could be over two hundred. Is that true?"

"The police are chasing leads and investigating reports," Dale stated. "I cannot tell you much more than that, but we do expect several charges over the next few weeks."

"Does anyone know if his victims suffered these types of symptoms?" the doctor asked.

"I doubt it," Myra offered. "From the information I have been provided so far, I doubt his victims lasted long enough to succumb to any illness."

"That's terrible! I pray the victims' families can find peace," the doctor said. A nurse came up and handed the doctor a slip of paper. "The chopper is en route and will be here in a few minutes," he told them, looking up from the note.

Chapter 39

Three hours later, Myra was finally walking into her hotel room. She and Dale had waited with Mrs. Garrett in the waiting room until family members started arriving. Unfortunately, there had been no change in the status of either Mr. Garrett or Detective Wilson.

They also met a great number of Detective Wilson's family in the waiting area. They had discussed the confusing symptoms and their sudden appearance in great detail. None of the doctors had yet stumbled on a diagnosis. Seeing both men pale as the sheets they were lying on, swamped by tubes and surrounded by batteries of electrical equipment, had been heartbreaking. Looking over the sea of stress and anxiety riddled faces in the waiting room had been more so.

Myra was bone-tired. It had been an emotional roller coaster of a day. Six long hours of listening to the psychopathic Heirwick drone on about his supposedly past lives and his insatiable need for murder and mayhem had been draining in and of itself. Top that off with worry and concern for Officer Garrett and his family and then meeting with Detective Wilson's distraught family. And that wasn't even considering the underlying tension she felt with Dale.

She peeled off her clothes and headed straight to the shower. Perhaps a steaming hot shower would wash off the events of the day, she thought. Regardless, she needed the warmth for her soul. Myra didn't want to admit it, but Canton Wayne Heirwick was getting to her. She had learned long ago to steel herself against the atrocities she encountered, read about, and heard firsthand from the people that committed them. Even then, it could still drain her energy, but not like Canton Wayne Heirwick. It felt suffocating when he simply walked into the room. When his eyes fell on her, she instantly felt cold. When he talked, his voice was like a knife to the heart. Whether he was responsible for the ills of the officers and guards, she was not certain. But he was dangerous, of that there was no doubt.

Two long days and he had yet to discuss any of the South Carolina victims. For that matter, he had yet to discuss any of his present life. She was edgy…frustrated with the lack of progress. She had to continually remind herself to be patient. He would eventually tell her what she wanted to know. However, it was going to be in his own sweet time. He was in control for now, but only for as long as it took him to finish his storytelling.

She forcefully cleared her mind of Heirwick and the events of the day. She needed to think of something else. She needed to call her mother, she thought. It had been a couple of weeks since they had spoken, and she knew her mother would be worried. She also needed to keep tabs on the state of the senate campaign. She didn't want to get blindsided by a reporter.

Ah, the reporters! How she hated when they got in your face and grilled you with questions. If her stepfather did run, his whole family would be considered fair game. She was not looking forward to that at all. The hot water ran over her body, and her thoughts turned to her father. How she missed him! *How different our lives could have been*, she thought. She definitely would not be here talking to…she mentally shook herself. She definitely did not need to start thinking about that again tonight.

She turned off the water and grabbed the soft white towel from the rack. She quickly dried herself and padded back into the bedroom, grabbed her pajamas from the dresser drawer, and wearily put them on. Once dressed, she crawled between the cool sheets and fell asleep almost instantly.

Chapter 40

The ringing of her cellphone woke Myra. She glanced at the bedside clock—6:00 a.m. She was so exhausted that the large digital numbers on the clock were blurry. Two hours. That's how long she had been asleep.

"Hello?" she answered the phone sleepily, expecting to hear Dale's voice giving her a patient update.

"Good morning, my darling! You sound a bit sleepy. I hope I didn't wake you."

Myra, instantly awake, disconnected the call. Her stalker! How had he gotten her cellphone number? Had the police detective in charge of her case been right? Was it someone she knew? Darrell immediately came to mind. At first, she had not even considered the possibility it could be someone she knew, especially not someone at her office. But the more she began to learn about Darrell, and after his behavior of late, she was seriously reconsidering the idea.

After sending the e-mail to Charleston's Police Chief Lorenzo Decemi about the comments she had overhead Darrell making in regard to the case of Father Zachariah and the two boys, she had also sent a quick e-mail to Detective Parks, who was handling her stalker case. Thinking about it now, she realized she had not heard from either of them. She assumed Chief Decemi was swamped with the Alphabet Killer case. Detective Parks, however, was another matter entirely. She was a bit peeved she was not getting updates from him on how the case was going. She would have to send him an e-mail later in the day. Right now, she decided she was going to try to get a couple more hours of sleep.

She dropped her cell phone back on the nightstand and closed her eyes. *Ring…ring.* Her cellphone went off again. She picked it up and saw Dale's cellphone number calling. "Hi, Dale. How are the guards doing?"

"It's not polite to hang up on people, love. Perhaps it was my mistake since it's a bit early and you were at the hospital so late with those worthless beings. I guess I can forgive you for that. Have you missed me?"

Myra gritted her teeth. If she ever discovered who this stalker was, she would probably strangle him herself. "How did you get my cell phone number, and how have you accessed Dale's number?"

"Now, now, love. I can't give away all my secrets. Have you enjoyed visiting Mr. Heirwick in the prison? His is an interesting case, isn't it?"

Myra sat straight up in bed. Only a few individuals knew about her working on the Heirwick case. That considerably narrowed her stalker suspect pool. "How do you know about the Heirwick case?"

He laughed a low rumble. "My darling, it's all over the television. His is the largest case in history!"

"What do you want?" she snapped.

"Only you, my love."

"I don't think so!" Myra retorted bitterly.

He laughed again. "I do so love it when you play hard to get, my love. It makes the chase all that much more interesting and fun."

"I'm not playing hard to get. I'm just not interested. Goodbye." She hung up on deep rumbling laughter.

"Well, I'm certainly not going back to sleep now," she muttered, kicking off the covers and climbing out of bed. The room felt tainted now. She stumbled into the bathroom. The reflection in the mirror was ghastly. Her eyes were bloodshot like she had been on an all-night bender, her hair was a tangled mess, and she was pale. Growling at the mirror, she turned on a cold shower and grabbed her toothbrush.

"Damn the man!" she growled, shoving the toothbrush into her mouth.

By seven thirty, she was entering the prison with a cup of strong black coffee and her equipment. Within a couple of minutes, she was through the scanning process, had collected her badge, and was stomping toward her temporary office. Dale's office door was closed. The guards at the front had said he wouldn't be in this morning. They had not heard from the hospital, so she told them what she had learned prior to leaving the medical university hospital in the wee morning hours.

She unlocked her office door and settled at the desk. After setting up her equipment, she decided to contact Detective Parks. When he didn't answer his phone, she sent him an e-mail updating him about the early morning cell phone call and how he had called from Dale's number, but she knew it wasn't Dale. And she gave him a list of the people who knew she was working on the Heirwick case.

At that top of her list was Darrell. Her office, Dr. Hull, the judge, a couple of doctors at the two hospitals, and the guards at the prison. As an afterthought, she included Captain Harover and her staff, though she didn't really seriously consider anyone from her staff, the prison, the hospitals, or Dr. Hull. She was now convinced the culprit was at her office. She listed each male at her office and typed out notes next to his name in the e-mail.

Darrell Moore—worked at office for a year. Trying to integrate himself with office staff on a personal basis. Belligerent. Argumentative. Confrontational. Narcissistic? Manipulative. Moved to area from northwest.

Nathan Daniels—worked at the office since she, Stephanie, Elaine, and Joseph opened it several years ago. Friendly. In a relationship. They talked often. Never showed any romantic interest, even before he entered his current relationship.

Joseph Baldachi—married to Elaine since college. Met Joseph and Elaine in graduate school. Attended their wedding. Joseph and Elaine had just had a baby two months ago, and they were both still out on maternity leave.

George O'Malley—Stephanie's husband. Not affiliated with office in any way. Married for two years. Prosecutor for Richland County.

James Allen—worked for office for three years. Quiet. Reserved. In a homosexual relationship with boyfriend for several years. Intelligent. Great with patients. Frequently requested by new LGBTQ patients.

That was all the men affiliated with the office in any way, as far as she knew. A few of the support staff were married, but she didn't know the spouses. Rhonda was not married, nor was she in any exclusive relationships. Eugene Hull was like family, and it was a given the judge was not the stalker. She had only met the prison guards a few days ago. By process of elimination, that meant that one of the men she just listed had to be her stalker, didn't it?

She pressed send on the e-mail and copied both Stephanie and Elaine on the e-mail. Then she sent a group e-mail to Stephanie and Elaine on her suspicions. She asked them to keep an eye on Darrell, especially while she was out of the office. She also mentioned the confrontation they had in her office last Friday.

As an afterthought, she also included the events that had been happening at the prison. If something happened and she fell ill, they would need to be prepared to fill in her position at the office a little longer. She also sent an e-mail to Rhonda with a list of things she needed completed on her behalf. She also asked Rhonda to go by her apartment and check on things for her.

After catching up on her e-mails, she went back to the entrance. She needed to contact Dale on a secured line, and she couldn't trust the number in her own phone at this point. One of the guards lent her his cell phone.

A woman answered on the second ring. "Dale Jones's phone. Can I help you?"

"This is Dr. Myra Christie. Is Dale available?"

"He's asleep. What do you need? I hate to wake him up. He's only been asleep for about a couple of hours," the woman responded.

"Are you his wife?"

"Yes. What is this concerning?"

"I'm working on an evaluation at the prison. I received a phone call from his phone number at six this morning."

"My husband was asleep at six this morning. You must be mistaken."

"Mrs. Jones, I can assure you, the number reflected on my cell phone was his phone number. What concerns me is that I have a stalker. He's been calling, sending letters, etcetera, for a couple of months now."

"Dale would never stalk anyone!" Mrs. Jones snapped.

"I know that, Mrs. Jones. The problem is that my stalker called me at six this morning, and somehow the number that showed up on my cellphone was Dale's number."

"How is that possible?" Mrs. Jones asked, obviously confused.

"That's my point, Mrs. Jones. I don't know how he did it, and it concerns me greatly. I'm not sure if he has somehow messed with my phone or if he has somehow messed with Dale's. Whatever the case, I think it's important that Dale knows this immediately. Somehow, my stalker is very aware of my activities, and he knows I'm working on a case that involves an inmate in Dale's prison."

"That's horrible. You poor thing! What do you need me to do?"

"I'm calling from someone else's phone at the moment. Could you please tell Dale as soon as wakes up? He may need to go by his cell phone carrier's office and have his phone looked at. I'll be doing the same thing when I leave here today."

"I will certainly do that for you. Have you contacted the police, Dr. Christie?"

"I have, but they have not made much progress yet."

"I can't imagine what you must be going through. I hope they catch him soon."

"Thank you. I appreciate your help."

Myra rang off and gave the guard back his phone. Thanking him, she then asked that he have Mr. Heirwick brought to her temporary office for his session.

Chapter 41

"You are looking particularly ravishing today, Dr. Christie." His dark eyes were all but devouring her.

She longed to be back in the shower in her hotel room to wash off his penetrating gaze. She knew Dale was going to be angry when he found out she was at the prison this morning without him present, but this was her job. Myra was exhausted and sleep-deprived. She was worried about her stalker and the guards, but she needed to get this over with as soon as possible.

Originally, she had intended to arrive after lunch, as Dale had suggested when they left the hospital. Unfortunately for her, the stalker decided she needed to wake up at six. So far, her day was going great! Two hours of sleep, awaked by a lunatic stalker, and now doing an evaluation on another depraved lunatic.

"Why don't we focus on your story? Let me see, you were discussing—" she began before being interrupted.

"How are Officers Garrett and Wilson today?" he asked with a bemused look.

Her head snapped up, and she stared at him. "What do you mean?" she asked carefully.

He laughed. It was a hideous sound that grated on her ears. "You know exactly what I mean, Dr. Christie. Don't play games with me." He paused. "On second thought, yes, let's play games. I do so love a good game, even though I always win." He flashed a smile at her.

"Games?" she asked blankly.

"Oh, you can do much better than that," he chided.

She narrowed her eyes at him. "Is that what you have been doing the last couple of days? Playing games?" She already knew the answer, but she wanted him to admit it, needed him to admit it.

"What do you think?" he asked.

"I asked you first." She tensed.

They stared at each other. Finally, he spoke. "I sometimes play with victims. I sometimes play with my food. I always play with my lovers. I would love to play with you. I could give you pleasures you have never had before," he spoke softly.

"I would rather discuss what you know about Officers Nickerson, Garrett, Ameson, and Wilson," she stated. She studied him closely. Body language always told her more than the person's words.

He laughed again. "Afraid I'll pleasure you too much, Dr. Christie? I assure you, you would never be satisfied by another man after I made love to you."

"We were discussing the officers, I believe. We need to stay on topic, if you don't mind. Our time may be shortened today."

His eyes bore into her, and he smiled. "The warden doesn't know you are here today, does he? He is very protective of you. I've heard some of the guards discussing it, and I noticed it yesterday when he was in here. You were lovers at one point."

A faint blush crept up her neck. It had been a long time ago. They had been high school sweethearts at one point, till Loretta Anderson had strolled into school one day. Her family had just moved to Fredericksburg, and the voluptuous redhead had turned many heads. Dale had been one of those heads, and he was smitten at once. A week later, she and Dale had broken up.

She had been heartbroken all of one day. Mostly she had been heartbroken she had lost her virginity to someone who had taken her so casually. They had only been dating a couple of months, but by the time of the breakup, she had already known they didn't want the same things. She quickly cleared her mind. "We are not discussing me. We are here to discuss you, remember?" she cautioned.

"But it is so much fun discussing you. I know quite a bit about you, actually. My father has been whispering to me at night about you. Top of your class in all your degrees, quite the accomplishment!

You've published several papers, making a real name for yourself. And all because your daddy died—was killed actually. No love interests because you are too focused on your job. A well-known forensic psychologist working part-time for the state, and you work with several other psychologists in a growing practice treating trauma-related cases."

She was more than a little shaken by his knowledge of her and was trying desperately not to show it. "You are so much more interesting. Let's talk about you," she redirected his attention.

"You hold black belts in taekwondo, kenpo, and Shotokan. Very impressive! You even competed a little in martial arts and was quite successful during your youth." The maniacal smile was back. "You never fail at anything, do you?" he asked, though it was more of a statement than a question.

"And you kill people just for the sheer pleasure, don't you?" she stated likewise.

"And you have a one-track mind." He laughed. "Very well, we will discuss me for a while, but I warn you, we will discuss you in detail very soon," he warned.

"What do you know about those officers?" she tried again, relieved to finally have him back on topic. It was more difficult to shake off that veiled threat.

"Officer Ameson was punished because he was a bad officer. He was a dirty cop," he stated rather a matter-of-fact. "Took bribes, was working with one of the biggest drug distributors in the State of South Carolina. If you look deep enough, you will find his hidden accounts and the safe deposit box where he kept several hundred thousand dollars for emergency. He kept his undercover IDs and used them to open up bank accounts to hide his endeavors. His wife and children live comfortably, too comfortably for a cop's salary, and yet she never asked where the money was coming from."

"A new half-million-dollar home completely paid off, a Mercedes for the wife, a new Mustang for the teenage daughter, and a new Porsche for the teenage son about to graduate," he continued. "Private schools, the wife does not work. Country club living with golf course and clubhouse memberships. Well-manicured yard done by a service, fully landscaped yard with in-ground pool and hot tub combination with service contract, not to mention the full-time housekeeper. Tell me, Dr. Christie, how does a menial cop with eighteen years of service afford all that in one of the nicest neighborhoods in the area?" he asked.

She made a few quick notes on her pad but did not respond.

"I'll tell you," he continued. "He was dirty, and I punished him. How dare he call me lowlife scum during the arrest when he was a dirty cop!" he thundered. "Yes, I punished him, and now he resides with my father in Hell."

"And the others?" she asked when he paused.

"Officer Nickerson was very unpleasant and sanctimonious. He called me a crazy bastard and told me it was just a matter of time before I got the electric chair. I simply gave the bastard a taste of his own medicine." He shrugged.

"As far as Officers Garrett and Wilson, well, all in due time. It just wouldn't do to tell you all my secrets at one time now, would it? You would get bored and not want to listen to the rest of my story. And since I've already started telling you, I must finish my story. After all, you have been so patiently waiting to hear about my recent victims."

"Why don't we talk about them now?" she invited, still making notes on her pad.

"All in due time, my dear. All in due time." He paused and waited for her to look at him. Then he continued with his story.

Chapter 42

Day 3 of Canton Wayne Heirwick's narrative of his life

My next life saw me born in a time of great reform in Russia. My earthly parents were barely more than peasants, but I came to wield much power. I was born in Moscow to bakers. I was one of the eldest of several siblings, and as such I was expected to assist in the vending of my family's baked goods. Most often, I assisted my father while my eldest sister attended to the baking with my mother during the day.

Moscow at that time was under great strain. The current czar, Peter, had ideas about bringing Mother Russia out the old ways and into a more competitive style with the rest of the world. Alas, the vast majority of Russians felt betrayed and resisted the change. My earthly parents were among them.

Quite ironic, as it would turn out, as I would become a part of that change. I had known it since the day of my birth. My father—Abaddon, Apollyon, Satan, Devil, Lucifer, the Prince of Darkness, oh, you humans have so many names for him—whispered in my ear so many nights of the role I would play in history. No, my work in this life was not to end life. In fact, he forbade me to kill during this life. My role was too important to jeopardize with a kill.

This time, I was to be placed in a position of power that would ultimately lead to distrust and chaos for the better part of a century, perhaps even the demise of the emperorship of Russia. It all started because a young man loved my mother's pirozhkis. I have to admit, they were delicious—the best I have ever had, in fact. This young man was Alexander Menshikov, once a vendor of the delicious treats himself as a child and young adult.

His life changed dramatically when he had a chance meeting with Franz Lefort, who had visited the vendor for some baked goods. So taken was he with Alexander's charm and intelligence that he offered him a position as one of his assistants. Lefort was, at the time, Peter the Great's right-hand man, as it were, but he was beginning to ail. Shortly after their collaboration, and just before Lefort's death, he introduced Alexander to Czar Peter I's service.

Alexander was a quick study and earned the czar's respect and friendship. They became close friends, and Alexander was rewarded generously. By my seventh year, just before my eighth birthday, Czar Peter I made plans to move the capital to Saint Petersburg, a place he fashioned out of lands he had acquired. He needed someone to watch over the area as massive construction was underway, so he bestowed the position of governor-general on Alexander.

The czar had brought contractors and masons from all over Europe and demanded service from every family in Russia for this mammoth undertaking. The area would be in need of guidance and policing with so many persons working long hours to build the future of Russia. My Alexander was just the person to do it. Alexander had been a frequent visitor to our corner to purchase our pirozhkis. Knowing that the czar would demand a person for service from our family, he offered to take me into his service for my father.

My father readily agreed, and so the next day, I left my family to embark on my new journey. I spent the next few weeks learning my new tasks of running errands for Alexander and being his junior assistant. It was a busy time with Alexander's household packing belongings for our new venture, settling as much business in Moscow as possible before we left, and both of us learning what our new duties would entail. Just over a month later, we were on our way to Saint Petersburg.

It wasn't much to look at when we first arrived. A house had been built for us near the czar's Winter Palace, which was under construction. It was little more than a swamp, so earth was being moved to backfill the entire area before buildings could be constructed. Land was being cleared, and services were being brought in to provide for the mass of construction personnel. It was beautiful chaos.

It took roughly ten years to complete the Winter Palace for the czar, but a smaller residence had been built for him and his family in the interim. The czar made many trips there over those initial years, and I had reason to meet him. He was impressive. Just a few inches shy of seven feet tall, he was a force to be reckoned with, yet kind and generous. He and Alexander became best friends, and I had the best seat in the house!

By 1712, I think, Saint Petersburg had officially been declared the new capital by the czar, and people flocked there. In line with Peter the Great's vision, it was undoubtedly a very European city. There were plans for a great museum and wonderful university to be built. He had done Russia proud, and Alexander and I were right in the middle of it.

By this time, I was on the threshold of becoming a man in my own right. I had the ear of Alexander and his trust. My opinions and ideas were valuable to him, and my influence was becoming apparent to me. I encouraged him to befriend his men by participating in their gambling ventures. This was looked upon unfavorably by other men in power, and soon his actions were reported to the czar. The czar, however, paid no heed to idle gossip, and so my Alexander was safe from prosecution.

This encouraged me to flex my power over Alexander. More and more of my ideas were making their way to the czar's ear, and Alexander was being rewarded handsomely. Within a few short years, Alexander had been bestowed the titles of Duke of Cosel, Duke of Ingria, Prince of the Russian Empire, and Prince of the Holy Roman Empire for his service and my ideas, but my assignment was just getting underway.

In the background, I was pulling political strings that were causing hate and discontent between the factions. Peter the Great was aging, and it would not be long before a new leader would be needed. Alexander was prone to the occasional bad decision that drained him of his finances. I knew this would be a problem in the future, so I encouraged him to pad his coffers with money from taxes collected.

Over time, he became a wealthy man, but again, he was reported to the czar.

Admitting to a fraction of the sum actually taken and feigning illness, the czar overlooked his indiscretion, and Alexander paid back a lowly sum. Not long after, our great leader died, and another was needed. I convinced Alexander to back the czar's wife, Catherine, as the new leader. She was easily manipulated, which meant that Alexander would ultimately be making the leadership decisions for all of Russia. Using my expertise, I manipulated political positions once again to back Alexander and Catherine. It worked famously.

Catherine was instituted as empress. Finally, my plan was in action. Alexander followed my advice religiously. I was taking him to new heights of power. On my counsel, he promoted himself to generalissimus, the most superior position in the military. This gave him unprecedented power of the military forces regardless of who was emperor or empress.

Catherine, regrettably, died just two years after being declared empress of Russia. Attempting to save his position and hide his fraudulent ways, Alexander, at my insistence, forged a will that placed Peter II, Peter I and Catherine's grandson by Alexei, on the throne. This meant that Alexander would continue to rule Russia until Peter II was of age.

Some thought power went to my Alexander's head, but it was really I who was giving the orders. My orders enraged the nobility as I knew it would. It was finally time to shake things up and expedite my true objective. I began to slowly poison Alexander, not to kill him but to make him sick. Taking advantage of his illness, the nobility conspired against him. They stripped him of his power, lands, and wealth before imprisoning him and his family in Siberia, where he died.

Peter II now became my focus. I had many friends in the nobility and factions by this time, and I continued my expertise. I was no one's man now. I had my own power without the need for Alexander. I came and went from the palace as I wished, paying homage to young Peter II and providing women for his youthful lust.

I needed to create a chaotic atmosphere, so I was constantly pitting the factions against one another. Then, I exposed young Peter II to smallpox, and shortly thereafter, he died—on the day of his expected wedding, no less! Once again, a search was on for a new czar. The only logical choice was Ivan, the son of Peter I's half brother, Alexis I. He was to rule jointly with his brother Peter I, with his older sister Sophia being the ruling power until they were of age. I will spare you the details, but suffice to say that I created a huge power struggle within the family for years. There were five different leaders of Russia over the next thirty years.

I continued to meddle in the Russian affairs of state until my death as an old man in 1784. That was the longest life I have lived to date. I lived as a noble with great wealth and power. Such an interesting life, I think, but not the greatest. The greatest is yet to come. You will see! But first, let's move on to my next life.

Chapter 43

She glanced at her watch and realized it was eleven thirty. She stopped their session to take a much-needed break and told him they would resume at two o'clock. She needed to get away from the prison for a while—away from him. She ached with the need and exhaustion. She motioned for the guards to come take him to his cell, and she turned off her equipment as dread crept over her.

She was not looking forward to seeing Dale and hoped she could slip out without his seeing her. She had caught his disapproving stare earlier though the windows of the office and could tell he was not happy. Well, she wasn't happy with the situation either, but she had a job to do. He was just going to have to get over it, she fumed to herself.

As the guards removed the inmate Heirwick, she grabbed her briefcase and wallet, locking the door to the office and leaving her electronic equipment in place for the afternoon session. She was headed down the hallway to the front door of the prison when she heard a voice from the office she had just passed.

"Want to tell me what you are doing here today?"

She ignored the voice and continued into the foyer and to the front door. She had just exited the building and was turning toward the parking lot when a hand grabbed her upper arm with firm pressure. Startled, she jerked around and realized it was Dale. "What do you think you are doing?" she demanded, trying to tug her arm away.

"I asked you a question, and I expect an answer. Don't pretend you didn't hear me," he growled as he slipped on his sunglasses and more or less dragged her to his SUV.

"I'm doing my job. Where are you taking me?"

"Wherever I want," he challenged as he forced her in his vehicle and quickly circled the SUV, climbing into the driver's seat.

She glared at him in fury. "I don't appreciate being manhandled."

He ignored her as he backed out of the parking space. "Put your seat belt on," he ordered.

She automatically complied but was not happy about it. "I demand to know where you are taking me!"

"To get something to eat! You look like you are about to collapse. There's a little diner not far from here," he finally told her as he turned onto the main highway.

"I am not about to collapse," she grumbled. "I'm just tired."

"I wonder why? Did you even get any sleep?"

"Yes. I got about two hours," she explained.

"Yes, I heard about that from my wife when I woke up. That's not nearly enough," he chastised her. "Why didn't you tell me you have a stalker?"

"I am not a child, and you are not my father!" she all but exploded. He was making her feel like a guilty child caught red-handed being disobedient.

"This is going to be a huge case, and you need to be on top of your game. That man is extremely dangerous, and you need to be well rested and alert when you are dealing with him," he cautioned.

"I know," she responded, rubbing her eyes and stifling a yawn in the warm vehicle. The sun was beating down on her through the windshield.

He glanced at her and tightened his grip on the steering wheel. After all this time, he still cared for her, he realized. He was sorry he had hurt her so many years ago. They had both been so young, and he had been so stupid. It hadn't taken him long to realize Loretta Anderson had been a player and a user.

By then, however, it had been too late. Myra had refused to talk to him. He couldn't really blame her. He had been a jerk to her. They graduated a couple of years later, and he never heard from her again—until she walked into his prison. What were the odds? He was married now—a complicated relationship, but he was also disturbed by the feelings he was having toward Myra.

She finally relaxed back into the seat and closed her eyes. She had darkened circles under her eyes that she had cleverly covered with makeup, but from his angle and the sun hitting her face, he could still make them out. Last night had been exhausting for him too. He could only imagine what she was going through after talking with that psychopath all day yesterday and spending all morning with him today.

He had to admit that he admired her dedication and strength. She had really blossomed from that tall thin leggy teen he had once known. She had been pretty back then, but now...she had metamorphosed into a very beautiful bombshell. He was surprised she wasn't married. There must be a trail of heartbreak wherever she went, he thought.

A few minutes later, they were pulling into a gravel parking lot, and she opened her eyes. A weathered building stood in front of them with several cars in the lot. He was out of the vehicle and opening her door before she even got her seat belt unbuckled. She grabbed her wallet and briefcase then walked with him into the building.

A hodgepodge of rusty collectibles and signs decorated nearly every square inch of the inside. Several tables with red and white checkered tablecloths dotted two different rooms and several people were already seated, some eating, some waiting for their food, and some looking at menus.

An older woman with an equally weathered faced approached them from the counter with two menus in hand. "Hi, Dale! Who's your friend?" she beamed, wagging her eyebrows suggestively.

"Sapphire, meet an old friend, Dr. Myra Christie. We grew up together," he introduced them.

Sapphire? Myra thought. She would never have guessed that name in a hundred years. "It's nice to meet you." She smiled, shaking the waitress's hand.

"A doctor, hmmm. Didn't know you knew anybody that smart, Dale." Sapphire laughed as she led them to a table in the second dining area. No one else had been seated in the area, so they would have some privacy.

"Very funny, Sapphire." He grinned. "You might be surprised at some of the people I know. I know a lot of people in a lot of high places."

"And a lot more in really low places." She laughed again as she slapped him on the shoulder and handed them their menus. "What y'all want to drink?"

"Ice water, no lemon," Myra stated.

"Two sweet ice teas," he told Sapphire. "She needs something to keep her going today. She had a rough night last night followed by a long morning," he explained.

Sapphire gave him a long look with an even longer smile before disappearing through a door in the back of the room.

"Sapphire and her husband, Frank, own this place. The food is great, and it's close to Lieber," he explained.

She perused through the menu before putting it down. He was busy looking at his text messages on his phone. She grimaced as she realized she had been too tired to look through her messages yesterday. She would have to cut her session with Inmate Heirwick short again today so she would have time to review all her messages and respond to them in a fairly timely manner.

"Did your wife tell you my stalker called me this morning from your phone number?"

Dale looked up at her. "Yes. I stopped by the cellular phone store on my way in. They said there's a computer program that allows telemarketers and scammers to call cell phones using familiar numbers to the recipient. They do that so that people will actually answer their phones. Once they answer, they are caught off guard by the telemarketer or scammer, giving the telemarketer or scammer a better chance of success."

"I don't understand. How do they know you called me before?"

"It's part of the computer program they use. Apparently, when they call your number, an instant relay is set up between their device and your phone. It can pick up and display any phone number the caller wants to display."

"So you're saying that it was just happenstance that it was your number he chose to call on?"

"Exactly." Dale smiled and put his phone down.

"That might be the usual case, but not in this one. He knew he was calling using your number. He knew who you were, Dale. He knows I'm working the Heirwick case."

"With that program, he could use any number he wants. He might have just assumed I called you last and went from there."

"Perhaps, but I'm still not convinced. Dale, this guy knows things he should not know."

"What do you mean?"

"He knows things about me, things about you. I didn't tell anyone except my staff that I was going to be here working this case."

"Someone from your office might have let it slip, or the judge, or Dr. Hull. Hell, even one of my guards could have let it slip that you are here working on the case."

Myra was resting her elbows on the table and staring at her interwoven fingers. "Perhaps. I just have a bad feeling about this."

Dale reached across the table and took her hands in his. "Don't worry about it. That's exactly what the stalker wants you to do. Don't accept his calls."

"I don't have a choice if he can call on any number he so chooses now, do I?"

"You know what I mean." He lightly squeezed her hands. "Hang up on him when you realize it's him."

"I do. He just continues to call back. He's called me on my home phone and my cell phone. He writes me letters and has them delivered to my office and to the courthouse during the Johnson trial. Hell, he's even entered my dreams somehow!" She gritted her teeth.

Sapphire returned with two sweet teas and an ice water, placing the water in front of Myra with a smile and sidelong glance at Dale. "Do you know what you want?" she asked Myra.

"I'll take the double-decker BLT with a side salad. Could I also get an order of that fried okra?" Myra asked.

"You sure can, honey. My Frank makes the best fried okra around!"

Dale ordered chicken fried steak, mashed potatoes, gravy, and green beans, which sounded really good to Myra, but it made her sleepy just thinking about eating such heavy food for lunch. With their orders in, Myra took a few minutes to really take in her surroundings. An old yellow and green John Deere sign was on the wall next to her with a faded framed photo of a farmer on a tractor plowing ground just above it. A rusted band saw was hung just above the oversized doorway. There was so much paraphernalia on the walls and ceiling, it made her dizzy just looking at it.

"So how has it been going with Heirwick?" Dale finally asked.

"Long and arduous," she said simply. Opening her briefcase, she took out her notepad. "I can't discuss everything he has said so far because it is a court ordered evaluation, but he did tell me something about Detective Ameson that I thought you should know."

"Detective Ameson? Who is that?" he asked.

"Detective Ameson was one of the arresting officers I told you about last night. He died suddenly and mysteriously shortly after the arrest. And when I say shortly, I mean hours. I spoke to a Captain Harover at the precinct where he worked. I still need to talk to his superior officer. He was out when I called last night."

Dale was quiet as he absorbed what she was telling him. She could tell he was thinking about his prison guards who were hospitalized and worrying about the rest.

"The other officer, Detective Wilson, is the other arresting officer. We met his family last night. I know it was a long and stressful night. He's the one that is at MUSC with the same symptomology as Officer Garrett."

"So you're saying that every officer that comes into contact with this maniac suddenly falls ill or dies?" he asked incredulously.

"I'm saying that there is a coincidence. Nothing more, nothing less. I'm not really sure what is going on yet. I did ask Inmate Heirwick if he knew anything about those cases and...well..." She paused, not quite sure how to continue.

"Well what?" he prompted her, his brows furrowed.

"You have to understand that this guy likes the attention he is getting and will tell me anything to keep getting it. The outlandish story he has been telling me is the thing of horror fiction." She paused as their lunch was delivered, and Sapphire left to check on her other customers.

She took a bite of her BLT and chewed thoughtfully as she watched Dale cut up his entire steak before eating a single bite. "So there are a lot more murders out there," he stated with resignation.

"I don't know yet. We haven't gotten that far yet. I can tell you he is extremely depraved."

"Depraved? That's putting it mildly!" he told her as he chewed a piece of steak.

She popped a piece of okra in her mouth and moaned her delight. "This is really good." She smiled at him.

"I told you it was good. I come here every chance I get. One of the guards told me about it when I first started at the prison."

They ate in silence for a few minutes. Sapphire refilled their drinks and left before Dale asked her, "So what about this Officer Ameson?"

"Heirwick claims he was a dirty cop."

"Dirty cop?" he asked in surprise.

"Took bribes, worked for a big drug lord here somewhere. He also said he had multiple bank accounts with hundreds of thousands or more in several banks under various names he had used while undercover years before," she informed him as she looked over her notes. "He and his family lived way beyond the means he earned as an officer, and his wife supposedly does not work. Kids in private schools with their own sports cars."

"Do you put any stock in his ramblings?" he asked.

"To be perfectly honest, I'm not sure. He claims he punished him by putting him to death, but how could he? He was in lockup at the time. He may just know some dirt on the officer and made up the rest when he heard he had died. I'm sure it was all over the jail when it happened. It shouldn't be too difficult to look into Officer Ameson a little to see if anything was suspicious and deems further investigation," she suggested.

"When we get back to the prison, we will call the Berkeley County DA and see how she wants to handle that. I agree that it wouldn't hurt to look into Ameson a bit. If he's clean, then no problem. I just don't like the idea of finding out he's dirty by that scumbag. That prison is full of depraved killers, but there is something about Heirwick. That guy is the worst and most insidious man I have met. And trust me, I've met a bunch in the federal system," he declared.

"He said Detective Ameson had a safe deposit box where he kept his records and cash on hand. Since his death was recent, his wife may not have accessed it yet if there is one," she continued as she put her notes up and focused on enjoying the rest of her meal.

As their plates were taken away, Dale requested Sapphire's famous brownie al la mode covered with homemade vanilla bean ice cream and drizzled in hot chocolate fudge over Myra's protests. It was heavenly. She tried not to think about all the calories she had just consumed. She would worry about that later, she thought, feeling like she was wobbling as Dale paid the bill and they left. So much for having a light meal. She yawned. It was all she could do to keep her eyes open on the return trip to the prison.

Chapter 44

Back at the prison, Myra sat across the desk from Dale as he dialed the phone number of the county prosecutor. Myra had her notes in front of her so she could accurately tell the prosecutor what had transpired during their conversation. She tried to stifle a yawn and gently rubbed her eyes as a voice picked up on the other end.

"Berkeley County Prosecutor, Charlene Ebbs's office. How may I help you?" a rather squeaky female voice responded.

"Is Mrs. Ebbs in? This is Warden Jones at Lieber," Dale informed her.

"One moment, please," the voice replied before placing him on hold.

"If I had to listen to that voice every day, I would be an inmate here myself," Dale drawled, causing Myra to collapse into a fit of giggles.

"Charlene Ebbs, can I help you?" a sultrier voice came over the line.

"Mrs. Ebbs, this is Warden Dale Jones of Lieber Correctional Facility. I have Dr. Myra Christie here with me, and you are on speakerphone," he informed her.

"Ah, Warden Jones! How are you? I haven't seen you in a while," she all but purred.

Myra cast him a questioning look and a sly smirk. He narrowed his eyes at her in warning. "Doing well...and you?" he asked. The pleasantries always had to be made in the South before business could be conducted.

"I can't complain. Life is good. What can I do for you?" she asked.

"Dr. Christie is working on the Heirwick case. She is the evaluating psychologist, or at least one of them. Dr. Christie, would you like to explain to Mrs. Ebbs the nature of this call?" he asked.

"Hello, Mrs. Ebbs. Some interesting events have been taking place in the vicinity of Mr. Heirwick," she began.

"How so?" Ebbs asked.

"A couple of guards have collapsed around him, and both are in the intensive care facilities. The latest is Officer Garrett, who has an unusual symptomology and was transferred to MUSC last night."

"What does this have to do with the Heirwick case?" Ebbs persisted.

"Mrs. Ebbs," Dale interjected. "If you could be patient for a minute and let Dr. Christie explain. It's rather a complicated matter."

"Of course. I do apologize if I interrupted you," Ebbs drawled, though she sounded a bit peeved.

"Mrs. Ebbs, considering the nature of the symptoms, the attending physician last night asked if there were other cases. On a hunch, I contacted the arresting police officers and found that one had mysteriously died within hours, and the other, a Detective Wilson, was also at MUSC with similar symptoms. Fearing a possible contaminant, the hospital has put both men in quarantine. Their situations are very grave," Myra explained.

"I'm so sorry to hear this. I had heard Officer Wilson was ill, but I had no idea it was that serious," Mrs. Ebbs replied, sounding concerned.

"This morning, Mr. Heirwick inquired about the conditions of both Officer Garrett and Detective Wilson without my mentioning either of them. He then proceeded to discuss some rather…well… inappropriate behavior on the part of the other arresting officer, Detective Ameson. Detective Ameson died shortly after the arrest. Mr. Heirwick claims to have killed him because he was…um…" Myra hedged, searching her brain for the most nonderogatory adjective.

"A dirty cop?" Ebbs supplied for her.

"Yes," Myra acknowledged.

"Did he give you any specifics?" Ebbs asked in monotone.

"Mrs. Ebbs, I doubt these allegations are true, and frankly, I question everything that Mr. Heirwick has been telling me," Myra rushed.

There was a silence on the other end of the line for moment as though the prosecutor was debating something internally. Finally, she resigned to share information. "Warden, Dr. Christie, what I am about to tell you stays between us. Is that clear?" she asked sharply.

"Yes," Dale replied, giving Myra an uneasy look.

"Yes, Mrs. Ebbs," Myra agreed.

"Detective Ameson has been under investigation for some time. He was moved to the homicide division from the narcotics division about six months ago. The only reason he was moved was because, although we know he was dirty, we could not prove it. What has Mr. Heirwick told you?" she asked again.

"He said that Detective Ameson was working with the top drug distributor in the state, but he didn't mention any names. He also said that Detective Ameson has several bank accounts and a safe deposit box with incriminating information in it," Myra supplied. "He did not give me any specifics, I'm afraid his wife may not be aware."

"A safe deposit box, eh? We didn't know about that. I'll have SLED officers look into it. Anything else?" Ebbs asked.

"No, but I'll be sure to contact you if he tells me anything else," Myra promised.

"Thank you. This information could prove very useful if we can find the key to that box," Ebbs said. "Thank you for not keeping this information to yourself. I know no one likes to rat out a cop, especially if they are unsure of the information. I appreciate your candor in this matter, Dr. Christie," she continued.

"I hope it helps you," Myra offered as she and Dale exchanged looks.

"We will leave you to it, Mrs. Ebbs," Dale announced as he readied to end the call.

"Please call me Charlene." She surprised Myra. "I have asked you several times, Warden. We work together, and it makes things easier. You too, Dr. Christie," Ebbs invited.

"Very well, Charlene. Have a great day," Dale said as he hung up. He leaned back in his chair and gave Myra a thoughtful look. "Well, well, so our boy knows things after all. I wonder how he knows those things?" he pondered.

"Good question. I'll see if I can get any more out of him," Myra offered as she stood and stretched. "I can't believe Detective Ameson is...was," she corrected, "a dirty cop."

"It happens, unfortunately. You can question him more tomorrow. You are going home or to your hotel or wherever you are staying now. You are about to drop, and you need rest."

"I'm fine," she lied.

"If you don't go willingly, I'll drive you myself. You are not going to talk to him anymore today," he said emphatically.

Myra was too tired to argue. She glared at him for a moment before grabbing her briefcase. "I still have to gather my equipment," she began, but he cut her off.

"Leave it here tonight. It will be fine. It's locked up. Only the psychologist and I have the key to that office." Standing, he took her elbow and escorted her to her vehicle.

Chapter 45

Myra had been forced to cut the interview session short by Dale. Though if she were honest with herself, she was ecstatic and hadn't put up much of a fight. She had been tired before lunch. After lunch, she could barely keep her eyes open. She really wanted to get the evaluation completed, but exhaustion was not conducive to good work. Even more so, working with someone like Heirwick could be downright lethal. Guards were posted outside the door, and he was confined in the chair, but if he was able to get out of those restraints, the guards might not even be able to get to her in time.

After the conversation with the prosecutor, she realized she needed to think before she talked with Mr. Heirwick again. She had to design a line of questions to determine how much he knew about Detective Ameson and how he knew it. Myra also realized he might know more about other people in the area.

How long had he been in the Charleston area? His kill files, or at least the one's in Dr. Hull's possession, indicated that he moved around a lot. What if he stayed in an area doing his research on several potential victims, then came and went frequently over a period, killing here and there as he went? It would appear as though he was merely passing through an area when he was really hunting an area. In two hours, he could be in Savannah, Georgia. In three hours, he could be in Wilmington, North Carolina. *He could have been staying in Savannah and killing in Florida, Georgia, South Carolina, and North Carolina at the same time!* she thought.

Right now, however, her mind was muddled with lack of sleep and anxiety. She was past exhaustion, and she knew Dale was right, as much as she hated to admit it. He had escorted her to the front door and would have escorted her all the way to her SUV had she allowed him. Instead, he stood in the doorway, watching to make sure she left.

More annoyed than angry, she snapped her safety belt and grabbed her cell phone. Since cell phones were not allowed in prisons, she left hers in her vehicle on the charger. She had fifteen voice mails since yesterday morning waiting on her cell phone. "Great! Just great!" she muttered to herself.

She sighed as she scanned them quickly and noticed three from her mother. She might as well call her instead of wasting time listening to them all. It would be faster that way. She pressed her mother's phone number and hit call. When it started ringing, she pressed the speaker option before backing out of the parking space and headed toward her hotel in Summerville.

They talked the entire fifteen-minute trip to her hotel. Apparently, her stepfather finally made the bid to run for the senate in the next election. His campaign was now underway, and funds were rolling in from various supporters. As a lawyer and a judge, he had a reputation of getting things done. He was a fair and upstanding guy, and it didn't hurt that he had a military background and served with the FBI for a few years as well. Myra was confident he would win the senate seat.

She informed her mother about consulting with Dr. Hull on the high profile case and that she would be out of her office for another few days. She never discussed anything pertinent concerning the cases she worked. Rather, she mentioned non-specifics—high profile case, working in a prison, not able to access a telephone. It didn't matter, however, because her mother knew well enough not to press her for any details.

Her mother loved her dearly and supported Myra in any endeavor, but she did not understand Myra's nor Myra's father's choices to work with what she called "the lower echelons of society," meaning the criminals. Myra's mother grew up in a wealthy family. Myra's grandfather felt she had married below her station when she married Myra's father. He had been in the military at that point. When he joined the FBI, he marginally improved his station in life, according to Myra's grandfather. He had died when Myra was young, and she couldn't help but wonder what he would think of her and her choices. Would he have looked down on her like he had her father for choosing to protect the public?

Myra was nearly at the hotel before her mother brought up the real reason for her call. Her cousin Lydia was getting married. Lydia had been trying to get in touch with Myra. Myra was expected to be in the wedding party. That meant that she also had to return Lydia's message before she could sleep.

Hanging up with her mother, she gathered her things and headed for her hotel room. As she entered her room, her phone beeped with a text message. It was from Dale. She set down her things and quickly scanned it. There was no change in Officer Garrett yet. Scans showed normal brain activity, but he was still on a ventilator.

She kicked off her shoes and decided she needed a quick shower. She always needed a shower after talking to Heirwick. His story was so fanciful yet so sordid. She shook her head in disgust and caught her pale reflection in the bathroom mirror. Her eyes were still blood-shot from lack of sleep. Dark circles had appeared under her eyes despite her artistic makeup. She looked every bit as exhausted as she felt. No wonder Dale had insisted on her leaving for the day!

Ten minutes later, she was curled up in her bed with her laptop on her lap, scrolling through her e-mails. She found a couple of updates from Nathan and Elaine, who had taken over her normal cases. A quick scan of them assured her that everything was going well so far. She e-mailed them back with some notes on upcoming appointments they would be filling for her. She also let them know this case was high profile, and she wasn't sure yet when she would be returning. She hoped that she would be finished by the end of the week. Wishful thinking? Boy, she hoped not!

Myra responded to her pressing e-mails, deleted the scams and advertisements, and saved the rest for later. She picked up her phone to review the rest of her phone messages. Nothing of importance, she realized, as she listened to a few of them. Lydia had called with her good news, but Myra was just too tired to deal with the hour-long conversation she knew they would have. Lydia deserved more than that, and she just couldn't give it right now. Instead, Myra texted Lydia her congratulations with an apology that she was wrapped up in a case and would call her next week. With that, she sat her laptop on the nightstand with her phone and promptly fell asleep.

*****

Insistent knocking on the door awakened her. She looked at the clock as she climbed from beneath the covers. It was 4:00 p.m. Two and a half hours of sleep. "What now?" she mumbled. She looked through the peephole in the door then stumbled backward in shock.

"What are you doing here? How did you know where I was?" she asked, swinging the door open.

"Hello to you too! Rhonda told me. We had a bad storm up in Columbia, and lightning struck the electrical substation and damaged something. Power is out over several blocks. Elaine called the electric company, and they said we wouldn't have power back until late tomorrow, so we had to close the office early."

"Okay, but you still haven't answered my question. What are you doing *here*?"

"Rhonda said you were down here. Since the office is closed, I thought I would drive down and we could have dinner together. I'll even let you show me Charleston." He breezed by her and made himself comfortable in the armchair placed by the window.

"I'm not here on vacation, Darrell! I'm *working*!" she emphasized.

"Looks like you were sleeping to me. I checked in at the front desk when I got my room, and they said you were in."

"I have been up for over twenty-four hours, Darrell. I need sleep! Now get out and let me get some sleep!"

"You're grouchy!" he sneered.

"I'm not grouchy! I'm exhausted and sleepy!" she defended.

"Hmmm... I could use a nap too, I guess." He waggled his eyebrows at her and began unbuttoning his shirt.

Myra's mouth fell open in shock. "What in the hell do you think you're doing?"

"Getting undressed. I don't want to get my clothes all wrinkled. Besides, we can't have any fun if we're fully clothed." He smiled at her.

"I am not sleeping with you. I am not having dinner with you. And I am not going to give you a tour of Charleston! I've been working my ass off down here, and I'm not finished. I have a lot going on down here. You need to get the hell out of this room or I will call security!"

"Come on, love...you don't mean that. We don't have to do a tour tonight, and we can eat here if you like."

Myra gritted her teeth in anger. She felt like she was in an episode of *The Twilight Zone*! "Darrell, you need to stop calling me love. Nothing is going to happen between us. I'm not eating dinner with you, and you are not staying in this room! Now...get...out!" She held the door open, shooting daggers at him with her eyes.

Darrell walked across the room and stopped in front of her. He raised a hand and reached for her face, but she pulled back out of his reach. "Why don't we shut the door, darling?"

"I will close it just as soon as you step into the hallway. And don't call me darling!" she snapped.

"It's just us here, Myra. You don't have to play so hard to get now," he said softly.

"I'm not playing hard to get, Darrell. I am not interested. Frankly, you should be concerned right now. I am one of your bosses, and I could fire you for this. Get out! Now!"

He looked into her eyes as though he were searching for something. When he saw she was not going to back down, he dropped his head and stepped into the hallway.

She immediately closed the door behind him and latched the chain. Shaking with fury, she paced back and forth in the hotel room, muttering to herself. Myra realized something was going to have to be done about Darrell, and soon. A partner's meeting was going to have to be called as soon as she got back to Columbia. Right now, she had more important things to deal with, namely a psychopath sitting in prison that needed her evaluation. Darrell, the office, her stepfather's campaign, Lydia's wedding, and her stalker case were just going to have to wait.

Pausing in front of floor-length mirror, Myra saw the dark circles were still under her eyes. Just looking at her reflection made her tired. How Darrell had felt amorous toward her was beyond her. She looked terrible.

The bed was beckoning to her. She flipped the lights off, crawled into the bed, and nestled back into the covers. It took a lot of tossing and turning, but she finally drifted back into sleep.

Chapter 46

Myra, now well rested, entered a prison in pandemonium the following morning. Guards were rushing around. Three ambulances were out front, along with the coroner's van. Dale looked haggard as he entered the psychologist's office where she was setting up her electronic equipment and downloading the previous day's interview from the video recorder to her laptop.

"Would you please forego your interview today? I'm asking as nicely as I can," he asked her.

"What's going on? It's crazy in here today!" she stated.

"Last evening, one of the guards noticed an inmate lying on his floor. When he called for backup, they found him unresponsive. Medical personnel started working on him, but he died about an hour later on his way to the hospital. Three other inmates have suspiciously fallen ill during the night, and another just fell dead at my feet less than twenty minutes ago. We are on lockdown and pending an investigation," he explained as he lowered himself into the chair across from hers.

"And you think it's the same thing that affected Officer Garrett, don't you?" she asked.

"We're not sure yet. These guys were foaming at the mouth, fluid coming out of their ears. Seizures. Damned if I know what's going on around here! I wanted to catch you before you came in today, but I lost track of time. We have all been quarantined pending further review, and you shouldn't have been allowed in here."

"Quarantined? You mean the inmates or everyone in the prison?"

"All of us. I have to add you to the list since you have been here interviewing Heirwick."

"Wait! You mean I'm quarantined too?" Myra asked, astonished.

"Duh, Myra! Yes. All of us. That means you will be living here with the rest of us until the Centers for Disease Control and Prevention [CDC] tells us we are clear. By the way, were you with anyone yesterday after you left or this morning?"

"No. I went back to my hotel room and promptly fell asleep. Wait, one of my coworkers came down last night and came into my room briefly. We argued, and he left."

"Did you come into contact with anyone at supper last night or breakfast this morning?" he asked, leaning forward.

"I was too tired to eat last night, and I had a granola bar for breakfast. I keep a stash of them in my vehicle. Wait, are you telling me I cannot leave the prison?" she asked. What he was saying was finally starting to sink in. She slowly sank into her own chair.

"That's what quarantine and lockdown mean, Myra. Are you all right?" He leaned forward and placed his hand on her forehead.

"I'm just fine," she snapped, pushing his hand away. "It's just a lot to take in. When will the CDC be here, and how long do they expect us to be in quarantine?"

"CDC is on their way. No inmate is leaving their cell today. Their meals will be delivered to them for their own safety as soon as the CDC checks out our food supplies. That's all I know right now. I guess it will depend on what they find here."

"I've never heard of such a thing in a prison." She stared at him.

"Nor have I. I know this is a major issue for you. I have informed my staff that you have access to my office and my computer if you would like. I just can't let you do your interview today. Not until this has been resolved," he explained.

"I understand. Thankfully, I have my laptop. I have a number of things I need to get done." She noticed for the first time the anxiety and exhaustion in Dale's face. The last few days had been hard on him. "Are you okay?" she asked.

"Just tired…exhausted. I haven't seen my family for three days. I was on my way back from Columbia from talking with Officer

Nickerson's doctor and wife the other day when I got the call about Officer Garrett. After we left the hospital night before last, I went home and crashed for a few hours before returning here. I've been here ever since."

"Have you called your wife? She must be so worried."

"That's on my to-do list this morning. You need to contact your coworker and tell him to quarantine himself for two weeks, at least."

"I'll message him, but I doubt we were close enough for him to be exposed to anything. He was only in my room for a couple of minutes before I threw him out."

"Trouble in paradise?" He gave her a tired smile, but it spoke volumes.

"He has a misplaced infatuation, but I think he finally got my message loud and clear," she stated. "Is there anything I can do to help around here?" she offered.

"I'm not sure yet. Have you noticed anything?"

"Noticed anything? You mean about Heirwick?" she asked, and he nodded. "He doesn't appear to be sick or having any symptoms of anything. All he does is go on and on with this bogus story of his. He always has an answer for everything I ask him. He's one of a kind! I'll give him that. But no, I haven't noticed him being sick, and the only thing I've been is exhausted the last few days. Oh, and repulsed by some of the things he tells me." She smiled.

They sat in silence for a few moments, each pondering their own thoughts. Myra racked her brain for any clue. She would go through the clips today to see if she missed something, some vital clue about these mysterious illnesses and deaths.

Myra cocked her head. "Have any other inmates exhibited any symptoms?"

"Not yet. Not that we have noticed, anyway," he stated. He dropped his head and shook it. "Five inmates and two guards in two weeks. Isn't that enough?"

"What about mental illnesses? Anyone showing any unusual or out-of-character aggression, anxiety, or hearing voices?"

"Not that I know of, but I'll make sure the guards keep a look out for that." The radio on his hip crackled. He grabbed it and spoke into it. "On my way." And with that, he was gone.

She took her things into Dale's office and sat them down. Clearing off a section of his spacious desk, she set up her laptop and stacked all the reports on Heirwick beside it. She popped her head into his secretary's office and asked if they had any folding tables available. The secretary was uncertain but said she would find out.

A few minutes later, the secretary entered Dale's office informing Myra that the warden was on the phone for her. She crossed to the desk, picked up the receiver, and pressed a button on the phone. "Warden? One moment please." She handed Myra the phone and left the office, closing the door behind her.

"Yes?" Myra asked into the phone.

"It's me. Why do you need a table?" he asked.

"I also need a white board if you have one somewhere. I was thinking that setting up a command position with a list of the sick and deceased inmates with their symptoms might be of some help," she offered.

"Actually, that's a great idea. All of my guards are here with me. Hang on a sec." She could hear him talking to someone next to him but could not understand what they were saying. "Tell Amelia that medical has whiteboard in their supply room. There is a folding table down the hall past the cage in the second room off to the left. The key is my desk. I have to go," he said abruptly and hung up.

She had no idea who Amelia was, so she once again headed next door to his secretary's office. "You wouldn't happen to be Amelia, would you?" she asked.

"Yes. I guess we haven't been formerly introduced." She laughed.

"No, we haven't. I'm Dr. Myra Christie, but you can call me Myra. It looks like we are going to be seeing a lot of each other for the next few days."

"Yes. I heard as soon as I walked in this morning. Good thing my husband is a truck driver and out of town right now. I would hate to have to tell him he was quarantined because of me." She made a funny face.

Myra laughed. "I guess that might be a bit difficult to explain. "Dale...er... Warden Jones, I'm sorry," she apologized. "I've known him for years, and it seems so foreign to me that he's a warden now."

Amelia smiled. "Most of us are on first-name basis around here except when company comes."

"Thank you." Myra smiled her appreciation. "Well, I was hoping to set up a sort of command post. I need a folding table and a whiteboard. Dale said the whiteboard was in the medical supply room."

"Okay. All the medical staff are with him right now, but I know the combination for the door. You'll need some of those erasable markers too, won't you?"

"Yes, if you don't mind. He said the table was down the hall, so I can get that myself," she replied.

"I'll be right back," Amelia said as she disappeared down the hall toward the medical department.

With Amelia on her way to get the whiteboard, Myra rummaged through Dale's desk drawers until she found a key ring with three keys attached. One of the keys was marked supply room. She grabbed the keys and headed across the foyer and down the opposite hall. She found the folding table easily and another whiteboard tucked behind a set of shelves.

Feeling lucky with her finds, she lifted the table and headed back to Dale's office. Amelia had leaned the whiteboard against his desk and placed a pack of new markers on Myra's stack of files. After she finished setting up the table, Myra headed back to the supply room for the other whiteboard. With all of her finds now in the same room, she placed the keys back where she found them before looking around the office. The wall adjacent to the door was the best place for the six-foot table, but a bookshelf was in the way.

She hated to rearrange his entire office, but there was a crisis in the mist, and she reasoned moving a bookshelf was but a small inconvenience. She got busy with her plans, and before long, she had moved the bookshelf to the wall beside his desk. After setting up the table and whiteboards, she asked Amelia for a list of the sick and deceased inmates. An hour passed before she saw Dale again. She was hard at work with her back to the door, so she didn't hear him enter and visibly jumped when he commented.

"Nice," he mused as he studied the whiteboards. She had listed all the officers who had fallen ill as well as all the inmates, along with the symptoms as she knew them. She had even called the hospital in Columbia to check on Officer Nickerson and reported those findings on the boards as well.

"Thanks. I called MUSC and checked on both officers. They are still the same, no changes. I also called the police department and talked with Detective Ameson's and Wilson's supervisor. Unfortunately, he didn't have much more to add. I called Dr. Hull, but I didn't get an answer. There was a recording on the office phone that simply said the office was closed for the next few days and to leave a message. I couldn't reach him on his cell phone either, which worries me." She frowned.

"He was here a couple of days last week before all this started. We need to get in touch with him. Jeez, this is a nightmare. The only good thing is that I haven't been around my family enough to have to quarantine them. Last week, I was at a conference and well...this week has been..." He trailed off.

He didn't need to finish his sentence. She knew all too well what the week had been like for him. The stress and strain were written all over his face. "What else can I do? I was looking on the computer for similar cases, but I couldn't find anything." She shrugged.

"I don't think there's anything else to be done at the moment. CDC will be here shortly." He ran his hand through his hair and sat on the sofa across from the large windows.

He was exhausted and in need of a shave. A haircut wouldn't do him any harm either, she thought. It was a little longer than the current fashion. Still, it was much shorter than he had worn in high school.

"Why don't you lie down and take a nap?" she suggested.

"I can't. I won't have time," he replied with eyes closed, head resting on the back of the sofa.

"What about a shower then? It might revitalize you a bit. It's going to be a very long day, I'm afraid."

He slowly opened his eyes and ran them over her like a sweet caress. "You are even more beautiful than you were when we were in school," he said. "I'm sorry I hurt you. I didn't mean to, you know. I was just a really dumb kid full of himself."

That had been the last thing she expected to hear from him, and she wasn't exactly sure what to say. A blush crept up her neck, and she turned away from his prying eyes. She grabbed the stack of files and her notepad from his desk where she had been working.

"I'll just go work in the other office so you can get some rest or whatever."

When she turned around, he was already up and closing his office door. "Are we never going to talk about this?" he asked, sounding frustrated.

"Talk about what?"

"Us." He raised his hands in exasperation.

"There is no us and never was," she said drily.

He walked toward her slowly, eyes staring deeply into her own, making her uncomfortable. "I remember a time when there very much was," he said softly.

He was standing not more than a foot away from her. Shifting everything to one arm, she put the other up to stop him from advancing further. His chest was hard and hot as her hand made contact. "Dale, if we ever did have anything, it was a very long time ago and was over just as quickly as it started." She tried to sound all business. "I don't blame you for anything. I never have. If I didn't seem overly upset back then, it was because I wasn't. I realized we were never meant to be because we wanted different things out of life," she patiently reasoned with him.

"I've often wondered what would have happened if we never broke up. I've kicked myself for years over it." He grasped her hand in his. "I used to think about you often over in the war. I still have your picture in my wallet, and it helped through some pretty rough times over there."

"My picture? You mean your wife's picture, right?"

"No, I mean yours. Truth is, Sonja and I were already having issues before I left. I really didn't think she would be here when I got back, but she was. We've tried to make it work…been to counseling and everything. I thought bringing her back to her family and where we were happiest might help, but it's not."

"I'm sorry to hear that, Dale. I truly am, but I'm not the answer either."

"Why haven't you married? Is there someone special?"

She walked over to the sofa and sat down. "No, there's no one. I haven't dated anyone in some time. I've just been too busy. First it was because Dad died. I was in a serious relationship at the time, but Zach got frustrated because I was too wrapped up in grief to give him the attention he thought he deserved. I know he deserved more than I was giving him, but I was grieving, and I needed attention.

"It was a tough time. Mother and I both fell into depression, but mine got out of hand. I took a semester off from school because I just couldn't handle anything. After that, I found a new focus. I needed to be a forensic psychologist so it didn't happen to anyone else. It still does, but at least I know that I'm doing something to lessen the chances. First there was school, then there was the internship, the papers I wanted to write for publication, and then it was working in a big firm handling my own patients and working part-time for the state doing evaluations. Once I got established, a couple of friends wanted to open their own practice, and they asked me to join them, so we started a partnership. The past few years have been spent trying to build our practice and make it a success."

She looked into his face and saw the question in his eyes and answered before he had a chance to ask it. "Oh, yes, there have been a few offers, but I wasn't in love with any of them. My work was always more important to me than any relationship. Maybe someday that will change, but for now, I still feel the same way. I love what I do, and I feel driven to do it. I know you probably don't understand, and that's okay. Mother doesn't understand it either."

"I do understand. I felt the same way about the Marine Corps. I loved it, but in the end, it wasn't good for me. I still miss it, and I miss all the guys, but we all have to move on," he said.

"Exactly, Dale. I have moved on." She sighed. "Now here you are asking me about a past life that was so long ago."

He leaned forward and let his head fall into his hands, almost as though he were defeated. "I'm sorry. I guess I was just hoping that you still felt the same way I did. I've always loved you. I know that now. I only married Sonja because it was the next step in the relationship and she wanted it. We both realize what a mistake it was now."

"I'm sorry, Dale. I really am. I had no idea you felt this way even back then. I guess I was a little miffed when you went chasing after that new girl in school, but I realized she was the new and exciting thing in school. It's what guys do. If it had been a new guy, I may have done the same thing. Who knows? The point is, what we had was a simple crush. We were just learning about relationships in order to grow. I can't help you with your wife for two reasons. First, I wouldn't because of what you have just told me. Second, ethically, I can't help you because of our past relationship, as well as being friends. This is something that you two need to figure out together. You have a lot of things to consider, like your children too."

"They are the only things keeping us together, I think," he replied.

"Maybe there is more there than you realize, and you have just never given it enough attention because you were holding out for something that was never really there to begin with," she said as she patted his shoulder in comfort.

"So how do I get over you?" he suddenly asked, looking longingly into her eyes.

"By realizing it was never more than a fantasy you have built up. If you had really loved me all those years ago, you would not have been so easily swayed by what's her name." She smiled.

He continued to stare at her. He didn't say anything, just raised his hand and gently brushed her long soft hair over her shoulder before raking his knuckles along her jawline. "It's going to be hell locked up in here with you," he whispered.

She didn't respond to him. She couldn't respond. What did one say to that? He was right; it was going to be hell being locked up in there with him and everyone else for however long it took for the CDC to clear them.

"I think I need that shower really bad now," he said as he jumped to his feet. His long strides had him swinging open the door and disappearing down the hall toward the locker room before she realized what he had said.

Chapter 47

Within the hour, the entire prison facility was a beehive of activity. SLED (South Carolina Law Enforcement) officers, CDC (Center for Disease Control), representatives from the South Carolina Attorney General's office, DHEC (South Carolina Department of Health and Environment Control), and agent's from the FBI had descended en masse. All the newcomers were fitted with hazmat suits until the source, if there even was one, was found. It was virtually impossible to tell who was who.

SLED was the investigating party because it was a South Carolina facility. DHEC was there as the responding state department for unknown illness and as the initiator of the quarantine. The CDC arrived at the request of DHEC and the state to help in identifying a possible contagion, especially since one law enforcement officer had died and three others were in the hospital. The FBI was there for two reasons—one because it involved a suspect that had committed murders in multiple states, namely one Canton Wayne Heirwick, and the second to support the prison officers in maintaining security of the prison. The attorney general's office was in attendance mainly, as far as Myra could tell, for the publicity fallout that was sure to follow.

Shortly after arriving, complete physical examinations had been performed on all the staff, including Myra. Blood samples, nasal swabs, and oral swabs had also been taken, labeled, and logged for review by DHEC's laboratory personnel, as far as Myra knew. Now officials were bringing inmates to the medical department to do the same to them. It was a major undertaking.

Needing a breath of fresh air, she had made her way to the foyer at one point, only to find it swamped with people in white suits and masks. Giving up the effort, she headed back to Dale's office. She needed something else to work on for a while. Reviewing tapes, transcribing Heirwick's story, and reading all his files had her feeling raw and nerves frayed. In the hall, just outside Dale's office, she heard Amelia, his secretary, fretting over something. Thinking she might be of help, she entered the secretary's office.

"I can't deal with this right now, Ellen. I have a situation I am dealing with here. And before you ask, no, I don't know when I will be available." She glanced up to see Myra in front of her desk. "I have to go now, Ellen. I have someone in my office. I have to go. Yes, I love you too. Bye!"

"I'm sorry. I didn't mean to intrude. I thought maybe you needed help with something," Myra apologized.

"Thank you so much for your timely entry!" Amelia was all smiles. "That was my sister. She's going through her third divorce. She is so whiney and needy, and I have trouble dealing with her on a normal day!"

"Well then, glad to be of assistance. It's so nice in here. No bodies!" Myra breathed deeply as she crossed to the window.

"I kicked them all out. Told them I couldn't hear the phone ringing." Amelia laughed.

"Oh dear!" Myra said.

"What's wrong?"

"The media has heard about our predicament. There are at least two news vans out there," Myra informed her as Amelia jumped from her desk and crowded at the window with Myra.

Amelia was several inches shorter than Myra and probably fifty pounds heavier and at least twenty years older. Amelia pushed her glasses into her hair as she studied the chaos of the parking lot.

"Good grief! It looks like there are just as many people outside as there are in here," Amelia exclaimed.

"It's turning into a circus around here. I hope they have all the inmates in lockdown. It would be so easy for one of them to just walk right out now," Myra muttered more to herself.

"Don't you worry. Dale has that under control. All the guards know what to do," Amelia soothed. "The extra security will definitely be a big help."

"I feel so useless." Myra slumped into the only other chair in Amelia's office.

"Are you kidding? Dale said it was you that discovered the connection with the detective and Officer Garrett. If you hadn't made that connection, none of this would be happening right now. Your attention to detail could potentially save a lot of lives here, and I, for one, am very thankful considering that I am one of them!"

"It was just a matter of time before someone made that connection."

"Maybe...but you found it first. That means a lot, dear. It means a lot to the family of Officer Garrett, and before this is over, I'm sure a lot more families will be added to that list."

Myra smiled at Amelia. "Thank you. No wonder Dale calls you his hidden treasure."

"Now, dear, I'm going to tell you what I tell Dale. Flattery will get you everywhere!" She laughed as the phone began to ring.

Several hours later, a frustrated Myra was reviewing her notes and videos of Canton Heirwick. The prison staff had done a medical evaluation on him immediately upon his arrival. Nothing alarming had been noted. Blood pressure, sugar levels, and blood tests were all within normal ranges. Even his cholesterol and triglycerides levels were great. Other than narcissism and his antisocial behaviors Myra had noted, and of course the psychopathy, she could not find anything wrong with him.

He had scored extremely high on the psychopathy checklist she had performed, and Dr. Hull had come to the same conclusion. Still, she had found nothing in the recordings she had made either. When an exhausted Dale walked into his office, she was reviewing arrest records again. She had just hung up with the police department, who was e-mailing her updated reports on the status of the individuals in his scrapbooks.

She looked up as Dale collapsed on the sofa. His face indicated the strain he was under, and the black circles under his eyes conveyed it had been days since he had last slept rather than hours. She remembered seeing pillows and blankets down the hall in a duty room next to the supply room, so she quietly left in search of them. Returning a couple of minutes later with both in her arms, she found Dale sleeping peacefully. She slipped the pillow beneath his head without waking him and covered him with the blanket before slipping back out of the office with her laptop. She quietly pulled the door closed behind her and taped a Do Not Disturb note on it.

Restless, she made her way to the psychologist's office to work, only to find that all of her equipment had been stashed on top of the filing cabinets, and the room was being used as an extra medical room. A guard had been napping in the duty room, which marked that one off the list. Amelia's phone was ringing off the hook from reporters and family members of the guards and prisoners seeking information, which ruled her office out as well. The only room that did not have wall-to-wall bodies, sleeping people, or ringing phones was the supply room. She asked Amelia if she could borrow her key so she wouldn't wake Dale.

The room had a stale and musty odor from being locked up. There was no window and only a four-bulb fluorescent overhead light. It was harsh but adequate. With the door shut, it was quiet, and the best part, no one else wanted to be there. She found a folding chair and an empty two-drawer filing cabinet which she used as a makeshift desk. It would do.

She clicked on the video file from the day before and heard her own voice state, "Day 3 of Canton Wayne Heirwick's life story narrative." It was depressing. Three days' worth of video files and still she was no closer to hearing about the current deaths or those scrapbooks. Today was the fourth day in a row she had been at the prison, but somehow it seemed like she had been here forever. She was on first-name basis with a few of the guards and felt like she was old friends with Amelia.

Then there was Dale. She would rather not think about Dale. That conversation earlier had rattled her more than she cared to admit. She had no feelings for him. She had not lied. She would treasure their friendship if he could offer that, but she felt part of his renewed interest in her was because he was unsatisfied with his home life. She could not and would not help him with that.

Marriage counseling was too sticky for her. She preferred working in abnormal psychology issues, which made up a good portion of the inmates in the country. She also liked working with traumatized patients. For her, those cases were easy to decipher. Dealing with marriage counseling involved hurt feelings, mistrust, affairs, and children caught in the middle of two parents using them as weapons against the other. Nope! It just wasn't her proverbial cup of tea.

She worked diligently for some time before eye strain forced her to take a break. She left her makeshift work space, locked the door behind her, and made her way to the small break room. Amelia was chatting with a guard sitting at a table in front of a window. Evening was beginning to set in as evidenced by the late afternoon sun casting shadows from the foliage outside.

"We have coffee, hot tea, iced tea, and sodas," Amelia announced. "Gee, you look as exhausted as Dale. Can I get you something?"

"A hot bubble bath, a bed, a stiff drink, and Tylenol, and not necessarily in that order." Myra grinned as she rubbed her temple.

"Well, we have a shower. That's the best I can do for a bubble bath. I have some Tylenol in my desk drawer, and I think Dale might have something stiff hidden away in his desk drawer." She smiled.

"We have cots in the duty room you can crash on, but I have to tell you they are not that comfortable," Mike Galloway, the guard, spoke up.

"Just give me some floor space and a pillow and I'll be fine!" She laughed as she fixed herself a cup of Earl Grey tea. At least someone had some good taste around here.

A ripple of laughter flowed over the other two. Cup of tea in hand, she crossed to the vending machines. A pack of mint gum was the only thing remaining. "The vultures have already emptied the machine. It was gone by three this afternoon," Mike said in disgust.

"I heard someone say food was going to be delivered again in a bit. Everything in the cafeteria is being sterilized so they can resume cooking again tomorrow. The food stores have been mostly cleared," Amelia informed them.

"I hope they get here soon. I missed out on the sandwiches they brought for lunch, so I'm starving," Mike grumbled.

"I have granola bars I keep in my vehicle," Myra told him. "I would tell you to help yourself, but I don't think they are going to let us out of here anytime soon so I could get them for you."

"Thanks for the offer, at least."

"Who is offering who what?" an unexpected deep voice spoke from the doorway, causing Myra to jump.

"We are starving in here. Dr. Christie has some granola bars in her vehicle if you want to jump ship and rescue us, boss," Mike announced.

Dale sauntered into the room. He still looked exhausted, and his hair was rumpled, practically standing on end. A quick glance at the vending machines explained what he suspected. He filled a cup with coffee that looked more like motor oil and took a seat at the table with them.

"Any idea how long this is going to last?" Amelia asked him.

"Well, I was talking to the head DHEC guy earlier. He said we could be in quarantine for up to a month or more."

"A month?" screeched Myra and Mike together. "I can't stay here for a month. I have clients that I need to attend to!" she cried.

"It could take up to two weeks, or even longer, just to figure out what kind of contagion they are dealing with. If not, then we might have to stay longer than a month. They are bringing up clothes, cots, pillows, etc. to make the stay a bit more tolerable. Until then, we better pray they figure it out fast." He sipped at his coffee, his eyes downcast.

"Well, I guess I better call my office and explain the situation," Myra stated as she stood up.

Dale followed her out of the break room, Amelia and Mike watched with interest. "Use my office," he murmured as he caught up with her.

"Thank you."

"Where have you been hiding? I've been looking for you."

"I set up a makeshift office in the supply room or storage room, whatever you call it," she replied as she made her way through the sea of bodies toward his office. He was at her back, too close to her back in her opinion.

"I told you to use my office," he growled in her ear.

"You were sleeping. I didn't want to wake you," she explained.

"You will work in here whether I am in here or not. Is that clear?" he warned as they entered his office and rather forcibly shut the door.

"But—" she started.

"I mean it. I don't want to have to worry about you."

"Worry about me? What on earth are you talking about? There are so many people here I can't walk without bumping into a half dozen at least!" She was getting irritated with his irrational behavior today.

"Exactly! Anything could happen." He splayed his hand out in gesture.

"You are being irrational and paranoid. I am not your responsibility. I work for the court, remember?" she all but spat.

"How could I forget? You keep reminding me every time we have a conversation." His sardonic reply told more than he wanted to say.

"Have you talked to your wife? Told her what was going on here?" she asked with narrowed eyes.

"No. I doubt she's home anyway." He walked to the window, turning his back to her.

"Call her now. I'm sure she has a cell phone. She needs to hear from you. Your boys need to hear from you. Do it right this minute." With that, she walked out the office with a decisive click of the door.

She was so irritated with Dale. In her need to escape him, she stomped out the office and straight into a pair of piercing blue eyes dressed in a white disposable jumpsuit with a white mask and clear face cover. "Pardon me! I am so sorry." She was instantly apologetic.

"You can bump inta me anytime, honey," a deep Southern drawl flirted, the deep blue eyes smiling. She couldn't help but smile back. "Ya going my way?"

"Which way would that be?" she asked sweetly.

"I heard food arrived," he drawled. "I'm investagatin'. I could use some help."

She laughed out loud. "Then lead the way. I'm all yours!"

"I just mite take that literally, ya know." He chuckled.

She didn't say anything, but she was having trouble holding back a smile. She walked with him toward the foyer. A line of guards was starting to develop, heading in the direction of the break room. White-suited people were filing out of the front doors. The smell of something delicious was wafting in the air, and her stomach grumbled.

"I guess this is where we part." She laughed.

"Only temporarily, I'm sure." He winked at her, the blue eyes intense and smiling.

Chapter 48

The next morning, Myra was up before dawn. She had slept fitfully on the sofa in Dale's office with Amelia on a cot beside her. The men were taking turns at sleeping in the duty room. She had no idea where everyone in the white suits were sleeping, but they seemed to be working in shifts, monitoring and testing everyone in the prison.

She quietly slipped out of the office and made her way to the break room where she indulged in a hot cup of tea loaded with sugar, something she rarely did unless she was excessively stressed. She sat quietly by herself, watching the first streaks of dawn touch the dark sky. She had to contact her office, Dr. Hull, and her mother about the situation. Hopefully, Clara would go by the hotel to collect her things and check out for her. No sense in paying for a hotel room for a business expense when she was going to be holed up in the prison for an undetermined amount of time.

It reminded her that she still had not heard from Dr. Hull or his secretary, Reno, though she had left messages for them both the day before. *I guess I'll just call Clara at the house*, she thought as she sipped her tea. A rustle behind her caught her attention, and she turned expecting to see one of the guards.

"Good mornin', beautiful. I brought ya some donuts." Blue eyes sparkled behind the mask and white suit. He sat several boxes of donuts down on a nearby table before bringing one over to her. "I got a variety."

Her heart skipped a beat, and she felt a slight blush creep up her neck. "I love donuts!" She smiled as she opened the box to view the array of confections. "It's been ages since I've had donuts." She smiled at him. She grabbed a glazed sticky one and sank her teeth in it with a moan of pure pleasure.

"I would've brought ya some yesterday if I'd known I'd get that response." He laughed, watching her chew in pleasure.

"Mmmmm…these are so good but so bad for the waistline," she said between bites.

"Trust me, there ain't nothin' wrong with yaw waistline," he commented, wagging his eyebrows flirtatiously.

"Ha ha… I bet you say that to all the women after you feed them donuts," she replied, amused at his charm.

"Yaw're the first, actually. I'm Bret Myers, by the way," he introduced himself, holding out a gloved hand.

The introduction was meant to be personal in nature, but it felt antiseptic to Myra. White suite, mask, gloves, and rubber boots made her feel like a leper or something. It was hard to describe. Perhaps some of it had to do with being locked up under quarantine. She could only imagine how maddening it was going to get, especially since she had only been under quarantine for just under twenty-four hours.

She took his hand. "Myra Christie. So what agency are you with here?"

"FBI, Dr. Christie. Yes, I know who ya are. Everyone was briefed on staff members when we arrived. It's an honor to meet ya. Yaw dad is a bit of a legend around Quantico."

"Thank you. He was a pretty great dad." She smiled.

"It must be pretty annoyin' being cooped up in here," he mused as he sat down beside her.

"You could say that. I was just thinking about how trying it's going to be here until we are released. I think I might know how an inmate feels when they first arrive in prison. Think you can spring me?" She gave him a wicked grin.

He reached out and patted her hand. "I would if I could, trust me! I'm sorry yaw're in this position. They're working very hard to find a resolution to yaw situation. I wish I could do more to help ya." His blue eyes were penetrating, and his Southern drawl was downright sexy.

Myra suddenly felt exposed. It was almost as though he had just made passionate love to her, and she checked herself. Already the quarantine was making her crazy, she thought. "You brought donuts! That makes you a hero today," she said brightly.

He guffawed. "Well, gee, ma'am, it weren't nothing special," he exaggerated his Southern drawl and tipped an imaginary cowboy hat, which had her laughing. "It's been fun talking with ya, but I have to go relieve one of the guards."

"What happens with the guards who would normally have been on duty?" she asked, stalling him.

"Anyone who works here that has been in the facility since Mr. Heirwick arrived is under quarantine. The one's who aren't in the facility have been quarantined in their homes, along with anyone else who resides with 'em," he explained.

"Have you ever been through anything like this before?"

"Nope. First time for me," he replied. "How about you?"

"The first and hopefully the last," she stated. "I would tell you to have a great day under normal circumstances, but considering, I guess I should just say good luck," she offered, splaying her hands in a helpless gesture.

"I'm already havin' a great day because I got to see *you* again." Those piercing blue eyes of his darkened as his gloved hands took one of hers, gently caressing it.

Her mind went blank under the intensity of his gaze. She stared back at him, lost in the dazzling color and her emotional response. *Damn gloves!* she thought. Neither of them said anything for what seemed like ages before sanity reasserted itself in her brain. "Um… I…um…well…" Remembering the half-eaten donut in her other hand, she expressed her gratitude. "Thanks again for the donuts." She literally grasped at the first coherent thought that ran through her head. "I'm sure everyone will appreciate them." She felt like she was blabbering and struggling to make complete sentences as he continued to caress her hand.

"Just as long as *you* do, my day is complete. I'll see ya in a few hours," he promised, dropping her hand. He strolled to the breakroom exit, turned, and winked one of those beautiful blue eyes at her, then disappeared through the door.

Her heart had jumped at his promise, and now she felt bereft in his absence. *What is wrong with me?* she asked herself. *I need some serious psychotherapy*, she thought. She rarely flirted with anyone, rarely even felt physically attracted to anyone, and suddenly here she was, wanton about a guy she didn't even know. *Pull yourself together, you idiot!* she mentally berated herself. *You are here to do a job!*

By nine in the morning, she had already called her mother and her office to explain her situation. She talked a few minutes to Nathan about her cases then asked to speak to Rhonda. When Rhonda got on the phone, Myra began by informing her she was not to tell Darrell any information about her whatsoever. She explained the situation at the hotel room, leaving out the sexual advances. A thoroughly chastised Rhonda apologized and promised not to reveal any additional information to him. They discussed Myra's upcoming calendar and made appropriate changes.

Just before they hung up, Rhonda once again apologized for her behavior. "I guess that explains why Darrell didn't show up yesterday," Rhonda commented.

"What do you mean he didn't show up yesterday? I thought there was a power outage and the office was closed for a couple of days." Something wasn't making sense to Myra.

"Well, yeah. Lightning struck the substation and knocked out power for several hours, but they were able to get it and running sometime in the night. We opened at regular time yesterday, but Darrell didn't show up. Stephanie and I both tried calling him, but he didn't answer."

"Has he arrived yet this morning?" Myra asked. She was already in the process of typing out an e-mail to Stephanie and Elaine about Darrell's behavior in the hotel room and the confrontation she had with him the previous week.

"Not yet. Do you want me to have him call you when he gets in?"

"No. Don't worry about it. Just take care of those things we discussed. I also sent you an e-mail last night with a list of things I need you to do for me. Now that we're under quarantine down here, I'm not sure when I'm going to be able to get back to the office."

"Don't worry. We have things under control here. I hope they figure out what's going on there quickly," Rhonda offered.

"Me too!" Myra said as she hung up. *Me too!*

Her next call was to Clara. She asked to speak to Dr. Hull and was told he was sick in bed. Myra was immediately concerned, but Clara assured her it was just his sinuses bothering him. "We go through this every year." Clara laughed off Myra's concern. "He has a runny nose, itchy eyes, sore throat, and a headache, but he acts like he's dying!" Clara snorted.

Myra told her about the quarantine at the prison, but Clara was already aware. She and Eugene had been put under quarantine as well. A member of the CDC and one from DHEC had stopped by their house, ran some tests on both Eugene and Clara, and taken blood samples.

Realizing that Clara was not going to be able to go by the hotel on her behalf, Myra told her she was sending an e-mail to Eugene. It was nothing urgent, just work related. Would she please have him check it when he was feeling better? They hung up moments later. For the next half hour, Myra was stuck trying to figure out who could stop by the hotel for her. With no one in the vicinity to do it, she finally put a call into Rhonda. Rhonda readily agreed, but it would have to wait until after working hours since they were shorthanded. Darrell had not shown up for work yet. She had no choice but to leave it up to Stephanie and Elaine to deal with Darrell.

She had taken a shower and redressed in her same clothes, as well as put on fresh coffee for everyone. What she really wanted to be doing was continue her interview with Mr. Heirwick. Impatiently, she sat at Dale's desk, going over all the information she had gathered so far, the nails of one hand tapping incessantly on the desk.

Invested in what she was doing, she didn't notice Dale watching her from the doorway until he cleared his throat, making her jump. He looked weary and longing. She knew it was not going to be easy on him having her stuck in the same building with him for days on end, but he was going to have to put his built-up feelings aside and deal with it. What he really needed was sleep. Lack of sleep was affecting his emotional capacity. He had been snippy the day before with a few people. It was only going to get worse if he didn't get caught up on his sleep. "Sorry I disturbed you." He walked farther into the room.

"I'm just trying to find something that ties everything together, but I'm not having any luck. Hopefully they find something in all the tests they've been doing." She stacked the files together and closed her laptop.

"You look exceptionally beautiful this morning. Maybe it's because you're at my desk." He dropped to the sofa.

"How are your wife and sons?" she asked.

"Don't know. Haven't even thought about her since you arrived."

"How do you feel about that?" she asked, staring at him until he dropped his eyes.

"I don't know. A little guilty maybe? I keep finding myself having daydreams about you at inappropriate times."

"Why do you think you feel guilty?"

"Are you trying to psychoanalyze me?" he asked, cocking his head.

"Just answer the question, Dale. Why do you think you feel guilty?"

"Hell, I don't know. Because I can't stop thinking about you. Because I want to spend every second of the day with you? Because I can't give her what she wants anymore?"

"What does she want that you can't give her?"

"I wish I knew." He ran a frustrated hand through his hair. They sat in silence for several seconds. "She wants someone who loves her and cherishes her."

"You don't love her or cherish her?"

"Okay, now I definitely know you're psychoanalyzing me! I don't know what I feel for her. I haven't known for a long time. I take care of her and provide for her and the kids, but I'm not emotionally invested anymore. I haven't been for a long time. Things were good before the kids were born, but then they came along and everything changed. She was always busy feeding, changing diapers, doing laundry, and whatever else they needed."

"Is it possible that you may be jealous of the time she spends with the twins?"

"I know they needed a lot of work, especially in the beginning. But they're older now, and it still hasn't reverted back to the way things were."

"No one can live in the past, Dale. Things change. It's just the way it is. She had a lot of responsibility taking care of two infants at the same time. Did you help her?"

"I did when I could. I worked a lot, and she resented that."

"Are you sure she resented you working or the fact that you had an escape from taking care of two infants? Perhaps she wanted to spend some time relaxing with adults?"

"She did. She had me. A couple of her friends would come over on occasion, and once or twice a year her parents would come to visit."

"You think an occasional friend and seeing your parents once or twice a year would be enough adult interaction for you if you were spending twenty-four hours a day taking care of two infants?" She raised a questioning eyebrow.

"Hey, she wanted to have kids. It was a mutual decision." He became defensive.

"Okay. Was it mutual amounts of care once the babies arrived?"

"Of course not! One of us had to work." He became defensive.

"So you don't consider taking care of two infants as work?"

"Hey, that's not what I meant!"

"But you implied it," Myra gently reminded him.

"You're putting words into my mouth!" he snapped. "I know she was busy. One of them was always crying. It got on my nerves, especially when they were both crying nonstop."

"I'm sure it got on her nerves too, Dale."

He stared at her. She could tell he was angry and was trying to keep his temper under control.

"I didn't say it didn't. Why are we talking about this anyway?" he barked.

"Because you said you couldn't give her what she needed. It sounds like she only needs a break once in a while. You said the boys were six years old now. When was the last time you took some time off and just spent it with your wife? Maybe go away for the weekend, just the two of you?"

"We haven't been able to do anything like that since before the boys were born. Why?"

"Did it ever occur to you that she needs a break? That she might need a vacation from being a mother?"

Dale stared at Myra like she had just sprouted horns. She could tell by his expression that it had never occurred to him that Sonja needed a break. After all, she was home all day having fun, right? He didn't consider feeding the kids, bathing the kids, washing the laundry, washing dishes, sweeping and mopping floors, grocery shopping, cooking meals, or looking after the boys as work. "I think you need to put more thought into what she does all day, Dale. Her life is not an easy one like you think. In fact, I would recommend that you either take over all the household responsibilities for a week and send her on a vacation with her girlfriends, or you take the boys to their grandparents for a week or two and you and your wife go on vacation."

"You're kidding, right?" he asked sarcastically.

"I'm serious, Dale. I think you might be surprised at the response from your wife and yourself. For now, though, I think you need some sleep. You are sleep-deprived, which is leaving you cranky and has your emotions flying all over the place. I'm going to take my stuff to the little hole-in-the-wall I made for myself." Impulsively, she asked, "Since we are all under quarantine anyway, can I finish my evaluation with Mr. Heirwick? I'm restless and need something to do while I'm here."

"I'll talk to the powers that be about it. Some of the other inmates need counseling as well. Normally, Dr. Kendrick would see them, but since he's locked out of here…" He leaned back and stared at the ceiling.

"What type of counseling are we talking about?" she asked.

"Well, we have a couple battling depression. They are on meds, but Dr. Kendrick works with them weekly. Dr. Kendrick also has a program going for substance abuse and another that forces violent offenders to think about their victims. I'm not sure what he calls it, but it seems to help a little," he explained, rubbing the stubble on his jaw.

"I'm going to need contact information for Dr. Kendrick so I can discuss the cases with him."

"Sure. Amelia has his number. I'll be right back," he responded as he disappeared through doorway.

A few minutes later, he reappeared with an announcement. "You will be talking to Inmate Heirwick within the hour. Amelia has put a call into Dr. Kendrick for you. Anything else?" he asked as he stretched out on the sofa.

"Thank you," she answered. She gathered her things and left the office.

Chapter 49

"I've missed you," Heirwick ground out sexily.

"Has anyone explained to you what is going on around here?" Myra asked.

"Sure. They think I'm sick with something and giving it to everyone else." He laughed.

"What do you think happened to those other men?" she asked, referring to the inmates.

"The question is, what do you think happened to them?" he retorted. "I know what happened. I would think that you would, too, by this point."

"Meaning you punished them somehow for something?" she questioned, playing his game.

"Ah, you *are* catching on, I see. Very good! I'm continually impressed by you," he rejoined.

"Perhaps you could go into more detail for me? I don't understand how you punish them," Myra invited. She really needed him to talk about it.

"I simply want it, and it happens. I ask my father in hell to punish them for me. That's what he does. He punishes people. He gets credit for all sorts of things, evil things, but in reality, all he really does is punish those who deserve it. The evil things, the chaos of the world, the disease and pestilence, it is a product of my brothers and sisters and I. Those are our missions for our father. He rewards us sometimes, especially when we meet someone who needs his punishment."

She waited for him to go on, but he simply watched her. "So you ask for people to get punished and you're…ah…father in hell punishes them for you by making them sick. Is that correct?"

"Yes."

"And what about you?" she asked.

"I don't understand. What about me?"

"You don't think what you do is wrong and deserves to be punished?" Myra looked him in the eye, waiting for his reply.

"I do my father's bidding. He asks and I do. It's as simple as that. One day, I will rejoin him in hell when he desires it, but until then, I do as he requests."

Myra was getting frustrated. This was getting the investigation nowhere. "So how exactly does your father make people sick when he punishes them?" she tried.

"I don't know what you mean. He just makes it so. He has special messengers who do that for him. You can't see them unless they are coming for you, you know," Heirwick explained.

"A special messenger?"

"Yes. Like the grim reaper," he offered.

"Ah! An invisible person touches them and makes them sick," she identified with him.

"No. It is not an invisible person. It is one of my father's messengers. They are sort of like angels that do his bidding like my brothers and sisters and I. If they touch you, you die. If they breathe on you, you become very ill. If Father wants you to suffer in your punishment before you go to hell to live with him through eternity, then they breathe on you. Suffering is a form of his torture."

"So everyone who is terminally ill and suffering is being punished by your father in hell?" she asked, trying to understand the degree of his delusion.

"Of course not! Some people are just ill with various diseases. The messengers' breath is special with no cure. The only way it can be stopped is if I ask for it." He was becoming frustrated with her. Myra watched the muscle in his jaw twitch as he clenched his teeth in an attempt to stay calm.

"So if you wanted the people in the hospital to get well, they would? Would it be instantaneously?" she asked him.

"More or less. I guess you want me to prove it," he drawled drily.

"Well, it would go a long way in understanding," she hedged, trying not to buy into his delusion but rather to see how far he would take it.

"Very well. Officer Garrett and Detective Wilson will wake up. I was really just angry with them anyway. For the most part, they are both reasonable and good guys, I suppose. But those inmates will die because they deserve it! They are evil men who made false claims by claiming to also be my father's children! They will die for that! I will not tolerate it!" His wrists were tied down, but he still managed to make a fist in anger.

"Okay. Please calm down, Mr. Heirwick. What about Officer Nickerson? Can you heal him too?" she asked.

"I could ask for it, but I won't. He is not the man he claims to be, and so he will be punished for it." He swiveled his head to see Officer Bret Myers leaning against the wall outside the office. The door was closed, so he could not hear what was being said, but still he kept a constant eye on them.

"What do you mean he is not the man he claims to be?"

"I'm tired of this subject. Why don't we discuss the rest of my story?"

Chapter 50

Day 4 of Canton Wayne Heirwick's narrative of his life

In my seventh life on earth, I was born in 1784 in Santo Domingo. I was the illegitimate son of a Spanish sea captain and his island whore. I never actually met him that I know of. He was just a sperm donor, as you call them. I believe they call them baby daddies and baby mommas these days, but it's still the same.

My mother worked in the tavern as a prostitute, so I was raised there among the ruffians. Rum and fortunes flowed freely, I guess you can say. It was a pirate's haven by the time I got big enough to be interesting to anyone. I took to the seas as a young lad catering to my captain. I guess it is only fitting that I was on a pirate ship.

That was the life back then. The Spanish ships toting silver and gold back to Spain from South America and Mexico were the prizes everyone wanted. I was around six or seven when I first received my position as a cabin boy. I remembered my time from my previous life as a pirate, and I was willing to do it again, but it was not to be.

The ship I was on was caught in a violent hurricane. It survived in tack, but just barely. Many of the crew had been washed overboard. It is for this reason that we were an easy mark for a Spanish gun boat. They took us with little resistance. While the remaining men were locked up and shackled below deck, the captain of the Spanish ship took pity on me.

He declared that I was much too young to understand the folly of my ways and that I should be taken with a firm hand. We sailed for Spain behind a treasure ship, affording her protection. Along the way, I was taught the manners of a gentleman by the officers of the ship while acting as cabin boy to earn my keep.

It didn't matter much to me. I showed them I was a quick study, but in truth I was more curious about my new assignment. Father had not whispered it to me as of yet. We talked frequently, but he did not share that information. Once we arrived in Spain, I was taken to the court to stand trial with the pirates, but the captain spoke for me. He explained that I had had no choice in the matter. I had more or less been sold into slavery with my birth among pirates.

He asked for my charge, and it was granted. My life had been saved while my last crew hung from the gallows. I learned the captain was not married and so would not be taking care of me himself. He wanted me to be properly schooled. He had great ideas for me. Two weeks after our arrival in Spain, we climbed into a carriage and ventured to the northeast to Navarre.

Today, Navarre is called Pamplona and is famous for the running of the bulls in early to mid-July. To the north of Navarre are mountains and the French border. Hordes of beech trees cover the mountains. Navarre is a valley of sorts dotted with groves of olive trees and vineyards. The outlying areas are farming country, but the town itself is built within walls. Once upon a time, it had been its own territory, but the Spanish had taken to ruling it at some point in history before I arrived in the area.

I had visited it once with my Quintrala, a long, long time ago, and it was with melancholy that I was there once again. The captain's cousin, Maria Marguerite Teresa de Tudela Villanueva, was the only child of Countess Orphia Maria la Catalonia de Tudela, who had married Fernando Rafael Villanueva, Duke of Navarre. They had no children. It is to them that the captain took me to be raised. To live among your memories and not be able to talk about them is a curse. Quintrala and I had spent a fortnight there so many years before. Everywhere I went, I was reminded of her.

The duke and duchess were nice, and their residence was near Palacio de los Reyes de Navarra de Olite or Palace of the Kings of Navarre of Olite. The duke hated his cousins. He said they were only after his wealth and power. For that, he decided to groom me to take his place one day and often we visited the royal family when they stayed at the palace. It was a new experience for me. Not living in a life of luxury or even of privilege but being an only child. I was doted upon, and I found I rather enjoyed it.

I tried hard to blend in, considering that my assignment had yet to be explained to me. All I knew for certain was that I was to be patient. My time would come. And come it did! King Charles IV was considered by some to be a weak leader. I believe his weakness led to the fall of Spain. You see, Spain had an alliance with France's Napoleon. Yes, Napoleon Bonaparte was the emperor of France at this time.

He was a brilliant man when it comes to setting traps and war. Our king had insulted Napoleon and lost his trust. It led to his downfall. Without getting into too much politics or a vast history lesson, basically the king's son, Ferdinand, forced his father to abdicate the thrown to him. Napoleon, in a stroke of genius, gained permission to go through the alliance to move troops through Spain on their trek south.

Not paying much attention to these troop movements, both Charles and his son failed to notice that Napoleon was actually building his forces in northern Spain. Because the troops had been allowed to move freely, they took Madrid and a few other townships with virtually no resistance.

Napoleon then asked Ferdinand to meet him for discussions, but when Ferdinand arrived, he was taken prisoner. Napoleon then sent a message to Charles IV asking to meet with them for diplomatic discussions. The king and queen arrived at the destination, only to be taken prisoners as well. The Palacio de los Reyes de Navarra de Olite was burned, and Navarre was taken by the French. The year was 1808, and I was now twenty-four years old.

It was now apparent to all the citizens that Spain had been taken without a fight and was now a territory of France. My time had come. I knew what my assignment was. I became a part of the Spanish Resistance. I fell back upon my generations of training in order to train others on the art of battle. We hit when and where we could, small scrimmages here and there. Our numbers grew slowly.

I was one of the leaders of the resistance and was looked upon with high regard for my fearlessness in battle. It had been a long time, but now I was thriving on the carnage once again. I was a hero again, just like that! Stories abounded about my courage and fierceness. I was a legend in the flesh!

My people of Navarre whispered among themselves, but the French were unkind to them. We had to free Navarre and run the French out. The problem was the walls. It was difficult to get inside the town due to the large number of French troops. We needed to attack in a way that would drive the French out and free our people at the same time.

By this time, my adopted parents were older and being watched constantly by the French. They had even taken over my parents' home and the palace as their own residences. This gave me an idea. Because it was my home from the time I was eight, I knew my way around there well. I stationed my men strategically to provide a blockade, preventing supplies from reaching the French soldiers.

It was at this point that I slipped in under the cover of darkness and set fire to the palace, destroying much of the French's stores at the same time. For four months, we waited, entering the occasional scrimmage, preventing supplies from reaching the French. On October 31, 1813, the French troops finally surrendered and left Navarre. I was a hero to the people, but my victory was short-lived.

I made the mistake of turning my back on the French soldiers as they exited the town, and one shot me in the back with a musket. I did not die immediately. Instead, I lingered while the wound festered. I lived with my adopted parents in our home once again, treated with respect and honor by our people until my death from infection in early 1814.

Chapter 51

Myra needed a break, and she motioned for Agent Myers to move Mr. Heirwick back to his cell. After he was removed, she removed the storage disk from the video recorder and made her way to her storage room office. She slipped the disk into her computer and downloaded the video file. Then she took the disk back to her recorder before she forgot to replace it.

Agent Myers found her a few minutes later at her makeshift desk, watching the first part of the interview of the morning. "Any luck?" he asked, grabbing another folding metal chair from a stack behind her, placing it beside her.

His strong Southern drawl made her want to melt. She hated the anonymity of those white suits and masks. She wanted to see all of him. to see if he was as good-looking as his eyes and voice implied. "Not much," she said in disgust.

"What did he tell ya?"

"That he wishes it upon them and it happens, basically. The man is a delusional narcissistic psychopath," she spat in frustration. "He is so aggravating! He continually skirts the issues that he knows I want to hear and insists on this nonsense storytelling!"

"It's okay. Don't worry so much about it. We'll get to the bottom of it." He gently rubbed her back in soothing circles.

"He said that he would ask his father in hell to remove the suffering from Officers Wilson and Garrett, whatever that means," she said sarcastically. "He won't tell me what they have been exposed to or how he did it. He said the inmates got what they deserved and they would all die. Just more of the same bullshit, basically!"

"Why don't ya take a break from this here stuff for a while? Ya've been workin' on this case nonstop, from what I hear. Ya need to rest. Come with me." He took her hand in his gloved one and led her to the break room.

The midday sun was streaming through the windows, and she could see the red and white azaleas in full bloom. She loved this time of year with everything in full bloom, and here she was, locked up in a prison under quarantine! Her mother had been most sympathetic the day before when she called and announced her plight. At least the media hounds would not be able to get to her while she was in here, her mother pointed out, trying to make the best of her daughter's situation.

Rhonda had actually laughed about it when she was told. Stephanie and Elaine had been concerned, and Nathan, who was covering her patients for her, however, had not found it so amusing. He could not handle all his patients and hers for long. The best idea was to make a cancellation here and there when Stephanie, Elaine, or James could not step in to help.

She resented being in this situation. She resented Heirwick's attitude. Dale was already on her last nerve, and it had only been two days! *Jeez*, she thought, *what's it going to be like after a couple weeks of being here?* As far as she was concerned, the only high point at the moment was the guy holding her hand and leading her to the break room.

She felt stranded and bereft amid the sea of people in the prison. It was difficult to feel optimistic. She sat down at a table near a window, propped her chin on her folded hands, and stared out at the parking lot beyond the colorful azaleas, watching people discuss the plight of those inside. It was depressing, she thought.

"Here." Agent Myers handed her a cup of hot tea.

"Thank you." She smiled. She took a sip and made an awful face.

"Too strong?" he asked.

"No, it's way too sweet! What did you do, add a little hot water and a tea bag to a cup of sugar?" She all but gagged.

He laughed. "No, I just made it like I drink mine. Well, almost like mine. I like mine in a glass with ice instead of hot. I noticed ya like yaws hot."

"You did, did you?" She cocked an eyebrow at him.

"I notice a lot of things, like ya needed a break. Ya got take more breaks in these types of situations." He waved his arm around to indicate the quarantine. "They are stressful by themselves. Add in a couple of hundred criminals of the most dangerous kind and a serial killer that needs evaluation and ya get the perfect storm for goin' crazy."

"I don't know about crazy, but it does resemble a circus." She laughed. She loved listening to him talk. His strong accent dragged out certain vowels.

He took the seat next to her. "I've read yaw dossier, but why don't ya tell me a little about yawself? What's not in the report," he invited.

"You have me at a disadvantage. You know all about me and I don't know anything about you," she challenged.

"Fair enough, I guess," he mused. "I grew up in San Antonio. I have three brothers. We drove my ma crazy, but she loves us anyway. My dad had been in the Air Force but was injured, so he got out and worked on Randolph Air Force base there as a civil service. My oldest brother, Jake, followed in our father's footsteps and joined the Air Force. Ben, my next oldest brother, decided to become a doctor. My twin brother, Lee, joined the FBI with me."

"You have a twin brother?"

"Yup! And before ya ask, yeah, we're identical."

"That's so cool. I'm surprised your parents didn't give you rhyming names."

"Actually, they did. We all have a biblical name from the Old Testament—Henry Jacob, Benjamin Daniel, Zechariah Lee, and Elijah Bret. Lee is two minutes older than I am, which makes me the baby. I use it to my advantage every chance I get too." He grinned. "But it's hard to do when yaw a twin." Myra could not see the grin because of the mask, but she saw his eyes crinkle with amusement.

"You're a man of opportunity, are you?" she posed.

"I guess ya could say that." He chuckled. "My ma would probably agree with ya. Hey, whatever works, right?"

She shook her head, laughing. She could just imagine the handful he had been to his mother growing up. "Tell me more."

"Lee and I have been in the FBI for ten years. We've done several assignments together, which really trips people up sometimes. We've done a couple of undercover assignments and were able to trip up international criminals because of the twin factor. Right now, Lee's in the field tryin' to track down information on the people in Heirwick's scrapbooks."

"So how did you pull this duty?" she asked.

"I was on another assignment 'til a few days ago. I was guardin' a witness in a federal case. The case ended earlier this week, and US marshals took custody of the witness for relocation. So here am I. My brother called me last night to gloat because I got stuck here. Then I told him about *you*, and now I get to gloat." His eyes were sparkling mischievously.

"Sounds like he got the better duty, if you ask me." She sipped on sweet tea. "Have they made any progress?"

"So far, they've confirmed twenty-seven victims. It was nice of him to keep notes and maps on where the bodies were buried. Sadly, everythin' has been accurate in Heirwick's scrapbook files. It makes it easier to find 'em and identify 'em. I'm afraid they will be working on this case for years though. Lee said they counted over a thousand driver's licenses and identification cards in those books."

"Over a thousand? I thought they said it was four or five hundred!" Myra was aghast.

"Originally, that's what they thought, but some of the older files have multiple victims in 'em. Looks like he went through a time of invadin' homes and killin' entire families."

"Holy crap! I can't believe he wasn't caught before now! I don't even know what to say… I hope he starts telling me something about that soon. So far, I have four days of narrative from him and still nothing about the victims. Normally, I would've been just about finished with my evaluation by now," she explained.

"Well, ya have plenty of time to pick him apart now. My boss and Warden Jones didn't want ya to continue yaw evaluation with all this going on. I pointed out that ya'd already been in close quarters with him for nearly a week and had not fallen ill as yet, so why not continue to see if he might tell us somethin' useful."

"Thank you for that. I've been getting a lot of opposition from Warden Jones since the problem with Officer Nickerson. I really appreciate your helping me out. I couldn't handle being in here without something to do. Warden Jones asked me earlier if I would consider working with the other inmates in their treatment programs and counseling since I was here. That ought to help with the boredom."

"Well, part of the deal was that I guard ya when yaw talking to inmates, especially Heirwick." He became serious, and his blue eyes were penetrating, almost as though he could look right into her soul. "Ya don't talk to anyone unless I'm outside that door, understand?"

"You mean Mr. Heirwick, right?" She was feeling like she was getting lost in his blue eyes.

"I mean any inmate from this prison, and that definitely includes him."

Lost in the depth of his intense blue eyes, she nodded in agreement. She didn't understand why it pertained to all inmates, but if it meant that she had something do, she would agree. At least it would keep Dale out of her hair. A commotion in the hall grabbed their attention. Several people in white hazmat suits were carrying platters of food into the break room. It was lunchtime.

Chapter 52

Day 4 continued of Canton Wayne Heirwick's narrative of his life

New Orleans is a beautiful city, don't you think? I absolutely enjoy that city. It's more of a melting pot than any I have visited over the centuries. I was born there on Valentine's Day, 1814, and immediately felt at home. The French influence combined with the Caribbean, Spanish, and Irish, among others, gives it an atmosphere like none other. Sprinkle in the American Southern charm and you have an illusion of peace, harmony, and lots of wealth.

Of course, it has changed much over the last couple hundred years. For one, virtually all traces of my earthly family of long ago have disappeared, save for a few street names and the family mausoleums in the cemetery. The only reminder of our existence is the legend of me. Before I explain my legendary existence, I first need to explain the family dynamics.

This life was my reward for being so contained in the last one. My father in hell gave me free reign during this one to do whatever I wanted. But even I knew I had to bide my time in this one. You see, my family was extremely well-known. My earthly mother was Celesté Baptiste St. Sauveur, daughter of Xavier Thebodeau St. Sauveur and his wife, Abelle. Her father, my grandfather, was an important man in France and had been well rewarded by the king to come to New Orleans.

He was awarded nearly two thousand acres between the Bayou St. John and the Bayou Tchoupitoulas along with the position of handling the king's financial interests there. My grandfather was the wealthiest man in the area, in all of Louisiana, as a matter of fact. He loaned so much money to others that he eventually opened the first financial institution in New Orleans, which brought him even more wealth.

He had a huge mansion built on the property which actually faced the intersection of both bayous with well-tended yards dotted with live oak trees draped in Spanish moss. A variety of flowers and shrubs bloomed nearly all year long in the vast gardens. Oh, how I enjoyed it this time of year. The sweet smell of the purple wisteria that clung to trees. The heavy scent of gardenias floating in the air. My favorite was the jasmine that grew up the rock boundary fence of our estate.

It was so beautiful and peaceful. I remember lying on the edge of the bricked pond he had filled with Japanese koi, watching the fish on a lazy day. The pond and gardens were filled with numerous statues. They actually lined the bowling green. Between the statues, our live oaks that lined the drive up to the property, and the massive gardens, those grounds were the most well-known and coveted in all of the South. Grandfather used to think it funny how many people tried to copy his taste. Of course, they were never able to manage his caliber because none were as wealthy.

The house itself was magnificent! Three stories painted all in white with large black hurricane shutters on every window. All three stories had wrap-around porches bedecked with gingerbread trim and scrollwork balusters. It was a sight to behold. The interior was even more delicious with parquet flooring in every room! Golden oak, cherry, walnut, and mahogany woods were cut into all types of geometric designs. Fireplaces in matching woods went straight up to the ceiling, decorated with shelving, scrollwork, and a playful use of mirrors.

My favorite room was the music room that was used for dancing during parties. Grandfather had sheets of mirrors placed cleverly on the walls that reflected the grand cut glass chandelier in the ceiling. When the candles were lit in the chandelier and the sconces, the room was blinding with so much light. Ah, to hear the ladies' heels clicking on the mahogany parquet floor of that room. A grand piano made entirely of ebony was in one corner, and a series of double doors opened onto the porch and led to a brick trail through the garden.

Grandfather also maintained a residence in the French Quarter for convenience that was very nice, but not as nice as the grand plantation home. It was also a large three-story house with porches on all sides, boasting beautiful gingerbread work. Even the cornices were decorated grandly. A beautiful wrought iron fence surrounded the property that took up a whole block by itself. Oak leaves with acorns stemming from double twisted trunks adorned each panel of the fencing. The gates were massive works of art that resembled the magnificent limbs of the great live oak trees of the region and had his initials intertwined in the motif.

Everything was grand where Grandfather was concerned. Even his coaches were grand. Everyone knew who he was simply by the coach and resplendent horses which pulled it. He had several different breeds of horses on the plantation, and all were the best of the best. Arabian, Quarters, Appaloosas, and Thoroughbreds. He had a variety of working horses for the plantation as well, but the ones I just listed were his favorites for display.

My earthly father, Pierré Delino Chalmet de Marceau, had great aspirations. He pursued my mother and won her hand, which joined the two most influential and wealthy families in all of Louisiana. I have heard it was the most lavish wedding New Orleans ever had, even by today's standards.

My father's father held a position in His Majesty's army and had been given a grant of land for his long service. The grant was a modest amount of acreage to the east and northeast of the French Quarter along the Mississippi River. My grandfather, Philippe Devereux de Marceau, made wise choices in crops for his many acres and soon bought out neighboring landholders to ultimately build a five-thousand-plus-acre plantation. It was a mighty and extraordinary feat considering he and his father before him had been military men, and not exposed to farming, as it were. He and my grandmother, Irene Gissell, had one of the largest mansions on the Mississippi River waterfront just a couple of miles outside New Orleans. It almost surpassed Grandfather St. Sauveur's home.

Despite both families having such large plantations, my parents decided to live in the French Quarter. They lived in Grandfather St. Sauveur's home so my father could work in the financial institution and handle his father's affairs in town. My father, you see, had studied law in France for a time before returning to New Orleans. It did not take him long to build immense wealth of his own. He opened a shipping business that transported all the goods in and out of the area. He also opened his own law practice that flourished handsomely.

I am, or rather was, the only living product of that union. My mother had several miscarriages and lost twin daughters and a son to illness while they were mere toddlers. I was the only one to survive. Unfortunate events occurred soon after, which also took a major toll on my mother's health, both physical and mental, when I was only four or five, when my mother's brother and only sibling, Dion, was killed in a duel. They had been extremely close.

That left me the only heir to my grandfather's great wealth. My mother had been so distraught over her brother's death and her own children that she refused to have any other children. It caused a great strain on my parents' marriage for a time. I was so young. They thought I didn't understand, but as you know, I am very wise from time.

My father's three siblings, Antione, Raphael, and Claudia Gisselle were much younger than he. Aunt Claudia was not much older than I. I believe they called her a change of life babe. My uncle Antione drowned as a teenager just after my birth, so I don't remember him. Uncle Raphael, however, was my favorite family member. We were kindred spirits in a way. No, before you ask, he was not one of my brothers from hell. He was just naughty and extremely mischievous. Uncle Raphael was in trouble so frequently that he was sent to France for proper training and schooling. I was around seven or eight when he left.

Regrettably, I never saw Uncle Raphael again. Apparently, he found a love for gambling and women in France. I hear he was in great debt, and grandfather refused to pay any longer. He also had a habit of getting caught in the beds of wealthy men's wives. Whether it was because he couldn't pay his debt quickly enough or that he was caught in the wrong bed, regardless, someone took care of him, permanently. My grandparents received a letter sometime later that his broken body had been found in the Seine. The family was devastated. They had not even been able to mourn the loss of their son and sibling, respectively. It was not lost on my father that he was the only male left to carry on the family name, and the burden would fall to me. I was the only one left to carry on the bloodlines of both my mother's family, save for Aunt Claudia who was not quite right in the head, and my father's as well.

I was a very congenial fellow and practiced it thoroughly. I made friends easily, was well respected, and trusted. Naturally, my family's wealth and influence played a part, I'm sure. I was indulged, perhaps overly so, by everyone on both sides of the family. The only grandchild any of my grandparents would ever see.

By my mid-teenage years, I had developed a plan of action for myself. I started by practicing on the poor and destitute Creoles around the town. Those of affluence didn't really care if any of those disappeared. My first endeavor was a prostitute Creole woman on her way to her shack after her evening's…um…work. I petitioned to partake of her services, which she readily agreed, her eyes sparkling over the few coins I held in my palm. We found a quite spot off Bourbon Street to do our business.

While she performed…um…a service for me, shall we say, I schemed. I don't really know why I did, but earlier on the way out of our villa, I had found a meat fork lying out on the buffet. One of the servants had failed to put it away. Somehow it had ended up in my hand as I exited our home. While the prostitute did her business, my fingers tightened about the handle of the fork in my jacket. As I climaxed, I thrust it in her neck.

I can't describe the pleasure that ensued while her eyes rolled back in her head in shock, and I was taken to new heights. It had been a long time since I felt that way. There are simply no words. I held her head in place as our bodies convulsed together. It was so erotic and intoxicating.

Her blood, as her life slowly ebbed away, I realized, had pumped like a spigot all over my hand. Not having a way to clean myself and to avoid possible exposure, I began to lick at the blood on my fingers. It was so warm and salty, a slight coppery or metal taste, and I discovered I rather enjoyed it. I even enjoyed it more than the human flesh I had consumed so long ago. She was delicious. Abruptly, I found my mouth attached to those two puncture wounds on her neck, drinking thirstily. I nearly drank her dry that night.

The commotion among the Creoles the next day when they found her lifeless, bloodless body on Bourbon Street was profound. Everyone was discussing the happening. That night after dinner in the study, my parents were even discussing it. Panic about a vampire in New Orleans was spreading like wildfire. After that, I was careful to hide the bodies and only attacked outside the French Quarter.

My next victim was a slave boy on Grandfather de Marceau's plantation. His body was never found because I threw it in the mighty Mississippi River after I drained him dry. I only attacked on occasion so as not to draw attention to myself. Some of the bodies were eventually discovered, and I had found the meat fork to be a very useful tool in my work.

As the panic spread in the area, I began to have a problem. Our villa was always locked up tight, and my earthly father had posted one of the slaves as a lookout during the night. It made sneaking out for a kill most inopportune. I needed a new plan. I was not particularly close to either of my parents. My father spent his life working, and Mother spent her life hiding in depression. At seventeen, I decided to end their suffering.

All of our family, meaning both my mother's and father's parents, including us and Aunt Claudia, had been invited to attend a party on a plantation up the river. We had to take a riverboat upriver and would be spending a few days there before journeying back down the river. I began to set my plan into motion.

Our arrival at the plantation was a huge event. We were treated like royalty and given the best rooms in the manor, which, compared to homes of both of my families, was adequate but quite lacking in adornment and size. It was a lovely ball, and I danced with many debutantes. I think my family thought I was shopping for a wife while there, and I did not want to disappoint their entertainment. It was early spring, and there was still a chill in the air in the evening. Our stay there was enjoyable yet fateful.

We left there several days later in the late afternoon. We boarded the riverboat laden with bales of cotton and several other passengers. I remember darkness came early that evening with an approaching storm, and the darkened skies prevented safe navigation down the river. Our captain anchored the boat for the evening till the storm passed, intending to get underway as soon as the clouds cleared and the waves settled down. Taking advantage, I made my way to the boilers.

It was a common knowledge that disasters sometimes befell these modern works of travel. I was just going to help this one along a little. The slaves running the boilers had taken a break, so I went to work rebuilding the fires in the three boilers. It didn't take long before the pressure was very great. I quickly went topside, strolling to the railing overlooking the side, enjoying an early evening cigar. A rumbling beneath my feet felt like the artillery shelling from war. Pandemonium broke out as the cotton quickly caught fire and guests were trying to escape their rooms. When the boilers had exploded, the lights of the vessel had also gone out, so the only light available was from the fire and the lightning of the quickly approaching storm. I slipped over the side and into the water as though I had been thrown by the explosion.

I remember calling out for help in pretense. A few others must have heard my cries and decided jumping might be their own salvation. The boat was sinking fast and listing to one side. Screams filled the air with panic and pain. In less than thirty minutes, the boat was gone and most of her passengers, including my parents and grandparents. Of course, my parents would not have survived regardless of whether the fire had been great or not. I had drunk my mother while my father played cards. When Father came back to the cabin early, I partook of him as well. The fire helped to conceal my misdeed. I was surprised all my grandparents had expired as well. Only about twenty of us struggled to shore and safety. At dawn, a passing boat heard our cries and picked us up.

Back in New Orleans, our story of horrific explosions and fire and hearing the screams and watching our loved ones die became news and spread all over the South and eventually to the North and west by way of other boats and newspapers. The town mourned my loss more so than me. I hid away for an ample amount of time as though in deep despair at having lost all my family in one final blow. I only exited late at night to drink various patrons, slaves from neighboring plantations, and Creole. I inherited the wealth and lands of both my grandfathers' plantations and my father's wealth and businesses. I was one of the wealthiest men in the world in a matter of minutes.

I was the new owner of two plantations consisting of over eight thousand acres, a bank, a large shipping company, and a law firm, not to mention two villas in the French Quarter, which I hated. Grandfather St. Sauveur had started a project of expanding New Orleans, which included the new Garden District, road constructions, and other neighborhoods in New Orleans. I immediately commissioned the building of a new home on Charles Street on the best and biggest lot. It would be the most magnificent house in New Orleans with luscious gardens.

I was now free and wealthy enough to do whatever I wanted. I stopped the slaves of guarding the premises at night and started hunting when I felt like it. I avoided, of course, from taking my own slaves and servants, and instead I focused on neighboring plantations and the vagrants in town. The Irish were beginning to flood the area, coming in poor and downtrodden. I hit a few of them as well.

For many years, I lived my life of wealth. I was a playboy enjoying his riches. I hired people to run my businesses for me. I didn't have to worry about anyone stealing from me. Once, a bank manager stole quite a large sum of money. I caught up with him in Texas on his way to California. I slaughtered his entire family in front of him before I slowly tortured him to death. I made sure word got back to New Orleans of his and his family's deaths and his stealing thousands of dollars from me. I left his brutal death hanging in the air with no proof that I had been involved. It was enough to deter anyone else from stealing from me.

I never married. Instead, I focused my attentions on my many women friends over the years. Everyone loved me. Women wanted me, and men wanted to be like me. Well, I have to confess that even a few men wanted me too. I frequently hosted lavish parties at all my houses, occasionally snacking on the blood of an attendant. Bodies would wind up in the river, bayous, and swamps, most never being found again.

A few years after my new home was completed, I decided to apply my own mark on New Orleans. I enlisted all those Irish to build my New Basin Canal from Lake Pontchartrain. It would open the area to more trade. Life was good for me. It became problematic, however, when yellow fever became rampant among my workers on the canal. We lost the Irish workers almost as fast they entered our city. Even worse was the fact that I had to curb my appetite. I didn't know who was infected, so I had to cease my unconventional toasting.

By the summer of 1860, my canal was complete. New Orleans was growing quickly by the thousands. Tensions, however, were beginning to build in the country, and the talk of war was spreading over the land like a great wind. As if we didn't have enough to worry about with the war, yellow fever was still rampant in the area, especially among the Irish citizens and other lower class.

I know this only too well because it led to my untimely death shortly thereafter. After going several months without a kill, I decided to dine upon a beautiful blond Irish maiden. Her husband had left her home alone while he worked a boat on the new canal. This was my misfortune as she had been stricken with yellow fever but exhibited no symptoms. Drinking the blood of sick victims is a painful way to die. Let me tell you! Those damn Irish, they got me again!

One wonderful thing about me survived though. I knew at once that her blood was tainted, and I left her where I killed her and drained her instead of using my energy to hide her. I made it home, but not before the discovery of her body. A new panic of vampires raged through the area as I lay dying in my bed. Even today, my legend of the vampire of New Orleans is known and celebrated, even if they do not know my identity.

Chapter 53

It was late by the time Heirwick had finished his vampire tale. At least, Myra thought, if he continued to stay with his timeline and storytelling, she would not have to listen too much more of his depravity. She was willing to grab at any blessing after being quarantined in this place! She locked the office behind Agent Myers and the prison guard as they escorted their quarry back to his cell for the night.

She stopped by Amelia's office and found the woman reading something on her computer screen. "I couldn't stand the boredom any longer." Amelia grinned when she saw Myra. "I downloaded a book to my computer to read. It's a good juicy love story, if you want to read it later."

"Thanks. If I have to listen to much more from Mr. Heirwick, I may have to take you up on that. I need a change of pace." Myra sank down in nearby chair.

"I fixed you a plate before all the food disappeared this evening. It's on top of the filing cabinet there." Amelia nodded.

"You are such a blessing! I'm starving," she said as she stood up to collect the paper plate and plastic utensils.

"I didn't know what you liked, so I grabbed a little of everything. You might want to warm it up in the microwave in the break room."

"That would take too long," Myra complained as she removed the paper napkin covering the food. There was a generous helping of fried okra, macaroni and cheese, green beans, baked chicken, and something else that Myra could not readily identify. She stabbed a piece of okra and moaned in delight as she chewed it. "Where did this come from?"

"Sapphire's Place down the road catered to us when they heard what was going on over here," Amelia explained.

"I love that woman!" Myra declared as she dug into the chicken. "Remind me to tell her, okay?"

"Sure. I have another surprise too, if you're interested."

"I don't know if I can handle two surprises today." Myra laughed. "Okay, share away. I can't stand the suspense," she begged.

"One of the ladies at DHEC took pity on us. She brought us some clothes and showering products. We guessed at your sizes, so I hope everything fits. I placed your bag of clothes in Dale's office. To protect our bathing products, I hid them in here from the guys. Bottom drawer of the filing cabinet." She giggled.

"Would it be improper to give that woman a hug?"

"I hope not. I gave her one from both of us. She said if we collect our dirty clothes and give them to her, she will have them cleaned for us. I gave her another hug for that too." She laughed with Myra. "Of course, they were air hugs. Even with that getup they're in, they are afraid to be around us."

"There's way too much fun a'gawin' on in here without me," a voice spoke from the doorway.

Myra almost choked on her food as she looked up into Agent Myers's blue eyes. She could tell he was smiling because his eyes were smiling at her.

"Well, by all means, come on in," Amelia invited. "The more the merrier, right, Dr. Christie?"

"I was a hopin' to talk to ya alone, Dr. Christie, but it can wait 'til yawr finished eatin'."

Myra stood and placed her plate back on top of the tall filing cabinet. "It's okay. I need to get something to drink anyway. Walk with me?" she asked.

They walked to the break room in mostly silence to find it occupied by a couple of guards. While she grabbed a drink, he waited in the doorway. Privacy was at a premium with so many people in the building at any given time. It gave her a new respect for her freedom and understanding of inmates suddenly finding themselves thrust into prison for whatever crime, never having any peace or privacy until they were released, if they were lucky enough to get paroled.

A bottle of water in hand, they walked back toward Dale's office. She realized it was off-limits as well when she found him on the phone. "How about the counseling office?" she asked Agent Myers with a smile. "I think it's going to be the only private place we can find."

"Well, I need to talk to ya and the warden, but since he's on the phone, I'll start with you. Lead the way to yawr domain," he said with a flourish of his hand.

A minute later, she was unlocking the door and turning on the lights. He took a seat where Heirwick typically sat, leaving her to sit in her usual place behind the desk. She closed the door and took her seat across from him.

"Ya look tired," he opened. "Ya need more rest."

"I think we all need more rest," she said, rubbing her itchy eyes.

"Yaw'r probably right about that," he agreed. "Listen, I wanted to talk to ya and the warden in private about somethin'. We're tryin' to keep it quiet fer the moment. I received a call from my associate at MUSC not long ago. He's head of the team providin' security for the guards and inmates in quarantine at the hospital."

"I didn't realize you had a team there. I guess I just assumed that since the inmates were unconscious when they left here, they were just being monitored by hospital security."

"Hospital security ain't qualified to guard inmates. I assigned a team there as soon as I was given the lead position over this. My team leader called me about thirty minutes ago to tell me dat both officers are awake. They don't remember nothin', but the hospital is still runnin' tests. We're not sure if they're out of danger yet."

"That's great news though! They are awake!" It was the best news she had heard in days.

"Yea, it is good news. He said the doctors are still bein' cautious. One of the inmates 'as died, however, and the other two are still in comas."

"Oh no! That's terrible. How does that affect us here?" she asked, more somber.

"We're still under quarantine 'til further notice. The hospital still has no idea wot we're dealin' with and neither does da CDC. DHEC and da CDC have taken blood, saliva, and urine samples from everyone here and have completed physicals. They've swabbed nearly all the surfaces and disinfected everythin', includin' da inmates," he explained.

"What about Mr. Heirwick's medical information? I know my associate, Dr. Hull, had requested a complete physical on him before all this started. Neither of us has seen a copy of the physical. I can't even find any medical information from before his arrest."

"I'll make sure ya get copies of everythang. I requested they start their search with 'em since everyone who 'as fallen ill was in direct contact with 'em, even the other inmates," he stated.

"The other inmates were in direct contact with him?" she asked, surprised.

"Yea. The warden said they all arrived in transfer here with 'im."

"Transferred? I thought he was the only one awaiting trial in here?" she asked, a bit confused.

"He is. One of 'um had been in the county jail and just received 'is sentence. The others were transfers from other facilities. I understand the one in county was transferred in the same vehicle with 'im. The others arrived separately but within minutes, so they were all processed together."

"The one that rode here with him, what is his status?" she asked.

"He's the one that died at the warden's feet," he replied

"Has an autopsy been competed yet?"

"Nothin' was out of the ordinary accordin' to the reports. Labs haven't returned yet. The pathologist said it could take a few weeks to get those results back."

"So essentially, we are still at square one," she brooded.

"For the time bein', I'm afraid. Even with a rush on everythang, it still takes time for da cultures to develop and testin' of everythang." He placed his gloved hand on hers.

Myra bowed her head in an attempt to hide the tears of frustration that had unexpectedly pooled in her eyes. She blinked rapidly, hoping they would vanish before falling. After a minute, feeling a bit more composed, she raised her head and unexpectedly met his intense gaze.

"I'm concerned about ya," he said simply. She could see it in his eyes without his forming it into words.

"I'm fine. I feel fine," she corrected.

"Ya look exhausted. I spoke with da warden. He told me what ya did for 'em and Mrs. Garrett at da first hospital and then what ya did for all the families at MUSC when all this started. I know ya haven't been sleepin', cuz I can see it in yawr face, in yawr eyes."

"I said I was fine," she said flatly as she pulled her hand from beneath his and placed it in her lap.

"These people need ya in here. I'm not just talkin' about the inmates. I'm also talkin' about the staff. It's their own people in those hospitals, and they need to talk to relieve some stress and anxiety about it. If yaw'r not well rested, ya won't be of much help to anyone," he reminded her.

"Don't you think I know that? That's why I'm trying to get this evaluation out of the way so I can focus on the rest." She jumped up to pace to the door and back.

"Did ya sleep at all last night?" he asked, watching her.

"Yes, a little… I guess I got about three hours. That sofa in there is not the most comfortable thing, and I doubt those cots are much better."

"I can understand that. I know it's challengin'. Is there anything I can get ya to help ya rest better?" he asked.

"Sure! How about my bed from home with my favorite quilt and pillow? While you're at it, a nice bottle of wine and some candles would also help with the relaxation," she snapped sarcastically.

"I don't know if I can pull the whole bed thing off, and I know the candles are a definite no, but I'll see what I can do about the wine." He smiled.

"I'm sorry. It's not your fault, and I didn't mean to take it out on you. You're right, I am tired and frustrated. I'll take a shower before bed tonight and see if that helps. It's just a transitional period, I'm sure," she apologized.

"I'm not so thin-skinned that I can't see frustration and exhaustion," he said. "I should also tell ya that I've spoken with Dr. and Mrs. Hull. As I understand it, yaw'r like family to 'em." He didn't share with her that Mrs. Hull threatened to castrate him, should anything befall Myra while she was stuck in the prison.

"Yes. I know he's been a little under the weather. How is he doing?"

"We got 'em checked out. Looks as though he only has a really bad sinus infection. He'll be okay. What I'm concerned about is that Y're not sleepin' well before all this happened. His wife told me about yawr stalker." He held up a hand to stop the tirade he knew was forthcoming from her. "She's concerned about ya. I contacted yawr office and the detective handlin' yawr case, and it looks like there's no real strong leads yet."

"No, there hasn't been. Recently, he has begun calling both my house and cell phone. I just wish I knew who it was."

"I didn't know about the cell phone calls. When was the last time ya heard from 'im?"

"Just before I wound up stuck in here. He hasn't done anything to hurt me. He just keeps leaving me creepy love letters, flowers, and now phone calls."

"Do ya mind if I have yawr cell phone monitored? I can have my guys monitor it for incomin' calls. If he calls, we can trace 'im and hopefully catch 'im."

"That would be great! What do I have to do?"

"I'll get a consent form for ya to sign. We'll take it from there. Now let's get some food into ya and get ya into bed." He opened the door and followed her out.

She made her way back to Amelia's office and picked up her plate. Amelia was not in there, and Myra realized she missed her. She enjoyed the female companionship in a building nearly full of men. She didn't feel very hungry any longer, but she forced herself to eat at least half of it. After eating all she could muster, she headed to the break room to dispose of the plate and met Amelia coming fresh from the shower in red silk pajamas.

"Nice!" Myra whistled.

Amelia did a pirouette and fluffed her still damp hair with one hand before bursting out laughing. "I feel almost human again!"

"Leave the goodies out. I'm going to throw this away and then jump into a nice hot shower too!"

"Okay. Meet me in my office." She did a little wave, and Myra made a beeline to the garbage can.

Amelia was rooting about in a large shopping bag when Myra walked in a minute later. "Shampoo, conditioner, and other essentials are in that basket on my desk." Amelia pointed out, continuing her search. "Ah, here they are!" she exclaimed, pulling out fluffy plush slippers and placing them on top of something in her chair that was hidden from Myra's view. She looked up at Myra with twinkling eyes of excitement.

"What?" Myra frowned.

Amelia picked up the items from her chair and placed them on her desk for Myra. "These are yours." She smiled, showing even white teeth.

On the stack were the blue plush slippers, a new toothbrush, new silk and lace underwear, white satin pajamas, and a soft blue towel. "Oh my! It's like Christmas!" Myra exclaimed as she ran a hand over the items.

Amelia was laughing. "I know! I feel the same way. How pathetic is it that we are so excited over new underwear and pajamas?"

"I'm not even going to analyze that one." Myra laughed. "If I'm not back in thirty minutes, you might want to check on me. I may put these on right after my shower and instantly fall asleep!" Myra gathered everything into her arms with the basket of bathing items and headed for the locker room. She locked the door behind her before turning and catching a glimpse of herself in the mirror. She stared at the stranger looking back at her. There were dark circles under unusually hollowed and tired eyes. Her face was bare of all makeup, and her blond hair hung limply at her shoulders. Even her clothes looked tired and disheveled.

No wonder Agent Myers was concerned about her welfare, she thought. She looked awful. She turned the shower on, undressed, and stepped under the hot stinging spray of the shower, washing as much of her troubles and exhaustion down the drain as possible.

Chapter 54

Day 5 of Canton Wayne Heirwick's narrative of his life

My next life is perhaps the most notorious of all. I say notorious because I received worldwide fame for the first time, thanks to a growing world population and media. Yes, the media made me famous. I was born to a surly woman in 1860 Massachusetts. I do not quite remember my earthly father because he left when I was very young, just an infant really. I heard later that he was killed in the great American Civil War.

I have to admit that my mother may have been even more short-tempered because I was quite the handful. It was not easy for a woman to be the sole financial supporter for a family in those days. With the war breaking out, everything once again in chaos, the women had to do much more than they were accustomed, regardless of community position or standing. My mother most likely had it worse than many as we were destitute prior to the war.

She worked long hours to provide for us, even before my earthly father perished. Fortunately, this gave me all the free time I needed to hone my skills in my new body. I started by practicing on animals—the occasional cat I was able to catch, the rat or mouse I trapped, the dog I coaxed with scraps of food. By the time I was twelve, I was extremely adept at manipulation and pain. I was even more fortunate that we lived in a large town, which gave me anonymity.

A young boy of twelve, you see, is just beginning to awaken into a man. My…um…sexual urges, if you will, were beginning to stir. Not ever being one to put them off, I acted on them. My first was a prostitute that I manipulated after catching her stealing. She educated my young body to the ways of the world. It had been a while, you know. Twelve years of celibacy sucks! I wanted more, much more, but in my position in life at the time, I was unable to acquire the means necessary for such endeavors.

Therefore, I made my own destiny. I manipulated girls my own age and younger to provide sexual favors for me. If they refused, well…pain has a way of motivating people, I have found. Everything was fine until a couple of little girls had second thoughts afterward—attack of the conscience, I suppose. There was this do-gooder boy on our street, Jesse Pomeroy, a real obnoxious loser always hanging on his momma's tit. He was always telling on all the other kids, so with a little pain, the girls told their mothers he was the culprit who took away their virginity at such a tender age instead of me.

It follows that I had to either curtail my…um…activities or find another way. For a while, I curtailed them as best I could. At a time where such devastation has been brought upon a country as happens in war, commerce was beginning to thrive. A shortage of able-bodied men meant young boys like me were likely to find occupations. I realized quickly that with so many injured and dying men from the war, and so many getting injured in other businesses, the medical field needed help.

As I obviously have no qualms with blood or indelicate sights, should I say? I volunteered to assist a local doctor who also did autopsies when the need arose. He instructed me in the ways of medicine and surgery. I was most gifted, and he secured me a post in medical school. I earned my degree and was ready to make my mark. I worked in a hospital for a couple of years, honing my new craft.

Sometimes I have to confess, I got a little carried away and did the unthinkable in the medical field. I actually killed my patients on purpose. I tried not to do it too often for fear of hospital staff noticing. In my spare time, I did autopsies. Still, they were not as much fun as working on live bodies. Before anyone could catch on to my secret activities, I decided to move on to another position. I missed traveling, so I took a position as a ship's doctor. What better way to fulfill my objective than on a vessel that travels the world, I ask you?

Pay close attention now because this is where I become famous! Our first stop was in England. London, England to be exact. Do you remember what happened there in 1888? What better place to start my activities? I decided to practice on prostitutes. Due to my being a traveler, I had no place of business or residence in which to do my business, so I simply practiced in the streets. The streets were quiet at night, and the frequent fog gave me the cover I needed.

The highly publicized story of my actions should make it obvious. They dubbed me Jack the Ripper! Can you believe it? Me! Though I have no idea where the name Jack came from in all this. Still, I did not get the credit I so richly deserved in spite of the fame. They only credited me with five kills. There were many more. The problem was that they were only looking in Whitechapel. You see, I killed another unfortunate soul, another prostitute, but I did spread it out over a few years.

I was traveling, mind you, on a ship that sails the world. I enjoyed my craft in every port we visited. What better way to hide and avoid being caught? A few days here, a couple of months there, time passes so quickly! I had to make the most of my time.

I butchered six female prostitutes in Managua, Nicaragua, which earned me the title of the Managua Ripper in January of 1889. Then we traveled to Germany, where I only had time to take in the sights on one victim. Such is the pity. There may have been a few others scattered about, mostly on islands, but they were of no importance. None of them were really, but the news hounds ate it up. I sold more papers around the world than anyone, even published authors at that time. How about that!

What strikes me the most, even to this day, is that normally the upper echelons of society could care less about prostitutes and vagrants. They treat them like roaches beneath their feet. They are, to those upper-class societies, barely more than the rats that roam the sewers. They are a drain on society that litters the streets with waste.

As you know, I was back in London by 1891 and up to my old tricks. What you don't know is that there was more, many more, during this time for which I did not get credit. Frederick Bailey Deeming, the stupid bloke, got credit for the rest. He was new to my ship and had been listening to idle gossip on board our vessel. In London, instead of going to visit his beautiful wife and four darling brats in Rainhill, he followed me instead. He witnessed my work on one of the simple prostitutes and threatened to go to the authorities.

He watched me as I bartered with her for services outside the bar. He spied from the shadows as I leaned over her, slitting her throat before she had a chance to scream. He cowered in the dark as I carved her open and removed her entrails. And then he watched me run as I was interrupted in my work. The recreant actually tried blackmailing back on the ship!

We were in port for several days, and he had family in the area, like I said. You would have thought he might be concerned with their welfare after what he had just witnessed, or at least his own. The stupid half-wit never saw it coming. The next day, I slipped off the boat in early morning while the fog was still thick and made my way to Rainhill.

I posed as an injured traveler in great need of help to gain access to his home via his wife at daybreak. The buffoon was still in bed, sleeping off his liquor. I gave his wife some money for medical supplies and sent her shopping. It was so easy tying him up and gagging him. While he lay in his bed, I slaughtered his children in front of him, one by one. They were too terrified to even scream.

I was waiting behind the door when his wife returned and immediately bound and gagged her as well. I couldn't very well have her screaming and alerting the neighbors. Dragging her in the bedroom through her children's blood was so satisfying. The horror on both their pale faces was pleasing as I made them look at the mangled bodies of the children.

I couldn't just stop there, though. He was going to pay for hiding and watching in the dark. I wanted him to see what I was capable of in the daylight. He wanted to watch me in the shadows, well, he was going to watch me in light. He was going to see everything very closely this time. I threw his wife across the bed. She fell over his bound legs. I ripped her clothing off her before I mounted and raped her, still lying across him. When I was finished gratifying myself, I slit her from vagina to throat and gutted her, right there in the bed with him. For good measure and pleasure, I took his hand, placed the knife in it, and sliced her throat. It was a really sharp knife and easily sliced right down to the bone.

I slowly untied his petrified body and dared him to make a sound. He thought I was going to kill him next, but I had better plans. It still amazes me at how clever I was in this instance. Since I had killed in the nude, it was relatively easy to clean myself. I bathed on the kitchen table, keeping a watchful eye on him as he cowered in his bed, weeping like a babe.

I dressed and quietly slipped out of the house. Making my way to the nearest constable, I immediately gave this fantastic account of hearing what sounded like a woman and children screaming for their lives while passing his house. Later, I heard that by the time the constable arrived, Frederick had already fled the home. It was a sensational story, and everyone aboard the ship was questioned as to his whereabouts.

We did not see him again before we left London. It wouldn't be long, however, before he crossed my path again. Alas, sometime later, my ship sailed for Australia, eventually arriving in Melbourne. There he was sporting a new wife under a different name, but I saw the fear in his eyes when he recognized me as we passed on the street. Just to make sure he had learned his lesson, I butchered her too and left her in his bed.

I heard later, according to the papers, that the authorities found her buried under the floorboards of their guest bedroom in his rental house. Essentially, he was named, found, and executed. I'm sure it didn't help his case any at trial when they received word that his first wife and four children had been murdered as well. The ass got what he deserved. He should have minded his own business!

I traveled a while longer on the ship, but growing tired of the sea life, I resigned my position in a French port. I wanted to visit my old homestead of so long ago. I traveled all along the southeast area of France, from Normandy to Provence, reminiscing my time there with Quintrala. I got so caught up in my recollections that before I knew it, I had already killed and butchered a woman and ten teenagers—five boys and five girls.

A privileged gentleman like myself, and a doctor no less, I was not even suspected. I was called to investigate one of the murders when I had a layover in one town and the resident doctor was under the weather. I was happy to oblige. It was so much fun getting to play with my kill all over again, and this time they wanted me to do it. Can you believe that?

Some poor mentally unstable creature that had already attempted suicide a number of times was credited with the killings and eventually guillotined, so I heard. A pity such an innocent like him already living his own private hell was condemned by people more interested in their own politics and reputation than actually solving the crime. Don't worry. I know they are with my father in hell now. It's a bit crowded there these days.

So there you have it! My life as a celebrity of sorts! I'm still in awe that I was world-renowned and they still write books about me every day—well, at least about my glorious actions. People act horrified by what I do, but secretly they are fascinated, you know. Why else are there so many shows, books, and movies about murder and mayhem?

Why are there so many professions like your own seeking to investigate and understand us? Yes, there are some that are true serial killers, but you should be able to see by now that I do not have one specific type. Moreover, I was sent here to do this job. I am an angel of hell, the maker of Death, not a serial killer. I help people find their destiny.

Those poor souls, the prostitutes in London, their lives were meager at best. I made them stars of the world. People hardly glanced in their direction, had never heard their names, and definitely turned their noses up at them while they were alive. But in death, well, now you see, suitably those same people mourned their death. They prayed for their souls. They blessed their hearts and made excuses for their livelihoods. Those poor women were merely circumstances of society, but after I got through with them, well, they were famous!

Chapter 55

Myra had grabbed a breakfast sandwich from a pile that someone had so generously provided early that morning before she started her day and a box of orange juice, but it was afternoon now. Breakfast had been worn off long ago, and her stomach rumbled just as she met Amelia coming out of her office.

"You were up and at it early this morning," Amelia noted.

"Yes, but for once I actually felt somewhat rested. I don't know if it was the relaxing shower or the silk pajamas." She smiled as they made their way to the break room for lunch.

"I know exactly what you mean." She nodded and took in Myra's appearance. "Looks like we guessed your sizes pretty close."

"You did a fantastic job! I was surprised when I tried them on this morning and they fit perfectly." She leaned toward Amelia and said in a conspiratorial tone, "After wearing the same clothes for several days, I would have worn anything that was sent in for us."

"Well, I simply told her to think tall and extremely underfed."

"I am not underfed!" Myra defended herself. "I have always had an athletic build and a fast metabolism."

"Oh, how I wish they could bottle that!" Amelia muttered, patting her backside. "I've discovered I can't diet."

"Why is that?" Myra looked quizzical.

"I love food too much!" Amelia answered.

They both stopped laughing when they walked into the break room and discovered the last laugh was on them. A salad bar had been set up. The first day she could have eagerly eaten two or three burgers in one sitting was the day a healthy menu was on the table.

"Why do we eat in here instead of the cafeteria where the inmates are eating?" Myra asked one of the guards she hadn't met who was filling his own plate behind her.

"No one is eating in the cafeteria. The Red Cross and local restaurants are providing food for us. Individual box meals of what we are eating is being provided to the inmates in their cells."

"I didn't realize that, but it makes sense." Piling her plate as high as she dared before worrying about spillage, she wandered to Dale's office. It was empty, so she sat at his desk, responding to her e-mails on her laptop. Mostly they were mundane things from work and few messages from friends and family checking on her plight. Closing her laptop, she studied the whiteboards she had set up.

Someone had updated the notes on Detective Wilson's and Officer Garrett's status. She also noted that one of the other inmates had passed away during the night. There was no change on Officer Nickerson's status. The only good thing she noted was that no further cases had been added to the boards. Whatever it was that had caused the illnesses she hoped had run its course.

With her salad finished, she caught herself staring out the window. The sun was shining, and the lush grass of the open areas was dark green and badly in need of cutting. Pangs of frustration and irritation at the quarantine cut through her. It would have made everything seem a bit more bearable, she thought, if it were pouring rain every day. She marveled at the irony that humans don't always appreciate things until they are taken away.

Instead of dictating the morning session with Heirwick to written form for her files, she propped her feet upon the edge of the desk, leaning back in the chair. Closing her eyes, she forced herself to relax using breathing techniques and imagery. She could feel the tension leaving her muscles.

She almost drifted to sleep when a slow Texas drawl brought her out of her reverie. "Well now, I'm glad to see ya relaxin' for a change. I thought I was gonna have to tie ya down somewhere and force ya." The blue eyes were smiling at her as their owner sat down in the chair across from the desk.

"Very funny." She stuck her tongue out at him in a childish fashion. "I think that hot shower helped tremendously last night. The lady that brought those clothes, pajamas, and showering essentials in is my hero."

"Hmmmm…well if that's all it takes to impress ya, just tell me yawr sizes and I'll go shoppin' rite now. Would a lacey teddy be out of the question as appropriate apparel in here rite now?" he asked, his Southern accent lending an appeal of sexiness that took her breath away.

"You're just a barrel of laughs today, aren't you? It's not nice to tease, you know." Myra was surprised to find herself flirting back.

"Who said I was teasin'? I'm still thinkin' about tyin' ya down. Just can't get that image out of my mind." He winked at her.

Myra could feel the heat creeping up her neck. It wasn't fair that he could see all her emotions and she was confined to his eyes only. Sexual tension was thick in the air, and her body was responding. "I guess they don't teach about sexual harassment at the FBI," she replied drily.

"Sure, they do, but it's mostly on how to avoid gettin' caught," he deadpanned. "Besides, I thought it was only sexual harassment if one of the parties didn't appreciate it."

"That's not quite how it works." She tried to give him a stern professional look but ended up laughing. "That sounds like a commercial slogan I think I've heard."

"I'll forgive ya. I know my charm has a tendency to affect a damsel's cognitive skills on a frequent basis," he bragged.

"Too bad I'm not one of those damsels then, isn't it?" She couldn't help snickering.

"We could work on that, ya know." He was laughing. "I'm going to go relieve the warden so he can get some rest. Did ya want to see Heirwick again today or start on the other inmates?"

"I think I'll talk with him a while, but I'm going to cut it short so I can get in one of the other inmates this afternoon. Is that all right with you?" she asked.

"Sure. Give me about an hour for turnover and then I'll bring him into yaw office." He winked then disappeared down the hallway.

She had enjoyed their lighthearted sexual joking even though it technically wasn't appropriate in the workplace. She felt drawn to him.

It was easy to get lost looking into his eyes. They were almost a neon blue color—so intense. She had never seen eyes that color before. She wondered if he wore contact lenses. And that Southern drawl of his. It just sucked her right in. She couldn't wait to see the rest of his face. She sighed. She wouldn't mind seeing the rest of his body.

Chapter 56

"Are you enjoying my life story?" Heirwick looked across the desk from his confinement chair and licked his lips seductively.

The gesture made Myra's stomach churn with disgust. "Not particularly. I'm interested in when you are going to stop this charade and start talking to me about those boxes you had in your truck."

"Not yet, my dear. You promised to hear my life story first. It is an interesting life story, don't you think?" he asked.

"You know your history, and you did a great job of matching up the dates of events. Beyond that, I think I'll withhold my analysis until we are finished with everything, including the psychometric testing Dr. Hull will be performing in the near future."

"I think I would prefer you do them. In fact, I insist. I won't work with Dr. Hull. It's you who will do the complete evaluation of me, Myra, or no one does it," he insisted.

"I'm afraid it doesn't work that way, Mr. Heirwick. The court requests evaluations, and the Department of Mental Health assigns a psychologist or psychiatrist to perform them for the court," she explained patiently.

"I'm well aware of how the system works, Myra. What I'm telling you is that I will not cooperate with anyone other than you."

"You will only be hurting your own case," she continued to try and explain.

"I'm sure the judge and the Department of Mental Health will conform to my request. In the meantime, shall we continue?" he asked.

"Please do," she invited despite not wanting to hear another word of his vile narrative. She was not allowed to ask any questions during his narrative or he refused to continue. She pulled out her notepad and gestured for him to continue.

*****

Day 5 continued of Canton Wayne Heirwick's narrative of his life

I am so happy you are enjoying the story of my life! There is so much more I need to tell you! So much more you need to understand.

My real father wanted me to see the Orient, you see. He wanted me to get a real taste of it for myself. So he took my life himself this time. I don't really know how he did it as he rarely travels to the earthly realm, but suddenly here I was being born in northern Japan in the year 1898.

Have you ever been to the Orient? It has an allure all on its own. I was born in early spring, just before the cherry trees blossomed. What a sight that is to behold! Pink and white blooms floating on the air everywhere, swirling in the wind like a colorful tornado, almost like pink and white snow.

I was the only boy with one older sister and three younger sisters. It was a great disappointment for my parents that with so many children and I, the only male child. Males were a source of pride and virility, someone to carry on the family name and bring honor to the family. Alas, my father ultimately felt he was disappointed in this area too. Disillusioned. Humiliated. Disgraced. Perhaps he was.

My sexual desires were strong in this body. Stronger than ever before, perhaps, or maybe because I had not focused on that in the previous life, who knows? By the age of ten, I was experimenting with my younger sisters. Mostly just fondling, you understand, at least in the beginning. I coaxed them into playing show and tell when our parents were not around. Soon I had them performing oral sex on me. Of course, I had to threaten them with the killing of our parents first.

I can tell you there is nothing like a sweet child's mouth. Before long, I was becoming more brazen. They were my built-in sexual objects. I took advantage of every moment we had alone. It was not enough. As the year passed, I secretly began watching my earthly parents during the night. I learned new moves, new positions.

I could not wait to try them out. Unfortunately, my younger sisters, I found, were too small for some of the positions. That left only my older sister, who I had not touched up to this point. She was mother's favorite, and to tarnish her risked her tattling to mother. I watched her closely until I had something on her, something with which I could manipulate her. From that day on, she was my sex slave.

Oh, the fun we had! Pure ecstasy and joy rolled together! She was beautiful and talented. I tried positions I made up myself. She was a year older than I, so our bodies melded together as one much better than my younger sisters and I. I still delighted with their bodies, too, but my older sister was amazing.

She had been taught by mother to be subservient to males, and she was so good at it. I can tell you she made some man very happy as a wife. I enjoyed her for almost a year every chance I got. Perhaps I enjoyed her a bit too much. She wound up pregnant with my child, you see. I didn't know that was possible since I had never fathered a child before. I thought being an angel of hell prevented that sort of thing. I guess my father in hell had other plans.

At first, she was just mildly sick, so our parents did not catch on. After a couple of months of sickness, my mother got suspicious. By four months, her belly was starting to expand, and then the secret was out. Crying, she broke down and confessed to our parents while I was out. Ironically, I was having some fun with our youngest sister when she was confessing.

My mother was horrified and beside herself. She had a nervous breakdown over it. My father, on the other hand, was so furious. Honor was most important to him—family honor above all else. He decapitated me in the yard with his family sword handed down from his grandfather. Great-grandfather was a guard once upon a time for the emperor and his family. Can you imagine decapitating your own child for the sake of your own honor? I was only eleven at the time. So he killed his own son, his only son.

Ah well, life goes on, right? At least mine did. And what a life my next one was. You humans have so much fun sometimes. You love to make war with yourselves, and there is nothing you won't stoop to doing. The year was 1910 when I was reborn in my Germany of long ago. Born in Berlin as one Joseph Richter. Society tries to sweep my accomplishments under the proverbial rug during this life when I should be even more famous than my time as the infamous Jack the Ripper!

Doctor of Hell, my constituents called me. I thought it was especially fitting, and I touted it with pride. But Joseph Mengele would get all my credit under the name Doctor of Death. How unflattering! I was recruited into the Third Reich as a young doctor and given carte blanche. I had been particularly interested in the research aspect of medicine as before and quickly garnered attention. I was praised and given multiple awards for my work. They were all richly deserved too, I might add.

I'm sure you have heard the tales, how I was later persecuted by the rest of the world for my advancement of the field of medicine for you lousy pathetic humans. I did phenomenal work. Exciting experiments! Organ transplants are possible today for the painstaking experiments I did on the people the Nazis were going to kill anyway. I don't understand why everyone got in such an uproar over it. Hitler was never going to let anyone live that did not meet his standards anyway.

My bothers from hell congratulated me on my successes. There were several of us working under the Nazi regime at the time. In fact, Joseph Mengele was one of my brother angels of hell. The Nazi regime was an organization that seemed to be made exclusively for us! Of course, Hitler was insane, but that was what made it so beautiful. He thought he was one of us.

It was in our best interest to let him think that, of course. He recruited so many of us. Not all of us, but many, and at the urging of two of our brothers who were his closest friends and advisors. He had a few of my sisters as well. It was grand to be reunited with them all working for the same cause. A few of my brothers ran the concentration camps. Two of my sisters actually worked the gas chambers that put so many unfortunate souls out of their misery.

There were occasions where Joseph and I did our research together. I especially liked working on twins and triplets. Twins were frequent enough at the camps, but triplets were rare. I removed organs from one to see how long it lived without a specific organ. Special diets to compare the two to see which was more beneficial was a huge topic Hitler especially liked for the betterment of our troops.

My favorite was the psychological games. I did not get to do many of those, but Joseph did, and I assisted him for a short time. We would take entire families and strap them in chairs with electrical currents running to their chairs. Then we would shock a member of the family repeatedly to see how long he or she could withstand the pain. When he or she could no longer stand it, he or she would press a button to defer the current to another family member.

I preferred starting with the mother to see how long she would endure it to protect her precious brats. I can assure you she never lasted long enough and would eventually electrocute her children to save herself—no matter the age of the child. The fathers were the same way. They could withstand considerably less than the mothers though. If I upped the electrical current, the parents would gladly fry those brats to crispy critters!

My specialty lay in surgical procedures—removing the eyes from one individual and placing them in another to see if they still worked, brain transplants, the measurement of how much pain an individual could take during amputations and surgical procedures without anesthetic. How much anesthetic was too much before a person succumbed? I could go on and on with my experiments, but I'm sure you get the drift. I switched limbs with twins to see if their bodies rejected them, and I liked working on children the best. Their tiny little bodies seemed to heal faster than adults, and it took less food to keep them alive.

Everything was wonderful for all of us, until Hitler began to make mistakes in his plans. The deterioration of his mental faculties led to the allies making gains on us. We started losing more battles than we were winning. I knew it was just a matter of time before the war would reach Germany and we would lose. Hitler got too confident and attacked Russia too early. He should have waited until he had all of Europe under his control, in my opinion. But he didn't, and suddenly our enemies were attacking us from all sides.

Making preparations to escape Germany, I funneled money and liquidated much of my wealth into gemstones—diamonds and jewelry. I sent my lover ahead to South America with some of the money and forwarded much more by trunks and other packages as quickly as I could. As the enemy neared my camp, I made a hasty getaway and left some of my personal items with my nurse.

Sometime after the fall of Germany and the end of the war, I came out of hiding with a new identity and collected my belongings before heading to South America to meet back up with my lover. My wife was left in Germany to deal with the fallout there. She thought I was dead, I'm sure. I had taken everything of value and left evidence that she was a member of the Nazi party assisting in our medical experiments. She had never been in the party, and she had only ever been a socialite. I can just imagine her face when they came for her!

In the South American jungle, I carved out a top-notch facility. A few of my siblings had made it out of Germany and met me there. Together, we built a facility where we could continue our great works. We had each escaped with large amounts of wealth, and we lived like kings among peasants.

We never killed anyone in our vicinity. Instead, we traveled all over South and Central America, kidnapping individuals for our fun. We even started the human trafficking that continues to this day. Yes, that was us, setting trends. I even started the drug trade. The land was perfect for growing various plants that, when cooked, made a variety of illicit drugs. The world is still fighting my constituents on that front!

I had lived there for nearly five years with my lover before I was approach by none other than Adolph Hitler himself! What a hoot that was! He had been hiding out in a castle of sorts that had been built for him years earlier by the Argentine government. Their president idolized Hitler and us. He gladly opened his borders for us and provided legitimate companies for us to invest in and to handle our goods for sale. I flourished in our new atmosphere for nearly thirty years. Thirty years!

I'm not sure how it came about, but someone from the Israeli secret service found us in Argentina. I think someone in the US government sold us out. Yes, the US government. I know that one caught you by surprise. The CIA had known from the beginning where we were, but they had relations with Argentina and other countries of South America, not to mention they were supplementing the US economy and making all of Congress rich with the drug trade. Anyway, the Israelis had been hunting my siblings and me for decades since the war. One of them recognized Joseph Mengele during one of our trips to get more individuals for experiments.

You see, we had discovered that we could grab people all over the world and make money on them. Some we used in sex trafficking, some we sold to the wealthy in the Middle East as slaves, and the rest we experimented on with our new drugs we were developing. We had found the world wanted pills of all types. Pills to make them thin. Pills to make them happy. Pills to make them sleep. Pills for everything! We had just found a new way to attack the world, and we were winning this war!

Unfortunately, we didn't realize the Israelis were on to us. Several of us were captured and had a grand publicized trial that was followed around the world, and then they executed us. Why is it when the Third Reich executed people, it was horrendous and an insult to humanity, but when the world executed us, it was considered justice, a gift to mankind? At any rate, they didn't get all of us, nor did they capture Hitler.

Chapter 57

It's rather extraordinary how quickly one can settle into a routine. It had only been a few days and already everyone, including Myra, had settled into an easy rhythm. She had quickly gained the respect of all the staff by filling in wherever she could and answering phones here and there. Amelia and Myra shared Dale's office at night for their sleeping quarters while he shared it with a couple of guards during the day.

In her spare time, she had also taken to reviewing the files of the resident psychologist's inmate patients so she could begin working with them immediately after the interview process was completed. She also set up a schedule to talk with every one of the staff in quarantine. Since they were all stuck together, they even devised a half-day off rotation twice a week to make up for no time off work. Sitting idly for an entire day was just too much for any of them to bear.

A television had been set up in one corner of the break room, though no one had even turned it on. Myra had just finished her session with Heirwick and made a beeline for the breakroom. Two guards and two people in white suits, masks, and gloves playing a card game and there was no food in sight—not even a crumb! She crossed her fingers and murmured a small prayer, detouring straight to Amelia's office. As usual, Amelia had saved her a plate of food and was watching her soap operas on her computer screen. Myra absconded with the plate of food and went to find a quiet space to enjoy her supper. As she ate and checked her e-mails and messages, Agent Myers entered Dale's office for their usual afternoon banter and mild flirting.

The evening sun was streaking across the sky with reds and oranges casting a soft glow in the office through the windows. She looked longingly outside. Just a few days into the ordeal and she already felt like a prisoner. How would she feel when they were a few weeks into it?

"Red sky at night, sailor's delight!" he quoted.

"Neither of us are sailors," she pointed out, still watching as the sun sank lower in the sky.

"We could pretend," he murmured.

"I wonder if sailors feel like prisoners when they are at sea for long months at a time?" she asked, more to herself than him.

"I'm sure they feel confined, although they still have freedoms on the ships with activities."

"Even inmates have activities and things in here," she argued.

"True, but they don't have the freedom to move around, and they are limited in what they can do and when."

"I suppose you're right. I guess even I have more freedoms than they do, but it still feels very confining." She ran a hand through her hair absently. Bret watched the golden strands turn a bronze color in the light and longed to bury his hands in the luxurious locks. For several seconds, they sat in amiable silence, lost in their own thoughts.

"I'm going to hit the shower," Amelia spoke from the doorway, startling them both.

"Okay. Let me know when you're out and I'll take mine," Myra said.

"Sure thing!"

"I guess I better get out of here and get my own shower and something to eat. See you in the morning," he said as he rose.

"Have a great night." She smiled as she watched him cross the office to the doorway.

"Sweet dreams, Myra," he said thickly just before he slipped out the door.

His mention of her first name took her by surprise. He almost always called her Dr. Christie or simply talked to her without mentioning her name. It was rather nice hearing it in his deep Southern drawl.

*****

It was dark and stormy. The crack of thunder hung heavily on the night wind. A flash of lightning snaked across the night sky, briefly illuminating the room. Something caught her attention, awakened her from her restless sleep. She strained to hear it again, but the storm was blocking it out. The eerie darkness was occasionally broken with the sizzle of lightning; explosions of clashing thunder was unnerving.

She felt tied to her bed, her entire body immobile. A cry rose involuntarily to her throat, but she swallowed it. Straining harder, she thought she heard the noise that had first awakened her again. It was difficult to make it out. Another flash of lightning lit up the room. Then she saw it. Saw it there in the darkness, at her feet.

Terrified, she struggled to break free from the bonds that tied her. Her sleep-dazed mind was suddenly clear. Her heart was racing with fear, her breathing shallow, eyes wide with fright, and a lone tear escaped unwillingly from her eye. There was another brilliant flash of lightning, the room rattled with a powerful rumble, and suddenly the face was looking straight down on her from above. It looked ghostly and human at the same time. A man's features smiling down at her in a bizarre fashion, but they were not clear, and she didn't recognize him.

It was saying something, but she couldn't hear it. Still struggling with the bonds, his maniacal laugh hit her ears like a scream. He was taunting her, teasing her, watching her! She could not get loose! The bonds were too tight! He was touching her!

She felt his rough finger trail down the side of her face, and she twisted her face away. His finger continued its slow torturous path down her long slender neck, across her chest to the rise of her breasts. His eyes stared into hers. It felt like she was losing her soul, her identity, her life.

He was saying something again, but she could not understand him. It was a language unknown to her. Frantically, she struggled harder to get free to no avail. The crack of thunder made her jump in terror. If only she could break free!

He was whispering her name in her ear. A raspy, throaty kind of voice grated against her tender ear. The same voice from the telephone calls! The horrific sound of the raging storm outside echoed inside her body as she struggled harder! Her hands felt wet from her struggles, and her wrists and ankles burned from the friction of the bonds.

He stood still, devouring her with his eyes. He was dressed all in black, a black robe covering his head and casting shadows across his face. He was talking to her again, but his mouth was not moving. How was he doing that? She still couldn't understand what he was saying! An evil smile spread across his face, his white teeth flashing like the lightning. Her eyes widened with fear! Something else flashed in his hands as he raised them above his head. It glittered in the flashes of lightning.

Myra screamed, but the sound was stuck in her throat. She tried again and again as he laughed over her. He was calling her name without moving his lips again. Louder and louder he called her name, and still she fought with her bonds. She screamed again with every fiber of her soul. It was an agonizing yet piercing scream.

The room was shaking badly, or perhaps it was her. She screamed louder as he raised the shiny object higher above his head! He was yelling her name now, almost as loud as she was screaming! Bloodcurdling scream after another, and still he stood paused above her, object in hand. What was he waiting for? She watched him with terrified eyes as he suddenly seemed to evaporate into thin air.

She was shaking badly. No, wait! Someone else was shaking her, calling her name. Limp and spent, she struggled to open her eyes. Disoriented, she blinked uncomprehendingly into the bright light of the room. Several people stood around her.

Amelia was at her feet, gently rubbing her legs. Dale was standing, looking down at her over the shoulder of someone dressed in white. Another prison officer stood in the doorway with a concerned look. Focusing her eyes closer, she gazed into deep pools of blue.

Agent Myers gathered her into his arms, cradling her. One hand was smoothing her blond hair, damp with sweat.

"There, there," Amelia cooed.

"I think she's gonna be okay now. Yaw'r all right, honey. Yaw'r safe," the deep Texas drawl whispered against her ear.

A flare of anger flashed in Dale's eyes momentarily, or did she just imagine it? Still shaken from the intense nightmare, she shivered. Myra knew she should push him away, but she was cold and shaking from fright. His warm body and strong arms felt heavenly around her. It felt so real! It was just like the other dreams, only this one had been extremely terrifying. She was not accustomed to nightmares. She rarely had them her entire life.

Amelia returned with a cup of hot tea. "Here, drink this. It will make you feel better."

Myra gratefully accepted the cup with shaking hands. She could feel the heat travel through her body as she took a few sips. She was practically sitting in Agent Myers's lap. Slowly, her mental facilities came back to her. The nightmare was fading, but the crashing of thunder was still in her ears. The fear was still in her eyes. Glancing at the windows, she discovered it was still dark and storming badly.

Finally finding her voice, she asked, "What time is it?"

"Six in the morning," Dale responded. "You're usually up by now."

Six in the morning? She still felt exhausted, as though she hadn't been asleep at all. "Seriously?" She peered around the room.

"Are you okay?" Dale asked, frowning over the fact that she was still in Agent Myers's arms.

"I... I...think so. I just feel extra tired for some reason."

"Probably that nightmare you had, dear. It was a doozy! We had a devil of a time waking you up. You started thrashing around, and I couldn't wake you so I fetched Dale here. Agent Myers heard you screaming before Dale could get here," Amelia provided.

"I'm sorry I caused so much trouble. I rarely have nightmares. In fact, the only time in my life I can remember having any was when my dad died. I don't know what brought this one on." She ran a shaky hand through her sleep-mussed hair.

"It's probably all the stress and lack of sleep. I want you to take it easy today," Dale ordered.

"I'll be fine," she argued as she hesitantly stood. She felt instantly chilled after the warmth of Agent Myers's arms and body.

"I would argue with ya, but I know it won't do any good." Agent Myers stood, taking her elbow to steady her. "I'll keep an eye on her personally, Warden." He gave a meaningful look at Dale as though the pair of them had taken up communicating telepathically.

A muscle worked in Dale's jaw as he bit back a retort. Instead, he simply nodded at the agent in charge. He had been outmaneuvered, and he knew it. He stared at Myra so hard that she unconsciously started checking the buttons on her pajama top.

"I think I just need a long shower to recover."

"You go straight there. I'll grab the shower stuff and a change of clothes for you," Amelia offered. She left the office. The guard at the door motioned to Dale, and he followed Amelia into the hallway.

Myra was alone with Bret. "So I take it you two have a history together?" He broke the silence.

She knew he was talking about Dale. "We dated in high school for a month or two. I hadn't seen or thought of him in years until I started this job with Heirwick." She ran another shaky hand through her hair and sat back down on the sofa.

"I'd be willing to bet he's been thinking about you a lot over the years," Bret replied as he sat on the cot across from her.

"I have no idea what you are talking about." She yawned. "What are you doing here so early? I usually have my shower before I see you."

"I had a feeling something was off this morning, so I came in early. Call it a gut instinct, if you will, but I've learned to trust it. Looks like it was right this morning! Amelia was all worked up when I saw her in the hallway. Then I heard you scream, and I came running. Amelia had been trying to wake you up for several minutes before I arrived. It took me several minutes too. That must have been some nightmare. Want to talk about it?" he asked.

"Not really." She gave an involuntary shiver. "It was so realistic... I just can't talk about it right now."

"Okay. How about some breakfast and then a shower? Maybe something on your stomach will make you feel better," he suggested. "Someone brought in breakfast croissants this morning. You sit right there and relax and I'll be right back." He took off before she could even reply.

She took another sip of her tea, curling her legs underneath her as she stared out the window into the stormy morning. Rain pelted the window so hard it sounded like hail. Pulling a blanket around her shoulders, she huddled in the corner of the couch like a little child. The nightmare had shaken her more than she cared to admit.

It was as if her stalker had been in the room with her, but his face was so distorted that she couldn't tell who it was. The eyes were the same as before, but the screeching laugh was different and was more like nails on a chalkboard. Even now, if she closed her eyes, she could still picture him standing over her, grinning with that shiny object held high over his head. Had it been a knife about to plunge into her soft flesh?

She opened her eyes and took a large gulp of the hot tea, burning the roof of her mouth and her throat. Unfortunately, it did not burn the scene from her mind.

Chapter 58

Day 6 of Canton Wayne Heirwick's narrative of his life

The year of my death and rebirth was 1976. Yes, that was my last death so far. I was born just outside of Sevierville, Tennessee, on a farm. My earthly parents were farmers and also owned an antique shop in Sevierville. I know by now that you have in your possession reports from my schools, police, etc., so I will just be upfront with you. I was a troublemaker in school, but I rarely got into trouble. No expulsions, but I was suspended once for ending a fight another started with me. I was a bit of a loner.

Humans are so difficult to understand sometimes, and the last few generations have been the worst. Their socialization skills are awkward, and narcissism abounds, in my opinion. So I stayed by myself mostly. When I did get in trouble, it was because I failed to follow some stupid rule or they claimed that I was inconsiderate to others. What do I care? They were all idiots anyway.

At a young age I started trapping various animals on the farm and in the forest for my own pleasure. Yes, I had to keep practicing my skills. I have extremely valuable skills, and I don't want them to get rusty. Sometimes I just gutted whatever I caught and brought them home for eating. Sometimes there was not enough left to eat when I finished my work. We lived in a very rural area, so I did not worry about being caught. Besides, many people in that area hunt and fish for food. I blended right in. Almost.

I made my first human kill when I was sixteen. I told my parents I was going to the movies, but in reality, I picked up a woman at a rest area off Interstate 40 and butchered her just for fun. They still haven't found her body. She was just passing through the state going somewhere unknown.

Her driver's license and information are not in my collection of files. I didn't start keeping that until I was in my late twenties. I made several kills in East Tennessee—mostly tourists, but some were natives that I either didn't like or they were disrespectful to me. I left home at eighteen to see the big wide world, or so I told my parents.

My elderly grandma was dealing with failing health, so I went to stay with her for a while in West Virginia. I think I stayed with her for four years, until she died. No, I didn't kill the old woman. She was my cover, my base of operations. I traveled all over the state of West Virginia while living with her.

She lived just outside of Huntington, which offered me the ability to also hunt in eastern Kentucky and southeastern Ohio. Marshall University was not far away, and it always provided a new selection of newcomers to have fun with. I enrolled there for a little over a year and got a bachelor's degree in criminal justice. I would have gone to graduate school, but there were just too many distractions there for me. Way too many women to have my way with. So many stupid guys to torture. There were many kills in those areas, but it wasn't until after Grandma died and I was going through her things that I stumbled on her scrapbooks. It gave me the idea to start my own.

She had changed her will and left everything to me for taking care of her those four years. Of course, I had a hand in the changing of the will. I cleaned out her bank account, loaded up a few valuables, sold what I could, and called my parents to take care of the rest. Traveling over to North Carolina, I scattered a few kills along the way. One or two here, one or two there. I left a trail of bodies throughout the state. I even hunted just outside one of the Marine Corps bases there. They talk about Marines being so tough, but I cut one down easily enough.

Creativity struck me with my kills over the years. I rarely do two the same way, and if I do, I do it in the same area. Law enforcement is so stupid. They seldom make connections with corpses unless the killer leaves a map behind for them. If all of your kills are alike, they can find you easily enough. If they are all different, no one connects the dots, and the case goes cold.

I spent a couple of months traveling all over the state before moving to South Carolina. Slowly, I made it all the way to Texas via the Southern states, staying in each one a few months. Limiting my kills in each state and never killing in the same town where I was staying reduced the risk of getting caught.

In Arkansas, I decided to become a cop. They are desperate for them in the small towns, and you can get hired easily enough. I worked in a small town there for a time. The problem was that I always seemed to be working because there were not enough cops to be able to take adequate time off. It cut into my uh...extracurricular activities. It was shortly after I left the police force there that I started keeping my scrapbook files.

My next stop was Oklahoma. Because I hadn't been able to express myself in a while, I had all this built-up tension. I needed to relax. I needed my own personal vacation. I needed multiple kills to make up for lost time.

My first stop on the way to Oklahoma was Hot Springs, Arkansas. I was visiting one of the fountains open to the public there and saw a family that I just had to have! I followed them back to the bed-and-breakfast where they were staying. That night, I invited myself to supper. It was a family of five—mom, dad, two girls, and a little boy. The bed-and-breakfast was run by an older couple in an effort to provide for their retirement. The funny thing was that the owners thought I was there to rent a room for the weekend!

Boy, were they surprised! When everyone sat down to supper, I pulled out my gun and made the dad of the family of five tie everyone to their chairs. We had some grand conversation, except for the part where the mom kept crying for her children. Stupid bitch! I got tired of listening to her and made sure I slit all the kids' throats while she watched. After that, things calmed down. No more crying and screaming from anyone.

I finished my supper with a good conversation. I couldn't decide whether or not to let the mom and dad or the older couple go. I felt like one of them should be free to brag about me. As it were, I got too jubilant in my fun and wound up killing all of them. Oh well!

Before long, I wound up in Texas. Texas was so big and rural. It demanded more time to cover it all. A little over a year or so later, I was out of funds and needed to work. Obtaining various occupations allowed me to spend more quality time in each area and more time with my victims before their slaughter. When authorities started noticing the bodies start to pile up, I simply moved on. I paid cash for everything and even purchased a camper to pull behind my truck so I didn't have to have the paper trail of rental properties.

I made my way over to California for a while, leaving a string of bodies all the way to the California coast. I just knew someone would figure it out, but they didn't. I was actually disappointed. I wanted a chase! When it didn't happen, I took a couple of months off then traveled to Napa Valley, where I had fun with a family that owned a vineyard. I did leave one of them alive—the eldest son. I have newspaper clippings where the son was charged with all those deaths. It's hilarious when that happens! You will find them all in my scrapbook, along with the dates of the kills and where I placed the bodies. Some I buried, some I didn't. Some I hid and some I left in their homes.

At any rate, the people in California were way too liberal for me, so I made my way up the coast to Washington and finally into Canada for a while. It was beautiful up there, but then winter hit. Cold weather and I don't get along too well. I hate snow. You can't kill without leaving tracks and trails. Thus, I made my way back to the Southern states.

I didn't make all my kills the same way, as you have probably noticed. That would indicate a serial killer was loose and draw way too much attention. Instead, I used several different MOs, and I don't care who I kill. The drive to kill and thrill of the hunt are so strong that it really doesn't matter about the body. I like to keep hair samples and other mementos for my own pleasure later. At the time of the hunt, however, it just depends on what my fancy is at that particular time. Sometimes I like sliding my sportsman knife in the abdomen and pulling upward to watch their expressions as their guts fall out in springy little ropes. It's quite fascinating.

Other times, I get all worked up and just go into a stabbing frenzy. If I'm short on time, I simply put a bullet in their head. If I have lots of time, I like to have sex with them repeatedly before torturing them. This one time, the guy gave me this hateful look and called me horrible names after I raped him, so I tied him up and cut out his tongue and his eyes. He didn't say anything else or give me anymore hateful looks when I raped him after that.

He was so much fun. I kept him around for a couple of weeks before I got tired of him. I dropped him off in some desolate forest somewhere and left him to die. I don't remember where that was. maybe Georgia or Alabama. Hmmm… I may have to go look him up. I don't remember if I put him in my files. I don't think I did because I didn't kill him.

Sometimes I dismember my kills and leave a little here and a little there. I took up crabbing in Mississippi once and used some parts in my crab traps. Crabs just love humans! Personally, I think crabs like humans much better than they like chicken in those traps. Just throw a hand or foot in a trap and watch them flock to it. They devour body parts faster than a kid eating peanut butter sandwiches. Filled my camper freezer and my cooler with crabs for months! Hell, I was even able to sell some of them.

I try not to eat my kills any longer. With so much disease and drugs these days, you really don't know what you are getting yourself into. It's a risk I just prefer not to take. I don't like dying too early. It just prolongs the time until I'm strong enough to kill again.

I guess you really want to know about crimes here, don't you? I've been in South Carolina this time for about eight months. I started upstate near Greenville, but by November, it was getting a bit cooler than I liked, so I moved down here to the Lowcountry where it has much nicer weather.

Everything was going great until a deer hunter saw me killing that woman and turned me in to keep from getting in trouble himself. That was down near Beaufort. I realized he saw me, so when he disappeared to call the cops, I moved her body a few miles with the help of Dad. When they didn't find a body or any evidence that I killed anybody, they had to let me go. Don't worry. I got even with the deer hunter.

There you have it. You are all caught up with the present. I don't think I left out too many details. I didn't think you needed to hear about each of my kills. I never knew their names, which is why I keep the driver's licenses. It's sort of my own personal historical record. This time has been my most prolific time yet. The population is so immense now that it is easier to hunt.

Chapter 59

It was not quite lunchtime when Heirwick ended his narrative. She asked him a few questions, but he only smiled. "I only agreed to tell you my story. Did you like it?" He winked at her.

"What do you think?" she challenged.

"I think it scares you to know that it could be true, but you don't want to admit it."

"Is it true or just a tall tale you came up with?" she asked, watching carefully for signs of lying. The body and eyes gave off all kinds of signs when someone was attempting to deceive.

"I told you I would tell you my story. It's up to you to decide now. I can't make that decision for you, love." He blew her a kiss.

"Where is your family? We haven't heard from them, and your arrest has been all over the news." She tried another tactic.

"Maybe you haven't looked in the right place if you can't find them." He grinned.

She made a quick note on her pad but kept her expression neutral. "How does killing people make you feel?" She purposely used the word *people* instead of *humans* to make the killings more personal. His cat and mouse game made her nauseous.

"I don't know. I don't really feel anything either way, except that I get stronger. I like watching their faces, their surprise turn to horror, then death creeps over them and the light goes out. It's a lot like killing animals, I suppose. Only animals are smarter." He leaned forward as far as his restraints would allow.

"What do you mean by that?" she asked.

"Animals are smart enough to run and do everything to evade being caught. Humans will come right to you, especially if they think they are going to gain something from it. Humans are greedy." He shrugged. "You aren't like that, are you? You intrigue me." He winked and blew her a kiss.

She ignored his gestures and personal comments. "Is that why your father in hell has you killing them? You kill them because they are stupid and greedy? Is that his way of punishing them?" She was still recording the session and would analyze his behavior more thoroughly later. It was not uncommon for inmates to flirt and make outlandish personal statements. For most, it was just a matter of amusing themselves; for others, it was like a personal conquest.

"No!" he all but yelled. She had definitely struck a chord there, Myra noted. He had slammed back in his seat, his face darkening with anger. "Father only punishes the bad and evil people." Heirwick took a few calming breaths. "He gave me a mission to create chaos, and death has a way of causing chaos. Wars have been started over less. I help Father when I can and kill those that are evil and bad, but I don't do it exclusively. Greed is one of the sins of God, but it does not necessarily make one evil," he explained.

"So what you are saying is that you're killing nonevil people. Does that not make you an evil person? Could you please explain this a little further for me so I can understand?" she asked, trying to keep him calm while pushing him to describe his delusion. It had been her experience that some delusional people bristle and feel trapped when they are asked to describe their delusion and defend it.

"I'm doing what my father sent me here to do. I don't consider myself evil because my father does not consider me evil. I am an angel acting on orders. I am his son! Everyone is bad to some degree. They are all full of sin, and most don't try to lead a good life. They think the occasional prayer will absolve them of their deeds. It doesn't work that way. I typically just end their sinning for them," he responded casually.

"I thought Jesus absolved people of their sins and God forgave them," she persisted.

"Ha! Don't make me laugh! God has always played my father to be a bad guy. His *precious* Jesus! Makes me gag! My father is so much better and more worthy than *Jesus*!" He was getting agitated and yelling.

Myra noticed that Bret and the other guard observed the marked difference in mood in Mr. Heirwick. They rose to their feet and watched Heirwick and her closely. She held up a hand to keep them at bay and show she had the situation under control while she considered her next step with him. She made a few notes on her pad and paused. It had not been the response she had expected when attacking his delusion. She decided to steer the conversation a little differently. "And what about the children? Were they sinners as well?" Finally, she was getting somewhere with him, but it was not exactly what she had anticipated. She felt she had to push him further.

He laughed, the sound grating as ever, and she cringed despite herself. "Children are innocents, you know. They learn bad things from the adults in their lives. I don't kill many kids, but when I do, it is to free them from their miserable little lives."

"You consider yourself an avenger, of sorts?"

"I suppose so, in some ways. Children all go to heaven to see my grandfather, anyway. It's not like they go to hell or anything. Look," he said as he splayed his hands as far as he could in the restraints. "It's not like any of the people I have killed have been innocent. In all my lives, everyone I killed was guilty of something."

"How do you know?" she questioned him.

"I feel like I'm talking in circles here. If you want me to keep talking, you need to come up with something better than that. I've already told you that answer. I guess you're one of those that buys into that whole 'Oh, she was so innocent and pure. How could someone do this to her?' Or the 'Oh, he was such a nice boy. Never did a thing wrong in his life. I can't believe someone could hate him enough to murder him' routine."

"It bothers you when family members make those types of comments?"

"No, actually, I think it's hilarious. They are lying just so they can be in the news. Everyone wants their five minutes of fame. They will say anything and do anything to get in the news." He rolled his eyes for emphasis. "The media feeds them what they want them to say. Can you just imagine if a father was being interviewed about his son getting shot during a drug deal? Oh, he was a jerk and deserved to die! Stupid motherfucker! He was lazy and dumb as a doorknob! That doesn't make for good news."

"And you want your five minutes of fame as well." She made a flat statement to get a reaction.

"I couldn't care less. If I wanted my five minutes of fame," he said using air quotes, "I wouldn't have gone so long without being caught. I would have taunted the police or turned myself in. It's funny when my fame gets broadcasted, but I don't really pay any attention to it." He was looking bored.

"Why not?" Myra asked, genuinely curious.

"Why should I?" he asked back. "Most of the story is fabricated anyway to get readers or listeners. The entire purpose of the news and media is to make money. What they don't know, they make up. The sensational headlines just to hook the audience, it's all just a big scam. A get rich quick scam! I prefer not to participate in the scam."

"Yet you placed newspaper clippings and flyers in your scrapbooks next to the corresponding victim. Why?"

He laughed loud and long. "Not for my own narcissism! I remember every person I have ever killed throughout the centuries, but I didn't personally know most of them. I don't have a record of my own exploits. I was intrigued by the way my earthly grandmother kept a record of her memories. I decided to try it myself. I found I like reviewing it on occasion and remembering faces and places. I've even revisited a few of them in their graves. When I was in New Orleans last year, I was saddened by all the progress of the city. I couldn't find burial sites, and some of the swampy areas where I placed bodies had been filled and constructed upon. Even my old homesteads were gone."

For the next hour and a half, it was more of the same type of conversation between Myra and Heirwick. He spoke freely with no compunction. He was an intelligent man, probably a really high IQ, she would give him that, but his bizarre and grandiose delusion stayed intact at all times. It was concerning and, in her professional opinion, warranted scrutiny by the court and other medical professionals. She was definitely interested in what his psychometric tests would reveal.

Later during lunch, Myra reviewed all her notes, reflecting that in the beginning she had felt that his delusional story was merely fictitious and a feeble attempt for an insanity plea. The law, she noted, regarding the insanity plea as a defense used in criminal trials such as this one to dispute the defendant, in this case, Mr. Heirwick, would not be responsible for his action due to mental illness at the time of the crime or an enduring and persistent problem. She was certain he had neither an episodic nor persistent issue. She was going to have to broach the subject in her report.

Recalling her conversation with Dr. Hull days ago, she now understood his reservations with this case. Mr. Heirwick was extremely intelligent, in the superior range on the intelligence scale. She knew he would score extremely high on antisocial personality testing and he had grabbed a perfect score on the psychopathy test. She was extremely interested in reviewing test results of a full battery of psychometric testing. Likely, if given the tests today, he would prove to be legally sane.

The other issue she had to review was if he was competent to stand trial. It was her personal opinion he was able to understand the law, assist in his own defense, and was fully aware of his circumstances and what a guilty verdict would mean for him. There was little more she could do except finish the transcription of all her notes and his video and audio narratives for her files to submit them to Dr. Hull. He would, in turn, perform the testing and submit the results with both his and her reports to the court. All of it would have to wait until she was out of the current situation.

Chapter 60

Myra had finished the interview with Heirwick that afternoon earlier than she had expected. True to his word, he had answered every question asked of him so far, since he had finished his monologue. She had found him mostly forthcoming despite his awkward attempts at flirting with her and his occasional mode of evasiveness. She still needed to do another interview with him in the morning to reiterate what he had finally been willing to discuss with her that afternoon. She also needed to ask him if he was the killer behind the ABC killings.

She was in her makeshift office, typing up notes regarding their conversation and making a list of future questions to ask him. Dale had taken to sleeping in the afternoons and working all night. They had found that the inmates began getting restless during the night when the quarantine had been issued. Dale liked to be active during that time to take control of the situation. He also felt that mornings were much busier than afternoons.

As a result, she, Amelia, and a few others had been eating their lunches in his office, and later she would type her notes in the storage room/makeshift office. It was typically quieter, and with no windows, it was less distracting than the psychologist's office. She was typing away and looked up to see a figure dressed in white in the doorway.

"Cozy," Bret drawled.

"I guess you haven't seen me in my office since that first day when I set it up." She grinned.

"Nope." He made pretense of looking around the small room that was not much bigger than a walk-in closet. "I like how ya decorated it." She couldn't help it. She busted out laughing at his corniness. He wagged his eyebrows at her and studied an outdated calendar on the wall like it was a painting by van Gogh, which made her laugh even harder.

"What brings you to my little hole-in-the-wall?" she asked, wiping tears of laughter from her eyes.

"Ya received a letter in the mail today. Amelia was lookin' for ya, so I told her I would deliver it to ya." He held out a white business envelope with block style lettering. She took it from him with shaking fingers and a pinched expression. "What's wrong?" he asked.

"It's from my stalker." She started to tear open the envelope, but he stopped her. "Hang on a second." He took the envelope from her and left. A moment later, he was back with a pair of latex gloves for Myra and a letter opener. He also had a plastic bag with him.

"Only hold it by the corners with your gloves on and only use the letter opener to open it."

She did as he instructed. When she pulled the letter out, small confetti hearts flew in all directions. She unfolded the letter and began to read with him leaning over her shoulder.

My Dearest Love,

I see much has been going on in your life lately. Being stuck in the prison under quarantine must be difficult for you, but you have been handling it like a trooper! I am so proud of you, darling. It does disturb me that you are there with your old lover, but I trust you emphatically.

Much has been going on in my life as well lately. Father and I converse nearly daily now. It's difficult to find enough alone time, especially with everything that has been going on, but like you, I do my very best. Father has even been taking more of an active role. I can't wait to see what the future holds.

The end of this journey to get to you is almost at an end. I promise we will be together in a few days. I know you are ecstatic as I. Being apart from you has been agonizing. I hate the way we left things a few weeks ago, but I promise I'll make it up to you. It was rude of me. My only excuse is that I am so excited to start our lives together that I did not consider how exhausted you have been the past couple of months.

Don't worry, my darling. Everything will calm down when you and I are together. I'll take you away with me, and you won't have to work with those lesser beings any longer. Until then, I remain,

Your loving servant and paramour

"Wow! This guy is really demented. I'm glad yawr in here where I can keep an eye on ya. At least in here yawr safe." Bret rested his hand on her shoulder, and she could feel his heat through his gloves and her top. Him touching her was distracting.

"Never thought I would hear that I would be safe because I was in a prison lockdown due to a quarantine. I need to get a copy of this letter before I forward it to Detective Parks in Columbia."

Bret moved just outside the door, waiting for her. She saved her work on the laptop and left the storage room, locking the door behind her. He followed her to Amelia's office. where she made a copy for herself.

"If ya don't mind, I'll take the original," Bret offered. "I can get my guys workin' on it faster than the crew in Columbia. Columbia has to send it to SLED for testin'. We can do that ourselves. It has passed county lines, and he's threatened you in a state-run facility now, while working on a federal case. I'm sure I can get a rush on it. I'll make sure the detective in Columbia knows we're workin' on it too."

"Thank you." Myra felt strangely calm. In the past, she had felt threatened, paranoid, nervous, terrified. Whether it was because she knew she was safe in the prison environment, or whether it was because Bret had been with her when she read the letter and had just taken the original to test it, she wasn't sure. Whatever it was, she felt comfortable now and was sure the FBI would catch the culprit quickly.

The following Monday arrived. Myra had completed the interview process with Mr. Heirwick, and she had performed counseling for several other inmates. The vast majority had been substance abusers, which led to criminal activities to support their addictions and landed them in prison. Six inmates had various psychotic disorders, and a number had been diagnosed with depression and other mood disorders. The last group had various notes from the resident psychologist in their records indicating childhood traumas of physical, sexual, and/or emotional abuse at the hands of their guardians or parents, which might have been contributing factors. For many of them, the added stress of incarceration had exacerbated those mood disorders.

According to the mental health records of the inmates, the resident psychologist preferred individual therapy, but Myra found group therapy more productive in some situations, especially substance abuse therapy and various mood disorders, respectively. It had been her personal experience in the groups she worked that individuals improve at a greater rate once they realize they are not alone in their battle, that others have the same or similar symptoms and demons, and they obtain the knowledge that recovery or at least improved quality of living can be obtained with treatment. Unfortunately, they were in the midst of a quarantine lockdown. She had no choice but to see each of them individually, but she would make notes in each of their records that she felt they would show more improvement in group therapy. Hopefully, the normal resident psychologist would see it when he was able to return.

Early morning appointments were scheduled for those needing daily individual treatments with the late morning blocked off for the quarantine program she initiated for staff members. She held a two-hour slot for individual staff seeking help as a part of a group. She also decided to hold two hour-long sessions in later afternoon after supper for staff that needed or requested individual sessions. Afternoon appointments were held open to perform wellness checks on some of the inmates, for which she was concerned about their mental health issues but who didn't need daily counseling.

The wellness checks consisted of her being escorted to actual cells to see how the inmates were responding to treatment. She had found in her own practice that inmates sometimes acted differently when they appeared in her office for therapy than when they did in their cells. It was not uncommon for some to claim illness they did not have in order to seek attention and to escape the confines of their cells.

With the lockdown in place, Dale had requested she keep the office appointments down to a minimum. Not only was everyone concerned about the possible spread of the contagion, they were all overworked and tired. That was when mistakes were often made. Afraid an inmate might accidently get out or injured due to the conditions, it was best to keep them in their cells as much as possible until the quarantine was over.

And so with this in mind, Myra made her checks in the individual cellblocks. One of the inmates requiring a wellness check was in the same cellblock as Heirwick. Myra was looking for the name of the inmate on the outside of the cell when she heard her name being called. Looking around, she realized it was Heirwick.

"What do you want?" she asked him. "I'm busy."

"I just wanted to tell you how nice you look today. You look absolutely radiant." He grinned.

"Thank you," she said politely. She started down the hallway.

"Any idea when we can get out of this quarantine and lockdown?" he asked.

"I'm sorry, I don't. I would suggest you speak to the warden about it."

"I would, but he avoids me. I think I make him nervous. Is he a good guy?" Heirwick watched her closely.

"As far as I know, he is."

"You know him well, don't you? I hear you know him carnally. When this quarantine is over, I'll know you carnally as well, and you can compare us to see which one is best," he persisted.

"Excuse me, I have work to do." She ignored his comments.

"How is Dr. Hull? Have you seen him lately?"

Myra looked up from the file of the inmate she was trying to locate and frowned. "I don't talk to him daily. We are doing independent interviews. Why do you ask?" she asked suspiciously.

A creepy smile lit up his face. "Maybe you should talk to him daily. You never know when something can happen to the people you care about."

A cold chill ran over her body. She didn't bother to respond to any more of his comments. Rather, she found the inmate she had been looking for and talked with him for a few minutes before moving on to the next patient.

The next day, Myra was just finishing a working lunch in the psychologist's office. She had been making notes on which inmates she needed to see that afternoon and the topic she wanted to discuss in the group therapy for the quarantined staff later that afternoon. She was clearing her space of her lunch debris and gathering the files of inmates she needed to see on the wellness checks when she heard a light rap on the door of the psychologist's office. She looked up to find both Dale and Bret, as she had finally conceded to refer to Agent Myers.

"What's up, gentlemen?" she asked.

"We have some good news and some not so good news," Bret responded, taking off his mask and pushing back the hood of his white hazmat suit.

"Should you be exposing yourself?" she asked, alarmed.

"It's okay. DHEC and the CDC finally discovered the cause of the illnesses. It is not contagious, but it is extremely dangerous." He smiled.

It had been over two weeks since they had been thrust into quarantine, and while she had been long awaiting this very news, she was having difficulty focusing on what he was actually saying. Myra was distracted by the sheer handsomeness of Agent Bret Myers. She had slowly been falling for those intense blue eyes and his slow Texas drawl and had caught herself on occasion fantasizing over what he looked like behind the mask and under the suit. Suddenly, she could see the real thing, and it was so much better than her fantasies. He had sort of a bronzed skin tone as though he had some Latino heritage somewhere in his ancestry and spent a lot of time outdoors. His hair was a dirty blond, wavy, and thick. Her fingers tingled to run through it. It was a striking combination that had her dazzled and a little out of breath.

"Can you believe it?" Dale asked. "I mean, I knew it was dangerous, but I never realized how deadly that stuff could be!"

"I'm sorry, could you repeat that?" She suddenly realized that she had been gawking at Bret and totally missed out on the important part of the conversation.

Bret smiled, and dazzling white teeth lit up his face. "I know it's hard to believe. They found traces of black mold in Heirwick's cell, but the majority of it was in Smith's cell. Smith was the inmate who died first. Apparently, a slow water leak has been goin' on fer some time inside the wall, and while the inmates noticed it, they didn't report it. I need to bring Heirwick in for interrogation. Could we use this office?"

"Why do you need to interrogate him?"

"Once it was discovered there was black mold, it was reported to the hospital. Apparently, the symptoms that Detective Wilson and Officer Garrett have are consistent with ingestion of black mold, which is not so common. We need to find out what happened, and I have my suspicions." Bret lightly tapped his fingers on the desk.

"Could we use your recording equipment?" Dale asked.

"Sure. Ah, what about Officer Nickerson? Any word on his condition?" she asked.

"DHEC contacted the hospital in Columbia and had him transferred to the medical bay for immediate treatment of black mold exposure. From his symptomology of hallucinations, disorientation, confusion, memory issues, and a constant tremblin', they think he was also exposed to the black mold. When inhaled in large quantities, it can have a devastatin' effect on the neurological system and most specifically the brain," Bret supplied.

"The other inmates were living with it for some time. All the inmates who fell ill or died were in cells around Heirwick's and

Smith's. We have been moving people around all afternoon to vacate that cellblock," Dale interjected.

"But why haven't any of the other guards or inmates in that cellblock fallen ill?" she posed to them.

"Some are sick. They have cold and flu-like symptoms from exposure. Two guards who were quarantined in their homes have symptoms, and three that have been here with us have light symptoms. The rest of us were wearin' these suits, which protected us, but Dale here has been havin' severe headaches and nosebleeds for a week." Bret patted Dale on the shoulder. She suddenly realized Dale's eyes were bright and his face a bit flushed as if he had a fever. "After the interrogation, he's going to be headed out on sick leave with the others to get treatment while the rest of us hold down the fort here."

"Why didn't you tell anyone, Dale?" Myra looked at him in disbelief.

"The other two guards have the same symptoms I do. They weren't the same as those officers in the hospital. We all have seasonal allergies, and we thought it was just something in the air." Dale shrugged. "We mentioned it to DHEC and the CDC and they tested us, but they just thought it was allergy related as well."

"So this means we can all leave?" she asked in disbelief.

"Yes, well, sort of," Dale began with a slight cough. "Would it be possible for you to hang out here for a couple more days while we transition all those who are sick? Some of the inmates are also sick and will be treated here in the medical department. We could still use your help."

"Sure. My office is not expecting me back anytime soon anyway," she volunteered. She was almost tingling with relief that she wouldn't have to leave the company of Bret yet.

"That's fantastic!" Bret stood. "Well, I think we better do this interrogation now if possible."

"Okay. I'll get everything set up for you. I was just about to do my wellness rounds anyway," she offered.

The men looked at each other as if silently communicating. Finally, Bret broke the silence. "Actually, Myra, we were hopin' that ya'd help with the interrogation. Ya know him better than anyone, and we could use someone studyin' his unspoken communication, as it were."

"Besides, we know he will talk to you, even if he won't talk to the rest of us."

"You are hoping to throw him off guard by having someone he's comfortable with in there," she guessed.

"Well, there is that too," Dale said sheepishly.

"Very well. I'll get everything set up and move the things around to make room for everyone while you fetch him."

*****

She could only imagine how a suspect felt when being interrogated by him. She would confess anything to him, even things she hadn't done. She would even confess to things she had done as a child under his interrogation. Myra almost felt sorry for Heirwick as Bret grilled him.

"Explain to me how two officers of the law came to ingest black mold within days apart and both had contact with you?"

Heirwick looked at Myra, and she nodded. "Coincidence?" Heirwick responded. "How should I know?" He was so calm, as though it was an everyday occurrence for him to get interrogated by an FBI agent. "Maybe they liked the taste of it?"

A muscle was working in Bret's jaw furiously, and she noticed that Dale's hands had knotted into fists so tight that his knuckles were white. She reached over and gently touched his arm in a calming motion.

"Agent Myers, are you insinuating my client had something to do with the illnesses of the two officers?" Ryder Kaspry, Heirwick's court-appointed attorney, interjected. He was a short and thin weasel-looking guy with close set eyes, dull brown hair thinning on the top leaving a ring around his head, and pale tired eyes. His dull brown suit, white shirt, and black tie looked worn and more tired than he did.

"Four officers actually, Mr. Kaspry," Bret corrected the attorney. "One is dead, two are critically ill, and one is seriously ill with neurological issues."

"I don't see how my client can be held accountable for their illnesses. I understand that black mold was found here in the prison in Mr. Heirwick's cellblock. Is that true?" he directed at Dale.

"Yes," Dale grudgingly admitted.

"And isn't it also true that several inmates fell ill and some have died from the same black mold being in their cells?" Kaspry asked.

"This is not a trial, Mr. Kaspry. You can stop with your courtroom theatrics. We have reason to believe your client purposely poisoned the officers and at the same time triggered illness in the inmates," Bret directed.

"He has been in a cell by himself as most of the inmates here. Please tell me what your reasoning is behind this idea, Agent Myers." The attorney was doing his job and preventing his client from talking.

"A witness, for one," Bret responded.

Ryder Kaspry actually had the gall to laugh. "You are taking the word of another inmate over my client who has not been convicted of anything? I think this interview is over, gentlemen."

"Who said the witness was another inmate?" Bret asked, halting the departure of the attorney.

"Are you suggesting another prison guard witnessed these actions and is just now coming forward? I demand to know his name! I will have him charged with negligence and manslaughter for the deaths of the inmates!" Kaspry puffed up like a peacock.

"I will remind you again, Mr. Kaspry, this is not a courtroom. It is an investigation, and I do not have to divulge my witnesses at this time. We would appreciate your cooperation—"

Kaspry interrupted Bret midsentence. "You do not want my client's cooperation! You want a confession so you can add more charges!" he accused. "I will remind you, Agent Myers, this interview is now over. If you have any further questions for my client, I would appreciate you contactin' my office in advance instead of calling me at home like you did this morning. If they are questions such as these, then they can wait until trial. Good afternoon, gentlemen, Dr.

Christie. Mr. Heirwick." He turned to his client, who had a bemused smile on his face. "I would advise you not to talk to anyone in the future without my presence. That also includes Dr. Christie, who can conduct any further interviews and tests in my presence."

The hostility in the room was thick and oppressing. Mr. Kaspry stood, indicating the interview was over.

"Excuse me, Mr. Kaspry," Myra spoke for the first time. "I don't think you understand my position here. I don't work for you or the prosecution. I work for the court. The judge ordered me to do an evaluation and interview on Mr. Heirwick. I don't need you to be here when I talk to your client." Mr. Kaspry started to interrupt, but Myra gave him a drop-dead look and held up her hand with a challenge that said he better think again before being rude to her. "Furthermore, I don't appreciate your threats. I understand you want what is best for your client. However, if you leave this room right now without Mr. Heirwick informing us how this situation arose, I will be forced to contact the judge and the South Carolina Bar Association and report that your personal actions led directly to the harming and possible deaths of several inmates and officers of the law. How do you suppose they will respond?"

Mr. Kaspry gave her a hateful look. A muscle was jumping erratically in his jaw. "Are you threatening me, Dr. Christie?"

"I never threaten anyone, Mr. Kaspry." She gave him a slight smile. "I'm simply telling you what is going to happen if you walk out of this office before we find out what has happened to nearly a dozen people working on this case."

"My client has been locked up the entire time in one of those cells. Why hasn't he come down sick?"

"Precisely, Mr. Kaspry. That's what we are trying to determine."

"You are treating him like a suspect instead of another victim. I won't stand for that!"

Myra had had enough. "Sit down, Mr. Kaspry!" she roared. "Obviously, it has escaped your attention either unintentionally or deliberately that Officers Ameson and Wilson were also exposed to the same contaminant. Officer Ameson died within twenty-four hours of arresting Mr. Heirwick. Officer Wilson was in ICU fighting for his life within forty-eight hours. That was *before* your client had even stepped foot in this institution."

Dale was staring at Myra with a slack jaw. Bret was fighting a smile. Heirwick was looking at her with admiration. Mr. Kaspry looked like he had been punched in the solar plexus. His thin lips were screwed up in a pinch. His eyes darted to his client while he tried to come up with a retort.

"Darling, I blew black mold dust in Officer Nickerson's face," Heirwick spoke up.

"I'm advising you to keep your mouth shut," Mr. Kaspry snapped as he sat back down.

Heirwick glanced at him and continued, "Nickerson may be young, but he is a bad man. He's been bringing contraband into the prison and selling it to the highest bidding inmate. Check his locker. You'll find an order for other items in there that he needs to sneak in, and you'll also find stuff he has stored until the bidding stops."

Dale stared at Heirwick. "And how do you know this?" he asked, a little pale.

"Word gets around the cellblock. That stabbing you had in here a few months ago? He brought the shanks in to the inmates," Heirwick offered. Mr. Kaspry was staring at the wall in front of him, furious with Myra and his client.

"What happened with Officers Ameson and Wilson?" Myra asked, ignoring the dirty looks she was getting from Heirwick's attorney.

"Ameson was a jerk. I told you he was a bad cop. I had some liquid black mold that I spilt on him when he was arresting me. Some of it got on my clothes but didn't make it to my skin. It was absorbed by Ameson through his skin. Officer Wilson must have either touched Ameson or my wet clothes, or Ameson touched Wilson. That's why Wilson is not dead. It was secondhand exposure for him."

"And the other officers?" Bret asked.

Heirwick ignored him and waited for Myra to ask him something else. Bret exchanged glances with Myra.

"And the other officers? How did they get exposed?" Myra asked.

"They were eating in the cafeteria with us. I had gathered some scrapings from my cell. I gave them to Smith and told him to put them into their food or I would kill him. Smith did as he was told. He just didn't know he was dying from exposure himself already. The rest of the inmates are all in my cellblock. It was easy to get it on them. Most of the time, I ground it up into a dust and blew it on them while they were asleep or I blew it on their food while they were eating."

"Are you responsible for the deaths of the priest and the two boys who were tortured and murdered here in Charleston a few weeks ago?"

"Wasn't that great! I knew it was going to go viral in the media before I did it. What did you think?"

"Why did you attack them?" Myra asked.

"Because I wanted to. I wanted to see how people responded to a priest and two boys going missing and then ending up murdered. Just as I expected, people immediately started blaming the priest. The media were the worst. If I hadn't put the priest out of his misery, he wouldn't have been able to hold his head up in society again. They had already ruined his reputation as a priest without even knowing the facts of the case or the priest personally. Even the parishioners turned on him. And they call themselves Christians! Ha! I ought to end the lot of them!"

"And the women and the teenager that Owen Johnson was accused of murdering. You murdered them as well, didn't you?" Myra asked, already knowing the answer.

"That was for you, Myra. I put a call into the Department of Mental Health and asked that you specifically be put on that case. You disappointed me."

"How did I disappoint you?" she asked.

"You didn't figure it out until after I killed Owen Johnson. He was already writing the letter when I went to him. I had him finish it, and then I finished him."

"It wasn't my job to determine guilt. My job was only to do an evaluation, which I did. How did you kill Mr. Johnson?"

"I hung him with his own sheet in his cell." At her skeptic look, he continued, "You mean you want to know how I got to him while he was in jail awaiting transfer to the prison. I posed as a police officer. You put on a uniform, and you can walk into any building and no one questions you. I walked right into the holding area with him. After he was dead, I simply walked back out. Check the videotapes if you don't believe me." He smiled, thoroughly enjoying all the carnage and sorrow he had caused.

"Do you have any additional questions, gentlemen?" Myra looked at both Dale and Bret, who shook their heads.

"I'll need ya to write this all out in yawr confession, Mr. Heirwick." Bret placed a notepad and an ink pen on the table in front of Heirwick.

"They haven't found the rest of the bodies yet, have they?" It was more a statement by Heirwick than a question.

"What bodies?" Bret asked.

"The rest of the ABC Killer's bodies. You won't find them in my files. I have a special spot where I keep their information."

"And where is that?" Myra asked.

"At my parents' house in Tennessee. Here, I'll make it easy for you," he stated as he wrote down the address and handed it to Myra. "You'll find the house key in the birdhouse in the side yard."

Myra took the paper with the address and raised an eyebrow at Bret. "Thank you for being honest with us," Myra thanked Heirwick.

"Are we finished?" Mr. Kaspry asked snottily.

"Just as soon as Mr. Heirwick writes out his statement," Bret responded.

"Well, since he didn't listen to me about opening his big mouth, I don't see why I need to be here while he's writing out his confession. You can just send a copy of it to my office." Mr. Kaspry didn't wait for any responses before he stormed out the door, practically slamming the door so hard Myra thought the glass in it was going to fall out and shatter.

It took Heirwick over an hour to write out his confession. All those days of his refusing to talk until after he had told his sordid story of reincarnation as an angel of hell, and now he was singing like a songbird. When he was finished with his statement, Myra and Bret read over it before having Heirwick sign and date it.

Heirwick had been watching Myra so closely that she felt like a bug under a microscope. As the others stood, he winked at her and blew her a kiss. She ignored him. Myra waited until Dale and two guards escorted Heirwick out of the office and back to his cell before she cut off the recording devices.

"Well, that went well," she said drily.

"I thought we lost it there for a moment when Kaspry got all wound up." He interlocked his fingers and stretched his arms in front of himself. "Then *you* spoke up and it was magical. The look on Kaspry's face was comical. I think ya know ya have an enemy in him."

"Oh well. I doubt we will ever have a case together again anyway." Myra brushed it off. "Do you really have a witness or was that just a bluff?" she asked, flipping off the lights and following him out into the hall where she locked the door.

"Yes, but it's kind of questionable, as the attorney guessed. My agent at the hospital questioned one of the sick inmates. He reported that the inmate told him either Heirwick or Heirwick had Smith scrape some of the black mold in his cell into an envelope, which Heirwick then gave to Smith. Smith was not in a position to contaminate the food with it without bein' caught, so he gave it to this other inmate. The inmate was on the cafeteria work crew and sprinkled the mold into a plate he fixed for Officer Garrett."

"That's awful! I can't believe people come up with such horrible ideas in order to harm others."

"Yeah," he agreed as they walked side by side toward Dale's office. "Black mold spores are exceptionally dangerous. When Smith scraped them, it released the spores into the air more than usual, which he and Officer Nickerson inhaled. Officer Nickerson was a smoker, so it affected him faster than Smith. Smith, however, inhaled it for a longer period, which led to his death. It's what also made the other inmates ill."

"I don't understand why Heirwick hasn't gotten sick though." She curled up on the sofa facing Bret, who took a seat beside her.

"Maybe he put somethin' over his face when he was scrapin' the black mold, or maybe he just had others do his dirty work."

"All these people injured, sick, or dying just because someone else wanted to be famous." She shook her head. "I wonder if Officer Ameson had known in advance that his arresting Heirwick would trigger all this, would he still do it? If he could have avoided contact with the liquid black mold."

"Officer Ameson had a brain aneurism. It just happened to coincide with the arrest. I got a copy of his medical report yesterday."

"Wow! I guess I just assumed he had the same symptoms as his partner. Wait, Heirwick lied to us then when he said Ameson was exposed to liquid black mold!"

"I don't think so. My lab collected his arrestin' uniform and tested it. They did find black mold on his uniform, but they couldn't explain why or how it was there. It seems that in his case, Heirwick is guilty of attempted murder but not guilty of the murder itself because it was actually natural causes."

"What about Detective Wilson? How do his symptoms play into this?" Myra watched Bret lean his head back and close his eyes. He looked tired too.

"We're not sure yet. That's one of the reasons why I wanted to interrogate Heirwick. It's my belief that with all that floodin' we had here a few months ago, Heirwick knew the dangers of black mold. He would have had access to it just about everywhere in this hot and damp climate."

"True. Do you think he got exposed like Heirwick suggested? I can't imagine him ingesting it? That is so gross, but I guess it would be hard to detect mixed in with something."

"So what are you talking about?" Dale asked as he joined them, pulling his comfortable office chair closer to the sofa.

"How Heirwick could have gotten Detective Wilson to ingest black mold," Myra explained with a shiver.

Dale shook his head in disgust. "We may never really know the answer to that, unfortunately."

"Are ya chilly?" Bret asked.

"Not really. It's just that poisoning is so cruel. The person dies slowly, or if he is lucky enough to survive, he has secondary medical problems for the rest of his life. It's just so tragic. How are he and Officer Garrett doing, by the way?"

Dale stretched in his chair and answered while Bret was in the middle of a yawn. "Slow in recovering, I'm afraid, but at least they're alive. Both of them appear to have some memory losses and breathing difficulty. Detective Wilson is still having seizures, so the extent of their recovery is still questionable."

"It doesn't look like either of 'em will be able to return to work," Bret added.

"Neither will Officer Nickerson. Nickerson and Garrett are both fine officers. It will be a shame to lose them around here." Dale had a faraway look in his eyes as he recalled his memories of working with the officers.

"Do ya believe Heirwick's account of Nickerson's behavior?" Bret asked Dale.

"I don't want to, but I have Amelia requesting a court order to open Nickerson's locker."

Chapter 61

The next few days were hectic, at best. The court order to open Officer Nickerson's locker came through and Dale cut the lock off the locker and searched it in the presence of Bret and representatives of the South Carolina Department of Corrections and the State Police. Just as Heirwick had stated, there were a number of contraband items in the locker including suboxone strips, shanks, and cigarettes. Despite his being in the hospital in serious condition, an investigation was immediately launched and the contraband taken into custody. If Officer Nickerson did survive and recover, he was looking at serious jail time for his endeavor.

After the search and seizure of the locker, Dale was finally able to go home with medications for a nice rest, and to see his family. They had been apart for almost a month, she realized. She was busy nearly around the clock. She was updating records, seeing inmates, replying to e-mails and messages, and to top it off, two of the inmates with psychosis had meltdowns which required her to be up with them all night two nights in a row.

On Friday morning, the resident psychologist reported to work, and Myra gave him an update on what she had been doing in his absence, including the results of the group therapy sessions she had initiated for the staff. By the time she had finished with everything and collected her belongings from Bret who had sent her laundry out for cleaning, it was late afternoon.

Bret had insisted on taking her out to dinner at a nice restaurant in celebration of her freedom from quarantine. She had been about to ask Amelia if she wanted to join them when she caught a glimpse of her exiting the building with a huge smile on her face. It had been weeks since any of them had seen friends and family, and a joyous mood was in the air.

It had been too late to catch up with Dr. Hull at his office after dinner. Instead, she headed to her apartment in Columbia. Myra was thrilled at the prospect of sleeping in her own bed, bathing in her own bathroom, and eating a homecooked meal. Even more thrilling, she reflected, was the fact that she would not have to see Mr. Heirwick again until his trial. On the flip side, she was disappointed her time with Bret had also come to an end.

By the time she reached her apartment, the excitement of being free again had worn off and was replaced with exhaustion. It had been nonstop work for the past few weeks, and she was beginning to feel the edges of burnout. She needed a vacation badly, she decided, and vowed to look into vacation ideas over the weekend. She just had to check in with her office first to plan some time off. The staff was just going to love her being out of the office again.

An hour and three trips to her vehicle later, Myra was sliding into a tub filled with hot water and fragrant bubble bath. Everything was unpacked; a load of laundry was in the washer and one in her dryer; her electronic equipment, notes, and records were in her home office; and she was happily sipping a glass of Moscato wine. A nondescript romance paperback in hand, which had been an impulse purchase at a gas station on the way out of Summerville, made her briefly think of Amelia. She had gotten Myra hooked on them. Now if she could just get Bret out her of head.

It wasn't long before Myra realized her folly. The romance novel, if it could even be called a novel, was putting ideas into her head about Bret instead of alleviating them. Her nice hot bubble bath had turned tepid, and the bubbles were all but gone. The wineglass was long empty, and what was supposed to be a soothing and relaxing book had left her tense and sexually frustrated instead. She climbed out of the tub, readied for bed, and she decided to call it a night. She had a lot of errands to do tomorrow and a lot of catching up to do!

Chapter 62

It was unusually dark. Rain had come through earlier, and another storm was fast approaching. Clouds blocked out the moon. She hadn't realized before just how much moonlight lit up the parking lot of her apartment complex and how few streetlights were there. It was weird, she thought, and a bit spooky.

She had been so behind in her work at the office after the fiasco at the prison that she had worked all weekend, trying to catch up so it wouldn't be so overwhelming when the workweek started. Even so, her first day back in the office had started at five that morning, and now it was after eight in the evening. It wasn't that late, but it was later than she normally arrived home and probably the reason for the parking lot being overfilled, she reasoned. The storms most likely had something to do with it as well.

An unknown car was parked in her assigned parking spot in front of her apartment building, annoying her. The residents of the apartment complex knew better, so it must be a visitor, she thought. Each apartment was assigned one parking space in front of the building. There were also non-assigned parking spaces for extra vehicles and visitors in an overflow parking area on the other side of the complex. She would have to walk approximately one hundred yards or so in the dark to her building.

Walking through a parking lot at night generally did not bother her, but tonight was different. A familiar place didn't seem so familiar without lights. A flash of lightning lit up the sky, momentarily adding to the air of creepiness. A nearby sound made her jump while she was collecting her things from her Jeep. She peered out into the darkness around her but couldn't see anything. Curiously, there were no other people in sight. "That's strange," she muttered to herself. The apartment complex was filled with mostly singles or newly married couples. A few were single parents with children, and one or two were complete families. It was most unusual to not see or hear anyone in the parking lot.

She walked a few feet and heard the crunch of glass under her feet. The lamppost light had either blown or been knocked out. That was one reason the parking lot was so dark. Then she noticed that several of the lampposts were out. It was almost as if someone had gone around breaking all the light bulbs in them. She made a mental note to let the management company know in the morning so they could replace them. Teenagers were notorious for doing mischievous things of that nature, though she didn't remember any living in the complex. But she had been gone for over a month, she reminded herself.

A loud thump somewhere in the darkness behind her spooked her. She hastened her steps then mentally berated herself for being so jumpy. It was probably just a cat or other nocturnal animal rustling around for food. She purposely slowed her gait.

A cool breeze sprung up unexpectedly, and a shiver ran down her spine. Her skin crawled as though someone was watching her from the shadows. She cast another look around but again saw no one. Halfway across the parking lot from her apartment, she thought she heard someone softly call her name. That was ridiculous, she reminded herself. She was imagining things, and she was jumpy because she had just finished working with the world's most prolific serial killer in history.

After a couple more steps, her name was called again. She distinctly heard her name that time! Whirling around, she stared into the dark abyss. "Who's there?" she called. No one answered. "Come out so I can see you!" she demanded, and still no answer. She gritted her teeth in fear while sliding her hand inside her purse. She always carried a bottle of pepper spray. It was something her father always insisted on from the time she turned twelve. She felt the familiar bottle, and her fingers wound around it.

Her arm kept her purse closely to her side, the bottle of pepper spray in her palm, ready if she needed it. She carried her briefcase in her other hand. She tightened her grip in case she needed to use it as a weapon. Approximately twenty yards from the stairwell leading to her apartment, her name was called again. It was a little louder this time. It sounded like it came between one of the cars she had just passed. Someone was definitely trying to scare her. She pretended to not hear it, but her ears strained to hear any approaching footsteps as she mentally prepared herself to fight.

A small sense of relief washed over her as she began climbing the steps to the third-floor apartment. The higher she climbed, the faster she climbed. She made it to the second-floor landing when she heard a thump below her. Pausing, she strained to listen. Was that heavy breathing she heard beneath the stairs? She broke out into a run, climbing the steps as fast as she could.

She dropped the pepper spray in her purse and felt for her keys. Terrified, she gulped air as she grasped her keys. She didn't see anyone below her, but she could hear them coming. She yanked her keys out of her purse and sorted through them for her apartment key. Another loud thump startled her. She stumbled and fell, scraping her knees and the palm of her hand. Her keys and briefcase went flying across the landing of the third story. Her purse had padded her chest in the fall. She struggled getting to her feet, her legs shaking, hands trembling. She stumbled again as she fought to maintain her balance while fumbling on the landing to grab her keys and briefcase.

Were those footsteps on the stairs below her? She couldn't see! Someone had broken all the lights but the far one on the landing! A cry escaped her lips. She cut her hand on a piece of broken glass as her fingers finally curled around her keys. Heart pumping furiously, she stabbed the first key her fingers were able to hold into the lock!

He was calling her name again. Over and over, she heard the deep husky voice! It was the wrong key! Tears escaped her wide, terrified eyes and ran down her face as fear gripped her heart in its icy hands. Collapsing against the door, she fought through her keys until she found the correct one. Her hands were shaking so badly she had difficulty inserting it into the lock. Glancing toward the dark stairs, she strained to see someone. It was too dark.

She was near hysteria. She tensed as the key finally fit into the lock! Twisting the dead bolt hard, she unlocked the top lock but still had another one to go! Chest heaving from her breathing, blood roaring in her ears, she labored to hear something, anything! Groping the lock in the doorknob with the key, she kept one eye on the stairwell. At last, the key slid into the lock and twisted.

Wrenching the knob with one hand, she yanked the keys out with the other. She kicked her briefcase into the foyer while pushing the door open. As she entered the apartment, an explosion of pain erupted in her head. She tried to push the door closed but found she was falling. Darkness closed in around her as she fell forward into nothingness!

With a start, Myra sat straight up in the bed. Her breathing was ragged. The cover and sheets were tangled about her legs. Her head was pounding almost as hard as her heart. It was just another nightmare, she realized. It disturbed her more than she cared to admit.

The illuminated lights on the alarm clock on the bedside table indicated it was a mere four in the morning. Extracting herself from the tangled sheet, she climbed out of bed and went to the kitchen for something to drink. It felt like she had eaten sawdust; her mouth was so dry. It was dark and quiet. The apartment was unnerving. The nightmare had shaken her badly, so she checked the door to make sure it was dead bolted. On impulse, she looked through the peephole. The landing was well lit, and no one was in sight.

A little relieved but still shaken, she reached for a glass in the kitchen cabinet and nearly dropped it. Her left hand was sporting a new bandage. She heard a roaring in her ears and immediately sat down in the closest chair and put her head between her legs to keep from passing out. It took a couple of minutes for the feeling to pass, then she carefully inspected her hand beneath the bandage. There was a slightly curved superficial cut about an inch long resembling a cut from glass. She could feel the panic rising in her chest and throat.

She frequently told her patients with posttraumatic stress disorder to drink ice water for the calming effect. The ice water shocked the body, so the metabolism had to go to work to rewarm the inner core. It distracted the brain so the intrusive thoughts abated. Following her own advice, she drank the water quickly. By the time she had finished the glass of water, she was feeling calmer. Her hands had quit trembling. Her breathing and heartbeat had returned to normal, but her hand was sore and she was still too scared to even think about what had happened and how she had obtained the bandage.

"Well, I guess going back to sleep is out of the question," Myra told her apartment as she poured herself another glass. Heading back down the hallway, she flipped on the light in her study. "Might as well get a head start on some of the paperwork." She refused to think about her injured hand. It was too terrifying to even consider the possibilities.

Her first task was to tackle the mountain of mail her assistant, Rhonda, had collected for her. Ever efficient, Rhonda had neatly stacked it in the center of Myra's home desk where it awaited sorting. She separated the bills and other pertinent things into one pile while shredding the junk mail. When that task was completed, she embarked on a more thorough inspection of the retained items.

She fired up her desktop computer while she sorted the bills and entered them into her handwritten ledger. It was more of a safety procedure keeping her financial accounts in a written journal instead of the computer, and she found that she enjoyed it. There were too many unscrupulous people hacking computers these days to steal personal information. She couldn't prevent someone from stealing her information or her identity, but she could take precautions that would slow it down. She always used a credit card to pay her bills and make purchases. Later, she electronically made a credit card payment from her checking account at another bank on the secure banking site. She strived to keep as much personal information from her electronic devices as possible. She also avoided storing passwords and login information on her devices.

Many of her past patients had been incarcerated for theft by various means and had willingly shared their secrets of obtaining information with her. Now she was a bit paranoid about her financial handling.

Completing that task, she set about reviewing the rest of the mail. There was a "thinking of you" card from her best friend from college. Myra made a mental note to call her later in the day. She had sent her an e-mail explaining her circumstances when the quarantine had first been initiated, but she had been so busy she had neglected to call her friend the entire time at the prison.

She found a few business letters, a couple of cards, one from her mother, two party invitations, one baby shower invitation, some miscellaneous things, and one letter with her name and address sprawled in familiar handwriting on an expensive quality envelope. There was no return address and no postmark. She slid her ebony letter opener, that had belonged to her father, under the corner of the flap with dread. She slashed the envelope open. The handwritten letter inside was of matching high-quality paper.

Chapter 63

Dearest Myra,

It has been difficult for me this last week not seeing you. I miss the glow of your silky hair...the
smell of your body. I know it has been difficult
for you too, this separation. I bet you have had
some sweet dreams about me lately. Absence does
that sometimes...it makes the heart grow fonder,
you know.

   Don't worry though. I'm on my way! I can't
wait to be reunited with you. To feel your body
pressed against mine. Our union will be a joyous
occasion. Make yourself ready for me, darling.
I'll be there as soon as I can. I know this is a short
note, but I have to go for now, love. Lots to do
before bed! Sweet dreams!

Forever yours in love

Myra was shaking as she read the letter. It was the first time she
had received one of the letters at her apartment. How had he sent
it to her without a postmark? Had he hand-delivered it to the main
office of the apartment complex? Had Rhonda unwittingly brought
it from the office? Could Darrell really be her stalker? Would it ever
stop? She felt dirty just reading it, and unexpectedly, she missed the
security of the prison.

It was only four thirty in the morning, too early to call Bret or Detective Parks. She paced the floor. Her first day back in her apartment was off to a great start! She assumed he was just trying to rattle her. If he was, it was definitely working!

Flushed with anger and agitation, Myra stormed her way to her master bedroom. She needed a shower to cool down. Maybe by the time she finished and eaten breakfast, it would be late enough to call one of the guys. She knew there was little they could do today with it being a Saturday, but at least it would be on record.

Though restless and agitated, Myra patiently waited until 9:00 a.m. before calling anyone. She tried Bret first only because she missed his voice, but her call went straight to his voice message. Her next call was to Detective Parks. He answered on the first ring.

"Detective Parks," he answered.

"Hello, Detective. This is Dr. Myra Christie. Have you made any progress on my stalking case yet?"

"Unfortunately, no. I reinterviewed your office staff, especially that guy you e-mailed me about. I had a little trouble tracking him down initially, but I guess you already know that."

"You mean Darrell?"

"Yeah. We've been trailing him for a few weeks now, but we haven't found anything yet."

"What do you mean about having trouble tracking him down? I've been out of town for a few weeks."

"Well, after I got your e-mail, I went by your office to talk with him. He wasn't there, and no one knew where he was. We went by his apartment, and he wasn't there either. His roommate hadn't seen him either."

"You mean he's missing? I talked with my office one day, and they said he had missed work without calling out, but they didn't mention that he was still missing." Alarmed, Myra started reviewing all her e-mails from her office.

"Not now. We finally found him. He had been in a car accident and was in the hospital," Detective Parks explained.

"Oh my god! Is he okay?" She was stunned. No one had mentioned Darrell being in the hospital.

"Yeah. He's fine. His car was totaled, and he hit his hard pretty hard. He was admitted with a severe concussion. His doctor said he had come in by ambulance really confused and not very coherent. I guess that happens with severe concussions. He spent a couple of days there and then was released. We talked with him after he was released. He was broadsided at an intersection by someone running a red light."

"Wow. I'm glad he's okay. I can't believe my staff didn't notify me of his accident."

"Well, anyway…it sounds like he has the hots for you, but he's denied sending you any letters or anything. He said he's talked to you a few times about the way he feels, and he knows you don't reciprocate his feelings. I think he may be telling the truth, but we've been trailing him anyway. He's the closest thing we have to a lead."

"Do you know if he's been near my apartment complex anytime over the past few weeks?" she asked.

"Not that I know of. My people know to notify me if he's ever in your area. Why?"

"I received a letter from my stalker while I was in Lieber Correctional Facility working a case, and I received another one here at my house while I've been gone."

"Lieber? Were you there during that quarantine that's been all over the news?" he asked interestedly.

"Yes, I'm sorry to say. It has not been fun."

"Do they know what caused all the problems?"

"Black mold from a water leak in one of the cellblocks. Apparently, one of the inmates realized what it was and decided to mix some scrapings into the food in the cafeteria. It made a lot of people really sick, but everyone is on the mend now."

"That's good to hear. I'm sorry we have not been able to grasp many leads in your case. I can stop by this afternoon to pick up the letter," he offered.

"Thanks. I'll see you then." Myra dropped her cell phone onto her desk. She was frustrated to hear there was no progress in her case and shocked to hear about Darrell. Why hadn't anyone in her office mentioned that Darrell had been in an accident and hospitalized?

With that taken care of, Myra looked at a list she had made earlier that morning while trying to pass some time. Her next call was to her mother. They caught up with family business, including the release of the quarantine at the prison. Toward the end of the conversation, her stepfather, Jack Carson, came on the line. They discussed the situation with the prison as well before he told her he would like to formally announce his candidacy for the senate as soon as possible. He wanted her in attendance when he made the announcement, which would be next Monday afternoon, just a little over a week away.

While she was happy and excited for him, it was a bit overwhelming for her with everything else going on. Thankfully, she would not be in the limelight much. Her mother would send her an itinerary after the announcement with events she would need to attend over the next several months. She had asked that they keep them to a minimum. But knowing her mother, she would have so many that she would be forced to thin them out herself.

She still needed to contact her cousin about the wedding details, but she decided to put that task off until the evening so they could have a long talk. Her more pressing matter was to do some much-needed grocery shopping. If she wanted to eat anytime soon, that had to be done immediately. She grabbed her list and headed out.

Myra's cell phone rang in the middle of the produce section. She had just started her shopping and was tempted to ignore the call until she saw Bret's name pop up on the screen. Her heart skipped a beat, and she suddenly felt giddy. "Hello?" she answered a little breathlessly.

"I'm on my way to Columbia. Where are you?"

"Well, hello to you too. It's nice to hear from you. I'm fine, thank you. And you?" she teased.

"I'm serious, Myra. Where are ya?"

"I'm at the grocery store. Why are you coming to Columbia?" She sincerely hoped it was to see her.

"To see *you*. We need to talk."

"Well, I just got here, and I need groceries or I'm going to starve. How far away are you?"

"About thirty minutes from Columbia. I left as soon as Dale called me."

Now she was miffed. "Dale called you?" She tried to act nonchalant. "What does that have to do with you coming to Columbia?"

"He didn't call ya?" He sounded surprised.

"Why would he call me? Last I heard, he was recovering at home from his contact with the black mold."

Bret growled into the phone. "We have a huge problem. I guess you haven't been watching television or listening to the radio either, have you?"

"You're starting to scare me, Bret. What's going on?"

"An inmate on Heirwick's block escaped sometime in the night. We're not sure how he got out or exactly when. There's a Nationwide BOLO [be on the lookout] out on him."

"Oh no! That's horrible! Is there anything I can do?" she asked.

"Yeah, listen to me and stay where ya're. I'm on my way."

"Why are you on your way to me?" She placed some bananas in her cart.

"Are you serious, Myra? Heirwick asked for you specifically before he would talk to anyone. He seemed fixated on ya during yawr sessions. Oh, and let's not forget that he made his confessions to ya against his attorney's advice. I'm concerned he's comin' for ya." Bret was obviously agitated and worried.

"Coming after me? Why on earth would he come after me? First of all, it's not Heirwick, just another inmate in his cellblock. Secondly, neither of them even know where I live, Bret." She placed some fresh spinach, romaine lettuce, cabbage, and kale in her cart before moving on through the produce section.

"I guess it never occurred to ya that he might have friends watchin' ya. Maybe someone to hurt ya for him or just to tail ya? Hell, we don't even know if he has an accomplice!" He was getting exasperated. "I need ya to stay right where yaw'r, Myra! I'll meet ya there. I just need the address."

"The address of the grocery store?"

"Yes! The address where yaw'r! I could find it myself, but if you give me the address, it will save me some hassle," he explained.

"I hope to not be here that long. I'm almost finished. Let me give you my home address and I'll just meet you there. I just need to drop some stuff off at my dry cleaners on the way home." She rattled off her address.

"I want ya to stay away from yawr apartment. I need ya to stay in a public place. If he *is* after ya, he'll be less inclined to grab ya in a public place."

"I have things I need to get done, Bret. You don't even know if he's after me."

"It's a gut feelin', Myra! Please listen to me!" he pleaded. "Are ya always so stubborn?"

"No." She smiled. "Sometimes I'm worse! See you in twenty!" She gave him the name of the grocery store and the name of the road for the location. "You better hurry up and get here!" She was so excited she felt jittery. A mischievous grin crossed her face, and she pointed her cart toward another part of the store. It was only then that she realized she had been so excited to hear his voice that she completely forgot to tell him about the new letter, and the mysterious cut appearing on her hand.

Chapter 64

Myra was waiting just inside the grocery store. She had already made her purchases, and everything was bagged up in the cart, waiting to be transferred to her Jeep. She peered out the automatic doors by the registers, looking for Bret. It had been twenty-five minutes, and she expected to see him at any moment.

"Hello, beautiful! I really didn't expect ya to listen to me and stay here," a voice said behind her.

Myra whirled around to face Bret, and her breath caught in her chest. He had on dark reflective sunglasses and looked like a bronzed superhero standing there in a faded and slightly too tight T-shirt that hugged all the right areas. His faded jeans clung nicely too. It was a nice change from the hazmat suits she had seen him wearing.

"I'm not stupid. He's a serial killer," she stated after she could breathe again.

"Are ya ready?" he asked. His deep Southern drawl rattled her to her core.

"Yes. I had planned on stopping by the dry cleaners, but that can wait until Monday," she responded. She glanced back at the registers as he pushed the cart toward her Jeep. All the women and a few men were staring at Bret like he was a juicy steak and they had not eaten in months. She smiled to herself and followed him out.

He had parked right next to her Jeep, which made it more convenient for them both. She unlocked the Jeep, and he quickly transferred the groceries into the back. "Ya get in the Jeep. When I'm finished, I want ya to take the long way to yawr apartment. I'm goin' to be followin' ya."

She did as he asked without argument. In fact, she rather enjoyed sitting in the Jeep, watching him flex those delicious muscles putting her purchases in her vehicle. *It should be a sin to be that gorgeous*, she thought. A slow smile spread over her face.

He looked up and caught her watching him with the smile on her face. She couldn't read his expression because his beautiful blue eyes were hidden behind those stupid sunglasses. "Ya ready?" he asked as he placed the last bag in the Jeep.

"Anytime you are." She involuntarily licked her lips. His lips twitched with an effort to hide his own smile. He shut the hatch door, pushed the cart to a holding area, then climbed into his black SUV. The windows were so dark with tinting, she had to assume he was ready for her to lead the way because she couldn't see him.

Normally, a five-minute drive to the grocery store took fifteen minutes on the way back to the apartment. Myra took the longest way she could think of and then tacked on a scenic route through another couple of neighborhoods. When they arrived at the apartment complex, she motioned where he was to park before pulling into her assigned parking space.

"Nice complex," he said, grabbing several bags of groceries from the cargo space of her Jeep. He followed her up the steps to her apartment, and she felt self-conscious in her brief denim shorts, deep V-neck top, and sandals.

"Did you drive all the way up here just to see the letter? I could have e-mailed a copy to you, you know," she went on merrily, oblivious to the havoc she was wreaking on Bret with the gentle sway of her hips and bare long legs.

"Can we just get your groceries inside first?" he asked more calmly than he felt.

"How long can you stay? I thought I would make us some lunch," she blissfully went on before he could answer. "I hope you haven't eaten yet." She beamed at him as they reached her landing.

He watched her long well-toned sleeveless arms as she fiddled with the key and dead bolt lock. She suddenly felt as nervous as a teenager on her first date. It seemed to take her forever to get both the locks unlocked and door opened. He followed her inside and made his way to the island bar as she closed the door behind them.

She stepped next to him, placing her two bags and her wallet on the bar as well. "I'll be right back with the rest." He slipped through the door, and she began putting things away. He was back within a couple of minutes. "I locked yawr Jeep for ya." He put the rest of the bags on the bar, locked the dead bolt, then leaned casually against the bar.

"Can I get you something?" She was rooting around in the bags for all the perishable items first.

"Ya sure can." He reached for her, pulling her into his arms and fastening his mouth hungrily on hers before she realized what he was doing. After a long breathless kiss, he murmured softly against her mouth, "Anyone ever tell ya that ya talk too much?"

Her senses were reeling, her heart pounding against her chest like a trapped butterfly, and her knees trembled so badly she was afraid they might buckle. She leaned into him for support, and he wrapped his arms around her. His tongue darted against her lips, igniting a sizzling fire that threatened to envelope her. Her lips parted involuntarily, and he deepened the kiss. His hands traveled down to her tight buttocks, pulling her into him.

His rock-hard body was tight with longing and excitement. She felt dizzy and exuberant. His kisses were speaking to her on a primitive level. Her fingers traveled up to twist into his wavy hair with a mind of their own. Hungrily, she pressed even closer to him, her head falling back as his lips trailed a line of kisses across her jaw and down her slender neck.

With one swift motion, he bent and caught her at the knees, lifting her into his arm, his lips never leaving her hot skin. "Where's the bedroom?" he whispered against her throat.

"Hmmm?" She ceased to think as pleasure rippled through her body.

"If ya don't tell me where the bedroom is, I'm going to take you right here in the kitchen." He nibbled on her earlobe.

"Down the hall on the right," she muttered as little sparks of electricity traveled through her body.

He walked with purpose as he carried her to the bedroom in his arms. All the while, she trailed little kisses along his jaw and chin. A low rumble sounded in his chest when her teeth lightly nipped the soft skin of his neck. He lowered her to the bed. His knuckles grazed the soft skin of her stomach, causing her to catch her breath as he fought with the button on her shorts. Myra kicked her sandals off as he tugged the shorts down her long legs, followed by a trail of heated kisses.

A hot tongue flicked across her navel, causing a sharp intake of her breath as he tugged her shirt over her head. He stopped and stood stock-still, staring at her long sinuous body dressed in only a creamy red lace bra and matching panties. His expression had her body blazing.

In quick succession, he kicked off his shoes, stripped off his shirt and jeans, and covered her body with his own. The kiss was more passionate than any she had ever had, and she moaned in delightful agony as his thumb teased her nipple through her bra. His hands seemed to be everywhere, liquid fire leaping from his fingertips. She nipped softly at his neck and his chin with her teeth, earning a grunt of approval.

She only ever had a few boyfriends over the years with the rare sexual encounter. This was a whole new experience for Myra. For many years, she thought there was something wrong with her sexually. She had never really enjoyed it before. Now as her body tingled and sizzled all over, maybe the problem had not been with her after all. She had never had an encounter like this before. It took her breath away.

Soft hands left feathery trails of flames along his back and arms. Her skin smelled of sweet vanilla and something else, something intoxicating to him. He could not get enough, and neither could she. Wriggling softly beneath him, legs wrapping around his, she pressed herself closer and nearly undid him.

He raised his head slightly and looked longingly into her eyes. "I've wanted ya since the first moment I laid eyes on ya," he whispered hoarsely. "It was hell being around ya every day and not being able to touch ya." His head dipped to taste her lips again.

A commotion in the kitchen caught them both by surprise. "Myra? Are you home?" a female voice called out.

"Are ya expecting anyone?" he asked.

"Oh God! It's the receptionist from my work. She's been collecting my mail for me. I guess she didn't get my message that I came home yesterday!" Myra wriggled out from under Bret and threw her clothes on. "Be right there, Rhonda!" she called out.

"Ya might want to turn your shirt right side out and around if ya don't want her to know she interrupted somethin'." He laughed, pulling lightly on the tag of her shirt beneath her chin.

"Shit!" she exclaimed as she tugged the shirt back off. She could feel the heat in her cheeks. "I'm coming!" she called out to stall. Feeling like a teenager caught kissing by her parents; she pulled her shirt on correctly and smoothed her hair. She looked longingly at him sprawled out on her bed before turning on her heel to meet Rhonda.

Chapter 65

"Hi! I didn't realize you were back yet. I collected your mail for you," Rhonda greeted her with a hug.

"Thank you. I hadn't gotten around to that yet today. Thank you for all you've done while I was cooped up in the prison under quarantine. I hope that never happens again!" Myra felt like she was babbling, so she started putting away her groceries.

"You are going to have to explain how all that happened. It sounds very intriguing, to say the least. You have missed so much at work too! Darrell is so stressed right now. I'm not sure what's going on with him. He's been very quiet at work, too. By the way, Samantha told us last week she was leaving at the end of August." Rhonda named off one of the other psychologists in the firm.

"You're kidding?" Myra paused in surprise.

"Nope, she said she couldn't handle working with the prisoners like you do. Elaine tried to get her to stay by offering to find someone else to take over the prison work, but she refused. Personally, I think she's been dating a psychologist in that big firm across town. There's also that long drive she has every day and fighting all that traffic to get her kids from childcare before it closes." Rhonda went on with her news. "Oh, and Leslie and Jake are getting married! He proposed around the time you went under quarantine."

"I'm so happy for her. They make such a great couple, and he's so good with her son. It's been really hard on her and her son since her husband, Derrick, died a couple of years ago," Myra replied. Leslie had done a summer internship with Myra's office two years ago. She had landed a nice job at a nearby hospital and stayed in contact with everyone. "Oh great!" she muttered as she realized the ice cream had begun to melt. She put the container in a plastic bowl before placing it in the freezer.

Rhonda snickered as she watched Myra. "Well, I think that's the majority of the important news of the office. I have to go for now. I have a big date to get ready for tonight. I'll try and stop by tomorrow to do some more catching up and to let you know how the date went!" Rhonda's bubbly voice and personality were infectious. She blew Myra a kiss as she walked out the door.

"I didn't think she would ever leave." Bret pouted from the hallway as Myra finished putting the last of the groceries away. She picked up the mail to drop it on her desk in the study. She intended to pick up where they had left off. He was leaning against the wall in nothing but his jeans. His chest and abs rippled with muscles at the barest of movement. She glanced at the mail so she could catch her breath. She paled as she read the top envelope in the stack. "What is it?" Bret asked.

"It looks like another letter from my stalker. I found another one in my mail Rhonda had collected while I was at Lieber," she said flatly as she tore open the envelope.

Hello, my beautiful dove,

I've missed you so much this past week. Those dazzling green eyes of yours looking deep into my soul…we are made for one another, you and I. I know you can feel it just as I do. Not being able to touch you has been almost more than I can bear.

Is it as difficult for you, my darling? It was not my intention that we should be apart this long. Have your bags packed, love! I'll be collecting you in a day or two. I promise you, love. I've been waiting a long time for you. Very soon, my darling. Just a little more patience, I promise!

With all my love

"Dear God, it sounds remarkably like the last one."

"Can I see the other one?" Bret asked.

Myra padded to her study with Bret on her heels. She crossed to her desk and handed him the envelope containing the first letter. She sank down in her chair as he read it and compared the two. He was leaning against her desk with nothing on but low riding jeans. Her heart started to hammer, and she stared at the ripped muscles of his abdomen.

The man was built like a superhero too, she thought. Her fingers itched to reach out and rake her long nails across those muscles. She wondered if he had that bronzed skin all over or if it was part tan. Biting her lip for a distraction, she retrained her eyes on his face. He was still studying the two letters, comparing them.

A muscle twitched in his jaw as he gritted his teeth. "I need these letters," he stated.

"Detective Parks will be stopping by this afternoon to pick up the first one. I called him about it this morning right after I left that message for you," she explained.

His eyes met hers over the letters. "I need the originals. We'll give him copies. Anybody else touch these other than you and me?" he asked.

"Not since I have opened them. I can't figure out how he got my home address."

"That's a good question. I'd like to know that too." He pulled a cell phone from his back pocket and scrolled through his contacts. Selecting a number, he put the phone to his ear and waited.

"It's me," he said into the phone as if he knew the person on the other end was expecting his call. "I'm here with 'er She just got two more of those letters in the mail. I'm takin' the originals to have 'em printed on Monday. They're both just like he said on the phone." He paused to listen. "Yes, he's still in lockup. The warden said he's to be notified before he leaves his cell for any reason." He paused again and listened. "Just what I was thinkin'…." He trailed off. She could hear a deep voice on the other end but could not understand what was being said. "Yeah, I was thinkin' we should put 'er under protective surveillance for a while. I can handle it, but I'm gonna need a team." Bret listened a while longer before abruptly ending the call.

"Did you just hang up on someone?" she asked, surprised.

"Hmmm?" He looked at his phone as if seeing it for the first time. "Oh! No, he was finished. It was my boss. He has a tendency to issue orders then just ring off." Bret looked like he was contemplating something.

"What's wrong, and what was that about protective surveillance?"

"We're puttin' ya under protective surveillance until further notice. We want to make sure the inmate is not after ya and that Heirwick has no accomplices out there. The problem is that we're spread thin until mid-next week, so I get to watch ya all by my lonesome till then." He smiled wickedly as he put the letters down on her desk and pulled her against him. "We have the whole weekend, and yaw'r not leavin' this apartment without me. My boss is callin' yawrs now to tell 'em ya won't be in the office until we get this resolved. We don't wanna to put *you* or anyone else in jeopardy."

"Um… I am the boss. Well, I'm one of the bosses. We have an equal partnership," Myra informed him.

"Really? Ya mean I'll be sleeping with the boss?" His tongue was doing naughty things to her neck and earlobe. *They are just going to love this latest development at the office*, she briefly thought as his mouth descended on hers. Suddenly, she didn't care what happened at the office.

Chapter 66

Monday morning dawned with a forecast of severe thunderstorms, both inside and outside Myra's apartment. The special agent in charge of the Columbia office personally arrived to introduce the protective team to Myra, only to find Bret in her bed. He was not happy about the turn of events and had removed Bret from the team for conflict of interest. It was a three-man team assigned to watch her at all times, although none were supposed to enter her residence unless there was a viable threat.

Bret had argued that having someone in the apartment was necessary since there were three stories of people going and coming. He had lost the battle and was ordered back to Charleston to assist with the investigation of victims and notifying their family members.

Myra had a splitting headache, and the argument did little to help, and neither did the aspirin she had taken. She ate a piece of dry toast, washing it down with tea to settle her stomach. How did everything seemingly go to hell so quickly?

She still had to go to Charleston to talk with Dr. Hull about the evaluation and to submit her report to him. She had promised Clara she would stop by the house. The problem was that the agent in charge wouldn't let her leave her house.

In the midst of everything, her phone was ringing off the hook from media outlets wanting her take on her stepfather's run for the senate. She had forgotten he was making the announcement that afternoon. It was just the perfect topper for an already wonderful morning, and it was barely eight in the morning. Her mother had scheduled a flight from Charleston to DC that was supposed to leave at 2:00 p.m. She was not looking forward to calling her mother to let her know she would not be able to make it.

After her own argument with everyone on her trip to Charleston, Myra climbed into her Jeep heading east on Interstate 26 to Summerville by eight thirty. She called Dr. Hull en route to his office so he could meet her there. Bret followed in his black SUV with a close tail of another agent who would be playing watchdog on the trip with his partner. It was not an ideal situation for her. Bret had demanded that she give everyone an itinerary of her day, and all shared cell phone numbers in case of changes or emergencies.

It was ten by the time she arrived in Summerville. Bret passed her on his way to his office as she exited the interstate with her tail in place. She took a few minutes to stop by a coffee shop before heading to Dr. Hull's office. Arriving before he did, she sat in her car sipping on a hot chocolate she had picked up earlier. A dark sedan was parked right behind her with the FBI agents, keeping close tabs on her. Flipping open her briefcase, she pulled out her report and reviewed it for at least the third time since she had completed it.

Moments later a red Lexus RX pulled up next to Myra's Jeep. The driver shut off the engine and gave her a little wave. She put her report back in her briefcase and grabbed her hot chocolate and a large coffee with light cream and extra sugar, just like he loved it, and a danish hidden inside a paper bag. His wife had him on a strict diet, which meant he cheated whenever he could. Dr. Hull gratefully accepted the coffee and the danish as he greeted her.

His secretary, Reno, looked up in surprise when they entered the office since he was not typically expected until almost lunch every day. Reno had been working with Dr. Hull for almost twenty years. She greeted them warmly. Not quite five feet tall, what she lacked in height, she made up for with her big bubbly personality. Dyed red hair, horned rimmed glasses blinged-out in rhinestones, and wearing multiple necklaces, rings, and bracelets, with outlandish brightly colored flowing clothing; Reno always reminded Myra of a 60s flower-child.

Following Dr. Hull into his inner office, Myra took a seat across from his desk. While he organized himself, she pulled the copy of her report from her briefcase. "I have my report for you. I'm sorry it took so long, but under the circumstances…" She trailed off as she slid the report across his desk for his review.

"So how was the quarantine? I was hoping to see you late last week."

"Well, I wouldn't jump straight to saying it was fun," she replied drily. "The FBI agent in charge asked me to stay a couple of days longer, and then I had to give a turn over report to the resident psychologist so he knew what I had been doing with his inmates in his absence. I didn't get out of there until late Friday afternoon, and you had already left your office," she explained.

"You should have called. Clara would have loved to have had you over for dinner," he lightly chastised, referring to his wife of many years.

"I'll have to take a rain check for that. I was so exhausted, and I couldn't wait to get home to my own bed. Sleeping on those uncomfortable cots is almost impossible." She made a face.

He smiled as he looked over the top of his reading glasses. "I'm sure. Well, at least you were there to finish the evaluation and keep an eye on the other inmates. It would have been most unfortunate if the place had gone on lockdown like that without a mental health provider in place to provide support. How did the guards and other staff take it?"

"They did pretty well. I talked to all of them on and off to make sure everyone was dealing with it okay."

"Did they ever figure out what the problem was in there?" he asked as he finally settled into his chair, sipping his coffee. He pulled the danish out and took a bite before pulling her report closer to inspect.

"Turns out it was black mold in a couple of the cells. Apparently, our Mr. Heirwick is one smart cookie. He suggested another inmate scrape some of the black mold in his cell into something to put in some of the food items. At least one guard ingested it, and another one inhaled the spores around the time it was being scraped. The scraping triggered the release of the spores and subsequent spread of the black mold that also made several inmates ill. It also resulted in the death of the inmate that scraped it. Another died because he had lung issues." She leaned back in her chair, sipping her hot chocolate.

"Black mold? That's some dangerous stuff! I didn't realize it could cause those kinds of problems if ingested."

"Yeah. They closed down the cellblock, and there's a hazardous removal company working in there to clean it up. I guess it could have been much worse," she replied.

"So let's see what you think about our man Heirwick." He rubbed his hands together as he began to examine her report. It took him a while to read it, making the occasional noncommittal noises as he read. She had also included a copy of the transcript of her interview with Heirwick, which he also read. After a considerable length of time, he looked at her with knit brows. "He rattled you, didn't he?"

"It was a most unusual interview, I will say," she allowed. "He is definitely inventive. I will give him that."

"Most unusual," Dr. Hull repeated thoughtfully. "Do you believe him?" he asked, looking directly in her eyes as though he was looking into the depths of her soul for the answer he sought.

"I believe we have had this conversation before. Yes, I know a great many people in the world believe in reincarnation, and there are instances that make you wonder, but I find it hard to believe any of his outlandish tales. He has illusions of grandeur, he is delusional, and he is narcissistic. He is very capable of assisting in his own defense, and he seems to completely understand his deeds. He crows over them, actually." Her last words were dripping in disdain.

He shrugged. "Everything you have just said is true, but perhaps the reincarnation is true as well. Who knows? Thank you for this. I had originally anticipated on submitting my own report as well, but Mr. Heirwick only told me part of his journey. He refused to answer my questions after a while and never discussed his recent crimes with me. That was why I contacted you. He insisted, actually."

"Who insisted?" She sat ramrod straight in her chair, alarm in her voice and on her face.

"Well, Mr. Heirwick, of course. He couldn't remember your name, per se, but he insisted on speaking with...let's see, how did he put it? Oh yes…the young beautiful blond collaborator. I didn't know what he was talking about at first, and then he referred to your father being an FBI agent and you being a psychologist that he knew I thought of you as a daughter. I knew it had to be you."

The color drained from Myra's face. Heirwick had known who she was before she walked in there to interview and evaluate him? What was really going on? "Did you ever mention me to him, even casually?" Concern and apprehension strangled her voice into more of a squeak.

"No. That's why I was stunned when he asked for you. He said he would only tell you everything. I didn't even get as far with him as the…um… Jack the Ripper story, I guess you would say."

Myra grabbed her briefcase and rounded his desk to give the very astonished Dr. Hull a daughterly hug. "I need to go. I need to talk to someone. Don't talk to anyone about me or this case for a while. An inmate in his cellblock has broken out. They have a nationwide BOLO out on him. I'm under FBI protection right now. I think it might be a good idea if we put you and Clara under it as well," she said as she hurried to his inner office door.

"Wait! We don't need protection, but now I'm really concerned about you. What exactly is going on here?" he asked, standing.

"I'm not sure yet, but I can guarantee you I'm going to find out one way or another," she promised as she slipped out the door.

As she hurried out of Dr. Hull's office, she called the cell phone number the FBI agent had given her to call to reach him in the car across the parking lot. He answered on the second ring, but before he could really say anything, she demanded to know Bret's location. The agent suggested the field office off Belle Isle Avenue in Mt. Pleasant, across the Cooper River.

She needed to talk to him in person and right away. She knew the local field office director was not going to like her showing up at the office, but oh well. Bret knew Heirwick and what he was capable of. He had seen him in action in the prison. The other agents assigned to her had never met him. Myra was bound and determined to get Bret back on the case! She just had too!

Chapter 67

One of the agents had followed Myra into the building and was sitting patiently in the waiting room. She met his eyes, and without a word, he rose and proceeded out of the building. Crossing the parking lot to her Jeep, she said, "I need to see Bret right now!"

"I'm not sure that's a good idea," he replied as his eyes scanned the parking lot. "I knew I should have been the one driving you."

"Too damn bad! I need to see him, with or without you," she snapped as she slipped into the Jeep and cranked the engine.

As he walked to the sedan behind her, she saw him pull out his cell phone. He was apparently informing the powers to be of the change of plans. Well, good for them! Nothing they could say at this point would sway her mind. Either she got Bret back on the case or there would be no FBI protecting her!

It was nearing one o'clock by the time Myra and the FBI agent walked into the FBI's Charleston field office. Bret was talking with the field office supervisory special agent when they arrived. A secretary ushered them in and offered them beverages before closing the door on her way out.

"Okay, Ms. Christie, what is this about?" the supervisory special agent, Paul Mims, asked, appearing bored.

"It's *Dr.* Christie, and I've stumbled onto some information that warrants Agent Myers to be back on the case," she announced, barely containing her fury over the agent's attitude.

"My apologies, Dr. Christie. I assure you I meant no disrespect. Agent Myers here was just telling me about the case you've been working on. I guess you met our special agent in charge earlier this morning out of the Columbia office."

"Yes, I did." She gritted her teeth at his patronizing tone. "I need to discuss the case with Agent Myers," she reiterated. "There have been some new developments."

"Agent Myers, as you know, is no longer on the case. What can I help you with?"

"You can start by reassigning him to the case." She was quickly losing her temper.

"I can't do that," he stated with a smug smile.

"Then you can explain to your superiors why I have refused my protective detail of a bunch of agents that do not know the case," she snapped. "And then you can explain to a congressional committee why I was not under protective detail. I'm sure my stepfather would like to hear all the details."

"Sir," Bret tried to interject.

"When I'm ready for your comments, I'll ask for them, Agent Myers!" Agent Mims bullied Bret. "Dr. Christie, why don't you have a seat so I can explain what a protective detail is. Then maybe you will understand why they are assigned to you."

That was it! Myra lost her temper. "Apparently, you don't know who I am, Agent." She hated to pull this, but this guy needed a slap in the face. "My father was Special Agent Michael Christie, agent in charge of the Richmond, Virginia, field office before he was killed in action and agent in charge of training at Quantico prior to that. My stepfather is Judge Jack Carson, running for senate in Virginia. Ring any bells? I am very familiar with the function of a protective detail. Furthermore, I am a forensic psychologist, and I was recruited by the FBI and turned them down once. I have a lot of friends in very high places that could make your life miserable, Agent, like the current deputy director of the FBI, my uncle Robert Dailey. Do I make myself clear?"

Agent Mims's eyes looked like they were about to bulge out of his head, and his face was so red she thought he might have a stroke. "Perfectly!" he spat. "But I'm still not changing my mind about this!"

"If you want this guy back behind bars, it's the only way you're going to catch him. You also need to get a protective detail on Dr.

Eugene Hull and his wife. Heirwick knows too much about Dr. Hull. I believe Dr. Hull and his wife are in mortal danger."

"I'll consider a detail for Dr. Hull and his family," Agent Mims finally spoke.

"You better do more than just consider it! He needs it immediately. Then make whatever call you need to make to get Agent Myers assigned back to my detail. I'll be expecting him at my apartment by the end of the afternoon."

"Dr. Christie, you are not my superior officer, and you don't make the decisions within the FBI. I respect your concern for Dr. and Mrs. Hull, and I appreciate your faith in Agent Myers, but do not think that just because you know a few people that you can come in here and demand special privileges."

"You are going to regret your decision, Agent!" With that, she spun on heel, yanked the door open, and proceeded out of the office, but not before she caught a glimpse of the smirk on her protective agent's face. What was his name again… Doug… Douglas? No, that wasn't right.

She was at her vehicle before she remembered it. Agent Dougin. He had enjoyed that show immensely by the look on his face. Agent Mims had a bad attitude. He had irritated her right from the start by calling her Ms. Christie when he knew very well her title was Doctor. Normally, that didn't bother her, but it was just his entire demeanor right from the start. He needed to be taken down a peg or two.

She immediately put a call into her uncle. The call went directly to his voice mail. She left a long message, briefly outlining the situation. She left her number for him and disconnected the call. *He's not going to be happy when he receives that message*, she thought.

She was still fuming when she hit Interstate 26 westbound twenty minutes later. Good grief, she hadn't even told Bret her uncle was the director. Most people wouldn't make the connection because he was her mother's half brother. He and her father had started out at the bureau at the same time. They had gone through the academy at Quantico together, and Uncle Robert had introduced her father and mother.

Her uncle had been after her since she graduated with her doctorate to join the FBI's profiling and psychology unit called the Behavioral Analysis Unit or the BAU. She enjoyed her job now, working with inmates and the private sector both. It left her time to do her own studies if she wanted. Plus she wasn't always on call like her father had been.

Before he had taken the position of special agent in charge of training, her father had always been traveling. It had bothered her when she was younger, not having her father around like the other kids. As she grew older, she understood it better and told her classmates he was a superhero. She still felt he was a superhero.

As if her mother could read her thoughts, her cell phone rang. "I'm sorry, Mom, but I'm not going to be able to make it to the announcement ceremony," Myra apologized.

"What's going on? I just got a call from Robert. He told me there was some kind of trouble down there that involved you."

"That serial killer case I was working on when the prison was put on lockdown due to the quarantine, well, Mom...one of the inmates in his cellblock escaped, and there's some information or an informant or something that has the FBI believing he's after me. I've got a security detail, but it's three guys who don't know anything about the case."

"I'll call Robert back."

"Hang on a second, Mom. There's more. The Columbia office and the Charleston office are not working together on this. I've been working with this agent by the name of Bret Myers at the prison. He knows the serial killer almost as well as I do. He came and watched over me all weekend by himself, and this morning they took him off the case. I just talked with the Charleston AIC, and he was an ass to me. They are not taking me seriously.

"I demanded that Eugene and Clara have a protective detail. Mom, this guy said something to Eugene. I can't remember how Eugene put it, but the killer knows way too much about him. I think he's been watching Eugene for a long time."

"Oh God! That's terrible."

"Agent Mims said he would *consider* getting them a protective detail, but I'm afraid by the time he gets around to it, it will be too late."

"I'm going to call your uncle Robert, darling," her mother told her. Leave it to her mother to try to fight all her battles for her. Myra told her she had already threatened him with that. "I'm not going to threaten, Myra. Robert knows Eugene very well. Trust me when I say he will have a detail shortly."

"Thanks, Mom. Why did you call in the first place?"

"I was calling to apologize. Someone let it slip that Jack was going to make his announcement tonight. It hit the news first thing this morning."

"I know. My phone has been ringing off the hook."

"I'm so sorry, dear. I wish I could do something about it."

"Don't worry, Mom. As soon as this stuff is all over, I'll gladly help out with the campaign as much as I can. I'm just sorry I can't make it there tonight."

"Jack will understand, darling. We need you to be safe. Now let me run. Jack is pestering me, wanting to know what is going on, and I need to call Robert immediately."

By the time her mother hung up, Myra was feeling much better and had left Charleston and its surrounding towns behind. It was a long boring drive back to Columbia. She turned her radio to pop music, turned up the volume, and tried to relax on the drive.

*****

Agent Dougin walked her up the steps and checked her apartment before she was allowed to enter, even though the dead bolt was still in place. It seemed rather silly and unnecessary to her, but Agent Dougin appeared more relaxed afterward. She invited him to stay in the apartment, but he assured her his replacement would be coming in soon. The director of the Columbia office had mentioned that morning that the agents would be primarily outside and, at their discretion, might check the interior of the apartment for her safety on occasion.

After today, there would be someone watching the apartment constantly, and one agent would be with her, if she had her way. If Heirwick did have an accomplice helping him with his deeds, they wanted to catch him or her in the act with Heirwick. She had no more than closed and locked the door behind Agent Dougin than her phone rang again. This time, it was Bret telling her he was on his way. Evidently, Agent Mims had been contacted by the director of the FBI about the incident in his office. The director of the FBI personally ordered Bret back on the case immediately. He had also ordered a protective detail for Eugene and Clara.

"Why didn't ya tell me the deputy director of the FBI was yawr uncle?" he asked. "It totally blindsided me in there."

"It just never came up in conversation. You knew about my dad, so I guess it just never occurred to me that you might not know they were brothers-in-law at one point," she explained.

"Now everyone will think I'm sleepin' my way to the top!" he complained.

Myra burst out laughing. "Serves you right for seducing me like you did!"

"Hey, I think it was mutual there, honey! By the way, you should have seen Agent Mims when your uncle called him. He was so rattled that he couldn't talk in complete sentences. I thought he was having a stroke!" Bret laughed.

"He's a pompous ass!" she stated emphatically.

"I was going to say he's always a dick, but hey, pompous ass works too!"

"Are you just now leaving Charleston?"

"Yes. I stopped by my place and packed a couple of bags first. I'm hittin' rush hour traffic here in Charleston, so it will be around six, I guess, before I'll be there. I have to check in with the Columbia office so they can put me up in a hotel."

"Do you really need to stay in a hotel?" she asked in a sultry voice.

"Afraid so, honey. We've got to keep this professional for the time being. At least ya got me back on the case so I can see ya." His

Texas accent was strong on the last part, and it sent shivers up her spine.

"Okay. Can you at least have dinner with me so I can catch you up with what I found out earlier today?" she asked.

"Yes, that we can do, at least meet in yawr apartment to discuss everything. No one has to know that yaw'r feeding me at the same time. What are we havin'?"

"I have a couple of rib eye steaks I was thinking of putting on the grill."

"You definitely talked me into it. I'll call you when I'm leaving the Columbia office."

"Sounds good! Be safe out there," she said as they hung up. She had anticipated working on some miscellaneous things that had been sitting on her desk for a while, but with the prospect of seeing Bret again, she decided to pamper herself instead. She felt almost giddy with excitement as she pulled the steaks out of the freezer to defrost before practically running to her bedroom.

At six o'clock, she was still working on the pampering. Hot rollers were in her hair, and she was fretting over what to wear. He had never seen her hair curled into long luscious waves. She had taken extra time with her makeup, another sight he had yet to behold. It had seemed somehow ridiculous in the prison to put on makeup and fix her hair in anything other than a ponytail, bun, or left straight.

She pulled a green sundress from the closet that matched her eyes and held it up as she inspected it in the mirror. She had already gone through half her closet. Her mother had purchased this dress for her last summer. She loved the fabric and the sway of the skirt with the flattering square neckline that cut across the top of her breasts, though she rarely wore the dress. It was just not professional enough to wear to the workplace, and she rarely went out. The last time she had worn it was to a friend's birthday party late last summer.

Finally making her selection, she was removing it from the hanger when her cell phone rang. Bret was on his way. He had just left the Columbia office and would check into his hotel after dinner. The giddy feeling returned, and she felt flushed as she hung up the phone.

Humming to herself, Myra sprayed herself liberally with her vanilla body spray before slipping into the dress and a pair of sandals. She removed the curlers from her hair and let the long blond locks fall about her shoulders. She lightly finger combed her hair to separate the curls. After double-checking her makeup, she blew herself a satisfied smile.

The doorbell rang while she was in the kitchen preparing the steaks for the grill. Immediately, her heart started thumping double-time in her chest. She saw him through the peephole before she opened her door. He looked delicious, she thought. Entering the apartment, he immediately swept her into his arms.

"I've missed you!" he whispered as his lips caught hers.

Chapter 68

After a nice dinner, Bret and Myra sat in her living room discussing her conversation with Dr. Hull. Bret, as she expected, was not happy. "So he definitely knew who ya were before ya even started workin' on this case?"

"Dr. Hull said he asked for me, but not by name originally. When I spoke with Heirwick in the prison on that very first day, I asked him why he had demanded my services. He acted like he knew exactly who I was, but he told me it was because he had seen me on television regarding the Johnson case. He told me he knew I treated my patients fairly. I thought it was a little odd at the time, but I couldn't put my finger on it. Then all that other stuff started happening, and I forgot about it."

"I don't like this at all." Bret frowned.

"Neither do I. I have no idea how he knew who I was, and it should have been just happenstance that Dr. Hull was asked to do the evaluation by the courts. But it's almost like Heirwick engineered the whole thing."

"Maybe ya worked with one of the other inmates before," he said thoughtfully. "Or maybe one of the inmates knew ya and mentioned ya to him?"

"No. While I was there, I checked in on all the inmates. I didn't know any of them. I'm really worried about Eugene and Clara." She twisted her hands in her lap nervously.

Taking her hands in his, he raised each one for a kiss. "Don't worry, honey. We'll get to the bottom of this somehow." He rubbed soothing circles on her hands with his thumbs.

"Something weird is going on. I just wish I could put my finger on it," she said. "I didn't get the impression that he had an accomplice during our talks. When I met him for the first time, it was like he was sizing me up. I had never seen him before, and I doubt very seriously if he had ever seen me." She shuddered, remembering those flat dull eyes of Heirwick.

"Maybe he just read somethin' about ya. Don't put too much emphasis on it for now. The main thing is that yawr safe. We're gonna catch Rodriguez again, and Heirwick is locked up. Don't worry."

Bret had not stayed in the apartment very long. They ate and then discussed Heirwick and his fascination with her, then he left. He didn't want to create any more problems with his chain of command. Instead, he took post outside the apartment complex to watch over her during the night.

Early the next morning, Myra was interrupted while making her ritual morning cup of tea by the ringing of her doorbell. Expecting Bret, she was disappointed to find Agent Maldonado from the day before. "Good morning, ma'am," he said as he flashed his credentials for her.

"Good morning. Is something wrong?" she asked.

"No, ma'am. We just wanted you to get used to seeing us around, to recognize us in the case of emergency. I'll be your chaperone for the day. There is another agent downstairs that will be watching your apartment in our absence in the event you have errands to do today."

"Actually, I do need to do something. I need to go to my office today." She smiled.

He frowned. "You were told yesterday to stay here as much as possible to reduce the threat. You are not going to make this easy for us, are you?" he asked.

"I'm sorry, Agent, but I have a job to do, too. I have been away from it for over a month due to unforeseen circumstances. My staff are overwhelmed, and my office is in turmoil," she patiently explained. "I'll be ready in an hour."

"Of course, but today I drive you everywhere. Is that understood?"

She smiled. "Very well. I can work with that."

"I'll be back up in an hour. Do not leave your apartment without me by your side," he ordered.

She nodded her agreement and locked her door as he turned on his heel and left. Oh, those FBI agents were just going to love her, she thought. By now, she was certain that word of mouth had traveled so that every FBI agent in the state knew who she was and to whom she was related. She expected a call from Uncle Robert very soon, chastising her for not conforming. Yes, it would not be long, she was certain.

Exactly an hour later, her doorbell rang. It was Agent Maldonado patiently waiting to escort her to his vehicle. She almost dreaded going into the office. It was in such disarray, according to Rhonda. They arrived before most of the other staff, so Myra put on the coffee and hot water for everyone. She was in her office going through a tremendous stack of mail when a throat clearing gained her attention. Darrell stood in her office doorway with a cup of steaming coffee in hand.

"Well, look who decided to finally show up," he said playfully.

"It's been a while." She laughed. "I would have traded with you any day of the week."

"Hmmmm… I think I'll pass." He grinned. "What are you doing here? I heard you were going to be out of the office for a while."

"I am, but I need to go through some things first." She sighed.

"Already causing them trouble, eh?"

"I try to keep them on their toes." She laughed. "So how are you feeling? I heard you were in a pretty nasty car accident."

"I'm good. Just got banged up a little. I was sore for a few days. I got a new car out of the deal!"

"Congratulations." She laughed.

"I guess Rhonda filled you in on everything that has been happening around here," he speculated.

"Yes. I saw her on Saturday. Sounds like you have had your hands full."

"Yeah, well, just another day at the office. I think we have most of everything under control here at the moment. You need to take care of this situation you are in and stay safe. We need you back here, but we can hold things down until this is over," he replied. "It sounds like a nasty business."

"It has been…" She trailed off.

"I'm sorry I added to your stress." He hung his head. "I've had the hots for you since I got here. When you finally started talking to me…well… I guess I just got it into my head that you were interested in me too. That you were just playing hard to get."

"I appreciate your apology. You need to learn that when someone says no, they mean no. Not everything is a game, Darrell."

"I know," he said. After a momentary lapse of conversation, he asked, "Is it really true you have a serial killer after you?"

"I don't know. Maybe. An inmate from the same cellblock where the guy I was interviewing was housed, escaped a couple of days ago. I think his name was Rodriguez, but I really don't know anything about him. I think the FBI is concerned he was sent after me by the other guy. Whether or not he is after me is anyone's guess. At this point, I think the FBI is just taking extra precautions until the guy is recaptured," she explained.

"Elaine and Stephanie held an office meeting and told us about that. The police have interviewed everyone in here, and no one has been giving any personal information out concerning any of our staff. It's hard to say how he got that information. You just take care of yourself."

"I will. I think I'll putter around in here for a while this morning to catch things up before I leave. If there is something that I can do from home, just let me know. It will be welcomed to take away the boredom!"

He threw her a mock salute as he continued down the hall to his own office. The office was abuzz with excitement over her return, even if it was only for a few hours. A small parade of staff came in to see her over the next couple of hours, slowing her progress. Everyone wanted to know all the details of what it was like being in quarantine in a prison. Thankfully, there had been no further letters or correspondence received at the office from stalker in her absence; though if she thought about it, somehow that fact was even more frightening.

As a result, it was much later than she intended when she finally left the office a little after two in the afternoon. To his credit, Agent Maldonado had not said much, except that he wanted her back in the apartment as quickly as possible. She sat back and enjoyed being chauffeured back to her apartment. As Agent Dougin had done the day before, she was escorted all the way to her apartment, although this time, Agent Maldonado did not inspect the entire apartment. There was really no need since the other agent was watching from somewhere in the vicinity.

*****

At five in the morning, Myra was awakened by the shrill of her cell phone. She sleepily answered the phone to hear Dale's voice on the other end. "Hi, Warden Jones. Miss me already?" She laughed groggily.

"Sure do," he replied flatly. "Are you sitting down?"

"In a matter of speaking." She yawned, flipping on the bedside lamp. "What's wrong? You sound horrible."

"I hate to tell you this, but Heirwick has escaped!"

"Oh God! What happened?"

"I'm not really sure. Everything is still chaotic down here from the quarantine fiasco. We have a construction crew in hazmat suits cleaning up in that cellblock. We had to move inmates around to make room for everyone with that block closed down for repairs. It appears he escaped sometime between midnight and the five a.m. shift change." When Myra didn't comment, he continued, "He killed an inmate and two guards and badly injured another guard who maintains the security cameras. I've been off trying to recuperate, and we are still short-staffed. My guards came in at five for the shift change and found the bodies with Heirwick missing. It appears he stole one of the guard's uniforms and walked out the front door. I can't believe this happened."

Myra was in shock. What were the odds that two inmates of the same high-security prison escaped within days of each other from the same cellblock? *Not good*, she thought. Was it possible Heirwick helped the other inmate escape so he could help Heirwick? He would not be arrested as easily a second time. The first time had been so incident-free that Myra was beginning to think maybe he had engineered it. Could all this be a part of some larger plan?

"Myra? Are you still there?" Dale asked. Myra nodded. "Myra? Hello? Are you there, Myra?" he asked again.

Realizing he couldn't see her nod through the phone, she squeaked out a breathless "I'm still here."

"I don't want to alarm you any more than you already are, but Myra, he has all kinds of drawings of you in his cell. His journal is full of comments and thoughts about you…more drawings. The FBI and local guys are here. They were called in immediately. Myra, Heirwick is fixated on you."

"Fixated on me?" she parroted automatically.

"We found more of those letters you've been getting from your stalker in his cell. I think he's going to come to you, Myra. I wanted you to be prepared. I have to go. I have to talk to all the authorities. I'm so sorry, Myra," he said as he hung up. Dale was genuinely distressed. The worst psychopathic serial killer the world had ever seen had just escaped a maximum-security prison and was fixated on her. Her worst nightmare had just come to life.

She sat huddled in her blankets, terrified to move for several minutes. Realizing she had to take some kind of action, Myra finally dialed Bret's number. He answered on the third ring and was suddenly alert when he heard the terror in her voice. "He's escaped! Dale just called, and he's gone!"

Bret knew exactly what she was saying and immediately took charge. "I'm on my way! Don't answer the door for anyone but me! Do you understand?" he barked into the phone.

"I won't. Please hurry!" she cried into the phone.

Chapter 69

Ten minutes later, Bret was pounding on her door. Myra was wrapped tightly in the comforter from her bed and was still shaking violently as she struggled with the locks. He burst through the door as soon as she had it opened and took her in his arms, holding her tightly. Her head was cradled on his shoulder.

He held her for a long moment before assisting her to the sofa where he sat her down. "I'm gonna make ya some hot tea. I've already called the local director, and he's on top of it. The Charleston field office has already sent personnel to the prison. An APB, all-points bulletin, has been issued for him and the car he stole. We'll find him," he assured her as he crossed to the open kitchen to put the kettle of water on to boil.

"Bret, Dale said they found more of those stalker letters in his cell. He's been my stalker all this time. How could he have sent those letters and made those phone calls while he was incarcerated?" she asked.

"I'm not sure, but I'll bet it's being investigated as we speak. They will be tearin' his life apart, especially since he's been in there." A few minutes later, he was back with her hot tea. He had added more sugar than she was accustomed to drinking, but she sipped it anyway. *He must really have a sweet tooth*, she thought. Then she began to question her own sanity. Who thinks about things like that right after they've been told a serial killer is fixated on them? Her hands were still trembling, but at least the initial shock finally started wearing off.

"When you were talkin' to Heirwick, did he ever say anything or indicate in any way that he may be interested in ya?" he asked.

She thought for minute, running several of their conversations through her head that had been suggestive. "He was challenging, like he was trying to scare me with his story. He flirted a bit, but I rebuffed him, stayed professional and focused on the interview. When I received those letters, I was stunned. They seemed so... I don't know...like he was trying to rattle me for some reason."

She looked at Bret pleadingly. "You have to understand that he excels at manipulation and loves to play games. It's all a game to him," she reasoned. "He knows or at least suspects the authorities have read those letters. He knows you will expect him to come here. I don't think he will. I think those letters were a red herring."

"He told ya he was comin' soon, and he just broke out of jail. I would say that he was sendin' you a message, sweetheart." Bret was peering out the blinds to parking lot. It was almost six o'clock, and the sky was beginning to streak with pink, purple, and yellow hues from the rising sun.

"This feels just like those nightmares I've been having lately," she muttered, annoyed with herself for being reactionary in this instance.

Bret's head swiveled around, and his eyes locked with hers. "What do ya mean?"

"I've had several since that one at the prison, and a few before. Mostly they were all along the same lines. I guess subconsciously, he had more of an effect on me than I thought." She sipped at her tea.

"Why didn't ya tell me you were still having those?" he asked softly, sitting beside her and pulling her close to him.

"They are just nightmares. I don't even know what sparked them."

"What are they like?" he asked in the same soft tone. When he spoke like that, all loving and concerned, she knew she could deny him nothing. That deep Texas drawl of his sounded like warm honey with streaks of sunshine running through it. Women must find it devastating to be interrogated by him, she thought. "Were they like the one ya had in Dale's office?"

"Just your typical nightmare, I guess. I feel like I'm being hunted, chased in the dark, then attacked. I can hear his voice in my dreams and that horrible laugh of his. It's so grating and irritating to me." She shrugged. Then she added as an afterthought, "His laugh, I mean. It's extremely irritating."

"I talked to Dale on the way over here. He said Heirwick wrote *angel of hell* on his cell wall in blood. Does that mean anything to ya?" he asked.

She shivered involuntarily. "Yes, he kept telling me that. You will need to contact the court for a subpoena, and request a copy of my report and transcript from the court of the interview. I cannot discuss anything with you until you present me with a subpoena. I'm sure the judge will immediately sign a subpoena for you, considering he just escaped."

Bret rose from the sofa and walked into her study to make a phone call. A few minutes later, he returned. "The local director is obtainin' a copy and will be here shortly. He thinks we need to move ya to a safe house. I agree with him."

"I just got home, and now you want me to leave again?" she asked in disbelief.

"It's just for a few days until we catch him," he tried to persuade her.

"And what if he goes underground and you don't catch him? Am I supposed to just live in fear for the rest of my life that he *might* come after me?" She was being irrational and she knew it, but the words just sort of spilled out of their own accord.

"Why don't we wait and cross that bridge if we get there?" he placated. "It'll be easier for us to watch ya there and to make sure yaw'r safe."

She sighed in frustration. Her life had totally been turned upside down of late, and she felt on the verge of tears. "Can I at least tell my family?"

"It's not a good idea, but we will give you a disposable cell phone to call them on if you'd like. Considerin' yawr stepfather just announced he's runnin' for the senate, it might be a good idea to put a couple guards on yawr parents as well for the time being."

She hadn't even considered them being targeted! Alarm spread over face. "I'll make a call about it as a precaution, and *you* go pack yawr bags." He coaxed her off the sofa with the promise of another cup of tea being delivered to the bedroom.

As she padded down the hallway, she heard him speaking into his phone. Oh, how did everything get so turned around? *Heirwick* was supposed to be in prison, and *she* was supposed to be getting on with her life. Now *she* was the prisoner and *he* was free!

She pulled a suitcase from the top of the guest room closet and headed for her bedroom. Well, she wouldn't need anything dressy since she would be locked up in a house or an apartment, she thought. She rummaged in her closet, pulling out several pairs of jeans and a few dressier tops. She was digging in a dresser drawer of T-shirts when Bret arrived with her tea. He sat it on her nightstand, smiled briefly, then went back down the hall to the living room.

Since she had no idea how long she would be locked up in the safe house or the amenities provided, she grabbed a couple pair of shorts and a few yoga pants, along with several sets of pajamas and practically everything in her underwear drawer. The doorbell rang as she was pulling a second suitcase from the guest closet. Deep voices traveled down the hall to her, and she assumed more FBI had arrived.

Bret ambled into her bedroom several minutes later to find her packing makeup and essentials into a carrying case. She threw the book she had been reading in the bag and zipped it up.

"Ready?" he asked, noting that she had also changed into a casual outfit.

"I have no idea how long I'll be gone or what I should pack. I just grabbed mostly casual things," she stated, dropping onto the bed.

"Sounds like ya packed just fine. Do ya need any help?" he asked.

"I think I got everything that I could possibly need from in here, but I need several things out of my study. It's going to look like I'm moving," she said as a lone tear trailed down her cheek.

Bret caught the tear with his fingertip before gathering her in his arms. "It's gonna be okay. This is just a precaution and not permanent. It's better to pack for a long time than to pack for a couple of days and then need somethin'."

A deep voiced called out from the other room, and he let her go. "Keep your head up, okay? I promise we will catch him."

She nodded as he planted a kiss on her forehead. He lifted the two suitcases off the bed and left the room. Taking one last look around, she threw the carrying case over her shoulder and left the room as well. Her living room was full of agents. One was looking out the window through the blinds and talking on his phone. Another was going over a map spread out on the island with Bret. The director, whom she recognized from the other morning, was talking to three other agents and nodded in her direction when she caught his eye.

Myra ducked into her study and took a deep breath. Her nightmare was definitely real now! She hurried about her study, placing her laptop and a couple of blank notepads in the computer bag. She added a couple more to her briefcase along with a stack of studies and other research materials she had been working on before all this had started over a month ago. For good measure, she also selected a couple of work-related books and a few mysteries from her bookshelf for leisure reading and threw them in her briefcase as well.

Her wallet was on the corner of her desk where she had left it the evening before, so she tossed it in the computer case because her briefcase was already bulging with material. She paused before she left the room to straighten her back and throw her shoulders back as an act of defiance to Heirwick. Even though he couldn't see the effort, it made her feel better. She collected her things and left to meet the agents.

Bret looked up as she crossed the room to stand next to him. "Ready?" he asked.

She didn't trust her voice because the emotion she was struggling not to show was firmly stuck in her throat, so she nodded instead.

"Yaw'r ridin' with me," Bret whispered to her as he nodded to the agent with whom he had been reviewing the map. Bret grabbed one suitcase and her carrying case. The other agent took the other suitcase and briefcase, leaving her to carry the bag with the laptop. He said something to the director that she didn't catch, and suddenly everyone in the room sprang into action.

The director and another agent preceded them out of the apartment, followed by Bret, then Myra, then the other agent carrying her belongings. He was followed by the rest of the agents. Another agent wearing plainclothes was stationed at the foot of the steps and was watching the parking lot. A dark SUV was parked directly in front of the steps so that it took up several parking spots. Three other identical SUVs were parked in the middle of the driveway, blocking the view of the one she was to ride in. All of them had windows so darkly tinted it was virtually impossible to see anyone inside the vehicle.

The men quickly ushered Myra into the closest SUV and stored her belongings in the back. Bret climbed in the front seat, and the plainclothes agent climbed in the front seat beside him. As they pulled away from the curb, she noticed they were following one SUV, and the other two were falling in behind them. It felt like she was in an action movie.

They drove aimlessly for a while, sometimes turning back on the way they had come before Bret drove into what looked like a more industrial part of town. She had explored most of Columbia over the years, but she didn't recognize this part of town. A silver automatic door opened in the side of a red brick building, and Bret entered. The door shut immediately behind them. He drove around another brick wall to reveal they were in an underground parking garage that had approximately ten spaces.

Bret parked in the space closest to the elevator. The plainclothes agent, whom he had introduced as Agent Hawkins, jumped out to open the door for Myra. They grabbed her belongings and stepped into the elevator. Bret pressed the button for the top floor, and the elevator swiftly began to climb. When it stopped, the doors slid open to reveal a foyer with an imposing steel door.

Bret punched a series of numbers into the pad next to the door before entering a key into a lock. The door slid open silently, revealing a spacious and well-decorated penthouse suite. Tinted windows climbed from the floor to the fourteen-foot ceiling. The furniture was a plush and modern brown suede sofa and matching recliners. The walls were left with the brick industrial look with highlights of stainless steel artwork and exposed beams throughout. She stepped farther in the room and was caught off guard at the spaciousness of the place. It was beautiful, yet it was going to be her prison for an indefinite amount of time. A beautiful prison, but a prison nonetheless.

The men carried her belongings into the master suite while she acquainted herself with the living space. The kitchen was alley style along the back wall to the right of the elevator. All stainless steel appliances, light maple cabinetry with recessed lights under the cabinets, and mirrored backsplash. Several teardrop stainless steel lights hung from the ceiling over the bar area. The floor was a dark hardwood that looked like it might be original to the building. It had a weathered and worked look to it. White shag area rugs were placed artfully in the living space. It was stunning.

The men came back in the room, and Bret handed her a writing pad and pen. "Make out a grocery list. Agent Hawkins will make sure it gets purchased and delivered to us today."

"Us? You're staying here with me?" she asked, very surprised.

"For today, I will. We'll be switching off every now and then," he said as he picked up a receiver from a wall phone next to the elevator she had not seen. He spoke into it and replaced it. "This phone goes directly downstairs to the control room. We have two agents in there monitorin' cameras and the garage door. If you need anythin', you just pick up one of the receivers throughout the condo here, and it will ring automatically on their end. Just let them know what you need and they'll make sure ya get it."

"This is much nicer than I expected," she stated with a small smile.

"We have several safe houses in the area, but this one is kept for VIPs." Agent Hawkins grinned sheepishly.

"I take it that I'm a VIP now?" She laughed.

"The acting director here in the Columbia office got a huge laugh over what you told Agent Mims yesterday!" He snickered. "Word has spread about your connections like wildfire."

"Uh-oh, that was not my intention." She gasped.

"That's what made it so funny. Ya should have seen him after ya left yesterday. He called up here while I was still in his office. Agent Stevenson had a field day with him. Between us, he's been trying to get rid of Mims for a while now. This may have provided him the perfect opportunity." Bret laughed.

"So then what is your position?" she asked Bret.

"I'm senior special agent. They've been after me for a while to take a more senior position, but I was havin' too much fun travelin' and competin' with Lee. I may have to reconsider now though," he said meaningfully as he wagged his eyebrows suggestively at her.

She smiled despite herself. "What about you, Agent Hawkins? What is your specific position?"

"I'm just an agent. One of those grunts that does all the hard work." He laughed.

She laughed. Agent Hawkins seemed to have a nice sense of humor. She needed that right now. Myra handed him a short list of groceries that she thought would hold her over for a couple of days. His eyebrows went up when he saw it.

"You sure you don't need more than this?" he asked.

Bret took the list and looked it over before adding several more things to it. "That should do it for now. Thanks, Lee!"

Agent Hawkins nodded as he accepted the list and headed to the door. "Let me know if you need anything else while I'm out," he called over his shoulder as he disappeared out the door.

Chapter 70

Myra debated on whether or not to unpack her things as Bret sprawled out on the sofa with the television remote in his hand. She finally decided she might as well get comfortable. It could wind up being a long stay. She finished unpacking and wandered back into the main room, which took up most of the condo space. It was a very spacious room that looked out over Columbia.

Bret was on the phone, talking in low tones. The groceries she had requested sat on the bar in bags. She put everything away and made lunch. She hoped he liked tuna salad because that was what she intended to fix. She needed something to keep her busy, but that was also fast to fix. A headache made its presence while she was putting her things away, and she realized she had not eaten anything since the evening before. She was rummaging through the cabinets for a toaster when he appeared beside her.

"Whatcha looking for?" he asked softly next to her ear.

She swallowed hard. It was difficult enough keeping her attention on a specific task with him in the same room without him whispering like that in her ear. His warm breath fanned her neck, sending her pulse racing. "The...um...um...toaster," she sputtered.

He laughed. He knew very well the effect he was having on her. He opened a few cabinets as well before he found it, setting it on the counter for her. "Need any help?" he asked.

"No. I hope you like tuna salad sandwiches, because that is what you're getting for lunch," she told him.

He laughed again. "Love 'em! I learned from my mama to always agree and eat whatever is put in front of me."

"I think I like your mother already." She grinned. She set about toasting bread as she chopped celery and red onions to add to the tuna salad. A few minutes later, she turned around to find him sitting on a barstool, watching her. "What?" she asked.

"Nothin'. I just like watchin' ya." He shrugged with a wicked smile on his lips.

She gave him an eye roll and turned back to finish making sandwiches. "Was that call related to my situation?" she asked after a pause, biting her lip.

"Sorta. They found the car at a rest area on I-95 just outside of Savannah. Looks like he's making a run for it and headed further south," he drawled.

"Or trying to throw you off his trail," she supplied, turning to face him.

"That's a possibility too. He stole another car from the parking lot. There's an APB out for that one now."

"He's very smart. He will trade that one off quickly as well. I guess the waiting game just got more intense."

"Maybe. The court sent over yawr report and a subpoena." He changed the subject. "Ya wouldn't happen to have a copy of it that I could read, would ya? Stevenson said it was just delivered to him via special courier. I could have him talk to ya if ya would like," he offered.

"I need to call the court to make sure I can discuss it first. The court is my client. Can I use my phone?" she asked.

"No. It could be traced. I turned it off and removed the chip while you were packin' this mornin', and yaw'r not to turn it back on. It's imperative that ya don't, understand?" he directed as he handed her his personal phone.

She nodded as she accepted his phone. She dialed the number of the judge's office and explained her situation to the judge's personal secretary. She put Myra on hold briefly before the judge came on the line.

"I hear you have a little problem," the judge acknowledged.

"You could say that," she agreed.

"Yeah, I got a call from an agent earlier, and then I saw the prison break on the news. Heard he has a bit of a thing for you," the judge stated.

"That's what I hear. They have me in protective custody right now. Because of ethics and all, I just wanted permission from the court before I discussed this case with anyone, Your Honor. I've never had anything like this to happen before," she explained.

"I doubt many people have, Dr. Christie. You have the court's permission to work with the FBI to bring this man to justice. I've sent a letter of authorization to the Columbia office. Good luck, Dr. Christie. I hope you catch him."

"So do we, Your Honor. So do we. Thank you for granting me permission. I appreciate it, and I know the FBI appreciates it too," she said.

With her phone call concluded, she handed Bret back his phone. She set a plate of sandwiches on the bar along with a bag of chips before disappearing into the master suite. A moment later, she came out holding a file that contained a copy of the report and transcriptions she had provided to the court. Wordlessly, she handed it to Bret before taking a seat next to him at the bar.

They ate in silence while he read the report. He was still reading later when she finished eating and retired to the sofa. She left him reading in peace as she flipped through the television stations. She rarely watched television and was unfamiliar with most of the daytime choices. Bored, she flipped the television off and began pacing.

She was trying to get inside Heirwick's head. Where would he go next? What was he thinking? She started reviewing all the conversations they had over and over in her head. Mostly they had discussed him. At times, they had discussed the officers who were ill and various other inmates, but all the conversations ultimately wound up coming back around to him. He was a true narcissist.

Something was nagging at her, just there on the tip of her brain. It was bugging her. Something she knew she had to remember. What he had said in passing one day that she hadn't really bothered to mention, she thought. Something she hadn't thought was important at the time. Something that was out of place in the conversation.

Bret let out a low whistle and turned to face her. "Is this guy for real? Does he really believe this load of crap he says?" he asked in disbelief.

"Yes, I believe he does, unfortunately. He's extremely smart but just as delusional as he is smart. Oh, with a healthy dose of narcissism thrown in for good measure. I suspect he was going for the insanity plea, but he's nowhere near," she said. She continued to pace back and forth absently.

"What's wrong?" he asked, taking a seat on the sofa.

"He said something to me one day in passing, and I can't remember what it was. It didn't have anything to do with the interview or evaluation. In fact, it was already done at that point. I was on my way to check on another inmate who was threatening to harm himself."

Bret said nothing. He just watched her pace back and forth. He knew how crucial this knowledge could be just as he knew how difficult it could be to get inside a criminal's mind at times.

"He said something about me looking especially nice that day. Then he said something else, something vulgar almost. Then he said..." She trailed off and stood perfectly still. A look of horror came over her face.

"What is it?" he asked, jumping to his feet.

"I remember! He asked me how Dr. Hull was doing, if I was keeping an eye on him. When I said I don't talk to him daily, he told me I should. He said, and I quote, "you never know when something can happen to the people you care about. Oh God, you don't think he's going after him and Clara, do you?" She grabbed Bret's arm. "You have to do something!"

Bret pulled his cell phone from his pocket and called Agent Stevenson. He relayed Myra's concerns and conversation she had with Heirwick a few days before the quarantine was lifted as well as Dr. Hull's office and home addresses and phone numbers. Myra resumed her pacing, this time with frantic anxiety.

The wait was grueling for Myra. The minutes ticked by like hours. She paced so much that she was making Bret edgy. His phone rang, but it was to inform her that they had contacted her mother and stepfather and they were under protective custody at their home.

She was thankful for the phone call, but it was nerve-racking waiting to hear about Dr. Hull.

Fifteen minutes crept by, then thirty, and still they heard nothing. Myra tried to sit down, but she was unable to stay still. She resumed her pacing once again. Back and forth across the room she went. When she got too close to the windows, Bret asked her to step back from them. He didn't want to take any chances.

Another fifteen minutes ticked by with no phone call. Myra was about to scream in frustration. She looked pleadingly at Bret, who could offer her no response. He felt helpless and frustrated himself. He hated seeing her stressed like this. She watched the clock on the wall like a hawk watched its prey. She was turning into a nervous wreck. Bret called downstairs to see if they had any brandy anywhere. Of course, they didn't but said they would call out for some.

Bret was even getting concerned when, an hour and a half after their initial call to alert everyone about Dr. Hull being a potential target, he and Myra still had not heard anything. He tried calling Agent Stevenson, but the call went straight to voice mail. He also tried calling Agent Mims, but he didn't answer either. In his gut, Bret knew something was wrong. One of the local Charleston guys should have called in by now.

The receiver on the wall buzzed, and both of them jumped. It was one of the guys downstairs alerting Bret that someone was on their way up with some brandy. Bret thanked him and waited by the door. A monitor by the phone showed a woman stepping off the elevator and pressing the code to open the door. Like Bret had done earlier, she inserted a key to work the lock, and the door swung open.

Meghan Clark, an FBI special agent that Bret had worked closely with before, entered the suite holding a brown paper bag. She held it out to him with somber eyes that darted to Myra and back to him. She knew something but didn't want to say anything in front of Myra. He introduced the two women then escorted Agent Clark to the door.

"What is it?" he whispered.

"We don't want to say anything until proper identification has been made, but they found three bodies at the business address you gave us. I've heard it's a very grisly scene. We have a forensic team there now combing the place. We are canvassing the area, but so far the reports have been that no one saw a thing."

A muscle worked in Bret's jaw, and he rubbed his eyes with one hand. Sometimes he really hated his job. He knew he had to prepare Myra for the worse possible news, and he was not looking forward to it. It looked like he had made a good choice in ordering the brandy. It was going to come as such a blow to Myra.

Chapter 71

A tearful Myra was curled up in the corner of the sofa. She was wrapped in a blanket, holding a glass of amber liquid, and rivers of tears flowed down her pale face. Bret had cuddled her in his arms for a long time after he delivered the somber news. It was unlikely the bodies in Dr. Hull's office were any other than Dr. Hull, his wife, Clara, and his secretary, Reno. They had no children to deliver such horrible news. Their only daughter had died from leukemia as a young teenager.

Myra was thinking about the last conversation they had. It had been about a monster. The same monster, she was certain, that had taken his life. Myra would not get to see Clara's smiling face again or have those interesting discussions with Dr. Hull on occasion. To her, it felt like she had just lost a part of her family.

She was furious with Agent Mims. He had dragged his feet in setting up a protective detail for Dr. Hull and Clara, simply because he hadn't liked her telling him what to do, and then reporting him to her uncle. He had been trying to make a statement. Well, he had made it loud and clear! And Eugene, Clara, and Reno had paid the price with their lives. Three lives lost, because an agent with a bad attitude on a power trip, had disobeyed a direct order and common sense. Bret had said that an investigation would be ordered into how Agent Mims had handled the case, especially after Deputy Director Dailey had personally called him and ordered the detail. Agent Mims's career was probably over, Bret had surmised, and she prayed it was true!

Phone calls would need to be made to Eugene and Clara's extended family and close friends. Myra didn't know any of their extended family. She didn't know if her mother knew any of them or not. Then there was Myra's mother. They had been family friends for years. She would have to call her mother and her uncle Robert. She was putting off those calls until identities had been verified. She wasn't certain if Uncle Robert would be notified through the official channels, but she felt he deserved to be told by someone in his family.

The wait for the inevitable had been going on for hours. With each passing minute, her heart broke a bit more, and the evil bastard was that much closer to her and the people she cared about. She had tried to think where he could possibly go next, and now her head hurt with the effort. Wherever he was, it was clear he was back in South Carolina.

Occasionally, Bret's phone would ring, and every time it did, her heart sank a bit lower and her stomach hurt. She was numb now. She was somewhere between being awake and being in a nightmare from which she could not awaken. She felt like she was drowning. A deep abyss engulfed her. Heirwick was winning, and he knew it.

The afternoon sky beyond the tinted windows was streaked with purples and pinks of the impending sunset. The colors of Mother Nature were spectacular, though Myra didn't notice. Bret's phone rang again. Myra turned pained eyes upon him, straining to hear the conversation he was holding in quiet tones.

The coroner had just confirmed the identities of Eugene, Clara, and Reno, Eugene's secretary. It didn't matter anymore. She had already known in her heart they were gone. She picked up the burner phone they had given her earlier from the coffee table and punched her mother's number into it.

The phone rang several times before she heard her mother's voice. "Hello?" came the tentative question of a woman not recognizing the number calling.

"Hi, Mom, it's me," Myra confirmed in a flat tone.

"Myra! Honey, what's wrong? What's going on? The FBI is here and said you were in some sort of trouble. I haven't been able to reach Robert. Are you okay? Where are you calling from? I don't recognize this number." Her mother was talking a mile a minute, not giving Myra time to answer a question before she fired off another one.

"Mom, I'm okay," Myra interrupted her. "I'm calling from a burner phone the FBI gave me. I can't use my phone because it could be tracked," she explained.

"Are you sure you're okay, darling? You don't sound okay." Her mother fretted.

"Mom, are you sitting down? I need you to be sitting down."

"Yes, darling. Jack is right here with me. We are so worried, honey."

"Mom, that serial killer I was doing that eval on at Lieber up until a few days ago? Well, he escaped in the early hours this morning. After he killed an inmate, two guards, and left another in critical condition…" She paused to swallow the lump in her throat that was the size of a softball. "Mom, he murdered Dr. Hull and Clara today!" she wailed.

"What!" There was a long pause as her mother processed the shocking information. "Murdered? Oh God! Oh, God, no! Not Eugene and Clara!" Her mother was shocked.

"I don't know any more details than that at the moment." The pain she felt made her voice crack. "He…he…" She broke. How could she tell her mother that a serial killer was after her? A fresh set of tears coursed down her face.

"He what, darling?" Her mother was choking on her own tears.

"He m-m-m-murdered them and Reno in the office. He… um…well, Mom, there's just no easy way to say this. He may be after me too."

There was silence on the other end. Myra waited, and still there was no response.

"Are you still there, Mom?"

"What do you mean by he's after you?" Myra could hear the chill of fear in her mother's whisper.

"Dr. Hull and the court asked me to do an interview and evaluation on him, which I did." She paused to take a deep breath.

"That's the case you were working on? The one that has been all over the news? The most prolific serial killer ever? You were working on his case when you were locked down under that quarantine?" her mother asked.

"Yes, it was. I didn't know him, Mom. I never set eyes on him ever, to my knowledge," she cried. "But he somehow knew me. He knew my relationship with Eugene and Clara, Mom. They have found evidence that he's also my stalker!"

"Oh, God, Myra! You poor thing! Do you have someone there with you, sweetheart? Wait, did you say stalker? What stalker?" her mother questioned in a demanding voice.

"Yes, I have an agent with me in a safe house and a couple more in the building. They are taking good care of me, but I'm not going to be able to call you on a regular basis. They took my phone so I couldn't be tracked. Mom, I didn't want you to worry. I've had a problem with receiving letters and phone calls for a few months. Since that other case, really. The police have been working on it since I received the first letter. They were basically just anonymous creepy love letters. The police thought it might be a fairly new guy in my office or a past client that had misplaced his feelings onto me because I treated him. Anyway, I'm sorry I didn't tell you before, but I didn't want you to worry, and you had so much going on with Jack's Senate run about to take off," Myra tearfully explained.

"Sweetheart, you should have told me," her mother admonished.

"I know, Mom. Anyway, I'm safe and well protected. I just wanted to let you know that I'm okay and well...about Dr. Hull and Clara. I can't stay on here any longer, but I'll call you as soon as I have more information. Please stay safe, and do everything the agents tell you, okay?" Myra pleaded with her mother.

"Don't worry about us, sweetheart. We are in good hands. You take care and stay safe. We love you. I love you," her mother said.

Myra was getting choked up again. "I love you too, Mom. Both of you. I'll talk to you later. Bye." She hung up the phone before her tears got uncontrollable again.

Bret was sitting on a barstool, waiting for Myra to finish her call. As she hung up, he crossed the room and sat down beside her. "Are you okay?" he asked, taking her hands in his.

She nodded. Her throat was tight with emotion. *This just could not be happening*, she thought.

"I need to go into the Columbia office first thing in the morning. We are spread a little thin right now, but we have agents coming in from other locations to help out. They will be here in the morning, and I need to go in to help brief them. We would love to be able to have you in there as well to give us a profile, but that would put you in too much danger. Do you think you could write up a profile for me between now and then?" he asked. "I know it's asking a lot, but any additional information, impressions, or thoughts you may have not put in your report could be very helpful."

She nodded, but didn't raise her head to look at him. It had been difficult talking to her mother as she had known it would be. She felt a bit empty inside except for the low simmer of hate that was building for Heirwick.

"Good girl. I think what you need right now is some rest." He lifted her into his arms from her cuddled spot, complete with blanket, and headed for the master suite. Gently, he lay her down and crawled into the bed with her, both of them fully dressed.

She curled into him, her head on his chest. His strong heartbeat beneath her ear was soothing. His arms wrapped around her tightly, comforting. Concentrating on the rhythm of the beat, she let go of her pain. Her eyes fluttered closed, and within minutes, she was asleep.

Chapter 72

Myra had drifted into a deep dreamless sleep and awakened to the smell of bacon frying. Her head was pounding, and her body ached from emotional stress. She rolled out of bed and into the shower. The water, as hot as she could stand, ran over her head and shoulders to relax and cleanse away as much of the stress as she could. The events of the last few days were taking their toll.

It was still early when she walked into the main room, carrying a pad of paper and a pen. Bret was in the kitchen cooking bacon, eggs, and toast for breakfast. She hoped he wasn't expecting her to eat any of that. Her stomach was in knots, and she still had that soft-ball-sized lump in her throat.

He was busy at the stove and didn't see her cross to the bar and take a seat. The folder containing her report still sat on the granite counter of the bar. She had reviewed the tapes so many times that she could almost quote part of his narratives word for word.

She stared at the pad momentarily before describing him in great detail for authorities. Bret, as a senior special agent, would be reading the profile to the other agents and law enforcement officials attending the meeting. Although they had a picture and basic information, it was not going to be enough to simply catch him again.

> Canton Wayne Heirwick. Suspect is a forty-four-year-old male who has a distinct lack of respect for laws, the rights of others, and lives. Extremely aggressive. Highly intelligent. Cunning. Manipulative. Tremendously narcissistic. Enjoys playing off the weakness of others (i.e., abuses

empathy of others for his own gain). May present with a superficial charm, especially to women, but is exceedingly deceitful. He is frequently impulsive, highly dangerous, and unpredictable. Suspect has a severe preoccupation with his own fantasy in which he is a powerful supreme being. He believes he is an angel of hell, the son of Satan, and is not afraid to die. He is convinced he is continually reincarnated. Subject enjoys theatre and may be able to professionally change his appearance. Suspect claims to have worked in law enforcement for a time and is well-versed in law enforcement tactics, investigations, and the law. He may use the stolen prison uniform to avoid recognition by authorities. He will exploit anyone, anywhere to achieve his own ends. He has a voracious appetite for killing with no remorse or empathy. He has no specific signatures and no discrimination in his killing. He kills for fun. Enjoys torturing victims and animals and loves blood. Crime scenes may be as simple as a strangulation to deplorable and deranged dismemberments. Subject also brags about enjoyment in cannibalism. This man is a psychopath by all descriptions, and great care should be used in his apprehension.

Wordlessly, Myra tore the sheet off her pad. Hearing something behind him, Bret turned in time to see her placing the profile on top of her file. "Good mornin', gorgeous. Did I wake ya?" he asked, pouring her a cup of hot water and moving the tea bags and sugar closer to her.

"No, I just woke up and smelled something delicious from this area, so I followed my nose." She smiled, but sadness lingered in her eyes. She was still pale with dark circles under her eyes.

"Well then, don't let me interfere with the lady's stomach." With a flourish, he looped a towel over his forearm and bowed to her. "Chef Myers has prepared a delicious breakfast for the lovely lady, complete with crispy bacon, scrambled eggs with cheese, toast, juice, and an assortment of fruit, donuts, and danishes for yawr pallet," he said in an exaggerated accent that had her laughing. He placed a plate of food in front of her, followed by a glass of juice and bowl of fruit he had arranged from the assortment that she had requested the day before.

"Looks delicious!" she complimented as she nibbled on a piece of bacon.

"I aim to please." He gave her a wicked grin before coming around to sit beside her. As he took his seat, he leaned over and nibbled on her neck.

"Keep that up and you won't be making it to your meeting," she threatened with her own wicked grin.

"Alas, I have found my perfect mate, and work gets in the way." He pouted.

She snickered, stirring her tea. "So what's on the agenda today besides your meeting?" she asked.

"I'm not sure yet. Yawr not to move from this place. I will hopefully be coming back here to protect ya, although I really want to be out there in the field to catch this guy," he growled.

"I still can't believe Dr. Hull and Clara are gone," she said, continuing to stir her tea as a lone tear ran down her face. Breakfast smelled good, but she really didn't have much of an appetite. She did her best to appease him by plucking a grape and popping it in her mouth.

"I know it came as a shock to ya, and I'm sorry for that. I'm just glad you were able to get inside his head yesterday. The guys said they think they just missed him there. It does prove that you were right though. He did try to deceive us about headin' further south by leavin' that car in Savannah."

"Any news this morning?" she asked.

"They found the other car he was drivin' last night in a parking lot not far from Dr. Hull's office. There have been no reports of another stolen vehicle yet. We have people all over the highways and interstate keeping an eye out for him," he assured her.

"What kind of vehicle could he have stolen that would not have been reported?" she asked more to herself.

"He could've walked to a factory parkin' lot and stolen the car of an employee that hasn't gotten off work yet," he offered.

"Or he could have simply killed the occupant and took the vehicle," she speculated.

"We haven't found any bodies, and there have been no missin' person reports filed since yesterday."

"Maybe no one knows the person is missing yet. It could be someone from out of state, a college kid, someone who lives alone. Knowing him, he would have put the body in the trunk of the vehicle or the passenger seat for all he cares. As long as no one realizes the person is dead yet, he's good to go." It was a chilling and disturbing revelation, but she realized it was true. The man had no compunction about killing anyone and everyone to achieve his goal.

A companionable silence fell between them while he ate and she nibbled at breakfast. "Is that the profile over there on the file?" he asked as he scooped eggs onto his toast to make a sandwich.

"Yes. This man is extremely dangerous, Bret. He's a psychopath with delusions about being a powerful and all-knowing supreme being."

"I've captured his kind before." He tried to lessen her worries.

"I doubt it. No one has ever captured his kind before. There are more bodies out there than is contained in those scrapbooks. The way he described his killing, he didn't start using the scrapbooks until after his grandmother died. He was killing long before that."

"Most of them do start out young," he offered.

"Bret, I'm not talking about torturing animals here. He used the hills of Tennessee, Kentucky, North Carolina, and West Virginia as his private hunting grounds for years before he started keeping those books. It wouldn't surprise me if he didn't kill his own parents and siblings."

"Has he said somethin' to you about 'em?" Bret asked quizzically. "We haven't been able to locate any of his family."

"Not really. He didn't really talk about them after he left to live with his grandmother. What do the people in that area say about him?" she asked.

"Not much. They said he was strange and everyone kept their distance. The family was quiet and just up and vanished one night. They even left most of their belongings behind."

"What if they never left?"

"You mean you think he killed them and hid the bodies?"

"That's exactly what I think. Is there any way an investigation can be done on the property where they lived? You know, like that ground penetrating radar or something?" she asked.

"I'm not sure, but I'll mention it to Agent Stevenson this mornin'. Will you be all right here by yourself for a little while? There are two agents downstairs, if you need anythin', and I think Agent Stevenson posted one on the outside to keep surveillance on the place from a distance."

"I'll be fine. He has no idea where to find me. I'll just curl up with a book or something till you get back." She smiled and leaned over to give him a quick kiss on the cheek. Sensing her intent, he turned at the last minute so that he caught her lips with his own to her surprise.

The kiss lingered for several moments before Bret finally broke the spell. "If I don't get out of here real soon, we're both gonna be in a heap of trouble," he murmured against her lips.

"Mmmmm…but you taste so good," she purred, trailing kisses up his jawline to nibble on his earlobe.

He groaned and gently pushed her away. "You are big trouble, lady." He emphasized each word. "Yawr gonna get me in trouble again." He laughed as he stood up. "I have to go make sure my lovely princess stays nice and safe in her red brick tower." He bowed to her.

"You just make sure you hightail it back here, Mr. Knight in Shining Armor. I need saving!" She gave him a small sad smile that made his chest tighten in pain as she handed him the folder and the profile.

He kissed her on top of the head as he accepted them. "I'll call you with an update. Try and relax if you can." He kissed her one more time before left.

Chapter 73

Myra, left alone in the penthouse condominium, tried to read one of the books she had brought, but she couldn't concentrate on it. She was jittery and worried about those in Heirwick's path of destruction and depressed and fatigued over the loss of her family friends. At noon, Bret's call had been transferred by the downstairs monitoring room to the condo's landline. He had informed her that a task force had been set up, and Agent Stevenson had requested his help in running it. Bret knew more than any of the others on this subject and was greatly needed.

She stretched out on the sofa to watch a movie, hoping it would distract her. Soon she was nodding off for some much-needed sleep. The late afternoon sun was streaming in through the windows when a sound woke her up. It sounded like someone was moving around. Still groggy from sleep, she sat up, expecting to see Bret. Instead, a voice spoke from the bar, freezing her heart.

"You are so beautiful, my love. I so wanted to wake you up, but I was torn with just watching you sleep. So perfect, cuddled up there on the sofa." He came toward her with a glass of brandy in his hand.

"How did you get in here?" she asked, trying desperately to sound calm. She was terrified.

"I've missed you. You mesmerized me every day you came to visit me. We are connected, you and I. A primitive sort of connection that ties our souls. I know you feel it too," he continued, ignoring her question.

"You didn't answer my question. How did you find me? How did you get here?" she asked again. She felt trapped. There was nowhere she could go. He had her trapped on the sofa.

"I haven't had this sort of connection with anyone except my sister, Quintrala," he continued. He casually looked around as though he were an invited guest. "Nice place." He smiled and sat in the overstuffed recliner across from her.

Myra stayed right where she was. Somehow, the coffee table between them made her feel just the tiniest bit safer. Random thoughts of how to escape and defend herself ran through her mind with lightning speed. Stealing a glance toward the door, she was wondering why the FBI agents had let him in here. A sickening feeling washed over her as she suddenly realized they would not have let him in willingly. She stood up.

"Why don't you sit back down and enjoy yourself? Relax. Would you like me to get you a drink? I have to confess, this is my second glass. You were sleeping so peacefully that I didn't want to wake you, so I just helped myself."

The thought of him wandering around the condo while she slept, him watching her sleep, made her even sicker. A cold fear washed over her, and she shivered. She had to remind herself to remain calm. She had a working relationship with him, and she could use that. She just had to stay smart about it until help arrived. Dear God, she hoped help would arrive in time.

"No, thank you. I'm not really a drinker of alcohol. I think I will get myself some water, if you don't mind." She casually walked to the kitchen, taking extra effort not to come into too close of contact with him.

He crossed one ankle over the other knee, obviously relaxed with no worries about being caught. "So how long have you been holed up in here?" he asked, looking around.

"Just since yesterday morning," she replied, trying to get a glass and fill it up while keeping an eye on him. Slowly, she slid a knife from the knife block on the counter and hid it in the back pocket of her jeans while wiping down the counter with a towel. She felt a little better having some distance from him.

"It's nice on the inside, but the outside is not much to look at, unfortunately. I like your apartment better," he replied.

"What do you know about my apartment?" she asked, startled.

He laughed. "You act like I've never been there." He rolled his eyes. "I like the layout and your taste in furniture. I even like that color scheme you have going on in there with creams and browns together, with splashes of primary colors here and there. I especially like the way you set up your study. So comfy and cozy. But I think you deserve a nicer place. I would love to see you in a bigger study with built-in floor-to-ceiling bookshelves. Maybe even a fireplace to settle next to when you're reading all those psychology books and studies." He gestured with his free hand as he talked.

A new wave of alarm spread through her. Had he been in her apartment at some point? How had he known she had been moved to this place? More importantly, how had he gotten into the building and then bypassed the electronic board outside the door?

"You have been in my apartment, haven't you?" she asked casually.

"Several times, actually. My father helped me."

"Your father?" she asked, bewildered.

"Yes. Oh, not my earthly father. My father in hell helped. I've been visiting you on and off for some time. I fell in love with you the first time I saw you. You can imagine my surprise when Father told me you were my gift! I just had to visit you immediately and make you mine. You are an extremely passionate lover." He gave her a smokey look. "We could always go another round now, if you would like." His smile did not reach those expressionless eyes of his, and it made the suggestion even creepier.

"Why don't you tell me about the earthly family you have this time? You really haven't mentioned them much to me," she asked, attempting to redirect the conversation.

"Ah, you want the excitement to mount some more. Okay, if you insist, but then you have to tell me more about yourself. We always talk about me, and I know very little about you. My father in hell has told me some, but he wanted me to discover the rest myself. He is very excited about our impending union. He selected you himself. You are my reward this time." He licked his lips, and she nearly gagged.

"Your life is so much more fascinating than mine," she stalled.

"I'm sure, but then I have had many more than you. I'm sure if we asked my father, he would make arrangements for us to continue our lives together for centuries to come."

"Before we get that far, are you going to tell me about your family?" she redirected him again.

"You have a one-track mind, don't you?" He laughed. "I like that about you, your dogged determination. Very well. I've already told you some about my current earthly family. What I haven't told you was that they were idiots. They were so stupid and backwards. My earthly father was a God-fearing man and believed in daily beatings to keep the soul healthy and clean. My mother was a mouse, afraid of her own shadow, and she did whatever her husband told her to do." He uncrossed his legs and leaned forward in his chair, his elbows resting on his knees.

"So he was abusive? Was it physical abuse only, or were there other elements of abuse?" she asked.

"That pig was smart enough to not touch me sexually and not smart enough to impose mental or emotional abuse. His fists and his words hurt bad enough. He took turns beating us kids and made us each watch as he beat the others. A few days before I left to go stay with my elderly grandmother, I put them all out of their misery. My earthly father was delivering hardwoods to the local sawmill. I killed our mother first while the others were out of the house doing chores. One by one, I killed the others. I buried their bodies in the woods behind the house." He stood and looked out the window, his back to her.

She calculated the distance to the door but knew the elevator door would not close fast enough to prevent him from catching her. She tried to remember if there had been a stairwell as he continued with his story.

"I cleaned up the house all nice and neat. Took what valuables we had, which were not much, and put them in the family car. It was a beat-up old piece of junk, but it ran. Then I sat back and waited for that piece of shit to come home. He came home, staggering, having spent a sizeable sum of the money from the sale of the hardwoods at the local bar. He was mighty surprised to come home to no wife and no dinner on the table. He started carrying on, hollering and yelling and such. I walked right up to him and sunk a knife dead center of his chest…and then I twisted the blade."

She should have been shocked by his revelation. She wasn't. Hadn't she already suspected that he had murdered his own family? He had brutally murdered her friends, and now he had come for her. He had just admitted to killing his entire family. If he could kill them so easily, then what chance did she have in surviving?

"He didn't even make a sound. He just stared at me in surprise. Surprise! Can you believe it?" he asked as he spun around to look at her. "He loved to make everyone else suffer for their shortcomings. I punished him for everything, just like my father in hell told me to do. That's my mission in this life. I'm here to relieve the misery of some and punish others. It's what I do best."

"And where exactly do *I* fit in with your…um…mission?" she asked.

He took a seat on a barstool. "You, my dear, are my reward for doing a great job. I told you that. Father decided I deserved a companion after all these years by myself. He has provided for us handsomely. We can go anywhere in the world you would like. Just name a place. We can even travel the entire planet if you would like. Maybe we could stay in a place for a few months or years so you can really get to see everything before we move on to the next location. Wherever you decide you want to go, my love, we will go."

"What do you mean he provided handsomely?" she asked, keeping the bar between them.

"He told me he has accounts for me around the world. We are rich, darling!" He flashed a smile at her.

"But where did the money in those accounts come from?" she asked more directly.

"What does it matter? Just go get your things and we can be off."

"It matters a lot to me," she hedged.

"Are you sure it matters to you, or are you just stalling, hoping that FBI agent guy you've been seeing will show up?" His eyes bore directly into hers as though he was reading her mind, and she looked away.

"Actually, I'm hungry. How about you?" she asked.

"You are a terrible liar, honey." He laughed. "But I will go along for a while. What are you going to fix us to eat?"

There were a couple of steaks she had intended to cook for Bret and her for dinner. There was also a package of chicken breasts. She chose the chicken. "How would you like chicken parmesan for dinner?"

"That sounds nice. Father said you were an excellent cook. He said you took after your mother. How are your mother and Jack, by the way?"

Myra froze, reaching for a frying pan. Ice slid over her heart. He knew her parents by name? She slowly stood up, the frying pan forgotten. "How do you know my parents' names?" she asked, staring him down from across the bar.

"I told you I know a lot about you. My father in hell told me. He said Jack is running for the senate seat in Virginia. He's a judge, right?"

She gritted her teeth so hard her jaw hurt. She would not give him the satisfaction of an answer.

"Oh, I've upset you. I'm sorry, dear. I didn't mean to upset you. Let me give you a hug to make it all better," he offered as he stood up from the stool.

"Don't you move. Stay right there!" she instructed. She was angry, but she didn't want him to know about the knife in her pocket.

"Why? He is a judge, right?" he asked. "I'm sure that's what Father told me. He said Jack was your stepfather. Your real dad, Michael, wasn't it? He was an FBI agent climbing the ladder of success. He was killed in action, right? I think you were in college at the time. That must have been tough for you."

How could he know so much about her? She couldn't speak; she just stared. She was beyond terrified at this point. Her options were limited on escaping. She was trapped, and he knew it. The only thing she could do was stall him and stay put. If she left with him, she would certainly die. If she stayed, she might have a chance. She offered up a small prayer.

"You look like him, you know."

"What?" she asked.

"I said you look like him."

"Look like whom?" What was he talking about now? she wondered.

"You look like your father. I met him once," he replied nonchalantly.

"You met my father?" she asked, astonished.

"Yes," he replied simply.

"Where did you meet my father?" she queried, not at all sure she wanted to know the answer.

"He and his partner came to West Virginia. They were investigating a series of murders across the state. Somehow, their investigation led them to me. My work was just starting at the time, so I couldn't very well let them stop me. I didn't have a choice, love. Your father had his gun on me and was ready to shoot. His partner was circling around behind the building. I didn't mean to kill him. I guess he moved just as I shot and the bullet lodged in his heart."

The color drained from her face. He had just admitted to killing her father. Her father! He killed her father! The words kept running through her brain over and over. Heirwick killed her father all those years ago! "You...killed...my...father?" She enunciated each word very clearly.

"It was an accident, love. He was not on my list. He just happened to be at the wrong place at the wrong time. Just like Dr. Hull and his wife. They were not supposed to be home. I just needed the cash he kept in his safe and his extra car. That was all. They just walked in on me. What was I supposed to do?" he asked, gesturing widely with his hands in an act of innocence.

"You killed my friends and my father! It was not an accident! You murdered them for your own personal selfish gain!" she screamed at him. "And you lie! They were not killed at home!"

"Now calm down, love! Everything is going to be okay," he said.

"Stop calling me that!" she spat at him. "I am not your love. I am nothing to you!"

"That's not true. You are my soul mate. My father brought us together. You are my opposite half." He was talking in a soothing voice, but it wasn't working. "And I don't lie. I have never lied to you. I was in Dr. Hull's house to retrieve the money from the safe, but they walked in on me, like I said. Dr. Hull started bargaining for their lives by telling me he had a lot more money in his office. I made him drive us there. There wasn't as much as he had let on. I couldn't just let them go at that point."

"Yes, you could have!" she shouted at him. "You just said your dad has money for you all over the world. Why didn't he give you some of that so you wouldn't have to kill my friends?"

"Because Dr. Hull was holding some of the money. He just didn't want me to have it." He spread his hands in explanation.

"You are delusional! You are sick, and there is no helping you! You are a psychopath!" she screamed.

"You don't mean that," he said as he rounded the end of the bar the farthest from the door.

This was it! It was now or never! She ran for the door and yanked it open as fast as she could. She was almost to the elevator when he caught her around the waist and hauled her back into the condo before the door shut. She struggled to free herself, but his arms were like vice grips.

"Oh no, you don't!" he said next to her ear. "You are not leaving without me. I've decided your FBI guy has been putting nonsense in your head about me. You know me, love. You know all about me. Now it's time to consummate our affection for one another. I've had you in your dreams. Now it is time I had you for real."

She struggled fiercely against his hold as he carried her toward the master suite. Halfway there, she managed to get her hand in her back pocket and pulled out the knife. It had been hidden by the long tails of her shirt. She threw her head back as hard as she could and heard the snap of his nose against the back of her head.

He let out a yelp, and his hold slackened. She pulled away, slashing at his arm with the blade of the knife at the same time. She put as much distance between them as she could in the couple of seconds she had. He was cursing as blood poured from his nose and the gash on his arm.

"You can fight all you want. It just makes it more fun for me." His hideous laugh bounced off the walls like echoes.

Myra made another effort to run for the door. In two steps, he had her by the shoulder. She tried to pull away, but something popped in shoulder, and she let out a cry of pain. Heirwick dragged her to the floor and covered her body with his. Blood running down his face splashed onto her neck as she struggled with her good arm to cut him again with the knife.

He was bigger and stronger than she was and soon had her good arm pinned above her head with the other one. Pain burned through her shoulder like liquid fire. Tears flooded her eyes, but still she fought. She kicked at his legs and tried desperately to plant her knee in his groin.

"Now I see why Father chose you for me. You are a worthy adversary, my dear. You fight hard. I like that," he all but purred against her neck as he licked and tasted her skin.

She was so repulsed she gagged. She was still trying to fight, but the pain in her shoulder was wearing her down quickly. Tears ran from the corners of her eyes and dampened the hair at her temples. She was just about to scream when she realized his ear was next to her mouth. Taking a deep breath and saying a prayer, she clamped down on his ear as hard as she could.

Cartilage snapped and popped between her teeth. She could taste the saltiness of his blood on her tongue and heard his yell of pain as he struggled to free his ear from her mouth.

"You bitch!" he raged, grabbing his ear or what was left of it.

She spat the rest of his ear in his face as she plunged the knife in his shoulder. He howled in pain, and she twisted the blade. He struggled to back away from her to remove knife. Myra was spent but still struggled to get to her feet. The injured arm hung limply at her side as she labored to an upright position. His blood covered the floor, and her feet slid in it. She kicked him in the groin for good measure.

He bent over, grabbing his groin, spewing curse words at her. Mustering the last of her strength, she did a roundhouse kick from her karate days and sent him staggering backward. She took the advantage and attempted to flee once again, but he caught her ankle, tripping her. She screamed in pain as her bad shoulder hit the floor first.

"You are mine! Do you hear me?" he yelled. "You are mine and you will always be mine!"

Heirwick hit her in the side of the face near the eye socket to keep her from fighting further. It felt as if an explosion had gone off in her head. The room went blurry, and spots of light detonated before her eyes. Her ears were ringing so loudly. The blow was so powerful that she was hallucinating. She was falling into a bottomless pit of darkness, and voices of the dead were coming to greet her. As she slipped into the dark abyss, she heard Bret's scream.

Chapter 74

Bret had tried calling the agents in the control room to give Myra a message that he was bringing takeout to the condo for supper, but there was no answer. He had tried a second time and got the same result. Realizing something was seriously wrong, he ran out of the Columbia field office, yelling officers down at the safe house. Everyone in his vicinity began running for the doors.

Agent Stevenson tried calling the agent he had posted outside the building. Alarmed that he also could not reach that agent, Agent Stevenson put out all-point bulletins for multiple officers down with the address. Federal and state agents swarmed the area with lights flashing and radios buzzing with information. Everyone was on high alert, knowing a possible serial killer was on the loose in the area.

Bret raced to the building. The outer garage door was in place and was not opening as expected. He stopped his car and ran for the emergency side door. Agent Stevenson had given him the key for the door only the day before in the event of an emergency. He would never have thought he would be using it under these conditions.

The lock clicked, and he swung the door open. Several agents had gathered at his back. They were dressed in their flak jackets and followed him inside, guns at the ready. As soon as they entered the building, Bret knew definitively that something was seriously wrong. The door to the control center stood ajar. On closer inspection, he saw both men down and motioned for someone to check for signs of life.

He and the rest of the agents moved forward. Bret took some of the agents and filed into the elevator, pressing the top floor button.

Other agents took the stairs, spreading out on each of the lower four floors to search for the assailant.

As soon as the door to the elevator opened, Bret could hear Myra screaming. He and the other agents rushed forward, pressing in the code and inserting the key into the lock on the steel door. The door swung open just in time for Bret to see Myra spit blood at Heirwick and plunge a knife into his shoulder. Then she was twirling in the air like the superheroes of martial arts films. She seemed to twirl in slow motion. Her hair framed her head like a golden halo. A leg flying out in a graceful kick met with Heirwick's head and sent him staggering backward.

His princess was turning to run, but the beast grabbed her ankle as he fell and pulled her down with him. Heirwick was struggling with Myra and got a punch to her face before Bret could get to him. She was stunned by the powerful blow. Enraged by the attack on his Myra, Bret charged Heirwick like a bull. Shoulder down, like he had been taught in all those football practices, he caught Heirwick where Myra had just stabbed him, driving the knife even deeper into the soft flesh just below the shoulder. Heirwick let out another howl and threw a fist toward Bret. The two men struggled. Other agents came flooding in behind Bret. Two dragged Myra to the safety of the elevator and called out for an ambulance. They carried her unconscious body out of the building and behind a road block to await one of the many ambulances en route.

Upstairs, Heirwick had managed to pull the knife out of his shoulder. He slashed at Bret but missed. Bret charged him again, and the knife fell to the floor. They were both grappling over the knife. Bret was able to get the upper hand, but just barely and knocked the other man back on his heel. Heirwick struggled to his feet, ready to charge. An agent who had followed Bret into the condo had his gun at the ready. He saw an opportunity and opened fire, planting several bullets in Heirwick's chest in quick succession. Heirwick's body thrashed violently as he fell to the floor at Bret's feet.

Bret stood over Heirwick's body until it stopped jerking then collapsed onto the floor. His breath was ragged from the intense fight. Adrenaline was still coursing through his body. He nodded at the agent who had just shot Heirwick. "Thanks, buddy!"

Another agent checked Heirwick's neck for a pulse and shook his head. "He's toast."

"Good riddance!" another agent spoke up from the doorway. "The bastard took out three of our guys!"

"Where is Myra?" Bret asked.

"They took her down in the elevator. She was unconscious," the same agent responded.

Bret rose to his feet with the help of the shooter and headed to the elevator. "I'll send forensics up here," he told them as he waited for the elevator. "You did good, Derrickson." He nodded at the agent who had shot and killed Heirwick.

The doors of the elevator slid open, and he stepped into it, pressing the button for the garage. As the elevator traveled downward, Bret caught a glimpse of himself in the reflection of the silver walls. He was covered in blood. He checked himself quickly, but as far as he could tell, it was all Heirwick's blood. Myra had done a number on the bastard!

In the garage, an ambulance had just arrived, and paramedics were checking out the FBI agents. One was still alive, but barely; the other two were dead. He asked the closest agent if he knew where they had taken Myra and was directed across the street to the barriers. Agent Stevenson and Deputy Director Dailey were huddled over her. In the street, another paramedic was checking the FBI agent in the car, who was also dead. He had been shot in the side of the head through the driver's side window. He probably had not even seen his assailant.

The other paramedic was calling a coroner to the scene. Bret walked over to Myra and told Agent Stevenson that a forensics team was needed upstairs, that Heirwick had been shot and killed resisting arrest and trying to kill another federal agent. Myra was still unconscious on the pavement, her blood soaked body cradled in her uncle's arms. He had flown in last night after Myra's mother called him to report that Myra was in jeopardy. Bret had spent the best part of the day with him in the command center, attempting to track Heirwick's movements through eyewitness reports. It had been a grueling day for all of them.

"Are you hurt, Myers?" Agent Stevenson asked him.

"I don't think so. I think it's mostly the subject's blood. Myra did a number on him before we got here. Is she hurt?" Bret asked, kneeling beside her.

"She's got some swelling on the side of her face here, but other than that, I don't think the blood is hers. We are waiting for the paramedics to assess everyone. I think it would be a good idea to get her to the hospital for tests," Deputy Director Dailey replied.

At that moment, a paramedic pushed his way into the crowd around Myra. He checked her vitals and agreed that she needed to be taken to the hospital. At the very least, she had a concussion.

*****

Later, at the hospital, both Myra and Bret had been checked out by medical staff. Myra was now conscious but was waiting to be taken back to surgery for a dislocated shoulder, torn rotator's cuff, and torn ligament in her left arm. They were minor injuries compared to what could have happened to her. She had given a preliminary statement to Agent Stevenson and her uncle, whom she was very surprised and happy to see.

They marveled over her forethought to keep Heirwick talking as long as possible. If it hadn't been for her quick thinking, he could have killed her and left or abducted her. As it was, they were shocked she had done so much damage to her assailant in her attempt to free herself. Her uncle was beaming with pride.

"As soon as you are out of here, we are having a proper date!" Bret informed her in front of her uncle.

Myra blushed and smiled at him.

"Oh my! I have to call your mother right now! She will be ecstatic! Not only are you okay, but you're actually dating!" Her uncle laughed.

Myra blushed harder and stuck her tongue out at him. Then she winced because the action made her face and head hurt where

Heirwick had hit her. "You're not funny!" She glared at him as best she could.

"Of course I am! I can't wait to see your mother's face when she arrives tomorrow morning and finds out you beat up a serial killer, got yourself some war wounds, solved the cold case about your father's killer, and managed to get a date all in the same day!" He rubbed his hands together in delight, causing Myra and Bret to laugh. "Jack will want you touring with him on his campaign! His poster stepdaughter takes down most prolific serial killer ever! I can see it now," he beamed. "Red, white, and blue banners with the slogan Tough on Crime!"

Epilogue

A dark-skinned, thin, and willowy beautiful aboriginal woman dabbed a cool compress against the forehead of her patient. She caught the eye of her daughter across the small bedroom. "It's time," she said.

Her daughter, equally as thin, willowy, and beautiful, gracefully crossed the room. She pulled the pillows from behind the patient's head and crawled into the bed behind the patient. "Lean against me for support." Her soft voice sounded like a soft melody. She took the patient's hands in her own.

The patient groaned and panted. Her belly with child ready to be delivered was a mound between them and the midwife. The dark-skinned older woman took her place between the patient's legs, ready to assist the mother in her delivery. The nearest hospital was many kilometers away, and the labor pains had come on too quickly to transport the patient in time.

"Take a deep breath and push," she ordered. The patient complied, her grunts and groans becoming louder as the delivery was in full process.

Outside, several pairs of eyes watched the man pacing back and forth on the porch. With each new groan and scream of pain, he became more worried, pacing a bit faster. One of the pairs of eyes belonged to the midwife's husband. "It's just a baby, mate. The Sheilas have got this. My Sheila is the best around," he bragged.

The pacing man glared at him even as the pacing continued. A small cry echoed from within the abode, and he stopped, staring toward the front door.

"One would think he was the one delivering the wee one," another man said, and laughter broke out among the men.

When the groaning and grunting started again, almost immediately, the worried man took up his pacing again. He heard the voices of the Sheilas from within but could not make out what they were saying. They had been in there for what seemed like hours. In reality, it had only been about forty-five minutes. This was his wife's first pregnancy, his first child. The baby was several weeks early, and he had a right to be concerned and worried.

Another woman had entered the bedroom while the men teased the father outside. She took the baby boy from the midwife and began bathing him in the basin of warm water she had prepared. His little body was shaking with his healthy cry. He was rather large for a premature baby.

Another woman had entered behind her and was eagerly awaiting the infant with dry towels. She glanced over at the midwife, who had a concerned look on her face. The midwife was busily issuing more orders to push harder. The patient was beginning to struggle. Twins? The patient had insisted for months that the doctor at the hospital had said only one baby. The midwife had been correct in telling her she was big enough for two babies.

She took the wet child from the bathing woman and gently dried him before wrapping him snuggly in a small blanket. She gazed down at the wee one and placed a gentle kiss on his forehead. "You're wiyanga is a little busy." She gently rocked him in her arms as she watched the midwife finally rise up with a squalling little girl in her hands.

After the midwife attended to the immediate needs of the second baby, she handed her off to the bathing woman, who had just returned with a clean basin of warm water. The midwife turned back to the patient, who was once again panting and groaning.

"I cannot believe this!" she exclaimed. "Most unusual!"

Her daughter was still supporting the patient, her eyes huge and worried. The patient was exhausted, and her strength was waning. She could feel it in the hands that gripped hers, the body that had been so rigid before leaning against her own. "Will she make it?" she mouthed to her mother.

Her mother shrugged her shoulders and issued more orders to the patient as she took up the delivery position again, ready to deliver a third baby.

Meanwhile, the man outside was still pacing and becoming even more worried by the minute. He had heard the baby cry for some time, and still no one had come to fetch him. Even the midwife's husband had taken on a pensive look. This was most unusual. It had been almost twenty minutes since they had heard the cry of the wee one. It rarely took this long to fetch the father unless there were complications. His wife was a very capable woman, but even she had her limits.

Even the midwife's husband was concerned. There were no soothing words for the father now. It had been too long. They all knew something was wrong. The teasing had stopped some time ago when the women had not come for the father. They could still hear the cry of the baby and the garbled voices of several women from inside. What could he say? Nothing. He could only wait like the father.

It was another five minutes before the midwife's daughter finally came to the door and motioned for the father to enter. As he entered the abode, she crossed to her father and spoke in her native tongue. Hesitantly, the father stood outside the bedroom doorway and tried to prepare himself—for what, he did not know. Another woman came up behind him and gently propelled him into the room. On the bed lay his wife, her damp and disheveled raven hair splayed out in contrast to the white pillow. She was very pale, and her eyes were closed.

"Is okay. She be resting. The wiyanga is very weak," she explained.

"Will she be okay?" he asked.

"It is too soon to say. She is even too weak to transport to hospital. Look." She tugged on his arm and indicated across the small room. Two women held three tiny infants in their arms. "They need to nurse, but she is too weak yet. I have sent my daughter to tell my husband we need a wet nurse and doctor immediately. He will fetch them," she explained.

The father tentatively crossed the room to look at the babies. They had only expected one child. Three? He could not believe his eyes. One of the women placed his eldest son in his arms.

"You're durung." She smiled at him.

He looked at the tiny bundle in his arms, afraid to move lest he drop the baby or hurt him. He looked up at the other woman.

"Duruninang and durung." She indicated with nods.

He didn't understand. The aboriginal language was too complex for him. He understood some words, but *durung, duruninang?* The young beautiful aboriginal daughter placed her slim hand with long delicate fingers on the child in his arms. "She says this is your son. The other two babies are another son and a daughter. This is your firstborn." She indicated the babe in his arms.

Two sons and a daughter at once! He could not believe it. Triplets! He looked lovingly at his sons and his daughter. They looked identical to him. Identical triplets, save for the sexes! He looked at his wife. She slowly opened her eyes and gave him a tired smile. He sat in a chair next to the bed provided by one of the women. He held their son in one arm, and one of the women placed their daughter in his other arm. The second son was placed in his wife's arm, supported by a pillow. He gazed lovingly into their children's eyes, their dark flat eyes, peering back at him, alert and knowing.

About the Author

AJ Easterling is a disabled American Navy veteran, a prior paralegal, and holds two psychology degrees, including a master's in forensic psychology. Originally from the hills of Kentucky, she has traveled extensively and lived in several different states, which she draws upon for inspiration in her writing. She currently lives near Charleston, South Carolina, with her husband and their two fur dog children. She and her husband also have a biological son, Bryant, and twin foster daughters, Starla and Shelby.

CPSIA information can be obtained
at www.ICGtesting.com
Printed in the USA
BVHW040349010622
638444BV00025B/22